FEARSOME
JOURNEYS

EDITED BY JONATHAN STRAHAN

Also Edited by **Jonathan Strahan**

FEARSOME JOURNEYS
THE NEW SOLARIS BOOK OF FANTASY

EDITED BY

JONATHAN STRAHAN

INCLUDING STORIES BY

SCOTT LYNCH

SALADIN AHMED

TRUDI CANAVAN

KJ PARKER

KATE ELLIOTT

JEFFREY FORD

ROBERT VS REDICK

ELLEN KLAGES

GLEN COOK

ELIZABETH BEAR

ELLEN KUSHNER

YSABEAU S. WILCE

DANIEL ABRAHAM

SOLARIS

First published 2013 by Solaris
an imprint of Rebellion Publishing Ltd,
Riverside House, Osney Mead,
Oxford, OX2 0ES, UK

www.solarisbooks.com

ISBN: 978 1 78108 118 1

Introduction and story notes and arrangement
copyright © 2013 Jonathan Strahan.
"The High King Dreaming" copyright © 2013 Daniel Abraham.
"Amethyst, Shadow, and Light" copyright © 2013 Saladin Ahmed.
"The Ghost Makers" copyright © 2013 Elizabeth Bear.
"One Last, Great Adventure" copyright © 2013
Ellen Kushner & Ysabeau S. Wilce
"Camp Follower" copyright © 2013 Trudi Canavan.
"Shaggy Dog Bridge: A Black Company Story"
copyright © 2013 Glen Cook.
"Spirits of Salt: A Tale of the Coral Heart"
copyright © 2013 Jeffrey Ford.
"The Dragonslayer of Merebarton" copyright © 2013 K J Parker.
"Leaf and Branch and Grass and Vine"
copyright © 2013 Kate Elliott.
"The Effigy Engine: A Tale of the Red Hats"
copyright © 2013 Scott Lynch.
"Forever People" copyright © 2013 Robert V S Redick.
"Sponda the Suet Girl and the Secret of the French Pearl"
copyright © 2013 Ellen Klages.

The right of the authors to be identified as the authors of this work
has been asserted in accordance with the Copyright,
Designs and Patents Act 1988.

10 9 8 7 6 5 4 3 2 1

A CIP catalogue record for this book is available from the
British Library.

Designed & typeset by Rebellion Publishing

Printed in the US

For Garth Nix and Sean Williams,
gentleman fantasists and dear friends,
with affection and respect.

ACKNOWLEDGEMENTS

ANY BOOK, AND especially a book like this one, is the product of the inspiration and perspiration of enough people to fill a small village. First and foremost, I would like to thank the brilliant team at Solaris Books – Jonathan Oliver, Ben Smith, and Michael Molcher – for their tireless work on this and my other books, as well as for some fine meals in Toronto last year. Second, I'd like to thank the baker's dozen of incredibly talented writers – Daniel Abraham, Saladin Ahmed, Elizabeth Bear, Ellen Kushner, Ysabeau S. Wilce, Trudi Canavan, Glen Cook, Jeffrey Ford, K J Parker, Kate Elliott, Scott Lynch, Robert V S Redick, and Ellen Klages – who were a joy to work with and delivered some wonderful stories. I'd also like to thank Tomasz Jedruszek for his very fine cover. I am fortunate to have the great Howard Morhaim as my literary agent and, as always, I'd like to thank him for his work on my behalf. I'd also like to thank Alice Speilburg and Beth Phelan from Team Morhaim, who are wonderful. Finally, a very special thank you to my wife Marianne and my daughters, Jessica and Sophie. Every minute spent working on this book was a minute spent not being with them, and their understanding and support is always an incredible gift.

CONTENTS

INTRODUCTION
JONATHAN STRAHAN

FANTASY. FANTASTIKA. CALL it what you will, almost any story can be made to fit within its boundaries and, like many of its finest texts, it's almost impossible to pin down or to define. As John Clute and John Grant rightly pointed out in their essential *The Encyclopedia of Fantasy,* fantasy is "a most extraordinarily porous term, and has been used to mop up vast deposits of story which this culture or that – and this era or that – deems unrealistic." Trying to home in on a usable definition, they wrote that:

> A fantasy text is a self-coherent narrative. When set in this world, it tells a story which is impossible in the world as we perceive it; when set in an otherworld, that otherworld will be impossible, though stories set there may be possible in its terms.

That definition sets out ground rules without clarifying much. A fantasy is a story set in a world where impossible things happen. Like fantasy itself, it's romantic and appealing but more than a little hazy at the edges. In fairness to Clute and Grant, they go on to devote a lengthy entry and, eventually, an entire encyclopedia to defining and understanding fantasy.

More recently, in *The Cambridge Companion to Fantasy Literature*, Edward James and Farah Mendlesohn note that "the major theorists in the field – Tzetan Todorov, Rosemary Jackson, Kathryn Hume, W.R. Irwin, and Colin Manlove – all agree that fantasy is about the construction of the impossible whereas science fiction may be about the unlikely, but is always grounded in the scientifically possible". While critics like Clute, Grant, James, Mendlesohn and most interestingly Brian Attebery, whose *Strategies of Fantasy* I strongly recommend to anyone interested in the academic discussion of fantasy, have a great deal of interesting things to say about the nature of fantasy and how it constructs the impossible, this book started from much more humble beginnings.

As many books I have worked on do, and in fact as many stories that I read happen to, this book started in a bar. I was at World Fantasy Convention in San Diego, California in the late fall of 2011 engaged in a passionate discussion about favourite writers and books, something I think every reader does when they find a like mind, and the subject turned to the work of the great Fritz Leiber. I had recently edited a collection of Leiber's work and was pontificating (the failing, perhaps, of having the discussion in a bar) on the depth and breadth of his work, from the beloved sword and sorcery adventures of Fafhrd and the Grey Mouser in Lankhmar to the humorous tales of a superkitten called Gummitch to dark and disturbing urban slices of fear like 'Smoke Ghost'. His collected fiction amounted, I argued, to nothing less than a library of fantasy that encompassed almost all of its possibilities.

While the convivial atmosphere of that bar no doubt encouraged some subtle exaggeration on my part, it also started me thinking about a book of new stories that might encompass as wide a range of types of fantasy story as possible, from 'traditional fantasy' to 'military fantasy' to quirky, strange tales of the impossible. The idea stayed with me and, when I was discussing possible new projects with Jonathan Oliver, my editor at Solaris, I mentioned doing such a book. He shared my enthusiasm and before I knew it we'd agreed that I'd edit a new anthology for Solaris that tentatively was to be called *Reap the Whirlwind* and would bring together a selection of all new 'mainstream' fantasy stories, for want of a better term, by some of today's best and most exciting writers.

It wasn't long, though, before we realised that title didn't really describe what we were attempting, and when the wonderful cover art from Tomasz Jedruszek arrived early in 2012 we knew the title had to change. After some discussion we came up with *Fearsome Journeys*, which I think aptly describes the beginnings of so many fantasy stories, including the ones that ended up in this book. Happily Jonathan also suggested that we should subtitle the book 'The New Solaris Book of Fantasy'. *Fearsome Journeys* was to be the first in a series of anthologies, not of 'new fantasy' but simply of fantasy, covering all of its many variations.

13

As the stories came in, first from Trudi Canavan, then K.J. Parker, Kate Elliott, Daniel Abraham, Glen Cook, and more, it became clear this first *New Solaris Book of Fantasy* was going to exceed my expectations. Those stories, and the ones from Saladin Ahmed, Jeffrey Ford, Robert V S Redick, Elizabeth Bear, Scott Lynch, Ellen Kushner and Ysbeau S. Wilce, and Ellen Klages have been a joy to read and I think make for a wonderful start to this new series. I'm already at work on volume two, which should be out late in 2014, but in the meantime I hope you enjoy these fine stories as much as I have.

Jonathan Strahan,
Perth, Western Australia
January 2013

THE EFFIGY ENGINE:
A TALE OF
THE RED HATS
SCOTT LYNCH

11th Mithune, 1186
Painted Sky Pass, North Elara

"I TOOK UP the study of magic because I wanted to live in the beauty of transfinite mathematical truths," said Rumstandel. He gestured curtly. In the canyon below us, an enemy soldier shuddered, clutched at his throat, and began vomiting live snakes.

"If my indifference were money you'd be the master of my own personal mint," I muttered. Of course Rumstandel heard me despite the pop, crackle, and roar of musketry echoing around the walls of the pass. There was sorcery at play between us to carry our voices, so we could bitch and digress and annoy ourselves like a pair of inebriates trading commentary in a theater balcony.

The day's show was an ambush of a company of Iron Ring legionaries on behalf of our employers, the North Elarans, who were blazing away with arquebus and harsh language from the heights around us. The harsh language seemed to be having greater effect.

The black-coated ranks of the Iron Ring jostled in consternation, but there weren't enough bodies strewn among the striated sunset-orange rocks that gave the pass its name. Hot lead was leaving the barrels of our guns, but it was landing like kitten farts and some sly magical bastard down there was responsible.

Oh, for the days of six months past, when the Iron Ring had crossed the Elaran border marches, their battle wizards proud and laughing in full regalia. Their can't-miss-me-at-a-mile wolf skull helmets, their set-me-on-fire carnelian cloaks, their shoot-me-in-the-face silver masks.

Six months with us for playmates had taught them to be less obvious. Counter-thaumaturgy was our mission and our meal ticket: coax them into visibility and make them regret it. Now they dressed like common officers or soldiers, and some even carried prop muskets or pikes. Like this one, clearly.

"I'm a profound disappointment to myself," sighed Rumstandel, big round florid Rumstandel, who didn't share my appreciation for sorcerous anonymity. This week he'd turned his belly-scraping beard blue and caused it to spring out in flaring forks like the sculpture of a river and its tributaries. Little simulacra of ships sailed up and down those beard strands even now, their hulls the size of rice grains, dodging crumbs like rocks and shoals. Crumbs there were aplenty, since Rumstandel always ate while he killed and soliloquized. One hand was full of the sticky Elaran ration bread we called corpsecake for its pallor and suspected seasoning.

"I should be redefining the vocabulary of arcane geometry somewhere safe and cultured, not playing silly buggers with village fish-charmers wearing wolf skulls." He silenced himself with a mouthful of cake and gestured again. Down on the valley floor his victim writhed his last. The snakes came out slick with blood, eyes gleaming like garnets in firelight, nostrils trailing strands of pale caustic vapor.

I couldn't really pick out the minute details at seventy yards, but I'd seen the spell before. In the closed ranks of the Iron Ring the serpents wrought the havoc that arquebus fire couldn't, and legionaries clubbed desperately at them with musket-butts.

As I peered into the mess, the forward portion of the legionary column exploded in white smoke. Sparks and chips flew from nearby rocks, and I felt a burning pressure between my eyes, a sharp tug on the strands of my own magic. The practical range of sorcery is about that of musketry, and a fresh reminder of the fact hung dead in the air a yard from my face. I plucked the ball down and slipped it into my pocket.

Somewhere safe and cultured? Well, there was nowhere safer for Rumstandel than three feet to my left. I was doing for him what the troublemaker on the ground was doing for the legionaries. Close protection, subtle and otherwise, my military and theoretical specialty.

Wizards working offensively in battle have a bad tendency to get caught up in their glory-hounding and part their already tenuous ties to prudence. Distracted and excited, they pile flourish on flourish, spell on spell until some stray musket ball happens along and elects to take up residence.

Our little company's answer is to work in teams, one sorcerer working harm and the second diligently protecting them both. Rumstandel didn't have the temperament to be that second sorcerer, but I've been at it so long now everyone calls me Watchdog. Even my mother.

I heard a rattling sound behind us, and turned in time to see Tariel hop down into our rocky niche, musket held before her like an acrobat's pole. Red-gray dust was caked in sweaty spirals along her bare ebony arms, and the dozens of wooden powder flasks dangling from her bandolier knocked together like a musical instrument.

"Mind if I crouch in your shadow, Watchdog? They're keeping up those volleys in good order." She knelt between me and Rumstandel, laid her musket carefully in the crook of her left arm, and whispered, "Touch." The piece went off with the customary flash and bang, which my speech-sorcery dampened to a more tolerable pop.

Hers was a salamandrine musket. Where the flintlock or wheel mechanism might ordinarily be was instead a miniature metal sculpture of a manor house, jutting from the weapon's side as though perched atop a cliff. I could see the tiny fire elemental that lived in there peering out one of the windows. It was always curious to see how a job was going. Tariel could force a spark from it by pulling the trigger, but she claimed polite requests led to smoother firing.

"Damn. I seem to be getting no value for money today, gents." She began the laborious process of recharging and loading.

"We're working on it," I said. Another line of white smoke erupted below, followed by another cacophony of ricochets and rock chips. An Elaran soldier screamed. "Aren't we working on it, Rumstandel? And by 'we' I do in fact mean—"

"Yes, yes, bullet-catcher, do let an artist stretch his own canvas." Rumstandel clenched his fists and something like a hot breeze blew past me, thick with power. This would be a vulgar display.

Down on the canyon floor, an Iron Ring legionary in the process of reloading was interrupted by the cold explosion of his musket. The stock shivered into splinters and the barrel peeled itself open backward like a sinister metal flower. Quick as thought, the burst barrel enveloped the man's arm, twisted, and— well, you've squeezed fruit before, haven't you? Then the powder charges in his bandolier flew out in burning constellations, a cloud of fire that made life immediately interesting for everyone around him.

"Ah! That's got his attention at last," said Rumstandel. A gray-blue cloud of mist boiled up from the ground around the stricken legionaries, swallowing and dousing the flaming powder before it could do further harm. Our Iron Ring friend was no longer willing to tolerate Rumstandel's contributions to the battle, and so inevitably...

"I see him," I shouted, "gesturing down there on the left! Look, he just dropped a pike!"

"Out from under the rock! Say your prayers, my man. Another village up north has lost its second-best fish-charmer!" said Rumstandel, moving his arms now like a priest in ecstatic sermon (recall my earlier warning about distraction and excitement). The Iron Ring sorcerer was hoisted into the air, black coat flaring, and as Rumstandel chanted his target began to spin.

The fellow must have realized that he couldn't possibly get any more obvious, and he had some nerve. Bright blue fire arced up at us, a death-sending screaming with ghostly fury. My business. I took a clay effigy out of my pocket and held it up. The screaming blue fire poured itself into the little statuette, which leapt out of my hands and exploded harmlessly ten yards above. Dust rained on our heads.

The Iron Ring sorcerer kept rising and whirling like a top. One soldier, improbably brave or stupid, leapt and caught the wizard's boot. He held on for a few rotations before he was heaved off into some of his comrades.

Still that wizard lashed out. First came lightning like a white pillar from the sky. I dropped an iron chain from a coat sleeve to bleed its energy into the earth, though it made my hair stand on end and my teeth chatter. Then came a sending of bad luck I could feel pressing in like a congealing of the air itself; the next volley that erupted from the Iron Ring lines would doubtless make cutlets of us. I barely managed to unweave the sending, using an unseemly eruption of power that left me feeling as though the air had been punched out of my lungs. An instant later musket balls sparked and screamed on the rocks around us, and we all flinched. My previous spell of protection had lapsed while I was beset.

"Rumstandel," I yelled, "quit stretching the bloody canvas and paint the picture already!"

"He's quite unusually adept, this illiterate pot-healer!" Rumstandel's beard-boats rocked and tumbled as the blue hair in which they swam rolled like ocean waves. "The illicit toucher of sheep! He probably burns books to keep warm at home! And I'm only just managing to hold him—Tariel, please don't wait for my invitation to collaborate in this business!"

Our musketeer calmly set her weapon into her shoulder, whispered to her elemental, and gave fire. The spinning sorcerer shook with the impact. An instant later, his will no longer constraining Rumstandel's, he whirled away like a child's rag doll flung in a tantrum. Where the body landed, I didn't see. My sigh of relief was loud and shameless.

"Yes, that was competent opposition for a change, wasn't it?" Tariel was already calmly recharging her musket. "Incidentally, it was a woman."

"Are you sure?" I said once I'd caught my breath. "I thought the Iron Ringers didn't let their precious daughters into their war-wizard lodges."

"I'd guess they're up against the choice between female support and no support at all," she said. "Almost as though someone's been subtracting wizards from their muster rolls this past half-year."

The rest of the engagement soon played out. Deprived of sorcerous protection, the legionaries began to fall to arquebus fire in the traditional manner. Tariel kept busy, knocking hats from heads and heads from under hats. Rumstandel threw down just a few subtle spells of maiming and ill-coincidence, and I returned to my sober vigil, Watchdog once more. It wasn't in our contract to scourge the Iron Ringers from the field with sorcery. We wanted them to feel they'd been, in the main, fairly bested by their outnumbered Elaran neighbors, line to line and gun to gun, rather than cheated by magic of foreign hire.

After the black-clad column had retreated down the pass and the echo of musketry was fading, Rumstandel and I basked like lizards in the mid-afternoon sun and stuffed ourselves on corpsecake and cold chicken, the latter wrapped in fly-killing spells of Rumstandel's devising. No sooner would the little nuisances alight on our lunch than they would vanish in puffs of green fire.

Tariel busied herself cleaning out her musket barrel with worm and fouling scraper. When she'd finished, the fire elemental, in the form of a scarlet salamander that could hide under the nail of my smallest finger, went down the barrel to check her work.

"Excuse me, are you the—that is, I'm looking for the Red Hats."

A young Elaran in a dark blue officer's coat appeared from the rocks above us, brown ringlets askew, uniform scorched and holed from obvious proximity to trouble. I didn't recognize her from the company we'd been attached to. I reached into a pocket, drew out my rumpled red slouch hat, and waved it.

About the hats, the namesake of our mercenary fellowship: in keeping with the aforementioned and mortality-avoiding principle of anonymity, neither Tariel nor myself wore them when the dust was flying. Rumstandel never wore his at all, claiming with much justice that he didn't need the aid of any particular headgear to slouch.

"Red Hats present and reasonably comfortable," I said. "Some message for us?"

"Not a message, but a summons," said the woman. "Compliments from your captain, and she wants you back at the central front with all haste at any hazard."

"Central front?" That explained the rings under her eyes. Even with mount changes, that was a full day in the saddle. We'd been detached from what passed for our command for a week and hadn't expected to go back for at least another. "What's your story, then?"

"Ill news. The Iron Ring have some awful device, something unprecedented. They're breaking our lines like we weren't even there. I didn't get a full report before I was dispatched, but the whole front is collapsing."

"How delightful," said Rumstandel. "I do assume you've brought a cart for me? I always prefer a good long nap when I'm speeding on my way to a fresh catastrophe."

Note to those members of this company desirous of an early glimpse into these, our chronicles. As you well know, I'm pleased to read excerpts when we make camp and then invite corrections or additions to my records. I am not, however, amused to find the thumbprints of sticky-fingered interlopers defacing these pages without my consent. BE ADVISED, therefore, that I have with a spotless conscience affixed a dweomer of security to this journal and an attendant minor curse. I think you know the one I mean. The one with the fire ants. You have only yourself to blame. —WD

Watchdog, you childlike innocent, if you're going to secure your personal effects with a curse, don't attach a warning preface. It makes it even easier to enact countermeasures, and they were no particular impediment in the first place if you take my meaning. Furthermore, the poverty of your observational faculty continues to astound. You wrote that my beard was 'LIKE the sculpture of a river and its tributaries,' failing to note that it was in fact a PRECISE and proportional model of the Voraslo Delta, with my face considered as the sea. Posterity awaits your amendments. Also, you might think of a more expensive grade of paper when you buy your next journal. I've pushed my quill through this stuff three times already. —R

13th Mithune, 1186
Somewhere near Lake Corlan, North Elara

RUMSTANDEL, BIG RED florid garlic-smelling Rumstandel, that bilious reservoir of unlovability, that human anchor weighing down my happiness, snored in the back of the cart far more peacefully than he deserved as we clattered up to the command pavilion of the North Elaran army. Pillars of black smoke rose north of us, mushrooming under wet gray skies. No campfire smoke, those pillars, but the sigils of rout and disaster.

North Elara is a temperate green place, long-settled, easy on the eyes and heart. It hurt to see it cut up by war like a patient strapped to a chirurgeon's operating board, straining against the incisions that might kill it as surely as the illness. Our trip along the rutted roads was slowed by traffic in both directions, supply trains moving north and the displaced moving south: farmers, fisherfolk, traders, camp followers, the aged and the young.

They hadn't been on the roads when we'd rattled out the previous week. They'd been nervous but guardedly content, keeping to their villages and camps behind the bulk of the Elaran army and the clever fieldworks that held the Iron Ring legions in stalemate. Now their mood had gone south and they meant to follow.

I rolled from the cart, sore where I wasn't numb. Elaran pennants fluttered wanly over the pavilion, and there were bad signs abounding. The smell of gangrene and freshly amputated limbs mingled with that of smoke and animal droppings. The command tents were now pitched about three miles south of where they'd been when I'd left.

I settled my red slouch on my head for identification, as the sentries all looked quite nervous. Tariel did the same. I glanced back at Rumstandel and found him still in loud repose. I called up one of my familiars with a particular set of finger-snaps and set the little creature on him in the form of a night-black squirrel with raven's wings. It hopped up and down on Rumstandel's stomach, singing:

"Rouse, Rumstandel, and see what passes!
Kindle some zest, you laziest of asses!
Even sluggard Red Hats are called to war
So rouse yourself and slumber no more!"

Some sort of defensive spell crept up from Rumstandel's coat like a silver mist, but the raven-squirrel fluttered above the grasping tendrils and pelted him with conjured acorns, while singing a new song about the various odors of his flatulence.

"My farts do not smell like glue!" shouted Rumstandel, up at last, swatting at my familiar. "What does that even mean, you wit-deficient pseudo-rodent?"

"Ahem," said a woman as she stepped out of the largest tent, and there was more authority in that clearing of her throat than there are in the loaded cannons of many earthly princes. My familiar, though as inept at rhyme as Rumstandel alleged, had a fine sense of when to vanish, and did so.

"I thought I heard squirrel doggerel," our captain, the sorceress Millowend, continued. "We must get you a better sort of creature one of these days."

It is perhaps beyond my powers to write objectively of Millowend, but in the essentials she is a short, solid, ashen-haired woman of middle years and innate rather than affected dignity. Her red hat, the iconic and original red hat, is battered and singed from years of campaigning despite the surfeit of magical protections bound into its warp and weft.

"Slack hours have been in short supply, ma'am."

"Well, I am at least glad to have you back in one piece, Watchdog," said my mother. "And you, Tariel, and even you, Rumstandel, though I wonder what's become of your hat."

"A heroic loss." Rumstandel heaved himself out of the cart, brushed assorted crumbs from his coat, and stretched in the manner of a rotund cat vacating a sunbeam. "I wore it through a fusillade of steel and sorcery. It was torn asunder, pierced by a dozen enemy balls and at least one culverin stone. We buried it with full military honors after the action."

"A grief easily assuaged." My mother conjured a fresh red hat and spun it toward the blue-bearded sorcerer's naked head. Just as deftly, he blasted it to motes with a gout of fire.

"Come along," said Millowend, unperturbed. This was the merest passing skirmish in the Affair of the Hat, possibly the longest sustained campaign in the history of our company. "We're all here now. I'll put you in the picture on horseback."

"Horseback?" said Rumstandel. "Freshly uncarted and now astride the spines of hoofed torture devices! Oh, hello, Caladesh."

The man tending the horses was one of us. Lean as a miser's alms-purse, mustaches oiled, carrying a brace of pistols so large I suspect they reproduce at night, Caladesh never changes. His hat is as red as cherry wine and has no magical protections at all save his improbable luck. Cal is worth four men in a fight and six in a drinking contest, but I was surprised to see him alone, minding exactly five horses.

"We're it," Millowend, as though reading my thoughts. Which was not out of the question. "I sent the others off with a coastal raid. They can't possibly return in time to help."

"And that's a fair pity," said Caladesh as he swung himself up into his saddle with easy grace. "There's fresh pie wrapped up in your saddlebags."

"A pie job!" cried Rumstandel. "Horses and a pie job! A constellation of miserable omens!"

His misgivings didn't prevent him, once saddled, from attacking the pie. I unwrapped mine and found it warm, firm, and lightly frosted with pink icing, the best sort my mother's culinary imps could provide. Alas.

Would-be sorcerers must understand that the art burns fuel as surely as any bonfire, which fuel being the sorcerer's own body. It's much like hard manual exercise, save that it banishes flesh even more quickly. During prolonged magical engagements I have felt unhealthy amounts of myself boil away. Profligate or sustained use of the art can leave us with skin hanging in folds, innards cramping, and bodily humors thrown into chaos.

That's why slender sorcerers are rarer than amiable scorpions, and why Rumstandel and I keep food at hand while plying our trade, and why my mother's sweet offering was as good as a warning.

In her train we rode north through the camp, past stands of muskets like sinister haystacks. These weren't the usual collections with soldiers lounging nearby ready to snatch them, but haphazard piles obviously waiting to be cleaned and sorted. Many Elaran militia and second-liners would soon be trading in their grandfatherly arquebuses for flintlocks pried from the hands of the dead.

"I'm sorry to reward you for a successful engagement by thrusting you into a bigger mess," said Millowend, "but the bigger mess is all that's on offer. Three days ago, the Iron Ring brought some sort of mechanical engine against our employers' previous forward position and kicked them out of it.

"It's an armored box, like the hull of a ship," she continued. "Balanced on mechanical legs, motive power unknown. Quick-steps over trenches and obstacles. The hull protects several cannon and an unknown number of sorcerers. Cal witnessed part of the battle from a distance."

"Wouldn't call it a battle," said Caladesh. "Battle implies some give and take, and this thing did nothing but give. The Elarans fed it cannonade, massed musketry, and spells. Then they tried all three at once. For that, their infantry got minced, their artillery no longer exists in a practical sense, and every single one of their magicians that engaged the thing is getting measured for a wooden box."

"They had fifteen sorcerers attached to their line regiments!" said Tariel.

"Now they've got assorted bits of fifteen sorcerers," said Caladesh.

"Blessed pie provisioner," said Rumstandel, "I'm as keen to put my head on the anvil as anyone in this association of oathbound lunatics. But when you say that musketry and sorcery were ineffective against this device, did it escape your notice that our tactical abilities span the narrow range from musketry to sorcery?"

"There's nothing uncanny about musket balls bouncing off wood and iron planking," said Millowend. "And there's nothing inherently counter-magical to the device. The Iron Ring have crammed a lot of wizards into it, is all. We need to devise some means to peel them out of that shell."

Under the gray sky we rode ever closer to the edge of the action, past field hospitals and trenches, past artillery caissons looking lonely without their guns, past nervous horses, nervous officers, and very nervous infantry. We left our mounts a few minutes later and moved on foot up the grassy ridgeline called Montveil's Wall, now the farthest limit of the dubious safety of 'friendly' territory.

There the thing stood, half a mile away, beyond the churned and smoldering landscape of fieldworks vacated by the Elaran army. It was the height of a fortress wall, perhaps fifty or sixty feet, and its irregular, bulbous hull rested on four splayed and ungainly metal legs. On campaign years ago in the Alcor Valley, north of the Skull Sands, I became familiar with the dust-brown desert spiders famous for their threat displays. The scuttling creatures would raise up on their rear legs, spread their forward legs to create an illusion of bodily height, and brandish their fangs. I fancied there was something of that in the aspect of the Iron Ring machine.

"Watchdog," said Millowend, "did you bring your spyflask?"

I took a tarnished, dented flask from my coat and unscrewed the cap. Clear liquid bubbled into the air like slow steam, then coalesced into a flat disc about a yard in diameter. I directed this with waves of my hands until it framed our view of the Iron Ring machine, and we all pressed in upon one another like gawkers at a carnival puppet-show.

The magic of the spyflask acted as a refracting lens, and after a moment of blurred confusion the image within the disc resolved to a sharp, clear magnification of the war machine. It was bold and ugly, pure threat without elegance. Its overlapping iron plates were draped in netting-bound hides, which I presumed were meant to defeat the use of flaming projectiles or magic. The black barrels of two cannon jutted from ports in the forward hull, lending even more credence to my earlier impression of a rearing spider.

"Those are eight-pounder demi-culverins," said Caladesh, gesturing at the cannon. "I pulled a ball out of the turf. Not the heaviest they've got, but elevated and shielded, they might as well be the only guns on the field. They did for the Elaran batteries at leisure, careful as calligraphers."

"I'm curious about the Elaran sorcerers," said Rumstandel, twirling fingers in the azure strands of his beard and scattering little white ships. "What exactly did they do to invite such a disaster?"

"I don't think they were prepared for the sheer volume of counter-thaumaturgy the Iron Ringers could mount from that device," said Millowend. "The Iron Ring wizards stayed cautious and let the artillery chop up our Elaran counterparts. Guided, of course, by spotters atop that infernal machine. It would seem the Iron Ring is learning to be the sort of opponent we least desire… a flexible one."

"I did like them much better when they were thick as oak posts," sighed Rumstandel.

"The essential question remains," I said. "How do we punch through what fifteen Elaran wizards couldn't?"

"You're thinking too much on the matter of the armored box," said Tariel. "When you hunt big game with ordinary muskets, you don't try to pierce the thickest bone and hide. You make crippling shots. Subdue it in steps, leg by leg. Lock those up somehow, all the Iron Ring will have is an awkward fortress tower rooted in place."

"We could trip it or sink it down a hole," mused Rumstandel. "General Alune's not dead, is she? Why aren't her sappers digging merrily away?"

"She's alive," said Millowend. "It's a question of where to dig, and how to convince that thing to enter the trap. When it's moving, it can evade or simply overstep anything resembling ordinary fieldworks."

"When it's moving," I said. "Well, here's another question—if the Elarans didn't stop it, why isn't it moving now?"

"I'd love to think it's some insoluble difficulty or breakdown," said Millowend. "But the telling fact is, they haven't sent over any ultimatums. They haven't communicated at all. I assume that if the device were now immobilized, they'd be trying to leverage its initial attack for all it was worth. No, they're waiting for their own reasons, and I'm sure those reasons are suitably unpleasant."

"So how do you want us to inaugurate this fool's errand, captain?" said Rumstandel.

"Eat your pie," said my mother. "Then think subtle thoughts. I want a quiet, invisible reconnaissance of that thing, inch by inch and plate by plate. I want to find all the cracks in its armor, magical and otherwise, and I want the Iron Ring to have no idea we've been peeking."

ENCLOSURE: *The open oath of the Red Hats, attributed to the Sorceress Millowend.*

> *To take no coin from unjust reign*
> *Despoil no hearth nor righteous fane*
> *Caps red as blood, as bright and bold*
> *In honor paid, as dear as gold*
> *To leave no bondsman wrongly chained*
> *And shirk no odds, for glory's gain*
> *Against the mighty, for the weak*
> *We by this law our battles seek*

ADDENDUM: *The tacit marching song of the Red Hats, attributed to the Sorcerer Rumstandel, sometimes called 'The Magnificent.'*

> *Where musket balls are thickest flying*
> *Where our employers are quickest dying*
> *Where mortals perish like bacon frying*
> *And horrible things leave grown men crying*
> *To all these places we ride with haste*
> *To get ourselves smeared into paste*

Or punctured, scalded, and served on toast
For the financial benefit of our hosts!

13th Mithune, 1186
Montveil's Wall, North Elara
One Hour Later

CANNON ABOVE US, cannon over the horizon, all spitting thunder and smoke, all blasting up fountains of wet earth as we stumbled for cover, under the plunging fire of the lurching war machine, under the dancing green light of hostile magic, under the weight of our own confusion and embarrassment.

We had thought we were being subtle.

Millowend had started our reconnaissance by producing a soft white dandelion seedhead, into which she breathed the syllables of a spell. Seeds spun out, featherlike in her conjured breeze, and each carried a fully-realized pollen-sized simulacrum of her, perfect down to a little red hat and a determined expression. One hundred tiny Millowends floated off to cast two hundred tiny eyes over the Iron Ring machine. It was a fine spell, though it would leave her somewhat befuddled as her mind strained to knit those separate views together into one useful picture.

Rumstandel added some admittedly deft magical touches of his own to the floating lens of my spyflask, and in short order we had a sort of intangible apparatus by which we might study the quality and currents of magic around the war machine, as aesthetes might natter about the brushstrokes of a painting. Tariel and Caladesh, less than entranced by our absorption in visual balderdash, crouched near us to keep watch.

"That's as queer as a six-headed fish," muttered Rumstandel. "The whole thing's lively with dynamic flow. That would be a profligate waste of power unless—"

That was when Tariel jumped on his head, shoving him down into the turf, and Caladesh jumped on mine, dragging my dazed mother with him. A split heartbeat later, a pair of cannonballs tore muddy furrows to either side of us, arriving just ahead of the muted thunder of their firing.

"I might forward the hypothesis," growled Rumstandel, spitting turf, "that the reason the bloody thing hasn't moved is because it was left out as an enticement for a certain band of interlopers in obvious hats."

"I thought we were being reasonably subtle!" I yelled, shoving Caladesh less than politely. He is all sharp angles, and very unpleasant to be trapped under.

"Action FRONT," cried Tariel, who had sprung back on watch with her usual speed. The rest of us scrambled to the rim of Montveil's Wall beside her. Charging from the nearest trench, not a hundred yards distant, came a column of Iron Ring foot about forty strong, cloaks flying, some still tossing away the planks and debris they'd been using to help conceal themselves. One bore a furled pennant bound tightly to its staff by a scarlet cord. That made them penitents, comrades of a soldier who'd broken some cardinal rule of honor or discipline. The only way they'd be allowed to return to the Iron Ring, or even ordinary service, was to expunge the stain with a death-or-glory mission.

Such as ambushing us.

Also, the six-story metal war machine behind the penitents was now on the move, creaking and growling like a pack of demons set loose in a scrapyard.

And then there were orange flashes and puffs of smoke from the distances beyond the machine, where hidden batteries were presumably taking direction on how to deliver fresh gifts of lead to our position.

Tariel whispered to her salamander, and her musket barked fire and noise. The lead Iron Ringer was instantly relieved of all worries about the honor of his company. As she began to reload, shrieking cannon balls gouged the earth around us and before us, no shot yet closer than fifty yards. Bowel-loosening as the flash of distant cannonade might be, they would need much better luck and direction to really endanger us at that range.

I enacted a defensive spell, one that had become routine and reflexive. A sheen appeared in the air between us and the edge of the ridge, a subtle distortion that would safely pervert the course of any musket ball not fired at point-blank range. Not much of a roof to shelter under in the face of artillery, but it had the advantage of requiring little energy or concentration while I tried to apprehend the situation.

Rumstandel cast slips of paper from his coat pocket and spat crackling words of power after them. Over the ridge and across the field they whirled, toward the Iron Ring penitents, swelling into man-sized kites of crimson silk, each one painted with a wild-eyed likeness of Rumstandel, plus elaborate military, economic, and sexual insults in excellent Iron Ring script. Half-a-dozen kites swept into the ranks of the charging men, ensnaring arms, legs, necks, and muskets in their glittering strings before leaping upward, hauling victims to the sky.

"Hackwork, miserable hackwork," muttered Rumstandel. "Someday I'll figure out how to make the kites scream those insults. Illiterate targets simply aren't getting the full effect."

The cries of the men being hoisted into the air said otherwise, but I was too busy to argue.

The war machine lurched on, cannons booming, the shot falling so far beyond us I didn't see them land. So long as the device was in motion, I wagered its gunners would have a vexed time laying their pieces. That would change in a matter of minutes, when the thing reached spell and musket range and could halt to crush us at leisure.

"We have to get the hell out of here!" I cried, somewhat suborning the authority of my mother, who was still caught in the trance of seed-surveillance. That was when a familiar emerald phosphorescence burst around us, a vivid green light that lit the churned grass for a thirty-yard circle with us at the center.

"SHOT-FALL IMPS," bellowed Caladesh, which is just what they were; each of the five of us was now beset by a cavorting green figure dancing in the air above our heads, grinning evilly and pointing at us, while blazing with enough light to make our position clear from miles away.

"Here! Here! Over here!" yelled the green imps. The reader may assume they continued to yell this throughout the engagement, for they certainly did. I cannot find the will to scrawl it over and over again in this journal.

Shot-fall imps are intangible (so we couldn't shoot them) and notoriously slippery to banish. I have the wherewithal to do it, but it takes several patient minutes of trial and error, and those I did not possess.

Fire flashed in the distance, the long-range batteries again, this time sighting on the conspicuous green glow. It was no particular surprise that they were now more accurate, their balls parting the air just above our heads or plowing furrows within twenty yards. This is where we came in after the last intermission, with the enemy bombardment, the scrambling, and the general sense of a catastrophically unfolding cock-up.

Rumstandel hurled occult abuse at the penitents, his darkening mood evident in his choice of spells. He transmuted boot leather to caustic silver slime, seeded the ground with flesh-hungry glass shards, turned eyeballs to solid ice and cracked them within their sockets. All this, plus Tariel's steady, murderous attention, and still the Iron Ringers came on, fierce and honor-mad, bayonets fixed, leaving their stricken comrades in the mud.

"Get to the horses!" I yelled, no longer concerned about bruising Millowend's chain of command. It was my job to ward us all from harm, and the best possible safeguard would be for us to scurry, leaving our dignity on the field like a trampled tent.

The surviving penitents came charging up a nearby defile to the top of Montveil's Wall. Caladesh met them, standing tall, his favorite over-and-under double flintlocks barking smoke. Those pistols threw .60 caliber balls, and at such close range the effect was... well, you've squeezed fruit before, haven't you?

The world became a tumbling confusion of incident. Iron Ring penitents falling down the slope, tangled in the heavy bodies of dead comrades, imps dancing in green light, cannonballs ripping holes in the air, a lurching war machine—all this while I frantically tried to spot our horses, revive my mother, and layer us in what protections I could muster.

They weren't sufficient. A swarm of small water elementals burst upon us, translucent blobs the color of gutter-silt, smelling like the edge of a summer storm. They poured themselves into the barrels and touch-holes of Caladesh's pistols, leaving him cursing. A line of them surged up and down the barrel of Tariel's musket, and the salamander faced them with steaming red blades in its hands like the captain of a boarded vessel. The situation required more than my spells could give it, so I resolved at last to surrender an advantage I was loath to part with.

On my left wrist I wore a bracelet woven from the tail-hairs of an Iron Unicorn, bound with a spell given to me by the Thinking Sharks of the Jewelwine Sea, for which I had traded documents whose contents are still the state secrets of one of our former clients. I tore it off, snapped it in half, and threw it to the ground.

It's dangerous arrogance for any sorcerer to think of a fifth-order demon as a familiar; at best such beings can be indentured to a very limited span of time or errands, and against even the most ironclad terms of service they will scheme and clamor with exhausting persistence. However, if you can convince them to shut up and take orders...

"Felderasticus Sixth-Quickened, Baronet of the Flayed Skulls of Faithless Dogs, Princeling of the House of Recurring Shame," I bellowed, pausing to take a breath, "get up here and get your ass to work!"

"I deem that an irretrievably non-specific request," said a voice like fingernails on desert-dry bones. "I shall therefore return to my customary place and assume my indenture to be dissolved by mutual—"

"Stuff that, you second-rate legal fantasist! When *you* spend three months questing for spells to bind *me* into jewelry, then you can start assuming things! Get rid of these shot-fall imps!"

"Reluctant apologies, most impatient of spell-dabblers and lore-cheats, softest of cannon-ball targets, but again your lamentably hasty nonspecificity confounds my generous intentions. When you say, 'get rid of,' how exactly do you propose—"

"Remove them instantly and absolutely from our presence without harm to ourselves and banish them to their previous plane of habitation!"

A chill wind blew, and it was done. The shot-fall imps with their damned green light and their pointing and shouting were packed off in a cosmic bag, back to their rightful home, where they would most likely be used as light snacks for higher perversities like Felderasticus Sixth-Quickened. I was savagely annoyed. Using Felderasticus to swat them was akin to using a guillotine as a mouse-trap, but you can see the mess we were in.

"Now, I shall withdraw, having satisfied all the terms of our compact," said the demon.

"Oh, screw yourself!" I snarled.

"Specify physically, metaphysically, or figuratively."

"Shut it! You know you're not finished. I need a moment to think."

Tariel and Caladesh were fending off penitents, inelegantly but emphatically, with their waterlogged weapons. Rumstandel was trying to help them as well as keep life hot for the Iron Ring sorcerer that must have been mixed in with the penitents. I couldn't see him (or her) from my vantage, but the imps and water elementals proved their proximity. Millowend was stirring, muttering, but not yet herself. I peered at the towering war machine and calculated. No, that was too much of a job for my demon. Too much mass, too much magic, and now it was just two hundred yards distant.

"We require transportation," I said, "Instantly and—"

"Wait," cried my mother. She sat up, blinked, and appeared unsurprised as a cannon ball swatted the earth not ten feet away, spattering both of us with mud. "Don't finish that command, Watchdog! We all need to die!"

"Watchdog," said Rumstandel, "our good captain is plainly experiencing a vacancy in the upper-story rooms, so please apply something heavy to her skull and get on with that escape you were arranging."

"No! I'm sorry," cried Millowend, and now she bounced to her feet with sprightliness that was more than a little unfair in someone her age. "My mind was still a bit at luncheon. You know that flying around being a hundred of myself is a very taxing business. What I mean is, this is a bespoke ambush, and if we vanish safely out of it they'll just keep expecting us. But if it looks as though we're snuffed, the Iron Ring might drop their guard enough to let us back in the fight!"

"Ahh!" I cried, chagrined that I hadn't thought of that myself. In my defense, you have just read my account of the previous few minutes. I cleared my throat.

"Felderasticus, these next-named tasks, once achieved, shall purchase the end of your indenture without further caveat or reservation! NOW! Interpreting my words in the broadest possible spirit of good faith, we, all five of us, must be brought alive with our possessions to a place of safety within the North Elaran encampment just south of here. Furthermore—FURTHERMORE! Upon the instant of our passage, you must create a convincing illusion of our deaths, as though... as though we had been caught by cannon-fire and the subsequent combustion of our powder-flasks and alchemical miscellanies!"

I remain very proud of that last flourish. Wizards, like musketeers, are notorious for carrying all sorts of volatile things on their persons, and if we were seen to explode the Iron Ringers might not bother examining our alleged remains too closely.

"Faithfully shall I work your will and thereby end my indenture," said the cold voice of the demon.

The world turned gray and spun around me. After a moment of disjointed nausea I found myself once again lying under sharp-elbowed Caladesh, with Rumstandel, Tariel, and my mother into the bargain. Roughly six hundred pounds of Red Hats, all balanced atop my stomach, did something for my freshly-eaten pie that I hesitate to describe. But, ah, you've squeezed fruit before, haven't you?

Moaning, swearing, and retching, we all fell or scrambled apart. Guns, bandoliers, and hats littered the ground around us. When I had managed to wipe my mouth and take in a few breaths, I finally noticed that we were surrounded by a veritable forest of legs, legs wearing the boots and uniform trousers of North Elaran staff officers.

I followed some of those legs upward with my eyes and met the disbelieving gaze of General Arad Vorstal, supreme field commander of the army of North Elara. Beside him stood his general of engineers, the equally surprised Luthienne Alune.

"Generals," said my mother suavely, dusting herself off and restoring her battered hat to its proper place. "Apologies for the suddenness of our arrival. I'm afraid I have to report that our reconnaissance of the Iron Ring war machine ended somewhat prematurely. And the machine retains its full motive power."

She cleared her throat.

"And, ah, we're all probably going to see it again in about half an hour."

ENCLOSURE: *Invoice for sundry items lost or disposed of in Elaran service, 13th instant, Mithune, 1186. Submitted to Quartermaster-Captain Guthrun on behalf of the Honorable Company of Red Hats, countersigned Captain-Paramount Millowend, Sorceress. 28th instant, Mithune, 1186*

ITEM VALUATION:

Bracelet, thaumaturgical...1150 Gil. 13 p.
Function (confidential)

Spyflask, thaumaturgical...100 Gil. 5 p.
Function (reconnaissance)
Total Petition...1250 Gil. 18 p.
Please remit as per terms of contract.

WATCHDOG— *Actually, I picked up your spyflask when you rather thoughtlessly dropped it that afternoon. I did mean to return it to you eventually. These minor trivialities of camp life do elude me sometimes. I hadn't realized that the company received a hundred gildmarks as a replacement fee. Do you want me to keep the flask, or shall I write myself up a chit for the hundred gildmarks? I am content with either. —R*

13th Mithune, 1186
Somewhere near Lake Corlan, North Elara

BUT THEY DIDN'T come. Not then.

Afternoon wound down into evening. Presumably, the Iron Ring thought it too late in the day to commence a general action, and with all of their sorcerous impediments supposedly ground into the mud, one could hardly blame them for a lack of urgency. The war machine stood guard before Montveil's Wall, and behind it came the creak and groan of artillery teams, the shouts of orders, and the tramp of boots as line regiments moved into their billets for the night. The light of a thousand fires rose from the captured Elaran fieldworks and joined in an ominous glow, giving the overcast the colors of a banked furnace.

In the Elaran camp, we brooded and argued. The

council ran long, in quite inverse proportion to the tempers of those involved.

"It's not that we can't dig," General Alune was saying, her patience shaved down to a perceptibly thin patina on her manner. "For the tenth time, it's the fact that the bloody machine moves! We can work like mad all night, sink a shaft just about the right size to make a grave for the damn thing, and in the morning it might spot the danger and take five steps to either side. So much for our trap."

"Have you ever seen a pitfall for a dangerous animal?" said Tariel, mangling protocol by speaking up. "It's customary to cover the entrance with a light screen of camouflage—"

"Yes, yes, I'm well aware," snapped General Alune. "But once again, that machine is the master of the field and may go where it pleases, attacking from any angle. We have no practical means of forcing it into a trap, even a hidden one."

"Has the thing truly no weak point, no joint in its armor, no vent or portal on which we can concentrate fire? Or sorcery?" said Vorstal, stroking the beard that hung from his craggy chin like sable-streaked snow. "What about the mechanisms that propel it?"

"I assure you I had the closest look possible," said Millowend. "It was the only useful thing I managed to do during our last engagement. The device has no real machinery, no engine, no pulleys or pistons. It's driven by brute sorcery. A wizard in a harness, mimicking the movements they desire the machine to make, a puppeteer driving a vast puppet. You might call it an effigy engine. It's exhausting work, and I'm sure they have to swap wizards frequently.

However, while harnessed, the driver is still inside the armored shell, still protected by the arts of their fellows. It's as easy to destroy the machine outright as it is to reach them."

"How many great guns have we managed to recover since yesterday's debacle?" said General Vorstal.

"Four," said General Alune. "Four functional six-pounders, crewed by a few survivors, the mildly injured, and a lot of fresh volunteers."

"That's nothing to hang our hopes on," sighed Vorstal, "a fifth of what wasn't even adequate before!"

"We could try smoke," said Rumstandel. While listening to the council of war he'd added flourishes to his beard, tiny gray clouds and twirling water-spouts, plus lithe long-necked sea serpents. Life had become very hard for the little ships of the Rumstandel Delta. "Or anything to render the hull uninhabitable. Flaming caustics, bottled vitriol, sulfurous miasma, air spirits of reeking decay—"

"The Iron Ring sorcerers could nullify any of those before they caused harm," I said. "You and I certainly could."

Rumstandel shrugged theatrically. Miniature lightning crackled just below his chin.

"Then it must be withdrawal," said Vorstal, bitterly but decisively. "If we face that thing again, with the rest of the Iron Ring force at its heels, this army will be destroyed. I have to preserve it. Trade territory for time. I want one hundred volunteers to demonstrate at Montveil's Wall while we start pulling the rest out quietly." He looked around, meeting the eyes of all his staff in turn. "Officers will surrender their horses to hospital wagon duty, myself included."

"With respect, sir," said General Alune, "you know how many Iron Ring sympathizers... that is, when word of all this reaches parliament they'll have you dismissed. And they'll be laying white flags at the feet of that damned machine before we can even get the army reformed, let alone reinforced."

"Certainly I'll be recalled," said Vorstal. "Probably arrested, too. I'll be counting on *you* to keep our forces intact and use whatever time I can buy you to think of something I couldn't. You always were the cleverer one, Luthienne."

"The Iron Ring won't want easy accommodations," said Millowend, and I was surprised to notice her using a very subtle spell of persuasion. Her voice rang a little more clearly to the far corners of the command pavilion, her shadow seemed longer and darker, her eyes more alight with compelling fire. "You've bled them and stymied them for months. You've defied all their plans. Now their demands will be merciless and unconditional. If this army falls back, they will put your people in chains and feed Elara to the fires of their war-furnaces, until you're nothing but ashes on the trail to their next conquest! Now, if that war machine were destroyed, could you think to meet the rest of the Iron Ring army with the force you still possess?"

"If it were destroyed?" shouted General Vorstal. "IF! If my cock had scales and another ninety feet it'd be a dragon! IF! Millowend, I'm sorry, you and your company have done us extraordinary service, but I have no more time for interruptions. I'll see to it that your contract is fully paid off and you're given letters of safe passage, for what they're worth."

"I have a fresh notion," said my mother. "One

that will give us a long and sleepless night, if it's practicable at all, and the thing I need to hear, right now, is whether or not you can meet the Iron Ring army if that machine is subtracted from the ledger."

"Not with any certainty," said Vorstal, slowly. "But we still have our second line of works, and it's the chance I'd take over any other, if only it were as you say."

"For this we'll need your engineers," said Millowend. "Your blacksmiths, your carpenters, and work squads of anyone who can hold a shovel or an axe. And we'll need those volunteers for Montveil's Wall to screen us, with their lives if need be."

"What do you have in mind?" said General Alune.

"A trap, as you said, is wasted unless we can guarantee that the Iron Ring machine moves into it." Millowend mimicked the lurching steps of the machine with her fingers. "Well, what could we possibly set before it that would absolutely guarantee movement in our desired direction? What challenge could we mount on the field that would *compel* them to advance their machine and engage us as directly as possible?"

After a sufficiently dramatic pause, she told us.

Then the real shouting and argument began.

14th Mithune, 1186
Somewhere near Lake Corlan, North Elara

JUST BEFORE SUNRISE, the surviving Elaran skirmishers fell back from Montveil's Wall, their shot-flasks empty, their ranks scraped thin by musketry, magic, and misadventure in the dark. Yet they had achieved their mission and kept their Iron Ring counterparts out of our lines, away from the evidence of what we were really up to.

Behind them, several regiments of Elaran foot had moved noisily throughout the night, doing their best to create the impression of the pullback that was only logical. A pullback it was, though not to the roads but rather to a fresh line of breastworks, where they measured powder, sharpened bayonets, and slept fitfully in the very positions they would guard at first light.

We slept not at all. Tariel and Caladesh passed hours in conference with the most experienced of the surviving Elaran artillery handlers. Rumstandel, Millowend and I spent every non-working moment we had on devouring anything we could lay our hands on, without a scrap of shame. My mother's plan was a pie job and a half.

The sun came up like dull brass behind the charcoal bars of the hazy sky. Fresh smoke trails curled from the Iron Ring positions, harbingers of the hot breakfast they would have before they moved out to crush us. General Vorstal had reluctantly sentenced his men and women to a cold camp, to help preserve the illusion that large contingents in Elaran blue had fled south during the night. We sorcerers received our food from Millowend's indentured culinary imps, their pinched green faces grotesque under their red leather chef's hats, their ovens conveniently located in another plane of existence.

As the sun crept upward, the Iron Ring lines began to form, regimental pennants fluttering like sails above a dark and creeping sea. A proud flag broke out atop the war machine, blue circle within gray circle on a field of black. The symbol of the Iron Ring cities, the coal-furnace tyrants, whose home dominions girded the shores of vast icy lakes a month's march north of Elara.

By the tenth hour of the morning, they were coming for us, in the full panoply of their might and artifice.

"I suppose it's time to find out whether we're going to be victorious fools, or just fools," said Millowend. We had taken our ready position together, all five of us, and rising anxiety had banished most of our fatigue. We engaged in our little rituals, chipper or solemn as per our habits, hugging and shaking hands and exchanging good-natured insults. My mother dusted off my coat and straightened my hat.

"Rumstandel," she said, "are you sure now wouldn't be an appropriate time to rediscover that chronically misplaced hat of yours?"

"Of course not, captain." He rubbed his ample abdominal ballast and grinned. "I much prefer to die as I've always lived, handsome and insufferable."

My mother rendered eloquent commentary using nothing but her eyebrows. Then she cast the appropriate signal-spell, and we braced ourselves.

Five hundred Elaran sappers and work-gangers, already drained to the marrow by a night of frantic labor, seized hold of ropes and chains. "HEAVE!" shouted General Alune, who then flung herself into the nearest straining crew and joined them in their toil. Pulleys creaked and guidelines rattled. With halting, lurching, shuddering movements, a fifty-foot wood and metal tripod rose into the sky above the Elaran command pavilion, with the five of us in an oblong wooden box at its apex, feeling rather uncomfortably like catapult stones being winched into position.

We leveled off, wavering disconcertingly, but more or less upright. Cheers erupted from thousands of throats across the Elaran camp, and musketeers came to their feet in breastworks and redoubts, loosing their regimental colors from hiding. Our North Elaran war machine stood high in the morning light, and even those who'd been told what we were up to waved their hats and screamed like they could hardly believe it.

It was all a thoroughly shambolic hoax, of course. The Iron Ring machine was the product of months of work, cold metal plates fitted to purpose-built legs, rugged and roomy, weighed down with real armor. Ours was a gimcrack, upjumped watch-tower, shorter, narrower, and wobbly as a drunk at a ballroom dance. Our wooden construction was braced in a few crucial places with joints and nail-plates improvised by Elaran blacksmiths. Our hull was armored with nothing but logs, and our only gun was a cast-iron six-pounder in a specially rigged recoil harness, tended by Caladesh and Tariel.

"Let's secure their undivided attention," said Millowend. "Charge and load!"

Tariel and Caladesh rammed home a triple-sized powder charge, augmented with the greenish flecks of substances carefully chosen from our precious alchemical supply. Rumstandel handed over a six-pound ball, laboriously prepared by us with pale ideograms of spells designed to ensure long, straight flight. Caladesh drove it down the barrel with the rammer while Tariel looked out the forward window and consulted an improvised sight made from a few pieces of wood and wire.

"Lay it as you like, then fire at will," said Millowend.

Our gunners didn't dally. They sighted their piece on the distant Iron Ring machine, and Tariel whistled up her salamander, which was taking a brief vacation from its usual home. The fire-spirit danced around the touchhole, and the six-pounder erupted with a bang that was much too loud even with our noise-suppression spells deadening the air.

Ears ringing, nostrils stinging from the strange smoke of the blast, I jumped to a window and followed the glowing green arc of the magically-enhanced shot as it sped toward the enemy. There was a flash and a flat puff of yellowish smoke atop the target machine's canopy.

"Dead on!" I shouted.

We had just ruined a cannon barrel and expended a great deal of careful sorcery, all for the sake of one accurate shot at an improbable distance. It hadn't been expected to do any damage, even if it caught their magicians by surprise. It was just a good old-fashioned gauntlet across the face.

"They're moving," said Caladesh. "Straight for us."

The Iron Ringers answered our challenge, all right. It was precisely the sort of affair that would appeal to them, machine against machine like mad bulls for the fate of North Elara. Hell, it was just the sort of thing that might have appealed to us, if only our 'machine' hadn't been a shoddy counterfeit.

"Forward march," said my mother, and I resumed my place at her side along with Rumstandel. This part was going to hurt. We joined hands and concentrated.

We hadn't had time to devise any sort of body harness for the control and movement of our device.

Instead we had an accurate wooden model about two feet tall, secured to the floor in front of us. On this we could focus our sorcerous energies, however inefficiently, to move corresponding pieces of the real structure. Ours was, in a sense, a *true* effigy engine.

Imagine pulling a twenty-pound weight along a chain in hair-fine increments by jerking your eyebrow muscles. Imagine trying to push your prone, insensate body along the ground using nothing but the movements of your toes. This was the sort of nightmarish, concentrated effort required to send our device creaking along, step by step, shaking like a bar-stool with delusions of grandeur.

The energy poured out of us like a vital fluid. We moaned, we shuddered, we screamed and swore in the most undignified fashion. Caladesh and Tariel clung to the walls in earnest, for our passage was anything but smooth. It was a bit like being trapped inside a madman's feverish delusion of a carriage ride, some fifty feet above the ground, while a powerful enemy approached with cannons booming.

We had to hope that our Elaran employers had strictly obeyed our edict to clear our intended movement path. There was no chance to look down and halt if some unfortunate soul was about to play the role of insect to our boot-heel.

Iron Ring cannonballs shrieked past. One of them peeled away part of our roof, giving us a ragged new skylight. Closer and closer we stumbled, featherweight frauds. Closer and closer the enemy machine pounded in dread sincerity.

Even fat and well-fed sorcerers were not meant to do what we were doing for long; our magic grew taut and strained as an overfilled water-sack. It was impossible to tell tears from sweat, for it was all running out of us in a torrent. The expressions on the faces of Tariel and Caladesh struck me in my preoccupation as extremely funny, and then I realized it was because I had never before seen those consummate stalwarts look truly horrified.

Another round of fire boomed from the charging Iron Ring machine. Our vessel shuddered, rocked by a hit somewhere below. I tried to subdue my urge to cower or hide. There was nothing to be done now; a shot through our bow would likely fill the entire cabin with splinters and scythe us all down in an instant. In moments, we must also come within range of the wizards huddled inside the enemy machine, and we were in no shape to resist them. Luck was our only shield now.

Luck, and a few seconds or yards in either direction.

"They're going," cried Tariel. "THEY'RE GOING!"

There was a sound like the world coming apart at the seams, a juddering drum-hammer noise, sharpened by the screams of men and metal alike. Everything shook around us and beneath us, and for a moment I was certain that Tariel was wrong, that it was we who'd been mortally struck at last, that we were on our way to the ground and into the history books as a farcical footnote to the rise of the Iron Ring empire.

The thing about my mother's plans, though, is that they tend to work, more often than not.

Given luck, and a few seconds or yards in either direction.

I didn't witness it personally, but I can well imagine the scene based on the dozens of descriptions I collected afterward. We had barely thirty more yards of safe space to move when the Iron Ring machine hit the edge of the trap, the modified classic pitfall scraped out of the earth by General Alune's sappers, then concealed with panels of canvas and wicker and even a few tents. A thousand-strong draft had labored all night to move and conceal the dirt, aided here and there by our sorcery. It wasn't quite a ready-made grave for the war machine. More of a good hard stumble of about thirty feet.

Whatever it was, it was sufficient. In clear view of every Iron Ring soldier on the field, the greatest feat of ferro-thaumaturgical engineering in the history of the world charged toward its feeble-looking rival, only to stumble and plunge in a deadly arc, smashing its armored cupola like a crustacean dropped from the sky by a hungry sea-bird. A shroud of dust and smoke settled around it, and none of its occupants were left in any shape to ever crawl out of it.

Millowend, Rumstandel and I fell to our knees in the cabin of our hoax machine, gasping as though we'd been fished from the water ten seconds shy of drowning. Everything felt loose and light and wrong, so much flesh had literally cooked away from the three of us. It was a strange and selfish scene for many moments, as we had no idea whether to celebrate a close-run tactical triumph, or the simple fact of our continued existence. We shamelessly did both, until the noise of battle outside reminded us that the day's work was only begun. Sore and giddy, we let Rumstandel conjure a variation of his kites to lower us safely to the ground, where we joined the mess already in progress.

It was no easy fight. The Iron Ringers were appalled by the loss of their war machine, and they had deployed poorly, expecting to scourge an already-depleted camp in the wake of their invincible iron talisman. They were also massed in the open, facing troops in breastworks. Still, they were hard fighters and well-led, and so many Elarans were second-line militia or already exhausted by the long labors of the night.

I'll leave it to other historians to weigh the causes and the cruxes of true victory in the Battle of Lake Corlan. We were in it everywhere, rattling about the field via horses and sorcery and very tired feet, for many Iron Ring magicians remained alive and dangerous. In the shadow of our abandoned joke of an effigy engine, we fought for our pay and our oath, and as the sun finally turned red behind its veils of powder smoke, we and ten thousand Elarans watched in exhausted exaltation as the Iron Ring army finally broke like a wave on our shores, a wave that parted and sank and ran into the darkness.

After six months of raids and minor successes and placeholder, proxy victories, six months of stalemate capped by the terror of a brand-new way of warfare, the Elarans had flung an army twice the size of their own back in confusion and defeat at last.

It was not the end of their war, and the butcher's bill would be terrible. But it was something. It meant hope, and frankly, when someone hires the Red Hats, that's precisely what we're expected to provide.

In the aftermath of the battle I worked some sorcery for the hospital details, then stumbled, spell-drunk and battered, to the edge of the gaping pit now serving as a tomb for the mighty war machine and its occupants.

I have to admit I waxed pitifully philosophical as

I studied the wreck. It wouldn't be an easy thing to duplicate, but it could be done, with enough wizards and enough skilled engineers, and small mountains of steel and gold. Would the Iron Ring try again? Would other nations attempt to build such devices of their own? Was that the future of sorcerers like myself, to become power sources for hulking metal beasts, to drain our lives into their engines?

I, Watchdog, a lump of coal, a fagot for the flames.

I shook my head then and I shake my head now. War is my trade, but it makes me so damned tired sometimes. I don't have any answers. I keep my oath, I keep my book, I take my pay and I guard my friends from harm. I suppose we are all lumps of coal destined for one furnace or another.

I found the rest of the company in various states of total collapse near the trampled, smoldering remains of General Vorstal's command pavilion. Our options had been limited when we'd selected a place to build our machine, and unfortunately the trap path had been drawn across all the Elaran high command's nice things.

Caladesh was unconscious with a shattered wagon wheel for a pillow. Tariel had actually fallen sleep sitting up, arms wrapped around her musket. My mother was sipping coffee and staring at Rumstandel, who was snoring like some sort of cave-beast while miniature coronas of foul weather sparked around his beard. In lieu of a pillow, Rumstandel had enlisted one of his familiars, a tubby little bat-demon that stood silently, holding Rumstandel's bald head off the ground like an athlete heaving a weight over its shoulders.

"He looks so peaceful, doesn't he?" whispered Millowend. She muttered and gestured, and a bright new red hat appeared out of thin air, gently lowering itself onto Rumstandel's brow. He continued snoring.

"There," she said, with no little satisfaction. "Be sure to record that in your chronicles, will you, Watchdog?"

The reader will note that I have been pleased to comply.

AMETHYST, SHADOW, AND LIGHT

SALADIN AHMED

"I JUST THINK it's a bad idea," Zok Ironeyes said as he sat down to a hilltop meal of oatcakes and pigeon eggs with Hai Hai. Below them, across a vast expanse of the greygrass that gave Greygrass Barrows its name, stood the small manor house under discussion. Zok popped a pickled egg into his mouth and turned his gaze from the bright green house to his partner's beady black eyes.

Hai Hai waved a dismissive white paw. Her long, pink-tipped ears drooped slightly, as they did when she was annoyed. "'A bad idea.' That's what you *always* say. That's what you said about the Mad Monk's Meadery."

Zok chewed and swallowed. "And we were nearly killed by the shade of a baby-eating cleric there."

"You were happy enough with the spoils, though —that case of rubywine and the two whores with the rhyming names." The rabbitwoman smiled wickedly and took a bite of her oatcake.

Zok also smiled in spite of himself. "Anyway, abandoned house, unattended loot that somehow hasn't been claimed yet—this all sounds too good. A beautiful beer-bottle with poison inside." But even as he said it, he was plotting out their approach in his mind.

The greygrass was tall enough that even Zok could approach unseen. The sweet-smelling blades swayed in the breeze, enough so that the duo's movement might be masked. It was either a perfect score or a trap.

Zok knew how that usually ended. Still, the Thousand Gods damn him, he'd never been able to resist a ripe peach dangling from a low branch.

He ate his last pigeon egg. Perhaps Hai Hai's mewling stooge had told the truth. Perhaps the place had been left unattended all season. The Legion kept a relative peace on the roads, even this far out, but bandits were hardly unheard of. Not to mention wolves and grasscats. The owners would have to be away to have left the ground uncleared so close to the front door.

Unless they had... other ways of keeping watch.

Zok took a long pull from his wineskin and turned it all over in his mind again. But there was little point. Either they went in, as quiet as they could, or they didn't. "This source of yours... you trust him?"

Hai Hai drained her own wineskin, and a thin red rivulet trickled down her chin, staining her white fur. "Foxshit and fire, Zok, no, I don't trust him! It's a fucking gamble, same as anything we do in this road-life of ours. How many Thousand-Gods-damned fool errands have I followed *you* on? Hunting that toad-headed demon you're always going on about? Peace and honor to your dead wife, man, but—"

Zok nearly growled at the blithe mention of Fraja's name. Out of habit, his fingers went into his purse and touched the earring that was his only memento of his wife.

Hai Hai saw the fire in his eyes. "I'm sorry, Zok. I know she was a fine woman, but she was nothing to *me*. I've helped you try to avenge her because you're my *partner*. That means something. So if I say 'here's a score,' you should..."

As Hai Hai spoke, Zok stood and strapped his bespelled broadsword Menace to his hip. By the time she finished her little speech, he was already moving quietly down the hill toward the manor house.

ZOK KNEELED AT the edge of the greygrass with Hai Hai, only thirty yards from the house.

The two-storey house was made of green-glazed brick, and had a flat, crenelated roof. Stables, a small barn, and a shed stood off to the side. Not a sound came from any of the buildings. No light from lamps, no smoke from fires. No animals about, either, other than the odd sparrow or squirrel.

The front door of the green house was a slab of etchwood covered in images of animals. Zok knew right away that it was genuine, and his pulse raced at the size and complexity of the nature-wrought scenes. Etchwood was prized for the naturally occurring images it held, but usually one found a single flower or a sun. A slab this size, with this many little pictures... Zok smiled, despite his unease. One part of the story was true, at least—there was great wealth here.

Beside him, Hai Hai sniffed once, and her ears stiffened. She gave him the *someone's here* hand gesture. Zok's muscles tensed. He looked before him, behind him. Nothing.

Something struck him hard from above. The quiet afternoon exploded with shouts.

A man had dropped onto him from the rooftop. Even as he crumpled to the ground, Zok shoved his attacker away. The man—no more than a blur of colorful robes to Zok's eyes—was on top of him again in an instant. *Where is Hai Hai?* Zok couldn't see his partner. Worse, he couldn't reach his sword.

Zok wrestled with his attacker. The man smelled of cloves, and his mustache was long and braided. *An Eastlander? What in the Three Hells is he doing here, besides trying to kill me?* Somewhere behind him he heard a woman shouting and Hai Hai cursing.

Menace's hilt dug into his ribs. Zok tried to gouge the man's eyes, tried to get space for a good head-butt. But despite being much smaller, the Eastlander was nearly as strong as Zok. Few enough men could say that.

Zok felt the battle-madness rise in him. *Enough of this.* He twisted and bit the Eastlander, tasting blood.

It worked. The man screamed and looked at Zok as if he had just become a giant viper. Zok seized on the Eastlander's surprise. He managed to flip the man onto his back, then sat astride him, pinning his wrists. A dozen yards away, Hai Hai was facing off against a small, dark-haired woman also wearing vibrant robes. The rabbitwoman had lost one of her sabers. The Eastlander woman wasn't armed, but a strange glow surrounded her hands, and they danced like weapons.

Zok looked back to his attacker. Now that he'd

shit in my stew! Not a Fatherpriest. Zok
mind the road-priests who, nominally at least,
ed every one of the Thousand Gods. But he
ver met a man who wore the shining tabard
asn't a pompous sack of scum. And they had
wer of the Empress behind them, which made
dangerous scum. A man with a sword at his
lowed the priest in, then closed the door and
silently beside it.

Fatherpriest studied Zok again for a long
t, as if he were considering buying a horse.
*n come check my teeth, then, and I'll bite off
king fingers.*

e stayed a good ten feet back from Zok. "My
ou are called Zok Ironeyes, yes?" he said at
am Father Gabrien, servant of the Fathergod.
.."

hawked up what wretchedness he could
e back of his throat and spit it at the man,
ching his pristine tabard and cutting off his
"What have you done with my partner?"
outed. "She had better be alive, shit-for-
"

had hoped to goad the man close enough to
n. But the priest showed no rage. He smiled
ssly, ignoring Zok's question.

ien ignored the question. "I am about to
n you, my son. Do not think to attack me. For
ommand, that necklace you wear—my little
you—will return to the size of a finger-ring.
ling on which command word I use, it can
ehead you as it does so, or reappear on your
s a harmless but valuable piece of jewellery.
understand?"

been pinned, the man didn't struggle. He just lay
there, staring at Zok as if at a mad dog.

Only then did Zok notice the man's necklace.
Around his neck was an incredibly thin band of what
looked like... amethyst. The stone of the Empire.

Zok could still hear Hai Hai and the Eastlander
woman, but he could no longer see them.

*Do they work for the Amethyst Empress? Why
in the Three Hells would Easterners be working for
the Empire? Who are these people?* They were good,
whoever they were. That rooftop blow would have
knocked most men cold.

But Zok was not most men.

"Stand down, woman, or I'll kill your friend here!"
he shouted. It was a bluff—as soon as Zok released
the man's hands he'd have a fighting opponent
again—but it was worth a try.

"Zok, don't—" Hai Hai's shout came from
somewhere behind him before it was cut short. Zok
turned, trying to keep hold of his captive. He saw
Hai Hai sprawled at the robed woman's feet.

Then the Eastlander twisted away hard, breaking
free of Zok's grip. Something—some sort of pink
light—blazed forth from the man's hand, catching
Zok full in the face. It burned his eyes, and he had
trouble breathing. In an instant, he felt the magical
light clouding his mind as well.

"Bind them," he heard the Eastlander say from far
away. Only then did he realize he was lying on the
ground. It was all Zok could do to keep his eyes
open. After another moment, he couldn't even do
that.

* * *

ZOK AWOKE IN chains. It had happened to him enough times that he did not panic. He was indoors, in a drafty building with a high ceiling. It was dark—the dark just before sunrise, his body told him, which meant he'd been out for hours—and his nose picked up the faded scents of horse and riding-beast nearby. He guessed he was in the stables of the house he'd just tried to rob.

He tested his bonds once, twice, thrice. But it was no use—whoever had chained him had known just how strong he was.

Just as his eyes were adjusting to the dark, a weasel of a man entered the stables. He carried a torch in one hand, and what looked like a jewellery box in the other.

"Who do you work for? Those Easterners?" Zok asked, his voice cracking. "And where is my partner? Best tell me now, little man. You know these chains won't hold me long. And as soon as I'm free, I'll snap that skinny neck of yours with my bare hands."

The little man didn't respond. He set the torch into a sconce and opened the small box.

Displayed within was a ring—impossibly delicate, and made of amethyst. It glittered with more than mere torchlight. *Sorcery.*

The man stepped close enough that Zok could smell his breath. Close enough that even a chained man could give him a good headbutt.

Zok lunged as best he could.

There was a pleasing crunch as Zok's skull connected with nose-bone. The man let out a howl and a sob as he snapped back, his ruined nose bleeding badly. He dropped the jewellery box, clutched his face, and ran screaming from the room.

An hour passed as Zok watched the torch burn.

Just as the chains were really [...] another man entered the stables. [...] the last, with cold eyes. He held a [...] in his right hand. Without saying [...] over and shoved it hard into Z[...] jammed it into Zok's balls. It hur[...]

"You ready to wear the ring [...] chance before I fuck you with th[...] been talking about the weather. [...]

Zok's eyes still burned with te[...] win, tough man. Just get me some[...]

The man said not a word. [...] jewellery box and drew the amet[...] Then he took hold of Zok's left ha[...] ring on his little finger.

As soon as he did so, the rin[...] disappeared, though Zok could [...] stone against his skin. There wa[...] and suddenly Zok felt something [...] around his neck.

A ring of amethyst, Zok guess[...] the Eastlanders had worn.

The man with the broomstick [...] *on here?* Zok tested his chains ag[...] he was still held fast.

A moment later, Zok heard the [...] wet huffing sounds of a riding [...] stable door opened again, and so[...] but when Zok's eyes adjusted to t[...] a man, not a beast that he saw en[...]

He was a head shorter than Zo[...] carried himself with the confide[...] And no wonder, given the shinir[...] over his armor.

Zok nodded once. Gabrien's men opened the locks on his chains. Zok suppressed his rage as best he could, keeping his hands from their throats. The Fatherpriest wouldn't have had the nerve to unchain Zok unless he were telling the truth about the amethyst necklace.

"Tell me what you know of the Shadow Weavers, Zok Ironeyes."

The Shadow Weavers? What is this madman about? Zok wondered. He spoke slowly. "The demon-men of the Old Far North, or so the stories go. Ages ago, led by the Dark King, The Man-Shadow, they swept over all of the lands of the Empire That Was. *Shadow, shadow, black as night / Grew until it murdered light.*" Zok spoke the words of the boyhood rhyme without quite meaning to. "Why are you asking me about children's tales? And WHERE IS MY PARTNER?"

"The children's tales tell more truth than you know, my son. Three thousand years ago, the Shadow Weavers—the spawn of man and demon—poured forth from the Plain of Ice and Iron. Northlands, Southlands, Eastlands, Westlands—everywhere they butchered men like animals and ate their souls. Entire kingdoms were slaughtered. Mankind was very nearly destroyed.

"Only the Twelve Clans survived, led by Virgin Queen Glora, whom the Fathergod, in His wisdom, chose as a messenger and a vessel. It was she who finally destroyed the Dark King in single combat, she who sent the Shadow Weavers scurrying back to their holes of cold and metal, but in the battle she was gravely wounded.

"When she died, the Fathergod brought her to His

side, to sit at His right hand and bask in the glow of His love, away from the painful world of men."

Zok yawned, perhaps more loudly than was strictly necessary. He had not been to a Church of the Fathergod in decades, but he remembered the stories well enough. They were no less dull to him now than they'd been as a child, but Gabrien surely had some point to all this blathering.

The Fatherpriest showed no sign that he'd heard Zok's yawn. "Queen Glora rejoiced to finally be in her Celestial Father's presence. But she knew that the Weavers would return one day, and that mankind would need a great power to defeat them. Thus she selflessly asked the Fathergod to..."

"...to pour her soul into the Diamond Diadem that our Empresses have worn for a thousand years. The Diadem proves the righteous rule of so on and so forth and so forth and so on. Get to the point, priest."

Gabrien smiled too broadly for Zok's liking. "The point, my son, is that the Diadem our Empress wears is a sham."

"And? Do you want me to act surprised? What does this have to do with me?"

"This concerns all humanity," Gabrien said quietly. His arrogance was gone. "For the Shadow Weavers are rising again. Indeed, a few of their number already live among us."

"You're mad." Zok said it as soon as he realized it, but he wished he'd held his tongue. The raving priest still held Zok's life in his hands.

"You'll see soon enough that I speak the truth, Zok Ironeyes. But there is hope. For I know where the *true* Diamond Diadem is. And you are going to get it for me."

Zok grunted.

"I have heard of your talents as a thief and a warrior, my son. And though the Fathergod frowns sternly on true thievery, I have need of your skills. As well as those of your... creature." Gabrien gestured toward the stable doors, and his lackey opened them.

Hai Hai walked in, a broad man with a spear following her. She was not chained. She even wore her sabers, though they were bound with peace knots. But glittering at her neck was a thin band of amethyst.

Creature. Ages ago, the beastmen—including Hai Hai's people—were born from dark sorcery. They did not have souls as men did. It was thus a doctrine of the Fatherpriests that the beastmen were no more than animals. But Zok would not let the insult stand, even if Hai Hai hadn't heard it.

"She is my partner, priest, not a *creature.*"

Gabrien waved it away, his gauntlet creaking. Hai Hai was brought to Zok's side, and he exchanged a silent nod with her. Gabrien still spoke only to Zok. "Let me, as you say, get to the point, Zok Ironeyes. I wish to hire you!"

Hai Hai made an obscene gesture with her white-furred paw "Hire? You're not *hiring* us." She touched her amethyst collar. "You're a slaver, *Father.* Putting a wig on the goat you're fucking don't make it a lady."

The priest snarled, finally letting his irritation show. Still, the man spoke only to Zok.

"Let me be as clear as possible, my son. You are house-breakers. The law of the Empire is unambiguous: the sentence for stealing from a manored family is death. But rare exceptions have been made for those who aid the Amethyst Empress. I offer you a simple choice: the swift, harsh justice you have brought upon yourselves, or service and fair payment for that service."

Something—something besides the obvious—wasn't right here. "If the Shadow Weavers are rising, if the true Diamond Diadem has been found, why doesn't the Empress just send the Legion in?" Zok asked.

"You men of the Blackhair North have strange ways. Here in the civilized world, a criminal does not interrogate an ordained Fatherpriest," Gabrien said, but Zok saw the answer in the man's eyes.

"The Empress doesn't know." Zok knew it was true as he said it.

Gabrien smiled and shrugged. "I will not weigh down our Empress's heart with these worries until I can report to her that I have acquired the Diadem."

Zok suppressed an urge to break the man's face. "You mean until *we* have acquired it. And you've taken the glory and earned yourself a Low Kingship."

The Fatherpriest shrugged again. "As you will. In any case, you leave in an hour. Now come, it's time you met your fellow servants of the Empire."

Zok stood outside the stables, where Gabrien's men prepared three riding beasts for travel. He wore a suit of scale armor that Gabrien had provided him. It was a very good fit, which was rare, given Zok's size. He tried to find comfort in this, tried to find calm in the familiar jangle of tack and harness. Hai Hai stood beside him, and the two Eastlanders who had ambushed them—their new allies, it would seem—stood a few feet away. Zok couldn't take his eyes off of the amethyst bands around their necks.

"You have met Ahmaddine Ahl and his wife already," Gabrien said by way of introduction. The Eastlanders nodded silent greetings, but they only held Zok's attention for a moment before a monster of a man stepped forth from the barn.

"This," Gabrien said, "is the Lockcharmer. He... is not one for words."

In all his adult life, Zok had only met three men larger than himself. Now it was four.

Zok could not tell the Lockcharmer's age, and he could not decide whether the massive, hairless man looked more like a cruel grandfather or a monstrous baby. Around the man's neck was another amethyst band.

But it was the Lockcharmer's hands that held Zok's attention. They... *were not his.* Tied to those huge wrists with strange bands of leather and metal, they were far too small for the Lockcharmer's body. Too small for any man's.

They were a child's hands, Zok realized.

"Each of you has been chosen for redemption through service," Gabrien said, speaking to the group now. Zok tore his eyes from the Lockcharmer's tiny fingers.

"A few hours' ride from here, in the catacombs of a ruined castle, a coven of Shadow Weavers has discovered the true Diamond Diadem of Virgin Queen Glora. In two days' time they will use the power of the new moon to spirit themselves, and the Diadem, away to the Far North. If that happens, mankind is doomed."

"So why don't *you* stop it, priest?" the Eastlander woman snarled.

"If I approach these creatures, they will sense the light of the Fathergod within me and know my approach from a mile away, the way a deer scents a hunter. But more impure souls—souls with dark spots upon them—the Weavers cannot smell such filth."

Ahmaddine Ahl snorted his contempt, and his wife narrowed her eyes, but they said nothing.

"In one night, my children, you can go from being the dregs of humanity to being its saviours. Heathens, thieves, abominations—each of you has your role to play here. And each of you can find redemption. Zok Ironeyes here shall be your field leader. The Eastlanders will be your greatest defense against the Weavers themselves, who fear light-magic more than any weapon. I don't doubt that the Weavers are keeping the Diadem in one of their legendarily impenetrable Ebon Chests. The Lockcharmer's task is to open it if so. As soon as you have the Diadem, return here. The riding beasts will know the way. Now go."

"A moment," Gabrien said, pulling Zok aside and handing him a map. He spoke quickly and quietly as the others prepared to mount up. "The Lockcharmer's crimes are greater than you can imagine, Zok Ironeyes. You will earn an additional reward if, in the name of the Empress's justice, you kill him after you acquire the Diadem. But only after! For he is the only man living who knows the secret of opening the Ebon Chests."

Zok glanced at Hai Hai and the others. "How do I know you haven't said the same to each of us? Maybe you're worried one of us will alert the Empress? Or will take the Diadem for himself? Maybe you just wish us to kill each other to save you some work. You want butchery done, you do it yourself, you soft-palmed dog-fucker. Now leave me be, so I can steal this thing you need stolen." He shook off Gabrien's hand and joined the others.

THE RIDING BEASTS' feet slapped rhythmically on the hard-packed dirt of the road. They rode in pairs, Zok beside Hai Hai, the Eastlander beside his wife. The Lockcharmer, who was either unwilling or unable to speak, rode behind them. Zok felt the huge man's stare on his back, like a beetle crawling up his spine.

"You come from the east," Zok said to the Eastlander, gesturing at the man's braided moustache and the pair's bright fighting-robes. "From beyond the Sea of Sand and Bones, if I don't miss my guess."

The man nodded. "We are people of Mokhul. In times of peace, I am called Ahmaddine Ahl." He touched the amethyst band around his neck, gave a bitter snort, and frowned hard. "But it would seem this is a time to use one's war-name. So you can call me the Rose. And this is my wife."

If anything the woman's look was harder than her husband's. "I am the Shrike, called Lasha Ahl in times of peace."

"And you are Gabrien's agents?" Hai Hai butted in.

"His agents?" Lasha Ahl spat. "Do you not see these bands around our necks? He ambushed us. We are his captives, same as you, Lady of the Hares." Zok knew little of Eastlanders, but he had heard that they respected the beastmen more than the men of the Westlands did.

Ahmaddine Ahl wore a deep scowl. "This thing needs doing. The Shadow Weavers nearly destroyed all of humanity once. You Westlanders have forgotten—you think the great Man-Shadow was destroyed for all time, if you believe he existed at all. Things are different on the other side of the Sea of Sand and Bones. We remember. And if the Weavers are truly rising again, no Mokhuli warrior worth her robes will refuse the call to battle. But this savage Gabrien dares to try and *compel* us to hunt the Weavers, in order to further *his* glory? When we are done with what must be done, we will return and kill *Father* Gabrien." He patted the curved knife that hung at his belt.

Zok turned to see if the Lockcharmer had heard the Rose's words, but the big man just sat his beast, holding the reins in those tiny hands, staring ahead, saying nothing. They rode on until late afternoon, the land rising as the miles passed.

Finally, the road crested a hill and they saw it—the small, ruined castle that Gabrien had described. A piece of wall or a rotted beam stood here and there, but Zok was only interested in the great, crumbling tower that dominated the horizon.

He reined in his beast and dismounted, gesturing for the others to do the same. "The entrance the priest mentioned is right there, inside that collapsed tower. Find a few sturdy trees, and tie the beasts to them. From here we go on foot, and we use only the silent signals that we rehearsed."

They picked their way down the other side of the hill, the thinning foliage providing dubious cover. Zok almost felt he was reliving last night's failed housebreaking, that he was walking into another trap. He winced at every jangle of his armor. But they each moved as quietly as possible, even the Lockcharmer who carried his bulk with a surprising grace.

The last fifty yards before the ruined tower held no trees or thickets big enough to hide them. But there was little they could do about it. Zok's fingers went to the amethyst collar around his neck.

Best get to it, then. He sniffed twice at Hai Hai and jerked his head toward the broken tower. She shook her head. She didn't smell anything suspicious. Zok waved his hand urgently and they all trotted toward the tower.

The rusty cellar door was just where Gabrien had said it would be, and it was open, as he'd also said it would be. No sentries met them, no alarms sounded. Room after ruined room held stagnant air, broken stone, or earth that had encroached past the shattered walls. Except for the eerie lack of vermin, it could have been any one of the dozen ruins Zok had seen over the years. Except that he didn't need his torch. Every room they explored, every hall they walked, was lit by a cold, flickering purple light. But there were no torches, so Zok couldn't say where the light was coming from.

Finally they found themselves facing a large, open chamber. It was hewn from dark stone and seemed too airy and open to be beneath a ruin. It had clearly been built with sorcery. The same flickering purple light that lit the halls filled the chamber and it revealed a grim scene.

A brown-skinned girl of maybe eight years—the first living thing Zok had seen in this place—stood on a dais, shackled to a post. At her feet sat a huge chest of ebon wood and black metal. Surrounding the dais were a half-dozen men who were not men.

They were tall and thin, shrouded in black rags and mail. Their strangely stretched faces were the yellow-white of moonlight, and their red eyes shone with a dull glow. Zok felt an unnatural fear seize him as he stared, and his guts twisted up until he felt like shitting blood.

Shadow Weavers. So it was true. And they were about to perform some sort of ritual. *That cannot be good.*

Beside him, the Rose and the Shrike sucked in simultaneous breaths. The Lockcharmer grunted and whined quietly. Only Hai Hai seemed unaffected by the unholy sight. She stood still as stone, studying the scene with those eyes of black glass.

And then, without warning, the Weavers spun as one, their red eyes searching the room. They knew that Zok and the others were there. One of them pointed with a thin, impossibly long finger, and let out a keening scream.

Then the demon-men flew forward.

Zok raised his sword, and Menace glowed in anticipation of the fight. Hai Hai shot forward, her sabers slicing out before her. Red and blue light danced in the hands of the Eastlanders. Behind Zok, the Lockcharmer whined.

The Weavers attacked. They moved like roiling clouds, but their red eyes only seemed to see the Eastlanders. Half walking, half flying, they shot around Zok before he could even swing at them.

"Get to the chest!" the Shrike shouted. Her hands danced madly, and a wall of sky blue light appeared, cutting the Eastlanders and the Weavers off from Zok, Hai Hai, and the Lockcharmer, who was wailing like a baby.

"We will hold them!" the Rose shouted. "Get the chest open! The Diadem will destroy them all!"

Zok didn't bother to ask how he knew this. He tried to push the Lockcharmer toward the Ebon Chest, but the big man just stood there staring at the girl in chains.

She was shackled at hand and foot, but appeared not to have been harmed in any visible way. The Weavers were soul-eaters. Perhaps they didn't care about the girl's body?

But it seemed the Lockcharmer *did* care. Zok did not like the look the man gave the girl.

"Open the chest, gimp!" Zok shouted, placing himself between the girl and the big man. "That's what you're here for!" Hai Hai was hacking at the Ebon Chest and fiddling with the lock, but she surely knew as well as Zok did that it was useless.

"The chest!" Zok cried again, but the Lockcharmer didn't move.

"You... you're a man!" the girl shouted upon seeing Zok. "You're not a monster. Please! Please help me!" Her voice trembled, but she did not cry. Most grown men would have. *Strong,* Zok noted with approval.

A quick, careful blow from Menace shattered the girl's chains. Then Zok heard the Lockcharmer shuffling behind him.

"Prize." It was the first word the Lockcharmer had spoken in a day. He took a step toward the girl, and her eyes went wide with fear. When she caught sight of his monstrous little hands, she screamed. The Lockcharmer took another step and began giggling. "PRIZE!" He shouted it this time, like an excited child.

Zok got in the big man's face. Menace was still in his hand. Zok had seen this kind of lust before—had learned more about it than any child should have to. He would not let the Lockcharmer have this girl. Zok decided he would kill the man, but not until the Ebon Chest had been opened.

"You fool, open the chest! The Eastlanders won't hold out forever!" Indeed, beyond the wall of blue light, Zok saw the Rose slumped on the ground. The Weavers—there were only four of them now—closed around the Shrike.

The Lockcharmer looked down at Zok—something few enough men could do. "PRIZE!" he bellowed again, angry this time. Gabrien had teamed Zok with a madman who couldn't control his lusts. The Lockcharmer wouldn't be talked out of this. He would have to die.

Don't be a fool, Zok told himself. *You need this one to get out of here alive!* But even as he thought it, he was flying at the Lockcharmer. The man was huge but unarmed, and with those weird hands of his, he wasn't much of a fighter.

It was quick work. The Lockcharmer screamed, then he died. The girl looked on in horror.

Hai Hai barely glanced at Zok before her shiny eyes went to the bleeding corpse. "Are you mad? You oaf! How in the Three Hells are we supposed to get out of here now? We..."

Zok nodded once toward the girl, then looked down at the body.

Hai Hai took his meaning. She spat and began to tap her foot. "We'll figure out something," she said.

Zok checked the Ebon Chest. It was worth a try. He started to set his hand on the lock but looked up when he heard the Shrike scream. He did so just in time to watch her fall. Three of the demon-men still stood.

Then the wall of light was gone. And the Shadow Weavers strode toward them.

As soon as those glowing red eyes were upon him, Zok heard words in his head.

They held light in their hands. They could not hear our voice. You can hear our voice.

The Great Man-Shadow shall be reborn. Be still. The Dark King will reign again. Be still. The voice seemed to come from all of them, and from none of them. It was male and female, high-pitched and low-toned.

Be still, it said, *be still.* The words were like a soft, long-fingered hand taking hold of his soul. And, in spite of himself, Zok felt his body obeying. His left hand fell from the Ebon Chest, and Menace dropped from his right.

A half-dozen more Weavers swarmed silently into the room like the shadows of swift-moving clouds. They massed at the foot of the dais but did not climb it.

You are better than the girl. You will be the vessel, the voice said.

"I will be the vessel," Zok said, unable to keep himself from speaking. Beside him, Hai Hai stood stock-still, as did the girl. Zok's feet began shuffling forward, and he could not stop his own body.

The voice spoke again, this time to Hai Hai and the girl. *You will be servants. You will leave this room and await us.*

The girl repeated the words and stepped down from the dais.

Hai Hai droned in repetition: "I will leave this room." She walked down the steps of the dais. "I

79

will leave this room," she repeated, "...after you cook my breakfast, eat my cunny, and die by fire!"

The Weavers were confused, their half-rotted minds unable, it seemed, to understand drollery. When Hai Hai flew at them with her sabers, though—they recognized that.

Zok felt his mind clear in an instant. The spell holding him had broken with the Weavers' concentration. The girl screamed and ran out of the room.

And then Zok heard another voice in his head. A woman's voice, as different from that of the Weavers as day was from night. *Place your hands on the Ebon Chest! Free me! Your worthiness will open the lock!* The voice was like sunlight and honey. Zok obeyed it instantly. His placed his hands on the lock.

There was a sound like a thousand chimes, and the lid flew open in a burst of golden light. All movement in the chamber stopped.

The Diamond Diadem floated up out of the Ebon Chest. It revolved slowly in midair, suspended in a beam of golden light, sparkling with the light of a thousand sun-dappled diamonds. Zok had been in the presence of powerful sorcery a hundred times, but nothing like this. He felt waves of pure power and grace wash over his soul.

Something very different happened to the Weavers when the light hit them. There was no flame, but they burned nonetheless. There was a horrible wailing, then robes and mail, flesh and bones all dissolved into ash. And just like that, Zok stood alone in the room with Hai Hai and the true Diamond Diadem of Virgin Queen Glora, which slowly lowered itself back onto the velvet cushion that sat inside the Ebon Chest.

Hear me, Zok Ironeyes! Hear the voice of the light! As with the voices of the Shadow Weavers, the voice seemed to come from everywhere and nowhere. But it was unmistakably a single voice— female, powerful, and clear as a clarion breaking a silent morning. Suddenly the Ebon Chest seemed more a throne than a box.

I am Glora, the Virgin Queen, servant of the Fathergod. I am the Diamond Diadem.

I was made to fight the Shadow Weavers, but they sought to use my power for evil. But you, in your worthiness, have freed me!

But you must not take me to the one who sent you. He means to serve the Fathergod, but he is consumed with pride and ambition. I release you from his power.

Zok heard a tinkling like glass. He felt the amethyst band around his neck crumble to dust. Beside him the same happened to Hai Hai's.

Over the centuries and millennia, granted glimpses by the Fathergod, I have watched humanity. And I have learned much. One of the things I have learned is that His servants sometimes take the most unlikely shapes. In your impurity, Zok Ironeyes, you are pure. And you have great strength. The strength that the world needs. That is why you must claim me.

Zok finally worked up the power of speech again. "You want *me* to wear you?"

No. The voice sounded like a pretty woman's sad smile to his ears. Like clouded sunshine. *No, you must destroy me. The power I bear is too great for men to wield. Only now do I see that. Now that I have been found again, this world is in grave danger.*

But saving this world of men will mean a long journey and great sacrifice. You must cast me from the peak of Broken Sword Mountain, into the fathomless depths of the Sable Sea. There, the tainted waves will devour me—and I will finally be beyond the reach of men and demons alike.

"And if I don't?" Zok asked.

There was a long silence. *If you do not, Zok Ironeyes, then evil will triumph!*

Zok stretched. It had been a hard few days, and he ached all over. "Sorry to say it, Majesty, but I really don't give a black bear's bushy balls about all that. Goodbye." He turned to go.

You do not understand! If I am not destroyed, some evil man—or worse, the Weavers—will find me! Darkness will cover the land! Children will die!

Zok shrugged, listening to the sound of his armor. It was good scale, and if he was lucky he could sell it for a few months' fancy boarding for Hai Hai and himself. That was about the best that he was going to get out of this miserable little adventure, it seemed. *Ah, well.* He'd had jobs that paid worse.

"Children die," he said at last. "The girl was in front of me. That's why I freed her. As for the rest of it, Majesty... well, the world will take care of itself. It always does."

Zok stepped to the Ebon Chest. Slowly, carefully, he closed the lid.

As Hai Hai and he walked out of the chamber, the muffled wailing of Virgin Queen Glora's soul sounded like a harp being played by an angry weasel.

They reached the outside, and footprints in the dust told Zok that the girl had done the same. *Good.*

Keeping an eye out for any more demon-men, they retrieved the riding beasts. For a long time, they rode in silence. Finally Zok said, "The Weavers' spell didn't work on you."

Hai Hai shrugged. "Soul magic. And, as the fox-fucking Fatherpriests will be quick to tell you, I ain't got a soul."

"But the Weavers were fooled. You could have fled alone."

Another shrug. "We are partners. That means something, right?"

"Right."

The tips of Hai Hai's ears drooped in annoyance. "Anyway, if you're going to burble like a woman about it, get it over with now, huh? We've a long ride ahead."

Zok smiled at his partner, spurred his riding-beast to a scurry, and said not a word.

CAMP FOLLOWER
TRUDI CANAVAN

CONTRARY TO WHAT the soldiers said, it was not after battle that Captain Reny enjoyed the services of the whore in his tent. After battle, he was too exhausted to do more than wash off the blood and gore, even if he only ever fought when the King decided to join the fight, or to protect his leader. Reny was too old for the victorious lustful celebrations the soldiers imagined their commanders enjoyed.

It was during the time between battles, after long meetings to discuss strategy, that he made use of the woman. Aside from the physical release and the sensual pleasure, he gained something even more valuable—a time in which he was free from thought and care. The past and the future did not penetrate his mind.

But all too soon he would be lying awake, his mind starting to dwell on matters best forgotten or ignored. As he was now.

To delay the return of those memories, he looked down at the woman sleeping on the floor beside his narrow stretcher-bed, and thought about her instead. She'd told him her name was Kala, but he doubted that was her true name. It was too common among the camp followers. Apparently it meant 'lucky charm', which was far too appealing a name in a time of war to be a real one.

Her waist was narrow, but she widened above and below in ways a woman ought to. He guessed she'd joined the other camp followers not long before he'd noticed her, or she would have been as skinny and wasted as they were. Yet he hadn't chosen her for her body alone. Something in her eyes reassured him. It was an *awareness* that told him she knew exactly what she was doing, despite her obvious youth, and wasn't tormented by it. It was the absence of desperation, loathing, horror or resignation in her face that had caused him to look twice, and invite her to join him.

All his doubts about her had faded as the days and weeks, villages and towns had fallen to the advancing army. She did not chatter, did not fawn or beg, and never complained. She was quiet, obedient and willing. She rubbed his sore muscles after battle. She had a skill with the cook pot that could turn the worst of rationed foodstuffs into edible fare.

Choosing her had been the best thing he'd done since joining the Conquest.

LOOKING DOWN FROM *the ridge, Reny felt the breath catch in his throat. Wavy, sinuous lines of trampled whetta ran between the forest and the farmhouse. A lot of people had passed this way. The sort of people who did not care if they ruined a crop. This could be evidence of their arriving or leaving. They could be gone or still in the farmhouse. Reny's anger at this careless destruction was overtaken by dread.*

Then he was at the house. He tried to shout but could not make a sound. I don't need to see this again. *Though he knew what he would find, he started searching.* I'm dreaming; I must wake myself up. *There was nobody in the kitchen where he knew he should find his wife... doomed to die after agonising days of pain and fever from infection within.*

Better they had killed her than left her like this. *The rooms upstairs were also empty. He ought to be grateful to not see, yet again, what they had done to his daughter and youngest son, but instead their absence left him fraught and hollow.*

They're gone. Where have they gone?

In the distance he heard the sound of horns—

He jolted awake.

And remembered.

His homeland had been invaded by the Henelan. The Laxen, his own people, had offered their empty throne to a sorcerer mercenary, Dael, if he would defeat their enemy. Within a year the Henelan, to the last child, no longer existed. A secret agreement was discovered between other neighbouring lands, who had planned to carve up Laxen among themselves once they defeated the Henelan. So a greater war started, until someone came up with the idea that lands united were lands free of warfare. And so, the Conquest began.

A retired soldier and former strategy adviser to the King of Laxen, Reny had offered his services to Dael at the beginning. When he had told Kala this, she had asked how long ago it had been, and he could not tell her the exact number of years with confidence. More than ten. Not as many as twenty.

The horns in his dreams rang out again, but his time he knew them to be real: the signal that the army was to pack up and be ready to march. Reny cursed and got to his feet. The woman looked up at him, a question in her eyes.

"Packing time," he told her.

She got up and started moving about, opening the trunks that held his belongings and putting what had been removed back inside them. He moved to the tent opening and looked out, then sighed heavily and turned back to see her watching him, her smooth brow wrinkling in mute enquiry.

"I should have been told about this," he answered. "Vorl is still punishing me for disobeying him."

She nodded and started folding the bedding, but her frown did not fade.

"It was something that happened before we… before I invited you to my tent," he explained.

The look she gave him was accepting, as if she didn't expect him to tell her anything more, but he thought he saw a glint of curiosity in her eyes.

He took a deep breath. "Vorl had just been promoted to General. He wanted to test his authority. In the wrong situation, that can make a man do needlessly cruel things. Or order others to do so. I refused."

She grimaced in sympathy and understanding. "Do you regret it?" she asked in her lilting voice. Her strange accent had been annoying at first, but now that he'd grown familiar enough to understand her he found it appealing.

He considered her question, looking away as he

remembered the incident. "No. Besides, I don't think I could have managed it anyway. Perhaps Vorl guessed that and wanted me humiliated." He turned back to find her looking bemused, and smiled grimly in apology. "Sorry, that won't make much sense to you. Dael sent Vorl to attack a place in the mountains. Though it was not directly in the path of the army, there was a risk people there could attack our rear if we didn't deal with them first. It turned out to be a temple run by women. Priestesses. No threat at all."

Kala went still, her face hardening as she comprehended the fate of the priestesses.

"And you refused to take part?"

Her voice was deeper and stronger than he had heard it before. It also had a tone of demand. Another man in his position might have punished her for that, he realised.

"Yes." He shuddered. To watch what had been done to his wife and daughter being done to others… He pushed the memory away and set his mind on packing. Kala, accepting his silence, said nothing more for some time; then, as the last tent rope loosened and the oilcloth collapsed on the ground, she glanced sideways at him.

"Dael hasn't got rid of you yet. You must still be valuable to him," she said quietly.

He shrugged, too astonished by her insight to be angry at her presumption. "Until Vorl convinces him otherwise."

"Vorl is a weapon, to be used and discarded when blunted. Advisers are like scrolls or books, to be consulted over and over. You don't hit your enemy with a book, then go consult your sword, do you?"

He stared at her in amazement, but she was walking away, stooping to take up one side of the tent and start folding it ready for travel.

THE STINK OF sweat, blood and gut juices permeated Reny's skin and clothing. These last were of an enemy soldier who had managed to dash through the front line of soldiers and Dael's guards only to impale himself on the captain's sword. Reny suspected he'd never forget the expression of surprise and dismay on the young man's face.

He reached the tent, staggered inside and stood there, swaying in the lamplight.

I'm still alive. Another battle survived.

Two buckets of water waited next to a neatly folded pile of clothing, ready for his return, but something was missing. He frowned and cast his eyes about the tent. Kala was absent.

Probably getting more water. Or food. Or something. He shrugged and started cleaning himself up. Long experience had taught him to start from the top of his head and work his way down, so that gore that might be trapped within his armour, clothing or hair would not drip onto parts already cleaned. Each piece of armour was removed separately; the soiled clothing stripped off and set aside. It was not easy this time, without Kala's help, but he felt a perverse determination to do it himself. *Do I think that if I show her I can manage this myself, she'll make sure she's here next time in case I decide I don't need her anymore?*

Once he was clean, he donned fresh undergarments, then set about putting much of the armour back on.

Fortunately the protective shell was not heavy. Most of it was hardened leather and when camped on the battlefield he avoided removing it as much as possible. The enemy might launch a stealthy night attack. It had happened in the past. The King's army had lost many good leaders.

Even though exhaustion usually overrode discomfort, it was torture to sleep in full armour, so Reny compromised by leaving off the back piece. When he was ready for sleep and found Kala still hadn't returned, something made him turn from the bed and replace the missing piece. He paced around the confines of the tent slowly, then went looking for her outside.

He trudged around the camp twice in the deepening night, even checking Vorl's tent. In the end, he found her, but only because he had overheard a watcher chatting to the man sent to replace him.

"...one with the yellow hair again."

"Same as last night. I searched her when she came back, but she wasn't carrying anything. She still out there?"

Reny had stopped to listen, his heart skipping at the mention of yellow hair. The two men were squinting out over the battlefield. His eyes followed their gaze. A thin sliver of moon lit a landscape that was far lumpier than it had appeared when the army had arrived a few days before. Figures moved about carrying lamps, bending and stooping over the dark mounds.

Reny had seen and watched this post-battle ritual many times before. Long after battle had ceased, the field remained a scene of activity. The wounded deemed to have a chance at recovery were carried from the field, but those considered unlikely to survive were given a quick and merciful death. Despite rules against the practice, whores also slipped out after darkness to take trinkets and small weapons from the bodies of the dead, though if they were spotted returning to the camp they risked losing the most part of their takings to the watchmen as bribes. Soldiers did not look favourably on those who stole from the dead—unless they benefited from it themselves.

Surely Kala was not partaking in this shameful trade? Reny had taken care of her as best he could, though admittedly hers was hardly a life of comfort and riches. Was she greedy for more? As Reny stared out into the darkness his eyes were drawn to a figure, familiar in the way it moved. Suddenly he did not want to know. *But if it is her and the soldiers hear I'm keeping a scavenger in my tent...*

Sighing, he set out onto the battlefield. As he approached the figure he felt his heart sink. It was Kala.

She hadn't seen him yet. He stopped, suddenly reluctant to approach. Perhaps he could try to pretend he didn't know what she had done. The thought of throwing her out and returning to an empty tent each night was surprisingly painful.

While he watched, she squatted beside one of the dark shapes. He heard a groan, and then a voice.

"Please. End it for me," the voice begged. "I can't... stand it anymore. *Please.*"

Kala reached out and touched the soldier's face gently. "I will give you peace," she said.

She moved her hand down and spread her fingers out over his chest. Reny could see that the man was shaking convulsively. The air between her hand and the soldier rippled, then her fingers slowly curled into a fist. The man gasped, let out a long breath and went limp.

Reny's skin pricked with cold. He felt the world shift around him like a wheel on a carriage slipping into a rut. He knew nothing would be the same again.

Kala got to her feet. She looked down at the soldier, then sighed and shook her head. Stepping away, she began walking among the bodies with slow and unhurried steps.

She is no thief, Reny realised. *She took nothing.* But he knew that wasn't true.

She had taken the man's life. Something within him *knew* this. He considered the shimmering air he'd seen between her hand and the dying soldier. It would be so easy to dismiss it as a bit of air heated by a campfire behind her, shimmering around her arm as she made a gesture of sympathy toward the man. But there was no campfire nearby.

Clearly she was not just a whore.

He had seen Dael perform magic, both subtle and dazzling. To deny the possibility that she was a sorcerer would be foolish and dangerous. Kala was walking away from him now. She hadn't noticed him standing there. He waited until she was too far away to hear or see him, then he made his way back to the camp. As he reached the watchmen, two soldiers overtook him, carrying a wounded man between them.

"We found him!" they called out to two other soldiers, who hurried to join them. "He'd been knocked out." They set the wounded man they had rescued down beside a campfire. Reny paused to watch as the man sat up and groggily accepted some water.

"I've seen Lady Death," the man said, his eyes wide. "And she's beautiful."

The four soldiers laughed.

"Must have been a good knock to the head."

"Just like you to have visions of pretty women."

"Well, if you're going to have visions, why not ones of pretty women?"

"I saw her," the wounded man said. "She saw me. But she let me live. She said I would live."

They laughed again.

Reny shook his head and continued on to his tent. From such talk, superstitions and legends might spring. He hoped Kala knew what she was doing.

If she returned tonight, he wasn't going to ask what it was.

IT MUST HAVE been torment enough to be dragged, defeated and in chains, to face one's enemy. But to have been given the freedom to walk to meet his conqueror, and then waste that small gift of dignity by stumbling and falling onto his face in the mud, was too much humiliation for the prince. There were smothered sniggers among the audience of army captains, though not from the captive locals brought to witness the surrender of their leader. He struggled to rise, but could not get his legs under him on the steep embankment. A low sob escaped him, then two guards came forward, hauled him back to his feet and half-carried him forward, forcing him to his knees before Dael. He sagged, all pride and fight gone, his head bowed.

Reny was surprised to find that, after the countless defeated men and women he'd seen brought before the sorcerer King, he still felt a stirring of pity for this particular man. Even in the fading light he could see that the prince was young, barely old enough to claim the princedom from his father, who had been killed in this nation's first battle against Dael.

"Your army is defeated, your cities have fallen," Dael told him. "Do you surrender your land and people to me? Do you give your remaining army into my hands, to fight in the glorious Conquest to unite the lands?"

The prince remained silent. He was still so long that Reny began to worry that the youth would not respond. Then suddenly the prince straightened his body and lifted his head. He glared at Dael with intense hatred.

"I do not."

Reny looked at Dael. The sorcerer's eyebrows had risen slightly. There was a strange, avid light in his eyes.

"You know that the penalty for refusing is death, for you and everyone in your land?"

"Yes." The hatred in the young man's face vanished and was replaced by a blissful, wide-eyed stare as he tilted his head to the sky. "The Goddess of Death will take us. She will bring us peace." His gaze dropped to Dael and his eyes narrowed again. "And she will avenge our deaths."

The Goddess of Death? For a moment Reny could not breathe or move, then his heart began hammering in his chest and his knees felt weak. Was this a deity these people worshipped? Or was it, as he suddenly feared, the whore in his tent? The woman who had returned to his bed and fallen asleep at his side, then prepared his morning meal as if nothing had changed? In the morning light, it was too easy to dismiss what he'd seen last night as an illusion, or a dream. He forced himself to stand still and breathe normally, not wanting to give any hint of the shock that the prince's declaration had given him.

Fortunately Dael was not looking at Reny. His gaze was fixed on the youth as he rose.

"Are you sure?" he asked. "I wouldn't want it to be known that I didn't offer you a choice."

The young man's eyes filled with fear as the sorcerer approached, but his voice was steady. "I am sure. As are my people."

Dael paused. "How disappointing," he said quietly. He nodded to the guards, who hauled the prince to his feet. Then he drew a long knife and plunged it into the young man's chest.

As always, Reny made his eyes stay focused on the scene, but not his attention. He'd grown adept at not *seeing* in these moments, and thinking of something else. Usually the whore. But this time, something caught his eye. Something strange and yet familiar. Something he might not have noticed if he hadn't slid down the ranks of Dael's favour in recent weeks, and been standing further down the slope, rather than in his usual place nearer to the King.

For the first time, he could see the knife protruding from the prince's chest, and the hand holding it... and more importantly, the air surrounding both.

It was shimmering.

The movement was barely noticeable, and he might have again dismissed it as an effect of the twilight descending upon the battlefields, or the heat from a fire or torch beyond the sorcerer and the prince. Now he knew better, and he wished he didn't.

But I do know, and it is dangerous to pretend otherwise. I must do what I would recommend to another man in this situation: consider every possibility, no matter how strange—because it is better to be over-prepared than be caught out by the unexpected—then deal with the problem.

He wished he could do his thinking alone and in peace, but, as ever, he didn't have that luxury. Now, after the prince's corpse had been removed, the sorcerer King and his captains retreated to the big tent where battle strategy was discussed and decisions made. Several hours had passed before all were sent to their beds. But as Reny reached the entrance of the tent he heard Dael call his name.

"Stay a moment, Captain Reny. I wish to talk to you."

As the tent emptied, the sorcerer King regarded Reny from the battered throne that was always dragged from battle to battle.

"Vorl doesn't like you," he said when they were finally alone. One thing Reny liked about the leader was how he always got to the point.

"I know," Reny replied, shrugging. "*I* don't like *him*."

"Why not?

"He is needlessly cruel."

"He is ruthless." Dael nodded. "Killing is what he does, and he does it well."

"Women and children?"

Dael's gaze became hard. "This is war. Nobody should pretend that it is merciful to the weak."

Reny opened his mouth to protest, thought better of it and nodded.

"He wants me to get rid of you," Dael told him. "He says you have rebellion in you, and your scruples will lose us battles one day. What do you say to that?"

Reny felt as if someone had dropped ice down the back of his armour, and it was sliding slowly down his spine. *I have a sorceress masquerading as a whore in my tent; a woman who both this army— and the enemy—think is some sort of goddess of death. The last thing I need is Vorl putting further ideas of betrayal in Dael's head.*

"I'd rather you got rid of Vorl," he replied, frankly.

Dael smiled. "Why should I do that?"

"Soldiers are like weapons," Reny found himself replying, "more useful in battle than hung on a wall. Advisers are like scrolls. You keep them so you can use their knowledge again and again." Somehow it had sounded more eloquent when Kala had said it.

Dael grinned, his eyes bright with amusement.

"*I* like you, Captain Reny. And that's most important. You may go."

Reny bowed, and hurried from the tent.

RENY WOULD HAVE liked more time to think, but he suspected that time was something he didn't have much of now. When he entered his tent and saw Kala waiting for him he felt a wave of relief, but it was followed by one of dread. And, unexpectedly, one of lust. She was regarding him with relaxed expectation from the end of the bed, with a small welcoming smile, and he was reminded once again that it was after strategy meetings that he most often used her services.

He knew that he never would again. That filled him with regret, but also determination. He drew in a deep breath, let it out slowly, and then sat down on one of the chests.

"What are you?" he asked. "Are you really a goddess?"

She showed no surprise, but her expression became serious, almost sad, and then the smile returned. "I am no goddess. What do *you* think I am?"

Reny met her gaze. "What *he* is. What Dael is. A sorcerer and... something else."

Her eyebrows rose and she regarded him appraisingly. "You've worked out more than I expected—or hoped."

"I've worked out nothing," he disagreed. "I have no idea what is going on. Am I keeping an enemy in my tent? Am I following someone ... some*thing* more than an ambitious and clever sorcerer mercenary-turned-King, with a love for war and a desire to unite the lands?"

Suddenly all trace of her smile was gone. She had that knowing, worldly look again, but this time there was anger burning in her eyes.

"I am from the temple," she said. "The temple Vorl attacked."

His stomach plunged to the floor. He stared at her and felt guilt and pity fill him all over again.

"I'm sorry—" he began.

"I lived there for over a thousand years," she continued.

Disbelief overtook guilt. He remembered the shimmering air between her hand and the dying soldier, and knew that he had to consider that something so incredible might be possible. If this was true... he felt the first spark of awe. *I bedded this woman...*

"But I am several thousands of years older than that," she added. She looked away, beyond the tent walls, and sighed. "When I was the age of the body you see before you, I developed more than womanly traits. I aged the same as other people, but then within a day or night I'd grow young again.

"Whenever I returned to youth, I found that I could heal from an injury in an instant, and I could use magic. But in time, I'd lose those abilities and start to age again. How could this be? I only worked out why when a sickness came and many of the local people died. It took many, many more years before I started to age again." She paused and looked at Reny meaningfully.

He frowned. "You... you can take magic from people who are dying?"

"I don't *take* it. It comes to me. When someone dies, magic is released and if I am nearby it flows to me. Or if there is someone else with the trait nearby, it flows to whichever of us is closest."

"So you are immortal."

She shook her head. "I am sure that, if I stayed away from death long enough, I would age and die like everyone else."

He thought about the temple, so isolated and only attended by a handful of young women. Healthy young attendees were less likely than older ones to die while serving the old woman they believed was a goddess.

"That's why you were there," he said.

She nodded solemnly. "I have lived too long. I am tired of it."

His mind took a leap of comprehension. "But if death gives you magic, why didn't you save the women in the temple?"

She blinked at the sudden shift in his questioning, then scowled. "It was their death that gave me magic. Once dead..." She sighed. "I cannot bring the dead back to life. I might have been able to heal one or two of them, if any had been alive after the soldiers left." There was bitterness in her voice.

"So you joined the camp followers of an army, which would surround you with a never-ending source of death and allow you to grow strong." He took a deep breath. "Is revenge worth delaying your release from this life?"

She smiled. "I am not seeking revenge. If I was, Vorl would have stopped being a problem for you months ago."

"Why are you here, then?"

She looked at him with an expression he could not name, and it sent a shiver down his spine. "All those years in the temple, waiting for death. I felt boredom beyond what you can ever experience. One thought kept me there, and kept me from giving up and leaving. One question that I will never know the answer to myself." She paused, and then smoothly rose to her feet. "Where does the death magic go, if sorcerers like me don't take and use it? What do you think, Reny?"

He stared at her as she walked out of the tent, and disappeared into the night, her words repeating themselves unceasingly in his mind, and rousing a deep, undeniable horror.

Soldiers believed in souls. They believed there was a life after death. They might not agree about the form that soul took, how it was judged, or who ruled the place souls went to, but they all held onto the same basic hope.

If they knew what she did, nobody would worship the Goddess of Death. They would fear her.

And Dael. Reny shuddered. Now that he knew the truth, some of the sorcerer King's more destructive decisions made sense. Dael was not trying to unify the lands in order to bring peace to them. He was harvesting fallen soldiers, his own and his enemy's, and keeping the lands in a perpetual state of war so that he might have eternal life and unending power over the living.

RENY DID NOT see Kala again that night or the next morning. He did not expect her to return. If her absence was noted, he planned to shrug and say he had grown tired of her, and sent her away. He considered finding himself a new whore to make this lie more convincing, but didn't.

He pretended to have an injury—a strain in his back—to avoid having to fight. It wasn't that he was afraid he would die and lose his soul to Kala or Dael. He simply didn't want to miss seeing whatever all this was leading to.

He pondered Kala's motives and her possible strategy to carry them out. She had all but told him she wanted to stop Dael, but was she strong enough to face him and win? He considered that perhaps she intended to lose, and achieve the death she longed for, but he doubted it. She would not have been gathering strength by walking the battlefield at night. Instead, she would have confronted Dael in a deliberately weakened state, ensuring her defeat.

*   *   *

AT MIDDAY DAEL led the army into the city to carry out his punishment for their defiance. To Reny's surprise, the King placed him among his personal companions, and sent Vorl ahead to rouse the citizens, who had not emerged to face the invaders.

Soldiers beat down a few doors before they realised all were unlocked. They emerged from the buildings, confused and pale, each group hurrying to report to Vorl, whose face grew darker and darker.

"What is wrong?" Dael called.

Vorl hurried over and knelt before his leader. "They're dead," he said. "All of them. Poisoned themselves, by the look of it."

Dael looked up, his eyes scanning the buildings lining both sides of the main city road. "Surely not all of them. I'd have… Keep searching."

Though soldiers roamed further and further afield, they found only corpses. Old men, women and children tucked in their beds or slumped in chairs. From the expressions on their faces, whatever poison they had taken had seemingly sent them to a blissful end.

It was then, in the silence of realisation, that a woman dressed in white stepped out onto the main road. Reny heard all the men around him draw in a sharp breath. She glowed faintly as she walked toward them. Her feet were bare. Her pale hair was long and unbound and much too familiar.

Reny could not believe this was the whore he had kept in his tent. She had been attractive, but not this vision of beauty. *She certainly never glowed like that when she was mine.* She must have gathered up the death magic of all the city's remaining citizens as they expired from the poison they'd taken. *Or did she poison them? Is this a part of her plan? Is she that ruthless?*

Unexpectedly, he saw through the glamour around her to a woman who must have suffered much in her long life, despite the magic that kept her alive and healed every wound. She was a woman who had not been able to escape the evils of the world, even when she had isolated herself in search of the peace of death. A woman who had no choice but to question if her own powers, over which she had no control, were evil. She must have cared deeply about the answer, he thought. Perhaps this was the true reason she sought her own death. *No, she did not kill these people.*

The soldiers shifted fearfully, muttering to themselves. Reny guessed they saw something else: the Goddess of Death. But Kala's eyes were fixed only on Dael. The sorcerer King was watching her, his eyes bright and smiling indulgently, as if watching children performing.

"Greetings, King Dael," she said, her voice echoing between the buildings.

"Greetings... whom do I have the honour of meeting?" he asked in reply.

"I have had many names. You may call me Saeyl."

He gestured to the buildings on either side. "Well, Saeyl. Did you do this?"

"Poison all these people?" She shook her head. "No. They arranged that all on their own. I don't know if they guessed what your abilities are and decided to deny you the magic you gain from the moment of their deaths," she shrugged, "or if they hoped their souls would go to me instead."

Dael's smile faded. She slowed to a stop a few paces away.

"I have not met anyone with my particular skills before now," he told her.

Her lips twisted with distaste. "I have met plenty."

"Where are they?"

"Gone. Dead."

"So we *can* die."

Her eyes brightened at his ignorance. "Yes, but only at the hands of another of our kind."

"So… you killed the others?"

She shook her head. "Not all of them. Most fought and killed each other. The last one I met wanted to go. He was very old, and tired of living." She lifted her chin. "How old are you?"

"Two hundred and forty nine."

Reny's skin prickled with cold. *I have been fighting for, and been loyal to, a man who is more than five times my age!*

Kala's eyes never left Dael. "So young. And with such skill in sorcery. When I discovered my power, few could or would teach me. Now there are *mortals* who know more than I did at your age."

"How old are you?" Dael asked.

"More than four thousand years," she said. "Less than five. It is hard to keep an exact tally, when counting systems keep coming and going with the civilisations that invent them."

"What do you want?"

Her eyebrows rose at his bluntness, then her expression became serious. "I want you to abandon this conquest of yours."

"Why?" Dael asked, his voice low and dark with defiance and anger.

"You don't need it." She took a step closer. "Look at me: I am proof that you do not need to wage war in order to live forever."

"Do you think that is my sole mission? What of power? What of peace? If I unite the lands there will be no more wars. We can do good things with our magic. And there will be no risk that you or I will be killed in some petty squabble between kingdoms."

She took another step, reaching out but not quite touching him. "How will you gather the power you need? Will you resort to slaughtering more innocent people? Will you breed people like livestock, to be a steady supply of sacrifices?"

"There are always criminals to be executed. And those who die of natural causes. If that's not enough... I'll think of something. You could help me," he said, reaching out toward her. His other hand shifted to his waist.

The movement was familiar, and even as Reny choked back a shout of warning Dael's dagger plunged into her chest under the ribs.

Trust that she knows what she is doing, he told himself. His heart raced. He stared at her face, seeing the pain and shock there, holding his breath and daring to hope. She was staring at Dael, her eyes dark with hatred.

"You said 'only at the hands of another of our kind'," Dael reminded her smugly.

She shook her head. "I did. But you are far too simple in your thinking."

Taking another step forward, she plunged her hand through his armour and into his chest, as if metal and bone and skin were the thinnest of paper. Dael's eyes went round; then, as she pulled her arm back, he looked down in disbelief at the bloody, pulsing mess of organs trailing from her hands back to his body.

Her hand held his heart, twitching and wobbling. Dael opened his mouth, made a faint, whimpering noise, then crumpled at her feet.

Kala waited until the first sounds escaped the watching soldiers. As the realisation that she had killed their leader sank into the minds of those watching, she raised her eyes and surveyed those standing closest. She gestured with the bloodied heart, beckoning them closer. Instead, all turned and ran, yelling and screaming their terror.

All except Reny. A movement in the air had drawn his eyes. The shimmer between Dael's body and Kala was so intense it was almost a sound.

Is it only her magic or does it come from all the souls he has taken?

He looked up and met Kala's eyes. Weariness and resignation had replaced her fierce grin of triumph. She grimaced as she let the heart drop to the ground.

"I can't stop myself taking it," she said sadly. "But I *can* do this…"

Then she turned and strode away, the rippling air stretching and slowly thinning between herself and the dead sorcerer until the effect was no longer visible.

WHEN HE LEFT, Reny took nothing with him but a large pack and his sword. While he would rather have left the weapon behind, he wasn't stupid. The road home would not be free of trouble. It would be full of ex-soldiers like him, and some would resort to theft and murder to get food, shelter and other essentials. He'd pass through lands that the sorcerer King had conquered, who would not welcome the men who had followed him, bringing so much suffering and loss.

At the end of the long journey was his home—and the ghosts of his family. If he made it, he would live the remaining years left to him there, and concern himself only with the strategies of crops and animal breeding cycles and bartering in the markets. He resolved to forget the war, and let all tales of his part in it fade from the memories of others, even if they would never leave his own.

Every day Kala was in his thoughts, and every night she appeared in his dreams, and he never stopped wondering where she was, and if she still sought her own death.

THE DRAGONSLAYER
OF MEREBARTON
K J PARKER

I WAS MENDING my chamber pot when they came to tell me about the dragon.

Mending a pot is one of those jobs you think is easy, because tinkers do it, and tinkers are no good or they'd be doing something else. Actually, it's not easy at all. You have to drill a series of very small holes in the broken pieces, then thread short lengths of wire through the holes, then twist the ends of the wires together *really tight*, so as to draw the bits together firmly enough to make the pot watertight. In order to do the job you need a very hard, sharp, thin drill bit, a good eye, loads of patience and at least three pairs of rock-steady hands. The tinker had quoted me a turner and a quarter; get lost, I told him, I'll do it myself. It was beginning to dawn on me that some sorts of work are properly reserved for specialists.

Ah, the irony.

Stupid of me to break it in the first place. I'm not usually that clumsy. Stumbling about in the dark, was how I explained it. You should've lit a lamp, then, shouldn't you, she said. I pointed out that you

109

don't need a lamp in the long summer evenings. She smirked at me. I don't think she quite understands how finely balanced our financial position is. We're not hard up, nothing like that. There's absolutely no question of having to sell off any of the land, or take out mortgages. It's just that, if we carry on wasting money unnecessarily on lamp-oil and tinkers and like frivolities, there'll come a time when the current slight reduction in our income will start to be a mild nuisance. Only temporary, of course. The hard times will pass, and soon we'll all be just fine.

Like I said, the irony.

"Ebba's here to see you," she said.

She could see I was busy. "He'll have to come back," I snapped. I had three little bits of wire gripped between my lips, which considerably reduced my snapping power.

"He said it's urgent."

"Fine." I put down the pot—call it that, no way it was a pot any more. It was disjointed memories of the shape of a pot, loosely tied together with metal string, like the scale armour the other side wore in Outremer. "Send him up."

"He's not coming up here in those boots," she said, and at once I realised that no, he wasn't, not when she was using that tone of voice. "And why don't you just give up on that? You're wasting your time."

Women have no patience. "The tinker—"

"That bit doesn't go there."

I dropped the articulated mess on the floor and walked past her, down the stairs, into the great hall. Great, in this context, is strictly a comparative term.

Ebba and I understand each other. For a start, he's practically the same age as me—I'm a week younger;

so what? We both grew up silently ashamed of our fathers (his father Ossun was the laziest man on the estate; mine—well) and we're both quietly disappointed with our children. He took over his farm shortly before I came home from Outremer, so we both sort of started off being responsible for our own destinies around the same time. I have no illusions about him, and I can't begin to imagine he has any about me. He's medium height, bald and thin, stronger than he looks and smarter than he sounds. He used to set up the targets and pick up the arrows for me when I was a boy; never used to say anything, just stood there looking bored.

He had that look on his face. He told me I wasn't going to believe what he was about to tell me.

The thing about Ebba is, he has absolutely no imagination. Not even when roaring drunk—whimpering drunk in his case; very rare occurrence, in case you've got the impression he's what she calls basically-no-good. About twice a year, specific anniversaries. I have no idea what they're the anniversaries of, and of course I don't ask. Twice a year, then, he sits in the hayloft with a big stone jar and only comes out when it's empty. Not, is the point I'm trying to make, prone to seeing things not strictly speaking there.

"There's a dragon," he said.

Now Ossun, his father, saw all manner of weird and wonderful things. "Don't be bloody stupid," I said. He just looked at me. Ebba never argues or contradicts; doesn't need to.

"All right," I said, and the words just sort of squeezed out, like a fat man in a narrow doorway. "Where?"

"Down Merebarton."

* * *

A BRIEF DIGRESSION concerning dragons.

There's no such thing. However, there's the White Drake (its larger cousin, the Blue Drake, is now almost certainly extinct). According to Hrabanus' *Imperfect Bestiary*, the White Drake is a native of the large and entirely unexpected belt of marshes you stumble into after you've crossed the desert, going from Crac Boamond to the sea. Hrabanus thinks it's a very large bat, but conscientiously cites Priscian, who holds that it's a featherless bird, and Saloninus, who maintains that it's a winged lizard. The White Drake can get to be five feet long—that's nose to tip-of-tail; three feet of that is tail, but it can still give you a nasty nip. They launch themselves out of trees, which can be horribly alarming (I speak from personal experience). White Drakes live almost exclusively on carrion and rotting fruit, rarely attack unless provoked and absolutely definitely don't breathe fire.

White Drakes aren't found outside Outremer. Except, some idiot of a nobleman brought back five breeding pairs about a century ago, to decorate the grounds of his castle. Why people do these things, I don't know. My father tried to keep peacocks once. As soon as we opened the cage they were off like arrows from the bowstring; next heard of six miles away, and could we please come and do something about them, because they were pecking the thatch out in handfuls. My father rode over that way, happening to take his bow with him. No more was ever said about peacocks.

Dragons, by contrast, are nine to ten feet long

excluding the tail; they attack on sight, and breathe fire. At any rate, this one did.

THREE HOUSES AND four barns in Merebarton, two houses and a hayrick in Stile. Nobody hurt yet, but only a matter of time. A dozen sheep carcasses, stripped to the bone. One shepherd reported being followed by the horrible thing: he saw it, it saw him, he turned and ran; it just sort of drifted along after him, hardly a wingbeat, as if mildly curious. When he couldn't run any further, he tried crawling down a badger hole. Got stuck, head down the hole, legs sticking up in the air. He reckoned he felt the thump as the thing pitched down next to him, heard the snuffling—like a bull, he reckoned; felt its warm breath on his ankles. Time sort of stopped for a while, and then it went away again. The man said it was the first time he'd pissed himself and felt the piss running down his chest and dripping off his chin. Well, there you go.

The Brother at Merebarton appears to have taken charge, the way they do. He herded everyone into the grain store—stone walls, yes, but a thatched roof; you'd imagine even a Brother would've watched them making charcoal some time—and sent a terrified young kid off on a pony to, guess what. You've got it. Fetch the knight.

AT THIS POINT, the story recognises (isn't that what they say in Grand Council?) Dodinas le Cure Hardy, age fifty-six, knight, of the honours of Westmoor, Merebarton, East Rew, Middle Side and Big Room;

veteran of Outremer (four years, so help me), in his day a modest success on the circuit—three second places in ranking tournaments, two thirds, usually in the top twenty out of an average field of forty or so. Through with all that a long time ago, though. I always knew I was never going to be one of those gaunt, terrifying old men who carry on knocking 'em down and getting knocked down into their sixties. I had an uncle like that, Petipas of Lyen. I saw him in a tournament when he was sixty-seven, and some young giant bashed him off his horse. Uncle landed badly, and I watched him drag himself up off the ground, so desperately tired. I was only, what, twelve; even I could see, every last scrap of flesh and bone was yelling, *don't want to do this any more*. But he stood up, shamed the young idiot into giving him a go on foot, and proceeded to use his head as an anvil for ten minutes before graciously accepting his surrender. There was so much anger in that performance—not at the kid, for showing him up, Uncle wasn't like that. He was furious with himself for getting old, and he took it out on the only target available. I thought the whole thing was disturbing and sad. I won't ever be like that, I told myself.

(The question was, is: why? I can understand fighting. I fought—really fought—in Outremer. I did it because I was afraid the other man was going to kill me. So happens my defence has always been weak, so I compensate with extreme aggression. Never could keep it going for very long, but on the battlefield that's not usually an issue. So I attacked anything that moved with white-hot ferocity fuelled entirely and exclusively by ice-cold fear.

Tournaments, though, jousting, behourd, the grand melee—what was the point? I have absolutely no idea, except that I did feel very happy indeed on those rare occasions when I got a little tin trophy to take home. Was that enough to account for the pain of being laid up six weeks with two busted ribs? Of course it wasn't. *We do it because it's what we do*; one of my father's more profound statements. Conversely, I remember my aunt: silly woman, too soft for her own good. She kept these stupid big white chickens, and when they got past laying she couldn't bear to have their necks pulled. Instead, they were taken out into the woods and set free, meaning in real terms fed to the hawks and foxes. One time, my turn, I lugged down a cage with four hens and two cocks squashed in there, too petrified to move. Now, what draws in the fox is the clucking; so I turned them out in different places, wide apart, so they had nobody to talk to. Released the last hen, walking back down the track; already the two cock birds had found each other, no idea how, and were ripping each other into tissue scraps with their spurs. They do it because it's what they do. Someone once said, the man who's tired of killing is tired of life. Not sure I know what that means.)

A PICTURE IS emerging, I hope, of Dodinas le Cure Hardy; while he was active in chivalry he tried to do what was expected of him, but his heart was never in it. Glad, in a way, to be past it and no longer obliged to take part. Instead, prefers to devote himself to the estate, trying to keep the ancestral mess from collapsing in on itself. A man aware of his obligations, and at least some of his many shortcomings.

Go and fetch the knight, says the fool of a Brother. Tell him—

ON REFLECTION, IF I hadn't seen those wretched White Drakes in Outremer, there's a reasonable chance I'd have refused to believe in a dragon trashing Merebarton, and then, who knows, it might've flown away and bothered someone else. Well, you don't know, that's the whole point. It's that very ignorance that makes life possible. But when Ebba told me what the boy told him he'd seen, immediately I thought: White Drake. Clearly it wasn't one, but it was close enough to something I'd seen to allow belief to seep into my mind, and then I was done for. No hope.

Even so, I think I said, "Are you *sure?*" about six or seven times, until eventually it dawned on me I was making a fool of myself. At which point, a horrible sort of mist of despair settled over me, as I realised that this extraordinary, impossible, grossly and viciously *unfair* thing had landed on me, and that I was going to have to deal with it.

But you do your best. You struggle, just as a man crushed under a giant stone still draws in the last one or two desperate whistling breaths; pointless, but you can't just give up. So I looked him steadily in the eye, and I said, "So, what do they expect me to do about it?"

He didn't say a word. Looked at me.

"The hell with that," I remember shouting. "I'm fifty-six years old, I don't even hunt boar any more. I've got a stiff knee. I wouldn't last two minutes."

He looked at me. When you've known someone all your life, arguing with them is more or less arguing with yourself. Never had much joy with lying to myself. Or anyone else, come to that. Of course, my mother used to say: the only thing I want you not to be the best in the world at is lying. She said a lot of that sort of thing; much better written down on paper rather than said out loud in casual conversation, but of course she couldn't read or write. She also tended to say: do your duty. I don't think she ever liked me very much. Loved, of course, but not liked.

He was looking at me. I felt like that poor devil under the stone (at the siege of Crac des Bests; man I knew slightly). Comes a point when you just can't breathe any more.

WE DO HAVE a library: forty-seven books. The *Imperfect Bestiary* is an abridged edition, local copy, drawings are pretty laughable, they make everything look like either a pig or a cow, because that's all the poor fool who drew it had ever seen. So there I was, looking at a picture of a big white cow with wings, thinking: how in God's name am I supposed to kill something like *that*?

White Drakes don't breathe fire, but there's this stupid little lizard in Permia somewhere that does. About eighteen inches long, otherwise completely unremarkable; not to put too fine a point on it, it farts through its mouth and somehow contrives to set fire to it. You see little flashes and puffs of smoke among the reed beds. So it's possible. Wonderful.

(*Why* would anything want to do that? Hrabanus, who has an answer for every damn thing, points out

117

that the reed beds would clog up the delta, divert the flowing water and turn the whole of South Permia into a fetid swamp if it wasn't for the frequent, regular fires, which clear off the reed and lay down a thick bed of fertile ash, just perfect for everything else to grow sweet and fat and provide a living for the hundreds of species of animals and birds who live there. The fires are started by the lizards, who appear to serve no other function. Hrabanus points to this as proof of the Divine Clockmaker theory. I think they do it because it's what they do, though I'm guessing the lizards who actually do the fire-starting are resentful younger sons. Tell you about my brother in a minute.)

SHE FOUND ME in the library. Clearly she'd been talking to Ebba. "Well?" she said.

I told her what I'd decided to do. She can pull this face of concentrated scorn and fury. It's so intensely eloquent, there's really no need for her to add words. But she does. Oh, she does.

"I've got no choice," I protested. "I'm the knight."

"You're fifty-six and you get out of breath climbing the stairs. And you're proposing to fight *dragons*."

It's a black lie about the stairs. Just that one time; and that was the clock-tower. Seventy-seven steps to the top. "I don't *want* to do it," I pointed out. "Last bloody thing I want—"

"Last bloody thing you'll ever do, if you're stupid enough to do it." She never swears, except when quoting me back at myself. "Just think for a minute, will you? If you get yourself killed, what'll happen to this place?"

"I have no intention of getting myself—"

"Florian's too young to run the estate," she went on, as though I hadn't spoken. "That clown of a bailiff of yours can't be trusted to remember to breathe without someone standing over him. On top of which, there's heriot and wardship, that's hundreds and hundreds of thalers we simply haven't got, which means having to sell land, and once you start doing that you might as well load up a handcart and take to the roads, because—"

"Absolutely no intention of getting killed," I said.

"And for crying out loud don't *shout*," she shouted. "It's bad enough you're worrying me to death without yelling at me as well. I don't know why you do this to me. Do you hate me, or something?"

We were four and a quarter seconds away from tears, and I really can't be doing with that. "All right," I said. "So tell me. What do I do?"

"*I* don't know, do I? I don't get myself into these ridiculous messes." I wish I could do that; I should be able to. After all, it's the knight's move, isn't it? A step at right angles, then jump clean over the other man's head. "What about that useless brother of yours? Send him."

The dreadful thing is, the same thought had crossed my mind. It'd be—well, not acceptable, but within the rules, meaning there's precedents. Of course, I'd have to be practically bedridden with some foul but honourable disease. Titurel is ten years younger than me and still competing regularly on the circuit, though at the time he was three miles away, at the lodge, with some female he'd found somewhere. And if I really was ill—

I was grateful to her. If she hadn't suggested it, I

might just have considered it. As it was; "Don't be ridiculous," I said. "Just think, if I was to chicken out and Titurel actually managed to kill this bloody thing. We've got to live here. He'd be insufferable."

She breathed through her nose; like, dare I say it, one of the D things. "All right," she said. "Though how precisely it's better for you to get killed and your appalling brother moves in and takes over running the estate—"

"I am not going to get killed," I said.

"But there, you never listen to me, so I might as well save my breath." She paused and scowled at me. "Well?"

Hard, sometimes, to remember that when I married her, she was the Fair Maid of Lannandale. "Well what?"

"What are you going to *do*?"

"OH," HE SAID, sort of half-turning and wiping his forehead on his forearm. "It's you."

Another close contemporary of mine. He's maybe six months older than me, took over the forge just before my father died. He's never liked me. Still, we understand each other. He's not nearly as good a tradesman as he thinks he is, but he's good enough.

"Come to pay me for those harrows?" he said.

"Not entirely," I replied. "I need something made."

"Of course you do." He turned his back on me, dragged something orange-hot out from under the coals, and bashed it, very hard, very quickly, for about twenty seconds. Then he shoved it back under the coals and hauled on the bellows handle a dozen times. Then he had leisure to talk to me. "I'll need a deposit."

"Don't be silly," I said. There was a small heap of tools piled up on the spare anvil. I moved them carefully aside and spread out my scraps of parchment. "Now, you'll need to pay attention."

THE PARCHMENT I'D drawn my pathetic attempts at sketches on was the fly-leaf out of Monomachus of Teana's *Principles of Mercantile Law*. I'd had just enough left over to use for a very brief note, which I'd folded four times, sealed, and sent the stable boy off to deliver. It came back, folded the other way; and under my message, written in big crude handwriting, smudged for lack of sand—

What the hell do you want it for?

I wasn't in the mood. I stamped back into the house (I'd been out in the barn, rummaging about in the pile of old junk), got out the pen and ink and wrote sideways up the margin (only just enough room, writing very small)—

No time. Please. Now.

I underlined *please* twice. The stable boy had wandered off somewhere, so I sent the kitchenmaid. She whined about having to go out in her indoors shoes. I ask you.

MODDO THE BLACKSMITH is one of those men who gets caught up in the job in hand. He whinges and complains, then the problems of doing the job snag his imagination, and then your main difficulty is getting it away from him when it's finished, because he's just come up with some cunning little modification which'll make it ever so slightly, irrelevantly better.

He does good work. I was so impressed I paid cash.

"Your design was useless, so I changed it," he'd said. A bit of an overstatement. What he'd done was to substitute two thin springs for one fat one, and add on a sort of ratchet thing taken off a millers' winch, to make it easier to wind it up. It was still sticky with the oil he'd quenched it in. The sight of it made my flesh crawl.

Basically, it was just a very, very large gin trap, with an offset pressure plate. "It's pretty simple," I said. "Think about it. Think about birds. In order to get off the ground, they've got very light bones, right?"

Ebba shrugged: if you say so.

"Well," I told him, "they have. And you break a bird's leg, it can't get off the ground. I'm assuming it's the same with this bastard. We put out a carcass, with this underneath. It stands on the carcass, braces it with one foot so it can tear it up with the other. Bang, got him. This thing ought to snap the bugger's leg like a carrot, and then it won't be going anywhere in a hurry, you can be sure of that."

He frowned. I could tell the sight of the trap scared him, like it did me. The mainspring was three eighths of an inch thick. Just as well Moddo thought to add a cocking mechanism. "You'll still have to kill it, though," he said.

I grinned at him. "Why?" I asked. "No, the hell with that. Just keep everybody and their livestock well away for a week until it starves to death."

He was thinking about it. I waited. "If it can breathe fire," he said slowly, "maybe it can melt the trap off."

"And burn through its own leg in the process. Also," I added—I'd considered this very point— "even without the trap it's still crippled, it won't be able to hunt and feed. Just like a bird that's got away from the cat."

He pulled a small frown that means, *well, maybe*. "We'll need a carcass."

"There's that sick goat," I said.

Nod. His sick goat. Well, I can't help it if all my animals are healthy.

HE WENT OFF with the small cart to fetch the goat. A few minutes later, a big wagon crunched down to the yard gate and stopped just in time. Too wide to pass through; it'd have got stuck.

Praise be, Marhouse had sent me the scorpion. Rather less joy and happiness, he'd come along with it, but never mind.

The scorpion is genuine Mezentine, two hundred years old at least. Family tradition says Marhouse's great-great-and-so-forth-grandfather brought it back from the Grand Tour, as a souvenir. More likely, his grandfather took it in part exchange or to settle a bad debt; but to acknowledge that would be to admit that two generations back they were still in trade.

"What the hell," Marhouse said, hopping down off the wagon box, "do you want it for?"

He's all right, I suppose. We were in Outremer together—met there for the first time, which is crazy, since our houses are only four miles apart. But he was fostered as a boy, away up country somewhere. I've always assumed that's what made him turn out like he did.

I gave him a sort of hopeless grin. Our kitchenmaid was still sitting up on the box, hoping for someone to help her down. "Thanks," I said. "I'm hoping we won't need it, but—"

A scorpion is a siege engine; a pretty small one, compared to the huge stone-throwing catapults and mangonels and trebuchets they pounded us with at Crac des Bests. It's essentially a big steel crossbow, with a frame, a heavy stand and a super-efficient winch. One man with a long steel bar can wind it up, and it shoots a steel arrow long as your arm and thick as your thumb three hundred yards. We had them at Metouches. Fortunately, the other lot didn't.

I told Marhouse about the dragon. He assumed I was trying to be funny. Then he caught sight of the trap, lying on the ground in front of the cider house, and he went very quiet.

"You're serious," he said.

I nodded. "Apparently it's burned some houses out at Merebarton."

"*Burned.*" Never seen him look like that before.

"So they reckon. I don't think it's just a drake."

"That's—" He didn't get around to finishing the sentence. No need.

"Which is why," I said, trying to sound cheerful, "I'm so very glad your grandad had the foresight to buy a scorpion. No wonder he made a fortune in business. He obviously knew good stuff when he saw it."

Took him a moment to figure that one out, by which time the moment had passed. "There's no arrows," he said.

"What?"

"No arrows," he repeated, "just the machine. Well," he went on, "it's not like we *use* the bloody thing, it's just for show."

I opened and closed my mouth a couple of times. "Surely there must've been—"

"Originally, yes, I suppose so. I expect they got used for something around the place." He gave me a thin smile. "We don't tend to store up old junk for two hundred years on the offchance in my family," he said.

I was trying to remember what scorpion bolts look like. There's a sort of three-bladed flange down the butt end, to stabilise them in flight. "No matter," I said. "Bit of old rod'll have to do. I'll get Moddo to run me some up." I was looking at the machine. The lead screws and the keyways the slider ran in were caked up with stiff, solid bogeys of dried grease. "Does it work?"

"I assume so. Or it did, last time it was used. We keep it covered with greased hides in the root store." I flicked a flake of rust off the frame. It looked sound enough, but what if the works had seized solid? "Guess I'd better get it down off the cart and we'll see," I said. "Well, thanks again. I'll let you know how it turns out."

Meaning: please go away now. But Marhouse just scowled at me. "I'm staying here," he said. "You honestly think I'd trust you lot with a family heirloom?"

"No, really," I said, "you don't need to trouble. I know how to work these things, remember. Besides, they're pretty well indestructible."

Wasting my breath. Marhouse is like a dog I used to have, couldn't bear to be left out of anything; if you went out for a shit in the middle of the night, she had to come too. Marhouse was the only one of us in Outremer who ever volunteered for anything. And never got picked, for that exact reason.

So, THROUGH NO choice or fault of my own, there were nine of us: me, Ebba, Marhouse, the six men from the farm. Of the six, Liutprand is seventeen and Rognvald is twenty-nine, though he barely counts, with his bad arm. The rest of us somewhere between fifty-two and sixty. Old men. We must be mad, I thought.

We rode out there in the flat-bed cart, bumping and bouncing over the ruts in Watery Lane. Everybody was thinking the same thing, and nobody said a word: what if the bugger swoops down and crisps the lot of us while we're sat here in the cart? In addition, I was also thinking: Marhouse is his own fault, after all, he's a knight too, and he insisted on butting in. The rest of them, though—my responsibility. Send for the knight, they'd said, not the knight and half the damn village. But a knight in real terms isn't a single man, he's the nucleus of a unit, the heart of a society; the lance in war, the village in peace, he stands for them, in front of them when there's danger, behind them when times are hard, not so much an individual, more of a collective noun. That's understood, surely; so that, in all those old tales of gallantry and errantry, when the poet sings of the knight wandering in a dark wood and encountering the evil to be fought, the wrong to be put right, 'knight' in that context is just shorthand for a knight and his squire and his armour-bearer and his three men-at-arms and the boy who leads the spare horses. The others aren't mentioned by name, they're subsumed in him, he gets the glory or the blame but everyone knows, if they stop to think about it, that the rest of them were there too; or who lugged around the spare lances, to replace the ones that got broken? And who got the poor bugger in and out of his full plate harness every morning and evening? There are some straps and buckles you just can't reach on your own, unless you happen to have three hands on the ends of unnaturally long arms. Without the people around me, I'd be completely worthless. It's *understood*. Well, isn't it?

We set the trap up on the top of a small rise, in the big meadow next to the old clay pit. Marhouse's suggestion, as a matter of fact; he reckoned that it was where the flightlines the thing had been following all crossed. Flightlines? Well yes, he said, and proceeded to plot all the recorded attacks on a series of straight lines, scratched in the dried splatter on the side of the cart with a stick. It looked pretty convincing to me. Actually, I hadn't really given it any thought, just assumed that if we dumped a bleeding carcass down on the ground, the dragon would smell it and come whooshing down. Stupid, when you come to think of it. And I call myself a huntsman.

Moddo had fitted the trap with four good, thick chains, attached to eighteen-inch steel pegs, which we hammered into the ground. Again, Marhouse did the thinking. They needed to be offset (his word) so that if it pulled this way or that, there'd be three chains offering maximum resistance—well, it made sense when he said it. He's got that sort of brain, invents clever machines and devices for around the farm. Most of them don't work, but some of them do.

The trap, of course, was Plan A. Plan B was the scorpion, set up seventy-five yards away under the busted chestnut tree, with all that gorse and briars for cover. The idea was, we had a direct line of sight, but if we missed and he came at us, he wouldn't dare swoop in too close, for fear of smashing his wings on the low branches. That bit was me.

We propped the poor dead goat up on sticks so it wasn't actually pressing on the floorplate of the trap, then scampered back to where we'd set up the scorpion. Luitprand got volunteered to drive the cart back to Castle Farm; he whined about being out in the open, but I chose him because he's the youngest and I wanted him well out of harm's way if the dragon actually did put in an appearance. Seventy-five yards was about as far as I trusted the scorpion to shoot straight without having to make allowance for elevation—we didn't have time to zero it, obviously—but it felt stupidly close. How long would it take the horrible thing to fly seventy-five yards? I had no idea, obviously. We spanned the scorpion—reassuringly hard to do—loaded Moddo's idea of a bolt into the slider groove, nestled down as far as we could get into the briars and nettles, and waited.

No show. When it got too dark to see, Marhouse said, "What kind of poison do you think it'd take to kill something like that?"

I'd been thinking about that. "Something we haven't got," I said.

"You reckon?"

"Oh come on," I said. "I don't know about you,

but I don't keep a wide selection of poisons in the house. For some reason."

"There's archer's root," Ebba said.

"He's right," Marhouse said. "That stuff'll kill just about anything."

"Of course it will," I replied. "But nobody around here—"

"Mercel," Ebba said. "He's got some."

News to me. "What?"

"Mercel. Lidda's boy. He uses it to kill wild pigs."

Does he now? I thought. It had occurred to me that wild boar were getting a bit hard to find. I knew all about smearing a touch of archer's root on a bit of jagged wire nailed to a fencepost—boar love to scratch, and it's true, they do a lot of damage to standing corn. That's why I pay compensation. Archer's root is illegal, of course, but so are a lot of useful everyday commodities.

"I'd better ask him," Ebba said. "He won't want to get in any trouble."

Decided unanimously, apparently. Well, we weren't doing any good crouching in the bushes. It did cross my mind that if the dragon hadn't noticed a dead goat with a trap under it, there was no guarantee it'd notice the same dead goat stuffed full of archer's root, but I dismissed the idea as unconstructive.

We left the trap and the scorpion set up, just in case, and walked back to Castle Farm. To begin with, as we came over the top of the Hog's Back down Castle Lane, I assumed the pretty red glow on the skyline was the last blush of the setting sun. As we got closer, I hoped that was what it was. By the time we passed the quince orchard, however, the hypothesis was no longer tenable.

We found Luitprand in the goose pond. Stupid fool, he'd jumped in the water to keep from getting burned up. Of course, the mud's three feet deep on the bottom. I could have told him that.

In passing: I think Luitprand was my son. At any rate, I knew his mother rather too well, seventeen years ago. Couldn't ever say anything, naturally. But he reminded me a lot of myself. For a start, he was half-smart stupid, just like me. Hurling myself in the pond to avoid the flames was just the sort of thing I might have done at his age; and, goes without saying, he wasn't there when we dug the bloody pond, twenty-one years ago, so how could he have known we'd chosen the soft spot, no use for anything else?

No other casualties, thank God, but the hay barn, the straw rick, the woodpile, all gone. The thatch, miraculously, burnt itself out without taking the rafters with it. But losing that much hay meant we'd be killing a lot of perfectly good stock come winter, since I can't afford to buy in. One damn thing after another.

Opito, Larcan's wife, was hysterical, even though her home hadn't gone in up flames after all. Larcan said it was a great big lizard, about twenty feet long. He got one very brief glimpse of it out of the corner of his eye, just before he dragged his wife and son under the cart. He looked at me like it was all my fault. Just what I needed after a long day crouched in a briar patch.

Luitprand played the flute; not very well. I gave him the one I brought back from Outremer. I never did find it among his stuff, so I can only assume he sold it at some point.

* * *

ANYWAY, THAT WAS that, as far as I was concerned. Whatever it was, wherever it had come from, it would have to be dealt with, as soon as possible. On the ride back from the farm, Marhouse had been banging on about flightlines again, where we were going to move the bait to; two days here, while the wind's in the south, then if that's no good, then another two days over there, and if that still doesn't work, we'll know for sure it must be following the line of the river, so either here, there, or just possibly everywhere, would be bound to do the trick, logically speaking. I smiled and nodded. I'm sure he was perfectly correct. He's a good huntsman, Marhouse. Come the end of the season, he always knows exactly where all the game we've failed to find must be holed up. Next year, he then says—

Trouble was, there wasn't time for a next year.

BY MIDNIGHT (COULDN'T sleep, oddly enough) I was fairly sure how it had to be done.

Before you start grinning to yourself at my presumption, I had no logical explanation for my conclusions. Flightlines, patterns of behaviour, life cycles, cover crops, mating seasons, wind directions; put them together and you'll inevitably flush out the truth, which will then elude you, zig-zag running through the roots of the long variables. I *knew*.

I knew, because I used to hunt with my father. He was, of course, always in charge of everything, knew everything, excelled at everything. We never caught much. And I *knew*, when he'd drawn up the lines of beaters, given them their timings (say three *Glorious Sun Ascendants* and two Minor Catechisms, then come out making as much noise as you can), positioned the stillhunters and the hounds and the horsemen, finally blown the horn; I *knew* exactly where the wretched animal would come bursting out, so as to elude us all with the maximum of safety and the minimum of effort. Pure intuition, never failed. Naturally, I never said anything. Not my place to.

So: I knew what was going to happen, and that there was nothing much I could do about it, and my chances of success and survival were—well, not to worry about that. When I was in Outremer, I got shot in the face with an arrow. Should've killed me instantly; but by some miracle it hung up in my cheekbone, and an enemy doctor we'd captured the day before yanked it out with a pair of tongs. *You should be dead*, they said to me, like I'd deliberately cheated. No moral fibre. Ever since then—true, I shuddered to think how the estate would get on with my brother in charge, but it survived my father and grandfather, so it was clearly indestructible. Besides, everyone dies sooner or later. It's not like I'm important.

MARHOUSE INSISTED ON coming with us. I told him, you stay here, we'll need a wise, experienced hand to take charge if it decides to burn out the castle. For a moment I thought he'd fallen for it, but no such luck.

So there were three of us: me, Ebba, Marhouse. The idea was, we'd follow the Ridgeway on horseback, looking down on either side. As soon as we saw smoke, Ebba would ride back to the castle and get the gear, meet us at the next likely attack scene. I know; bloody stupid idea. But I knew it wouldn't happen like that, because I knew how it'd happen.

Marhouse had on his black-and-white—that's breastplate, pauldrons, rerebraces and tassets. I told him, you'll boil to death in that lot. He scowled at me. He'd also fetched along a full-weight lance, issue. You won't need that, I told him. I'd got a boar-spear, and Ebba was carrying the steel crossbow my father spent a whole year's apple money on, the year before he died. "But they're just to make us feel better," I said. That got me another scowl. The wrong attitude.

Noon; nothing to be seen anywhere. I was just daring to think, perhaps the bloody thing's moved on, or maybe it'd caught some disease or got itself hung up in a tree. Then I saw a crow.

I think Ebba saw it first, but he didn't point and say, "Look, there's a crow". Marhouse was explaining some fine point of decoying, how you go about establishing which tree is the principal turning point on an elliptical recursive flight pattern. I thought: that's not a crow, it's just hanging there. Must be a hawk.

Ebba was looking over his shoulder. No, not a hawk, the profile's wrong. Marhouse stopped talking, looked at me, said, "What are you two staring at?" I was thinking, Oh.

I'm right about things so rarely that I usually relish the experience. Not this time.

Oh, you may be thinking, is a funny way of putting it. But that was the full extent of it: no elation, no regret, not even resignation; to my great surprise, no real fear. Just: oh, as in, well, here we are, then. Call it a total inability to feel anything. Twice in Outremer, once when my father died, and now. I'd far rather have wet myself, but you can't decide these things for yourself. Oh, I thought, and that was all.

Marhouse was swearing, which isn't like him. He only swears when he's terrified, or when something's got stuck or broken. Bad language, he reckons, lubricates the brain, stops it seizing up with fear or anger. Ebba had gone white as milk. His horse was playing up, and he was having to work hard to keep it from bolting. Amazing how they know.

On top of the Ridgeway, of course, there's no cover. We could gallop forward, or turn around and gallop back; either case, at the rate the bloody thing was moving, it'd be on us long before we could get our heads down. I heard someone give the order to dismount. Wasn't Marhouse, because he stayed mounted. Wouldn't have been Ebba, so I guess it must've been me.

First time, it swooped down low over our heads—about as high up as the spire of Blue Temple—and just kept on going. We were frozen solid. We watched. It was on the glide, like a pigeon approaching a laid patch in a barley field, deciding whether to pitch or go on. Very slight tailwind, so if it wanted to come in on us, it'd have to bank, turn up into the wind a little bit to start to stall, then wheel and come in with its wings back. I honestly thought: it's gone too far, it's not going to come in. Then it lifted, and I knew.

Sounds odd, but I hadn't really been looking at it the first time, when it buzzed us. I saw a black bird shape, long neck like a heron, long tail like a pheasant, but no sense of scale. As it came in the second time, I couldn't help but stare; a real dragon, for crying out loud, something to tell your grandchildren about. Well, maybe.

I'd say the body was about horse-sized, head not in proportion; smaller, like a red deer stag. Wings absurdly large—featherless, like a bat, skin stretched on disturbingly extended fingers. Tail, maybe half as long again as the body; neck like a swan, if that makes any sense. Sort of a grey colour, but it looked green at a distance. Big hind legs, small front legs looking vaguely ridiculous, as if it had stolen them off a squirrel. A much rounder snout than I'd expected, almost chubby. It didn't look all that dangerous, to be honest.

Marhouse is one of those people who translate fear into action; the scareder he is, the braver. Works against people. No warning—it'd have been nice if he'd said something first; he kicked his horse hard enough to stove in a rib, lance in rest, seat and posture straight out of the coaching manual. Rode straight at it.

What happened then—

Marhouse was five yards away from it, going full tilt. The dragon probably couldn't have slowed down if it had wanted to. Instead—it actually made this sort of 'pop' noise as it opened its mouth and burped up a fat round ball of fire, then lifted just a little, to sail about five feet over Marhouse's head. He, meanwhile, rode straight into the fireball, and through it.

And stopped, and fell all to pieces; the reason being, there was nothing left. Horse, man, all gone, not even ash, and the dozen or so pieces of armour dropping glowing to the ground, cherry-red, like they'd just come off the forge. I've seen worse things, in Outremer, but nothing stranger.

I was gawping, forgetting all about the dragon. It was Ebba who shoved me down as it came back. I have no idea why it didn't just melt us both as it passed, unless maybe it was all out of puff and needed to recharge. Anyway, it soared away, repeated the little lift. I had a feeling it was enjoying itself. Well, indeed. It must be wonderful to be able to fly.

Ebba was shouting at me, waving something, the crossbow, he wanted me to take it from him. "Shoot it," he was yelling. Made no sense to me; but then again, why not? I took the bow, planted my feet a shoulders' width apart, left elbow tucked in tight to the chest to brace the bow, just the fingers on the trigger. A good archery stance didn't seem to have anything to do with the matter in hand—like playing bowls in the middle of an earthquake—but I'm a good archer, so I couldn't help doing it properly. I found the dragon in the middle of the peep-sight, drew the tip of the arrow up to find it, and pressed the trigger.

For the record, I hit the damn thing. The bolt went in four inches, just above the heart. Good shot. With a bow five times as strong, quite possibly a clean kill.

I think it must've hurt, though, because instead of flaming and lifting, it squirmed—hunched its back then stretched out full-length like a dog waking up—and kept coming, straight at me. I think I actually did try and jump out of the way; just rather too late. I think what hit me must've been the side of its head.

I had three ribs stoved in once in Outremer, so I knew what was going on. I recognised the sound, and the particular sort of pain, and the not quite being able to breathe. Mostly I remember thinking: it won't hurt, because any moment now I'll be dead. Bizarrely reassuring, as if I was cheating, getting away with it. Cheating twice; once by staying alive, once by dying. This man is morally bankrupt.

I was on my back, not able or minded to move. I couldn't see the dragon. I could hear Ebba shouting; shut up, you old fool, I thought, I'm really not interested. But he was shouting, "Hold on, mate, hold on, I'm coming," which made absolutely no sense at all—

Then he shut up, and I lay there waiting. I waited, and waited. I'm not a patient man. I waited so long, those crunched ribs started to hurt, or at least I became aware of the pain. For crying out loud, I thought. And waited.

And thought: now just a minute.

It hurt so much, hauling myself onto my side so I could see. I was in tears.

Later, I figured out what had happened. When Ebba saw me go down, he grabbed the boar-spear and ran towards me. I don't imagine he considered the dragon, except as an inconvenience. Hold on, I'm coming; all his thoughts in his words. He got about half way when the dragon pitched—it must've swooped off and come in again. As it put its feet down to land, he must've stuck the butt of the spear in the ground and presented the point, like you do with a boar, to let it stick itself, its momentum being far more effective than your own puny strength. As it pitched, it lashed with its tail, sent Ebba flying. Whether or not it realised it was dead, the spear a foot deep in its windpipe before the shaft gave way under the pressure and snapped, I neither know nor care. By the marks on the ground, it rolled three or four times before the lights went out. My best estimate is, it weighed just short of a ton. Ebba—under it as it rolled—was crushed like a grape, so that his guts burst and his eyes popped, and nearly all his bones were broken.

HE WOULDN'T HAVE thought: I'll kill the dragon. He'd have thought, ground the spear, like boar-hunting, and then the tail hit him, and then the weight squashed him. So it wouldn't have been much; not a heroic thought, not the stuff of song and story. Just: this is a bit like boar-hunting, so ground the spear. And then, perhaps: oh.

I think that's all there is; anywhere, anytime, in the whole world.

I TRIED PRESERVING the head in honey. We got an old pottery bath and filled it and put the head in; but eight weeks later it had turned green and it stank like hell, and she said, for pity's sake get rid of it. So we boiled it out and scraped it, and mounted the skull on the wall. Not much bigger than a big deer; in a hundred years' time, they won't believe the old story about it being a dragon. No such thing as dragons, they'll say.

Meanwhile, for now, I'm the Dragonslayer; which is a joke. The duke himself threatened to ride over and take a look at the remains, but affairs of state supervened, thank God. Entertaining the duke and his court would've ruined us, and we'd lost so much already.

Twice I've cheated. Marhouse was straight as a die, and his end, I'm sorry, was just ludicrous. I keep telling myself, Ebba made a choice, you must respect that. I can't. Instead of a friend, I have a horrible memory, and yet another debt I can't pay. People assume you want to be saved, no matter what the cost; sometimes, though, it's just too expensive to stay alive. Not sure I'll ever forgive him for that.

And that's that. I really don't want to talk about it anymore.

LEAF AND BRANCH
AND GRASS AND VINE
KATE ELLIOTT

A HAND POUNDING on her cottage door woke Anna, just as it had that terrible night almost three months ago. Jolting upright, she wiped a hand across her mouth as if to wipe away the taste of fear and grief but it did not go away. Beside her on the wide mattress, her two youngest children slept like the dead, and she was glad for it. No sense in cringing and stalling; the bad news would come whether now or at dawn, and she did not want the children to wake.

From the other room, where she had long slept with her husband, rose a murmur of voices: her daughter and her new husband waking to the summons.

She wrapped her well-worn bride's shawl over her shift and padded to the barred door. Pointless to bar the door, really, since she had left the glass window unshuttered. The light of a full moon bathed the plank floor in a ghostly light, enough that she need not grope for a precious candle. By the measure of the shortened shadows, she knew it was barely past midnight.

She set a hand on the latch. "Who is there?"

"Anna, it is Joen. No trouble here, but I need you at once."

Her brother's familiar voice calmed the pounding clamor of her heart. She let him in just as the door into the other room opened and Hansi stuck his head out, holding a lit candle in one hand and his butchering knife in the other.

She said, "Holding a light in the darkness means the other man can see you but you can't see him."

Hansi chuckled. He was a good natured young man, slow to take offense to his pride. "My apologies, Mother Anna. Is that Uncle Joen I hear?"

"It is," said Joen, "and I would ask you to get everyone dressed."

Anna grabbed Joen's thick forearm. "I thought you said no trouble."

"There's been a skirmish fought in and around West Hall. Rumor says the Forlangers are involved. The family should hide in the caves until we are sure they've moved on."

Anna's daughter Mari appeared beside Hansi, resplendent in her bride's shawl and so heavily pregnant that she lumbered. Her face was solemn as she took the candle from her young husband and examined first her mother and then her uncle by its smoky light.

"We'll get the children up and go at once," Mari said.

Hansi brushed his fingers down Mari's forearm, and the gesture of affection made Anna glad all over again that her daughter had found a good man.

Joen nodded, shifting his crutch. His empty trouser leg swayed. "Take provisions, everything you can carry and cart, but be quick about it. But I need you,

Anna, if you will. There are dead and wounded at West Hall."

She turned on him, her mood gone bitter at once. "I will sew up none of those cursed Forlangers. They can die in their own rot."

"Truly," he said, patting her shoulder, "but it was General Olivar's men they fought."

"That changes matters then. For the sake of the general, I will do everything I can to help. I'll get my things."

Now that she was awake, the sour morning taste was rising in her stomach, a reminder that her husband's death had not left her entirely alone. But she did not speak of it. Mari suspected, but it was ill fortune to count on the harvest of fruit that might not ripen. If the gods willed it, then they would bless her with his last child.

Hansi rousted the children as Anna dressed and afterward collected her bag. She kissed them all and left, Joen shifting impatiently as he waited. The full moon bathed the world in a glamor. She had many soft memories of this time of night, for summer's tide had washed her youth in many sweet meetings. But now he was dead.

The houses of the village sprouted in clusters along a cart track that led to the tavern and the temple and, most magnificently, the new market hall built under the supervision of General Olivar ten years ago. She had to measure her pace to allow Joen to keep up without it seeming she could easily out-stride him and, because he was her older brother, she dared not joke with him about it; he would take it amiss, for he had been a soldier for ten years under the general's command before he had lost his foot.

Her husband would not have cared. His sense of humor had never failed, even as he was dying of a rotting wound her herbs and wise nursing could not heal.

The treacherous Forlangers had the king's ear and bragged that they were his most loyal subjects. But out here beyond the King's City people knew them for the greedy, cruel mercenaries that they were, always ready to steal from villages wherever they guessed the king would not notice. Only the general and his men stood between the villages and the raiders.

Someone had lit the crowing cock lamp atop the market hall's steep roof. This beacon called to the folk hurrying forward now, carrying their children, cages with chickens, and bags stuffed with grain and such produce as they could carry. It was not late enough in the season that beasts had been slaughtered for the winter's meat, so the older boys and girls were being dispatched to drive the animals out to the far pastures where they might hope to bide unseen until the danger was past.

The headman's daughter, standing among a cluster of whispering women, saw Anna and broke away from the others to meet her.

"Mistress Anna, if you will, can you go with my husband to West Hall? He is taking ten men."

"If the Forlangers walk the road, ten men will attract their attention. Give me your brother as escort, and we'll go through the forest. He knows the woods as well as I do. No Forlanger will see us."

"But alone, Mistress? My brother is no help in a skirmish. He will just run away and hide, but hiding did not save him then and will not now."

"He is braver than you think. Anyway, we cannot fight the Forlangers with swords and spears. If we have our wits, then that is our weapon against them."

THE COOL AUTUMN night air did not bite, but summer was irrevocably gone. Because it had rained the day before the leaves slipped instead of crackled underfoot, making it a quiet passage. With a clear sky and the moon's merciful light a bounty laid over the world, they did not bother with a lantern. Both she and young Uwe knew the nearby animal trails well enough that the full moon gave them all the light they needed to follow familiar ground. She kept her eye open for night-blooming woundheal, at its strongest here at the end of the year and especially under a full moon, but saw none of its pale blossoms.

Uwe slipped in and out of shadow ahead of her. The young man was light on his feet and very shy. He glanced back now and again to make sure she was on the right track, for there were places in the wood where a person might fall into harm's way and never know until it was too late to climb out.

That was the way of the world: usually the worst was already on you before you knew your throat had been opened and you were bleeding out. So her husband's death had come, its end determined before she had even known he was injured.

Ahead, Uwe halted, a hand raised in warning. Anna stopped, careful with her feet as she felt a branch bend beneath her shoe, shifting carefully so as to make no noise.

Men's voices shattered the silence with shouts and

a ringing clash of weapons. Sound carried oddly at night, seeming both near at hand and yet impossibly distant. Uwe merely shrugged and began walking again. This trail swung away from the main road and around the back of Witch's Hill to the back pastures of West Hall's cultivated lands. No one liked to go this way. As they neared the haunted clearing that sheltered Dead Man's Oak, Anna listened for the hooves of the Hanging Woman. All she heard were the last dying shrieks of a skirmish away north, then nothing at all except for the wind rattling branches and the chirp of a night-sparrow in a nearby tree.

Maybe the Hanging Woman walked elsewhere this night.

As they entered the big clearing with the oak, Uwe slowed his steps until he was walking beside her, keeping her between him and the ancient tree. An old reddened scar like a ring around his neck marked him as one of the few who had survived an encounter with the Hanging Woman. The meeting had changed him, for no one could meet the Hanging Woman and not be changed.

Uwe grabbed Anna's arm, fingers a vice of fear.

A body lay propped against the oak's gnarled trunk.

Uwe shrank back into the brush, but Anna knew better. You never retreated from what could not be changed. What was the point? If the Hanging Woman came, you could not hide from her.

Anyway, a sword rested on the ground at the body's feet, and the Hanging Woman always took weapons for she was a scavenger of lives. As Anna moved into the clearing, she crumbled a bit of dried lavender in her outstretched hand, letting its dust sweeten her steps, taking no more than three steps at a time, pausing between to whisper the old prayer that the old woman of the wood had taught her. "Moonlight make a shade of me, daylight make me whole."

So she came to the oak untouched. Its trunk was as wide as her cottage, and its bark wrinkled and knobby. The huge branches of the oak draped like arms waiting to crush her if she did one wrong thing.

The body was that of a soldier. He was alive, unconscious and bleeding, and at first glance, seeing an officer's sash bunched up across his chest, she thought he was a wounded Forlanger. She hefted her walking stick to bash in his head before he woke.

But then the light changed, shifting through the branches to illuminate his face clearly: an older man, dark hair sifted with white. A face she knew and would never forget, although she had only seen him once in her life, on the day ten years ago when the market hall had been dedicated and given over to the village.

She would never forget the crookedly healed nose taken during one of his first victories, the scar on his cheek, the metal brace he wore on his left leg. She knelt cautiously and eased the bloody glove off his left hand: yes, his left little finger was missing, as it said in the song—*He was last to get on the boat and yet all the Forlanger wolf got of him was his smallest finger.*

The wounded soldier was General Olivar.

Struck down and somehow abandoned or lost by his own men.

She was so stunned that she sat with a grunt and pressed both hands to her belly, panting softly as she tried to gather her scattering thoughts. Ten years had aged him, as it had aged her: ten years ago her eldest child Mari had been a mischievous girl always singing some silly song, her eldest son had still been alive for that was before the shivering sickness had taken the boy, and her two youngest not yet even born.

A hoof fall sounded, gentle as mist, and then another.

So the Hanging Woman announced her coming.

She looked up. At the edge of the clearing Uwe cowered under an evergreen bitterberry shrub, crouching with arms wrapped around knees. All she could see of him was his face like a frightened baby moon. Moonlight collected in the open space as magic into a bowl.

The hoof-falls touched as lightly as the light itself.

Shadows tangled, stretching and winding, coming into life.

The Hanging Woman's noose took shape as a rope of darkness coiling across the grass.

The old oak had a cleft, and in its hollow many years ago an old cunning woman well versed in herbcraft and mystery had lived for several winters. That was the old woman of the wood, the witch for whom the hill was named, although there had been another cunning woman before her according to the stories told to Anna by her grandmother when she was a child.

Anna glanced once more toward Uwe. He had not moved, trusting to the bitterberry's prickly scent to shield him. Rising, she grasped General Olivar by the armpits and dragged his limp weight halfway around the tree, whispering the chant of protection she had learned from the old woman: "Leaf and branch and grass and vine. Let me be like them, what the eye sees but does not notice."

Just in time she hauled him in through the cleft, into the dusty dry shelter of the tree's heart. The smell of smoke still lingered. He gasped softly, and his eyes opened.

"My sword," he said in a hoarse whisper, as if he already knew what she was about.

She had to risk it. The sword would betray their presence. The narrow cleft had been barely wide enough to admit the general's shoulders. She squeezed back through it now and to her horror heard the creaks of men shifting on saddles and the thump of many ordinary horses rather than the eight-legged steed ridden by the Hanging Woman. Pulling her bridal shawl up over her head gave her cover, of a sort, as she glided around the base of the tree. Four riders emerged into the clearing from the path that led, through thickets, to West Hall. They were too far away yet to see the ground clearly but if she moved again they would see her, so she did not run but instead placed herself to stand squarely over the fallen sword, letting her skirt cover it.

Their pale tunics and dark sashes marked them as Forlangers, a fine lord and three of his retainers to look at them all agleam in their pride. But the moonlight showed their hidden faces: a wolf and his gaunt and ugly brethren, hard of heart and bitter of blood.

Night and the ill-omened tree made them nervous. Battle had strung them taut. She had no trouble hearing their too loud voices.

"...said they saw someone running in this direction, my lord."

"I want him dead," said the lord in a high coarse voice. "This is all for naught if he is not dead."

"My lord, we came the wrong way," said a second retainer, his tone brittle with nerves. "This is the witch's tree, the hanging tree. It has an angry and hateful spirit."

The Hanging Woman was already here. Her shadows swelled with the rope of fear. The horses shifted nervously, ears flaring. In the sky above, clouds crept toward the moon.

Why not? What weapon had she, except her wits?

She raised her arms to make the shawl flutter like dark wings.

"Here are you come, so which is it who will offer himself to my rope?" she said in voice that carried across the clearing lit with a gauzy glamor. "I take one for my noose."

The moon slid beneath the cloud. A gust of wind shook through the vast branches. An owl hooted from the verge, and there came out of the forest the sound of a clop of horse's hooves, slow and steady as the approach of death.

The Hanging Woman was coming.

Night, and the oak's mighty shadow, did the rest.

The Forlangers turned tail and rode back the way they had come, toward the fields and buildings of West Hall. Brush rattled around them, marking their passage, and one man shouted as he lost control of his horse.

The cloud passed, and the moon re-emerged. The shadows untangled, and Uwe rose with wide eyes from the bitterberry where he had been hiding and dashed across the clearing to fetch up beside her.

She hoisted the heavy sword. "Was that you, with

the owl call? I reckon I have heard you test that other times."

He grinned, then popped his tongue in his mouth to make the clop-clap hoofbeat sound.

She laughed, then frowned, for it was dangerous to insult the Hanging Woman. "They will come back," she said. "If not at night, then at dawn. You must help me carry him to the rose bower."

Uwe did not want to enter the cleft. Into that cleft one night several years ago the Hanging Woman had dragged the person Uwe had been before, and he had emerged changed, become what he was now.

Anna grasped his elbow and shook him. "The wounded soldier is General Olivar himself. The Forlangers mean to kill him. If they do, there will be nothing but theft and indignity for us and all our kin. You see that, do you not?"

He nodded. They all knew it was true.

The general had fallen unconscious again although he was still breathing. They dragged him as gently as possible out of the cleft. In the moonlight, Anna unclasped his coat of plate armor and cut away padding and undertunic to lay bare the wound. It was just above his hip, in the meat and muscle of the torso. She bent to sniff at it, and while the scent of blood was strong, it seemed the blade had missed his gut for there was no fetid sewage breath from the cut.

That meant he might live.

If they worked quickly and covered their tracks.

They got his coat of plates off him, which woke him up, but he was a soldier who did not complain or panic. He just watched, eyes fluttering with pain, as she bound the wound with strips cut from his tunic.

Because he was awake, it was easiest to drape him over Uwe and let the slight man walk with the general's weight on him. Anna followed with the sword and the coat of plates. They halted beyond the clearing so she could go back with a branch and confuse the ground so no one would guess they had been there.

"Leaf and branch and grass and vine. Let them see but see nothing."

The old cunning woman had lived for six years in the wood, wintering in the oak and living the other seasons in a hidden refuge. During the time she had bided at Witch's Hill, the Hanging Woman had never once ridden out.

There is more than one kind of power in the world.

They made their way into the trees, following trails in the dim light all the way to a rocky spine of land where boulders made a great jumble of the forest floor. A stream burbled through the undergrowth, running low at this time of year.

In the other three seasons, the old woman had lived deep in the forest in this rocky dell, hidden by an astounding growth of sprawling evergreen rose-trees that were more shrub than tree. Sticks woven into the arched branches made a house of remarkable grandeur, one so artfully concealed that you could not see it unless you knew it was there.

Anna had herself lived here off and on for five years as a girl, because the old woman had demanded an apprentice from the village, someone to fetch and carry for her, and Anna had been the only girl bold enough to volunteer. She had been paid with learning, for the old woman had instructed her in herbcraft and many other cunning skills, although

Anna had not passed some subtle test and so had never been taught any deeper secrets. Most of all, she had been given the gift of freedom, able to speak her mind, to ask any question she had regardless of whether the old woman answered it, and to run where she willed on summer nights. She had met her husband in the forest, for he was a woodsman's son and became a woodsman himself in time. So they had set up house together after she got pregnant. By then the old woman had vanished, never to be seen again.

"Uwe," she said. "Go back and make sure no trace remains of our trail."

He left his heavy pack behind with its store of grain, for they had known they would have to depend on feeding themselves if the stores in West Hall were burned or looted.

Anna visited the rose bower several times a year to sort out its store of firewood, rake the ground, lay in grass, clear out any animal nests. The old woman had taught her that a fire must always be laid, ready to light. She was glad of that teaching now, for even in darkness she could start a fire on the old hearth. By its golden light she shifted the general onto a layer of grass.

His eyes were open but he did not speak. By the reckoning of his cold glare, she suspected he was in so much pain he dared not speak. Perhaps he was barely conscious, half sunk into the blinding haze that separates life from death.

She opened her bag and got to work. After peeling back the temporary bandage and his bloody clothing and giving him a leather strap to bite on, she cleansed the gash with a tonic of dog rose and whitethorn.

Afterward she sewed it up with catgut as neatly as a torn sleeve. A poultice of mashed feverbane leaves she bound over the wound with linen strips. That he did not pass out again during all this surprised her, but it took men like that sometimes: the heart would race and keep them wakeful despite the pain. She therefore lifted up his head and helped him drink an infusion of willowbark and courage-flower. She then fortified herself with the cider and bread she had brought for herself, since the old woman had also taught her that no one could keep their wits about them if they were starving or thirsty, especially not those who were needed to care for the ill and injured. He watched her from the pallet of grass. Being evidently a polite man, he did not speak until she finished eating.

"Where am I and how did you come to find me?" he asked in a voice made harsh with weakness and pain.

"You are in the forest between West Hall and Woodpasture, my lord general."

"You know me?"

"I live in Woodpasture, my lord. We have a market in our fine market hall every week."

"Woodpasture?" He murmured the word, seeking through his memory. "Ah. Bayisal."

"That is the name they call it in the king's court, I think," she said kindly. "But it is not our name. How came you to fall under the Forlanger sword, my lord?"

He breathed in silence for a time, measuring the pain in his hip or perhaps simply fishing back through the last few days. "Treachery. They and I are ever at odds in court. Lord Hargrim is ready to steal my command and my lands. I must get back to court. Have you men in your village who can convey me?"

"We have men, my lord. My husband died in your service, and my brother lost his leg."

He slanted a look at her, shifting a moment later to notice that she had placed the sword near his side, where he could reach it.

"I blame the Forlangers. Not you, my lord. In case you are wondering."

His smile had a force that cracked the distance between them. "Generously spoken, Mistress. May I know your name?"

"Anna, my lord."

"And the other one. There was another woman, was there not? The one who was supporting me as we walked?"

"No other woman. A man."

"I was sure, by the feel of her, for my arm was wrapped around her, though I meant no offense by it..." He rubbed a calloused hand over his eyes. "I suppose I was delirious. Perhaps I am roaming not on earth but in the shadows cast by the gods."

"No, my lord. You lie on earth. If men from the village convey you to the King's City, my lord, what is to stop the Forlangers from killing you all?"

"They could hide me in a wagon..." He shook his head at the same time she did. "They'll be watching the roads. They will not rest until Hargrim can throw my corpse before the king and claim me as a traitor."

"How will he claim you as a traitor when all know you serve the king loyally?"

"Men lie, Mistress Anna. They tell stories that are false."

"So they do, my lord. All but my husband. He was a good man and never lied to me, except for the time he had to come tell me that my son was dead."

"I hope your son did not die in my service too. I would hate to think I had repaid you for this by having measured so much grief into your life."

"No, my lord. He was a boy and died of a sickness, as children do."

"Sad tidings for a mother. What of you, Mistress Anna, do you lie?" He paused, a hand probing the linen bandage. "Can you heal me?"

"I have some knowledge of herbcraft and have done what I know how to do. I have a tea that should help with the pain and any fever. It is a bad wound, and you may yet die of it, but you may live. It is not for me to say. That is the choice of the Hanging Woman."

"Who is the Hanging Woman? Some country name for death?"

"Death is death, my lord, not a person. Do they not know that at court? The Hanging Woman has a rope and will hang you in it if she chooses to capture you. Those who are hanged are changed. Maybe that change will be life into death or maybe it will be something else, something you never expected."

He gave a rough cough, then winced. "This is not the work of your Hanging Woman, then, for I have been expecting an attack for months now. Ever since the poison has reached the king's ear, a rumor that I plan to raise my army against him and place myself on the throne."

"Do you, my lord?"

All at once the pain and exhaustion and blood loss overwhelmed him, or perhaps the infusion finally took hold. He looked so tired, as if the fight had dragged on too long and he wondered if he had the will to keep struggling. "No. Never. But it may be too late. The rot of that story may have already have tainted the king's heart."

"Can you rest, my lord?"

He twisted and turned as well as he could, restless and aggrieved. Lines of pain wrinkled his forehead. His lips were pale, and his eyes shadowed by the effort of speaking. "If only... if I could get to the king and not be murdered on the way. I was on my way to court now, and you see what has happened. Lord Hargrim's people control the roads. I will never get through."

"Have you no allies in court?"

"The king's sister has the king's ear. He trusts her. And I trust her." He paused and looked at her. A yellow-beak's whistle chirred twice from out among the leaves. "We were not lovers. It is nothing to do with that."

"I did not think it was," she said, surprised at how quickly he had hastened to deny an unasked question. "It is no business of mine."

"She was married to Lord Hargrim's brother back once. She knows what they are."

"Wolves," said Anna, for they had returned to a subject she cared about. "Winter wolves, on the hunt."

A smile tightened his mouth. "That's right. They are wolves. They want to kill me so they can eat the herd at their leisure once I am no longer there to protect those the king has given me to guard."

He looked up, seeing Uwe duck into view, but since Anna had heard the bird call she did not turn.

"This is Uwe. He is my friend, the one who carried you," she said.

The general stared for a long, uncomfortable while at Uwe's beardless face and the loose layers of clothing that hid his slender body.

Anna rolled up a blanket against the general's side. "Rest a little," she said. "You can go nowhere tonight or tomorrow or any day soon."

"Do me this one favor," he said, touching his throat.

There was a humble iron chain there, well made but nothing fancy. When he fumbled at the chain, she realized he had not the strength or dexterity to pull it out, so she hooked fingers around the links and eased it from under his tunic.

A hammered tin medallion in the shape of a swan hung from the end of the chain, odd to see around the neck of the general because it was a cheap trinket, the kind of thing peddlers sold when they came through the village with their carts in the summer and autumn. She turned it over. On the back were scratched markings.

"Do you see what it says?" he asked.

Uwe stretched forward to look and, like Anna, shook his head.

"I cannot read, my lord," Anna said. "I thought a lord like you would wear gold, not tin."

A smile brushed his lips. His gaze seemed to track back into memory, or else he was about to pass out.

"It says 'one foot in the river.'" His voice was hoarser now, fading as the infusion dulled the pain. "Elland Fort is where I saved the kingdom, even though people say my great victory was at Toyant Bridge. But the ones who I trust know the truth of it. They know I wear this to remind me."

"Who are those, my lord?"

"My young wife. My brother. My three captains, of whom one is now dead. My two aunts. The king's sister."

"And where are these people, my lord? Can they not rescue you?"

"The king's sister is at the palace, close to the king. The others are far from here, for we heard a rumor that the Forlangers were going to strike. My wife is pregnant, so I sent her to my aunts' stronghold in the south. I was riding to the palace with proof of the Forlangers' treachery. That is why they cut me down even so close to the court. Once the king knows, they will be ruined."

Anna pressed another swallow of the tincture down him. His breathing was getting a ragged edge as his body fought him down into the rest he needed if he wished to heal.

"They will lie about me, about what I did here, how I died here. They will lie about my disloyalty to the king. But whatever else, this is my token. Do not let it fall into the hands of the Forlangers. Better you should have it, if it cannot be returned to my wife."

She tucked the tin swan into his hand. His fingers closed over the medallion.

His eyes fluttered closed, as if the swan comforted him.

For a moment she thought he would finally sleep, but he struggled awake again as a man struggles to climb a slippery hillside. He glanced around the space but because of the darkness beyond the glow of the hearthfire he could see nothing except a glimmer of smoke pooling against the leaves as it sought a way heavenward.

"No one will find this place," she said. "And we will keep a watch over you. You can trust Uwe as you can trust me. The Forlangers killed my husband. I will not turn you over to them. I give you my oath by the water of the gods. Let that content you, my lord. You must rest if you are to have a hope of healing."

It did content him, or else blood loss and the herbs pulled him down.

Slowly, the sun came up although it remained dim beneath the leaves. The heavy cover of branches would disperse the smoke by so many diverse channels that it would be hard to see it, but a good nose might smell it and it was not yet cold. So she let the fire burn down and smothered its scent with crumbled leaves of lavender and fennel while Uwe fetched water from the nearby stream to fill the two covered jars she always left here.

She tidied herself and considered the situation.

"So here we are, Uwe," she said. "He will die here, or he will live. If he dies, then he is dead. If he lives, though, what then?"

Uwe rarely spoke for he preferred the forest and solitude, where he could live within the patience of the trapper and hunter and not have to trouble himself with the difficult passages that a changed man must negotiate among people. His voice had a lightness that made it hard to hear, but Anna knew how to listen. "My sister's husband can take him to the King's City in a wagon under guard of a company of men."

Anna shook her head. "No. They will be stopped and the general killed."

"They can carry him through the forest. I can show the way."

"The forest does not grow all the way to the gates of the King's City. They will still catch you."

"Then we can carry him to the other place he spoke of. In the south." Uwe bit a finger, sorting through thoughts. Anna had rarely seen him so animated. "The lord can write. We could fetch a bit of paper from the priest and have him write a message."

"One written word is like another," said Anna. "How can anyone trust that the message truly came from him and is no trick of the Forlangers? Ten men may write the same word and it will look the same, but each man speaks in a different voice."

The general's hand had relaxed in sleep and the tin swan slipped from his fingers, dangling just above the dirt where the chain caught and tangled through his lax fingers. His hands were calloused and scarred as by the lash of a whip. From far away, chased to their ears by the mystery of how the forest weaves sound, they heard a horn call, soldiers about their pursuit.

She fished the tin swan out of General Olivar's hand. "I will go."

Uwe blinked at her, then pressed a hand to his slender throat as if he wished to cry out that she could not, dared not, must not, but knew the words would be spoken in vain.

"Yes, I will go," she said more firmly, for she saw it was the only choice. "It is three days walk. I have food enough if I take all the bread and cheese. You know enough of herbcraft to stay with him."

Uwe nodded, silent, acquiescing because he had been her pupil once, learning the herbcraft handed down from woman to woman. That was before the troubled and despairing girl he had once been had tried to hang herself from the oak tree, but the

Hanging Woman had chosen life over death and had changed him instead into a man. So Anna felt assured he could care for the patient while she was gone. She thoroughly described the regimen necessary to keep the wound from rotting, and advised Uwe to brew up a stout broth from whatever grouse he could catch and boil up barley to thicken the general's blood.

"But only cook at night. Douse the fire in the day. Stay away from the village until you are out of food. If I am not back in seven days, then go to my brother Joen."

She did not like to think about Mari and her other children. She hoped they were well, hidden in the warren of caves where the villagers of Woodpasture had for generations taken refuge in times of strife. She hoped they would not worry on her behalf, but if the general died, then the steady depredations of the Forlangers would make life worse for everyone. West Hall would just be the beginning. Better they suffer a few days' anxiety now than a lifetime of misery after.

She took her humble bag and set off, skirting along the edge of West Hall's fields. No smoke rose, a better sign than she could have hoped for because it meant no houses were being burned. No doubt the Forlangers hoped to be given this grant of land once the general was disgraced and dead; only a fool burned the grain that would feed him. How many had died or been injured she could not know, but she hoped her relatives had been spared. The Forlangers knew that if they caused too much trouble the king would notice that strife troubled the isolated corners of his peaceful realm, so they prowled lightly and struck only for the necessary kill.

She knew the forest well and made good time on woodsmen's paths that wound through the trees and heavy undergrowth. Twice, on hearing men's shouts and horses, she found concealment and waited until all sound of soldiers' presence died away. Once she heard the ring of an axe, and she paused in a copse of trembling aspen. All the woodsmen in this region were some form of relation to her dead husband, sworn to aid each other. But the sound and presence of an axe might bring down the notice of the soldiers, so she walked on.

West Hall and Woodpasture lay on quiet tracks well off the King's Road, which led from the large town of Cloth Market direct to the King's City. Just after midday she came down out of the woods as if she had briefly retired there to relieve herself and was now simply resuming her journey. The traffic on the road was intermittent but steady for all that, no long stretches between a wagon drawn by oxen or a group of travelers striding along. She fell in behind a group of mixed journeyers, kinfolk by the look of them.

One of the women at the back of the group smiled tentatively at her, for Anna looked neat and tidy, no sores or sickness apparent on her skin.

"Good day to you, Mistress," said the other woman in a merry voice.

"It is a fine day," Anna agreed. "What a busy group there are of you, out in all your cheer."

"We are off to a wedding, my cousin's son." The other woman spoke with the clipped 'd' of the villages closer to Cloth Market, so the word sounded like 'wetting'. She glanced past Anna and saw no one walking behind her. "What of you, Mistress? Walk you alone?"

Anna gauged her interest and that of the other women, young and old, who turned to listen, for she was something new and interesting to pass the time. The men in the party saw her worn bridal shawl and drawn face and went back to their own conversations at the front of the group.

"I am recently widowed," she said in a low voice, and their murmured commiserations gave her the time she needed to settle on which story might be most convincing for such a company. "I am going to the King's City to get work as a spinner. My cousin said there are workshops there that will take a respectable woman like me."

They had opinions about that! They came from a village that lay athwart the King's Road near to Cloth Market and had heard many a sad story about girls and women from the villages being promised decent work and then finding themselves in far worse conditions, forced to work day and night for a harsh master who took all the profits for herself or, so one heard, sometimes even trapped into indecent work and abused by men. Yet other women did well for themselves! You had to be cautious, prudent, and hard-headed.

"But come walk along with us as far as Ash Hill," they said.

So she did, and heard about all the family gossip, and spent the night in comfort with some of the girls in the hay mow of the cousin's farm just outside the village of Ash Hill. Late that night a party of Forlangers clattered up to the farmstead, but after they spoke to the farmer and to all the men in the party, they rode away again.

Soon after dawn she took her leave and set out, pleased that the weather was fine. No friendly party of relatives appeared. She was careful to always walk close to or alongside other groups of people. For the entire afternoon she shadowed a suspicious group of carters pushing along baskets of apples who allowed her to walk close behind them after she explained that she was going in to the city to live with her sister who was a laundress. That night she slept rough, but it did not rain and it was not cold and she knew how to make a pleasant haven with a cushioned bed of old needles and grass under the evergreen branches of a thick spruce, although she badly missed her husband who would once have shared such a quiet bower with her.

In the morning she tidied herself as neatly as she could, braided her hair freshly back, and perfumed herself with a bit of lavender to hide the smell of forest. The road was quieter today, and she found herself a place to walk about a stone's throw behind a trio of wagons bearing threshed grain bound for the king's granaries. When the wagoners halted to take their midday break on a long spur of grass alongside the bank at the confluence of the Wheel River and the chalky colored White, she sat down away from them, far enough away that they would not walk over to question her but close enough that she was not alone on the wide road.

The last rind of cheese made a tough meal, and she was out of bread, but she hoped to make the King's Gate by nightfall. The sky remained clear and the air cool but not chilly, so hearing a roll as of distant thunder made her frown. Worse yet came the sudden appearance of outriders wearing the dark sash of the Forlangers. The wagoners quickly leaped up and raced to get their oxen unhobbled and their wagons moving, but it was too late. A company of Forlangers marched swiftly into view.

The outriders caught up with the wagoners before they could get out of sight down the road. A dozen soldiers searched the wagon beds, but most of the infantrymen swarmed the bank to take a drink of water and sit down to rest their feet and eat a bite from their stores. They were mostly young men, respectful in their way and quite uninterested in a careworn woman old enough to be their mother, but because there was only so much nice grassy space, a half-dozen seated themselves near to her and opened their kit to get out dried fish and round flatbread suitable for the march.

"A good morning to you, Mother," they said in the way of lads, politely offering her a quarter of bread. "Where are you off to?"

"The King's City to make my fortune as a herbwoman making love potions for the heartsick," she answered. "And where are you off to?"

They liked her cheeky reply.

One said, "Have you advice for me, Mother? For there's a girl who has said no to me three times. Is there any hope?"

She considered the youth's merry smile and dashing eyes. "Is she the only girl, or just the only one wise enough to refuse you when she sees you are quick to find solace from her hard heart elsewhere?"

His comrades laughed uproariously at that, and soon they were all telling her their troubles and asking her advice in the way of chance-met travelers who will confide to strangers what they would never tell their own kin, for it was sure she would never have opportunity to repeat the tales to anyone they knew. Despite their northern accents, she could understand them well enough. In truth, she wondered at them, for they were decent lads for all that they were Forlangers. Maybe it was their lord who made them wicked, not any of their doing.

A new party rode up at a canter, from the direction of West Hall.

Her heart froze, and her mouth turned as dry as the stubble of a mowed field in summer's heat. The lord she had seen in the clearing of Dead Man's Oak arrived with all his anger riding as a mantle draping him. He was accompanied by ten mounted soldiers. The infantry leaped to their feet, hastening to pack away their flasks and bread.

"Why do you loiter here?" he demanded. "We have reports of a remnant of General Olivar's company that escaped us and is even now making its way cross country to reach the court. Get up! Get up!"

He reined up by the flustered lads dusting off their backsides and shouldering their packs. His eye lit on her, sitting at peace among them.

"Who is this?" he asked them in a tone that snapped.

"My lord," said the merry one hastily. "Just an herbwife who chanced to be resting her feet here when we halted."

"Get on the march," commanded the lord.

As they hastened away, that stare came to rest on her. He had the eyes of a fish, moist and deadened, and thin lips that might, she hoped, never waken desire in a lover so that he would never know what it is to share true affection.

"What are you about on the road, herbwife?" he demanded.

Kindness would make no shift with a man like him. He could only see what he expected.

"I am but a poor widow," she said, pitching her voice to whine like her youngest would do in a tone both grating and harsh, "for my husband is dead of drink and my daughter married. The wicked girl promised I could live with her, though she didn't mean a word of it even though she took my marriage bed, so what am I to do when her ungrateful brute of a husband said he wanted nothing to do with me and him a drinker, too, I'll have you know. But mayhap you have a coin to spare for a sad widow."

"Which I daresay you will spend on ale the moment you reach an alehouse, you old shrew," he replied with a sneer. But he tossed her a copper penny and rode away. That quickly they were all gone, riding at speed away toward the city while she sat shaking.

Finally, when she could breathe calmly again, she picked up the copper for all that it had the taste of his evil hand on it. Old shrew! Not that old, surely, but then she looked at her work-chapped hands and she supposed her sun-weathered face appeared little different. There was certainly gray in her hair, for her comb told her that, although still plenty of the auburn that Olef had said was the fire washed through her that made his heart warm. Not just his heart.

She pressed a hand to her breast, feeling the tin swan tucked within her bodice.

A league more brought her to a small river whose name she did not know. She had only traveled to the King's City twice in the whole of her life, and while there were landmarks she recognized from her other trips, she did not know what they were called.

The road wound through coppiced trees. Ahead of her, she heard the harried voices and the grind of wheels just in time to step off the road. A shout chased along the wind. A half-dozen men trotted into view, pushing carts laden with sheepskins. They cast frightened looks back over their shoulders.

"Here, Mistress," called the eldest, seeing her. "Trouble at the bridge. Best you hurry back the way you came."

"What manner of trouble?" she asked, but then she heard thumping and screaming, and she knew.

"A fight on the bridge," said the oldest man, slowing to a walk as the rest kept moving. "Don't go down there."

"But I must get to the King's City."

He gestured in the direction of the carters as the last vanished around a curve in the road.

"Did you see the big ash tree with the blaze on its north-facing trunk? There's a trail there that carries on upstream to Three Willows village. They keep a small bridge, though they charge a penny for a crossing, so we don't like to go that way. But better a penny than dead."

He hurried on after the others, but Anna crept forward, careful to stay concealed in the undergrowth. She had to see.

The bridge in quieter times had a watchman and a gate flanked by two posts, each with a carved hawk on top whose talons held lanterns at night.

The watchman was dead, and dead and wounded men sprawled on the bridge's span, caught while crossing. A body bobbed in the sluggish water, dark hair trailing along the current. Several saddled but riderless horses had broken away and now

169

sidestepped skittishly through uncut grass, not sure whether to bolt or to await their lost riders.

The skirmish had swirled onto the other bank, a few last desperate men trying to break away from the Forlangers, but they were outnumbered. Anna stared in horror at the melee.

The outnumbered soldiers were the general's men by their colors: pine green and white. There were only six left, and two of those were badly wounded. A horse stumbled and went down with a spear in its belly. Lord Hargrim himself directed his men as they moved to encircle the last survivors.

At once, five of the general's soldiers charged with shrieks and shouts while the sixth drove his horse into the water and flung himself into the current to swim. It took a while for the Forlanger archers to loose arrows because the last of the general's soldiers had spread out, killing themselves by disrupting the Forlanger line for just long enough that the swimming man could get out of range.

Shouting curses down on their enemy, they too fell to lie bleeding at the feet of the Forlangers. The riderless horse made it across the river and stumbled up the bank, then headed straight for the other horses as for home.

"Follow him!" shouted the lord. "He must not get away."

A half-dozen Forlanger men were left behind to pick through the survivors, kill any who still breathed, and drag away their own wounded.

She turned her back on the slaughter and walked as quickly as she could, shaking, afraid at every sound, sure they would come galloping up behind her and lop off her head. But the ash tree with its half hidden blaze was still standing, and she cut into the forest and was well into the trees when she heard horses pass on the road. Her heart pounded so hard that she walked without tiring until at length she caught up with the carters.

The older man nodded to acknowledge her.

She said, "Your pardon, but might I walk with you the rest of the way? Seeing that blood-soaked bridge has taken ten years off my life."

"I pay no mind to the fights the king's men have among themselves," he said, "and nor should you. Not as long as they do not bother us. Why your haste to reach the King's City? You should just go home."

"I'm off to visit my daughter in the city, for she is to have her lie-in soon. Her first child. And while I do not like to speak ill of any woman, I must say that her husband's mother does not treat her in a generous way. Rather she lets my daughter do all the work while she sits in a chair and gives orders."

He was a chatty man, happy to talk about his own wife's mother and how she had been a scold unlike his own dear mother, both now long passed. He was just friendly enough that she did not mention she was a widow, and his younger kinsmen were polite but preoccupied at having seen slaughter done right before their eyes.

The path led upriver for about a league to a small bridge she would never have known existed but for the carters. A watchman at the bridge demanded the penny toll, and she handed over the coin the lord had thrown at her.

There was a party of Forlangers guarding the bridge on the far bank, but after they searched the carts for smuggled men, they let the wagoners pass and her with them, for no one paid her any mind in her worn shawl and with her worn face.

So she came to the city gates just as dusk was coming down, later than she had hoped. She knew well how to make a dry nest in the forest whatever the weather, but how to find a place to sleep in the city seemed a fearful mystery. The place was so crowded and so stony and so loud, and it stank.

She made her way to the river bank's stony shore. There, the last laundresses were heaping their baskets with damp cloth to haul back to their households.

"My pardon, good dames, but I'm wondering if you know where I can find my cousin's sister. She is laundress to the king's sister, so they tell me. I walked here from the village to let her know that her brother is gravely ill."

They laughed at her country accent and her ignorance.

"The king's sister's laundry is done indoors in great vats with boiling water, not out on these cold rocks," said the youngest of them, who was almost as pregnant as Mari. "Those women don't talk to us. You have to go round to the Dowager House beside the King's Palace. The king's mother has been dead these five years, so the sister has set up housekeeping there. And a good thing, too."

"Shhh," said the other women, and many of them hurried away.

"Why do you say so?" asked Anna, watching the others vanish into the twilight. Smoke made the air hazy. Everything tasted of ash and rubbish and shit.

"My pardon, I didn't mean to say it," said the girl. "It's dangerous to speak of the troubles in the court. You know how it is."

"I am up from the country. We hear no gossip there."

"Better if I say nothing," said the girl as she shifted the basket awkwardly around her huge belly.

"Let me help you," said Anna, taking the girl's basket. "It is a shame for you to carry such a heavy load so near your time."

The girl smiled gratefully and started walking. "The work must be done. Where are you from, Mistress?"

"Just a small village, no place you'll have ever heard of. By the forest."

"Isn't the forest full of wolves?"

"Yes, it is."

"Aren't you scared all the time that they'll come and eat you?"

"Wolves are no different than men. They hunt the weak. But maybe in one way they are kinder. They only kill what they eat."

The girl had a wan face, and hearing these words she looked more tired than ever.

"Here now," said Anna, regarding her sadly, for it seemed a terrible burden to be so young and look so weary. "If you'll tell me how to find the Dowager's House, then I will teach you some bird calls. Like this."

She trilled like a lark, and the girl laughed, so entirely delighted that she looked like a child on festival morning waiting for a treat of honey.

"If you'll carry the basket I'll walk you there. It's not so far from where I work and live."

"Do you wash all this laundry for a family?"

"That I do, Mistress. I'm lucky to have the work with a respectable tailor and his household. The lady of the house has said she will let me keep my baby in the kitchen during the day as long as I keep up my work." She named a name that she clearly thought would impress Anna, but Anna had to admit she had no knowledge of this well-known tailor and how he had once made a coat for the king's sister's chatelaine's brother. Anna's ignorance made the girl laugh even more. Anna was glad to see her cheerful.

So they walked along cobblestone streets as Anna taught her the capped owl's hoot and the periwinkle's chitter and the nightlark's sad mournful whistling 'sweet! sweet!' until some man shouted from a closed house "Shut that noise!" They giggled, and in good charity with each other reached a wide square on which rose the Dowager House, with stone columns making a monumental porch along the front and a walled garden with trees in the back.

The girl checked Anna with an elbow, keeping her to the shadows. "There are soldiers on guard," she said, bitterness staining her tone to make it dark and angry. "Those are not the king's men. They belong to the Forlanger lord. He has people watching the Dowager House. He licks the king's boots, so I wonder what he fears from the king's sister."

Anna knew what he feared, but she said nothing.

The girl took her hand, anger loosening her tongue. "My man soldiers with General Olivar's company, a foot soldier. That is why I do not like the Forlangers. I thought they were to be back by now. He and I are to be wed next month."

The words took Anna like a blow to the heart, reminding her of Olef's last day, of his last words, of his last breath. Of how the Forlangers had been responsible, of how they took their war against General Olivar to the back roads and the isolated places where their actions would remain hidden from the king.

She thought of the market hall, and how folk from all around came there on market day. Now that he could no longer push a plough, her brother Joen had been able to set up a stall selling garden produce that his wife and children tended, together with rope he braided from hemp. What went on in the king's court she did not know, but if the general trusted the king's sister, then the king's sister it must be.

But she could say nothing of this to the young laundress. She could only pray to the gods that the man who had escaped down the river might be her man.

A single guard wearing the mark of a white swan stood guard at the service door, around by the alley. When she touched the tin swan in her bodice, she knew she had to brave this last leg of the journey.

"Go on, child, go home, then, and my thanks to you." She handed over the heavy basket. "May the Hanging Woman loosen your womb and let your child come easily."

"My thanks, Mistress."

Anna watched the girl's waddling progress into the dusky streets and hoped she would get home without mishap, but the King's City was a peaceful place on the whole. Folk were still about, so she was able to cross the square by tagging along behind a pair of young apprentices hauling a butchered pig between them. The Forlanger soldiers glanced at the pig and made crude comments about what the lads were like to do with the sow, but their gaze skipped right over her. They took no notice of her at all, right up to the moment she cut sideways and strode up to the side gate and its single swan-marked guardsman.

"I pray you," she said in a low voice, not hiding her distress as a pair of Forlanger soldiers broke off to trot toward the gate, "if your lady wishes to save the life of General Olivar, then let me inside before they catch me. And tell them this tale, that I am ... "

Fear made her words fail and her thoughts sluggish. The guard was staring at her as the footfalls of the Forlangers closed in. The poor young man looked as stupefied as she felt. A breath of wind brushed her neck, like the stroke of a sword.

So she got mad, for she had not trudged all this way just to have her corpse tossed into a rubbish heap and the general left for dead in the forest.

"Stupid boy, let me in! Tell the soldiers I am your poor mother come to beg a loaf of bread in the kitchen and that I will scold you if you don't let me in. I will see that the lady knows you helped me. But General Olivar will die if you do not act now."

He was so surprised by her harsh tone that he opened the gate and, as soon as she slipped through, slammed it behind her.

The Forlangers ran up as she hurried across a courtyard to the servants' door. "You! Who was that?" they demanded.

The youth's voice was shaking, but it could as well have been from annoyance as fear.

"My mum, as if it's anything to you. Cursed woman keeps coming to beg bread off the kitchen. I'm that ashamed of it, but if I don't let her in she stands outside and scolds me. And she's drunk as usual. Best day of my life when I walked out of her cursed filthy hovel."

Their argument faded as she reached the door. She whispered thanks to the gods when the big latch pushed down easily, not locked. The door opened onto an entryway bigger than her cottage. She closed the door and stood there gaping at a high ceiling and wood paneling illuminated by oil lamps, the richest ornamentation she had ever seen, such fine carving as put the headman's house in the village to shame. The heat and smell of the oil in the lamps drenched her; the fierce light after the dark streets made her blink. A riot was happening somewhere down the hall, a clattering like a battle and many voices talking over each other.

Something about a roast.

A girl in a neat skirt and blouse covered by a linen apron dashed down a length of stairs with a tray in her hands. Seeing Anna, she stopped.

"Where is that careless girl?" bellowed a voice from the room where a mob was evidently destroying every piece of furnishing.

The girl ran into that other room. Anna tried desperately to get her bearings, but the long corridor, the many doors, the stairs, and the echoing sound confused her more than forest, road, or city streets had.

The girl appeared again, stared at her again, and ran down the corridor to vanish into another room. She reappeared with a radiantly handsome woman behind her who might have been Anna's age and was wearing the most fashionable clothing Anna had ever seen, a gold gown that shone like sunlight and a finely embroidered bridal shawl draped over her shoulders. Anna stood stunned, not knowing how to show honor to a great lady, the king's own sister!

The woman approached her with a stern gaze. "Who are you, Mistress? How have you gotten through the gates this night? I am surprised that

Roderd allowed you in, for he knows better. On the new moon, the lady gives out alms. You must come back then."

"You are not the king's sister?" Anna asked.

Those lustrous eyes opened wide, and the woman smiled. "I am her downstairs chatelaine, the keeper of the kitchen and lower hall. Where are you from? For you have a country accent and a country look about you."

Anna looked toward the girl, a little thing no taller than her second daughter but lively and as smartly-dressed as the headman's three proud daughters who liked to traipse around the village showing off their expensive garb.

"Go along," said the chatelaine with a gesture. The girl scurried off into what Anna at long last realized must be a kitchen so large that the headman's house would fit inside it. That explained the echoing clamor of many cooks and servants at their work, making ready for some manner of feast.

"Do not make me call a guard to throw you out, Mistress," said the chatelaine more kindly, as if suspecting Anna was slow of wit and perhaps drunk besides.

"I beg pardon for my manner," said Anna, recovering her tongue at last, "but I have never seen such a fine house as this one."

The chatelaine sighed.

She went on hastily, seeing the woman's patience wane. "I pray you do not throw me out. I am come many days' walk from a distant village with news I can only trust the king's sister to hear."

"You must imagine such a tale will fall coldly on my ears."

Anna did not know what to do. What if the Forlanger soldiers pushed past the lone guard and rushed into the house? She had to trust that the mark of the king's sister being a swan and the general's mention of her meant that the lady's servants were also loyal to the man. Her voice dropped to a whisper. "News of General Olivar."

The chatelaine's eyes opened wide. From the courtyard, shouting broke out.

Anna reached into her bodice and pulled out the tin swan.

The chatelaine gasped. "Hide it!" she said, then grasped Anna's wrist and tugged her along up the stairs in such haste that Anna stumbled twice before they reached the top. There, a pair of bored young men wearing swan-embroidered tabards straightened up as if caught doing what they were not allowed.

"Get down to the door and by no means allow any outsiders farther than the entry until I return," the chatelaine snapped. "Send Captain Bellwin to me at once in the library."

The young men grinned, like hounds eager to the scent, and pounded down the stairs just as some manner of altercation erupted at another door. But Anna had scarcely time to think, for the dazzling corridor down which they hurried was like a palace of the gods, all studded with gold and silver and color. There were people walking and standing and hunting and dancing along the walls too, so like to people that she wanted to reach out and touch them, only she knew they were paintings like the one in the market hall that depicted the king being anointed and crowned.

The chatelaine pulled her into a room so filled with books that it smelled different than any room Anna had ever been in. She did not know there were so many books. Even the priest at the temple, who bragged of his treasure-house of six books, would lose his ability to speak could he have seen the shelves and shelves of them. Who made so many books? What was their purpose?

What was going to happen now?

The chatelaine released her wrist and glowered at her until a neatly-clad servant girl peeped in. "Get me water to wash," she ordered.

They waited a bit longer. The girl returned with a bowl and pitcher and towel, and poured and rinsed the chatelaine's hand where she had touched Anna, then took everything away. As the servant went out, a soldier dressed in a swan tabard strode in.

"There is trouble at the gate. I did not know Roderd's mother is a drunk beggar." His gaze fell on Anna. A glint of humor in the slant of his lips gave her hope. "Is this the dame?"

"I am not the lad's mother," she said. "It was a lie so that the Forlangers did not take me."

"She says she has news of General Olivar." The chatelaine turned on Anna, and her fierce stare was the most frightening thing Anna had seen on her entire journey, for she could not tell if it promised or threatened.

It was only now that she realized it might all be for naught. She might have walked into a trap, and her life forfeit. Yet then she would join Olef on the other side. Mari and Hansi had the wit and strength to take care of the little ones. So be it.

She fished the tin swan out of her bodice and displayed it.

The chatelaine and the captain exchanged a foreboding glance.

"How come you by this token?" asked the captain. "What is your name, and where are you from?"

"I am called Anna, my lord. I have taken this token from the general. If you wish to save his life, then you must rescue him from the place where he is hidden."

"Word came last night that he is dead," said the captain in a flat voice.

"He is not dead. He lives, but is wounded and hidden. I brought this to show the king's sister, for he said that she would be able and willing to aid him. The Forlangers mean to kill him."

"They have already struck," said the captain to the chatelaine. "I thought it must be Lord Hargrim's doing, but we cannot establish he is the one behind the attack."

"General Olivar is proof," Anna insisted. "But the Forlangers control the roads."

The two servants conferred in low voices, and then the chatelaine left. Anna knew perfectly well the captain remained as a guard to make sure she did not escape. What surprised her was that he did not attempt to take the tin swan out of her hand. Nor did he speak. He went over to the desk and, still standing, opened a book and looked at the scratchings just as a priest could. Anna watched him but he did not move his lips as the priest did when he read; only his eyes moved, tracing left to right and then skipping back to the left and so on, a pattern as steady as that of a woman knitting.

The door opened to admit the chatelaine escorting two women. One was a magnificent noble beauty dressed in a gown of such splendor that she might as well have been dressed in threads spun of gold and silver. Her small, ordinary companion wore simpler garb sewn out of a midnight blue cloth so tightly woven it shone. They studied Anna, who did her best to stand respectfully, for she was not sure how to properly greet a king's sister.

The small, ordinary woman spoke to her, her speech so colored by odd pronunciations and words Anna did not recognize that she could make no sense of it. The king's grandparents had come from a distant place to establish their court here; that no doubt accounted for their strange way of speaking.

The chatelaine translated. "Her Serenity addresses you, Mistress. She wishes to see the token you hold."

Anna held out the swan. The tin badge was such a cheap thing, a trinket any girl could buy at a summer fair as a remembrance of her journeying there. Yet both ladies gasped, and the ordinary one stepped forward, took the swan out of Anna's hand, and turned it over. Her cheeks flushed when she saw the scratchings. Her gaze fixed on Anna in a fearsome way that made Anna see that she had mistaken the beautiful woman for the king's sister when it fact it was this unremarkable one who had the power and majesty.

Her snapped question had no word in it Anna understood, but she comprehended what the lady wished to know.

"The Forlangers attacked the village of West Hall, my lady. I went at night to give what aid to any wounded that I might, for I have some herbcraft.

We found the general lying beneath the Dead Man's Oak. I recognized him for he came once to our village to dedicate a market hall. Woodpasture, that is, but he called it Bayisal. Our people have always lent our support to the general. Our men fight when they are called. We have lost men in his service, killed by the Forlangers. My own husband..."

She faltered, choked by grief as she rested a hand on her belly.

The king's sister passed the tin swan to the beautiful woman, who perused it and handed it back, nodding.

The king's sister spoke and the chatelaine repeated it.

"How are we to know you did not find this token on a corpse and are come at the behest of the Forlangers to trick us into some rash action?"

"*One foot in the river* are the words he told me with his own lips. At Elland Fort he saved the kingdom, not Toyant Bridge. So he told me. He was wounded, and he may yet not live, but I did what I could to ease his wound and if the rot does not take him, then I think it likely he will live. I know where he is, and I can take you to him."

Even the silent captain looked around at that, first startled and then, as his wrinkled brow cleared, brightened by hope. The king's sister caught in a sob, grasped the beauty's hand, and shut her eyes. When she opened her eyes, the four of them fell into an intense discussion filled with many exclamations and objections and finally a forceful declaration by the king's sister that ended the argument.

She and the beauty left. The captain and chatelaine remained, looking as impatient as if Anna was the last chore that had to be done before a girl could run off to the festival night and the promises of a lover. Brisk footfalls sounded in the hall and a soldier appeared.

"The cursed Forlangers are still hammering on the front gate, Captain," said the man. Like the laundress he was a little difficult to understand with his quick rhythm and city accent, but he spoke the language she knew. "They demand to be admitted to speak to Her Serenity."

The captain nodded. "I will come in a moment and send them off with my boot in their ass." The soldier left. "She must be guarded without making it obvious we are guarding her. Make all ready. You heard what Her Serenity commanded. We leave at dawn. Lord Hargrim and his faction must be given no reason for suspicion."

The chatelaine said, "I will hide her among the servants."

So she did, giving Anna the finest clothes she had ever worn and feeding her the finest meal she had ever eaten, so rich with thick gravy that it made her stomach queasy. The meal ended with a sweet flour cake that was indescribably delicious, like nothing she had ever before eaten. She was given a pallet to sleep on among the other kitchen women, a decent bed but this at least was not as comfortable as the marriage bed she had shared with Olef.

She slept soundly but woke at once when the chatelaine rousted her. An impressive cavalcade of outriders, carriages, and wagons assembled outside. Anna was tucked in among the gaggle of women servants in one of the wagons, all wearing the same swan-marked midnight blue livery with their hair tucked away beneath cloth caps. With a great blaring of horns, the company rolled down the widest avenue in the city and out the main gate. The wagon with its padded seats was at first jarringly uncomfortable; Anna would rather have walked. But after a time she got the rhythm of it. The women around her gossiped and laughed for all the world as if this were a delightful excursion, and it did seem from their talk—those of them she could understand—they all believed their lady had suddenly taken a longing to visit the cloth markets of Ticantal, which name Anna eventually understood to be the same town she called Cloth Market.

But abruptly the whole long procession lurched to a halt. When she craned her neck to see, she realized they had reached the bridge where the last of the general's company had died. Soldiers blocked the bridge, and to her horror, Lord Hargrim himself could be seen in his sash and his brilliance speaking to the king's sister. The lady was riding a horse; he was standing, at a disadvantage because of the horse's bulk. The king's sister waved a hand, indicating her procession. Anna's hands tightened to fists as the lord walked down the length of the cavalcade, ordering his soldiers to peer into the closed carriage, to poke among the wagons carrying luggage. He ordered the wagon full of women servants to disembark, and Anna climbed down not ten strides from the man who had contemptuously tossed her a copper penny and called her an old shrew, but he looked right at her and did not recognize her. His soldiers looked under the benches and checked under the wagon, and yet when their rude inspection was over, even a lord as powerful as Lord Hargrim had to allow the king's own sister to pass for she was powerful in her own right.

Thus they came after two more days travel to the turning for West Hall and Woodpasture. Anna herself led the king's sister and Captain Bellwin and a few stout soldiers past the outer pastures of West Hall and down the overgrown trail to Witch's Hill and the Dead Man's Oak. The clearing lay quiet in the midday sun.

Now, after all this, the secret nest which she had cherished all these years would be betrayed, but it was in a good cause, surely. She hoped the old woman would forgive her the trespass.

Off her horse the king's sister strode along as well as any of the men as they pushed on into the forest. When they approached the rocky tumble and its dense watershed of thick rose-tree, Anna whistled the bird song she and Uwe had set for a signal.

There Uwe came, one moment hidden and the next appearing as out of nowhere, startling the captain so badly that the man drew his sword.

"He is a friend, the general's guardian," Anna said, anxious as Uwe shrank away, for the fear in his face might be fear of reprisal. Yet if the general were dead, why would Uwe still be here?

"Lives he still?" she asked.

"He lives," said Uwe.

She showed them the way in and allowed them their reunion in private, for it was what she would have wished, were it her own self.

They gave her coin, as such folk did, and although she and her family had never had much coin before, she was glad of it, for her brother Joen could use it to expand his rope-making and Mari had long wished for a new loom, her being clever with her hands and mind in that way, and now they could pay the carpenter to make one.

The general himself thanked her.

"I have thought much about our conversation," he said to her. "I cannot return your husband to you. Not even the gods can do that. But I have a thought that there is something else I can give you that may repay the debt I owe you."

Then they were gone.

After this the people of Woodpasture came out of the caves where they had hidden and life went on with the late season slaughtering and all the many chores that needed doing to get ready for winter. Mari had her baby, a healthy little girl, and they made a feast for the mother and child.

Over the next few weeks peddlers came through the village on their last pass through the area, selling needles, delicate thread much finer than what the village women spun for themselves, lamps, knives, and wool and linen cloth from Cloth Market, everything necessary for the kind of work women could do across the long closed-in days of winter. The traveling men had stories, too; stories made peddlers more friends than the goods they had to sell.

General Olivar, the hero of the country, had been treacherously attacked by the northern traitor, Lord Hargrim. Although wounded, the general had escaped by swimming down the river and had been rescued by his loyal captain Bellwin. The king had exiled Lord Hargrim for disturbing the king's peace and sent the Forlangers back home to the north.

It was a good story. Everyone told it over and over again.

One night a scratching on the door woke Anna out of a sound sleep. She checked to make sure the children still slumbered, then swung her feet to the floor and lit the fine oil lamp she had purchased. The shutter was closed against the cold but the lamp's warm light lit her steps to the door.

"Who is there?" she whispered.

"It is me, Uwe," said Uwe.

She set down the bar and opened the door. A full moon spilled its light over the porch. Uwe had on his familiar and well-worn wool cloak and a new sheepskin hat pulled down over his ears. The frosty chill made his beardless cheeks gleam.

"Can you come?" he asked, his forehead knit in a frown and his lips paled by cold.

It was such an odd request that she merely nodded and dressed in silence, waking no one. They walked the forest path, their path lit by the splendid lamp of the moon. An early snow had come and gone, leaving the northern lee of trees spotted with patches of white. Branches glittered, as beautiful as any painting on a wall. Dry leaves crackled under their feet, and in the distance an owl hooted.

She soon knew where they were going. When they came to the clearing, she saw that a man was hanging from the tree, naked, cold, and dead. It was Lord Hargrim. No sign of battle marred his skin, no wounds, no bruising, no broken bones. He was just dead, except for the crude mark of a swan carved on his back.

Uwe stamped his feet against the chill. Shadows tangled across the grass. Anna rested her hand on her round belly.

"Well, then, there comes an end to him," she said. "They'll make a good story of it. Now we have hope of peace."

She turned and, less cold than she had been before, set back for home.

SPIRITS OF SALT: A TALE OF THE CORAL HEART

JEFFREY FORD

THE SAGA OF Ismet Toler can only be told in pieces. Like a victim of his battle craft transformed to red coral by a nick from his infamous blade only to be shattered with a well-placed kick and strewn in a thousand shards, the swordsman's own life story is scattered across the valley of the known world and so buried in half-truth and legend that a scholar of the Coral Heart, such as myself, must possess the patience and devotion of a saint. It's a wonder I've not yet succumbed to the hot air of the yarn spinners of inns and royal courts. Oh, they have wonderful tales to tell—fanciful, heroic, daunting adventures— but their meager imaginations could never match the truth of what actually transpired.

Many of them will recount for you, as if they were there, the Coral Heart's battle on the island of Saevisha, against the cyclopean ogre, Rotnak, tall as a watchtower and ever ravenous for human flesh. They'll supply the details, no doubt—the whistling wind from the swing of the giant's club, the tremble of the earth in the wake of his monstrous stride, Toler's thrust to that single eye and the whole massive body crackling into a weight of red coral the size of a merchant ship. I hate to disabuse you, but the incident never happened. Please, an ogre? Remember we live in the world, dear reader, not a children's bedtime story.

One of the aspects of Toler's life most abused by these fabrications is the story of his upbringing in the Sussuro Mountains. Yes, they manage to capture well enough the location and the fact that he lived out his childhood in a cave in the side of a cliff—common knowledge—but that's about the extent of any accuracy. All of these tale tellers have him raised by a hermit, who taught him the art of swordsmanship. The old man was a master of the blade, a fallen knight who had fled the world for a life of contemplation. And even some of this is truth, because Toler was raised by a hermit. The difference between legend and truth, though, is that the hermit was a woman—an assassin who had spent half her life killing for the Alliance of the Back of the Hand, a clandestine society of the very wealthiest of aristocrats who pulled the strings of commerce and manipulated the fate of the powerless.

She was known, or more her work was known, under the alias, -I-. Even those in the secret council of the Alliance, those who sent her on her missions, had never seen her face. What they knew was her black cloak, her silk boots, the speed and grace of her sword. And they knew her mask, a blank white shell with two small circular eye holes and a small circle for a mouth. She killed swiftly, simply and accurately and moved like an eel through a sunken pasture in the escape. Most of her victims practiced sorcery.

The Alliance had secretly declared war on all magic, fearing its promise of hope to the powerless. In -I-'s years of killing, her prey had thrown spells at her, frightening illusions, distracting dreams, creatures of the imagination. She trusted in her sword, her darts, her leather club, and dagger. Once she parried with an enchanted hog, wielding a sword. Once she wrestled with an angel in the heat of the afternoon. She kept her focus as sharp as the blade, able to cut through illusion, sharper than magic.

In the summer of her 40th year, she was sent on a mission to kill a witch, the crone of Aer, who lived on the outskirts of the city of Camiar. There, in a small cottage, she kept a vast flower garden from which she drew her sorcery. The warm sun and cloudless blue skies did their best to distract the assassin as she rode out of the city to the edge of the Forest of Sans. Along the way, she repeatedly caught herself daydreaming. When she neared the spot where the council had told her she'd find the witches' cottage, she slipped off her horse and sent it silently away to graze in the pasture of tall grass. Moving against the breeze, she crept amid six foot stalks, swarming with yellow butterflies. Some small pest stung her on the back of the neck but she ignored the distraction. At the edge of the pasture, with the place finally in sight, she drew her sword.

She found the door of the cottage wide open and a black cat sitting on the top of three short steps. It never so much as cast a glance her way. Stepping through into the cool shadows of the cottage, she felt the adrenalin pulse and crouched into the fighting stance known as the fly trap. Her eyes immediately adjusted and she noted the basket of fruit on the table, the collections of animal skulls and cleaved rocks, displaying green and purple crystals at their centers. Melted candles and crudely fashioned furniture made from tree branches. Crystals hung by twine in the place's one window, blown glass bottles on the sill held nasturtiums. -I- moved cautiously from one room to the next till she'd searched all three. Then from the kitchen, through a back door, she let herself into the garden.

The aroma of the blossoms was relaxing. She felt the muscles in her sword arm slacken and released a sigh she'd not intended, which she knew was enough of a slip to get her killed. The garden had a fountain and diverging paths lined with egg-like stones, shining in the summer sun and radiating warmth through the soles of her boots. More butterflies and grasshoppers and thickets of flowers of all types and colors spilling onto the edges of the walk. Passing a shock of blue daffodils twice her height, she was startled by a figure, standing amid a bed of foxglove. Her blade instantly swept through the air, and stuck with a knock three inches in the neck of a wooden statue. Its eyes were sea shells, its heart a puffball. She pulled the sword free and spun around to see if anyone had heard. There was only a breeze and the sun in the sky.

-I- found her target further down the path, sitting in a wicker chair beneath an awning of huge, broad leaves. Beside the old woman there was a table on which sat a tea pot, two cups, a lit taper and a pipe. Upon noticing -I-, the witch smiled, and motioned for the assassin to join her. She pointed to the empty wicker chair across from hers. -I- was startled by the realization that she'd let herself be detected.

The witch pushed her grey hair behind her ears and said, "Come sit down. There'll be plenty of time for killing later. And take that ridiculous mask off."

Disarmed as she was, realizing that any chance of surprise was gone, she walked forward, sheathed her sword and sat down. "Did you hear me coming?" she asked.

"I smelled you two days off," said the witch. "Sweet enough but somewhat musty. Please, dear, the mask."

"Brave for a woman who's about to die," said -I-, unable to believe she was speaking to her prey. Until that moment, she'd never have conceived of the possibility. By every measure, it was bad form. Still, she removed her mask and set it on the table. The witch's glance made her blush.

"Do you mean me or you?" asked the crone of Aer.

"You intend to kill me?" -I- went for her sword.

"Easy, dearest," said the witch. "For someone who's killed so often, you know little of death."

-I- returned her sword and sat back. From her years of assessing her prey, her glance instantly registered the woman's lined face and hunched form, noted her strange beauty—ugliness made a virtue—and the grace with which she poured a cup of tea.

"If I'd wanted you dead, I'd have sent a thought form servant with a silver rope to strangle you in your sleep two days ago," said the witch. She pushed the steaming tea cup across the table.

-I- shook her head at the offering.

"Drink it."

She reached for the tea cup at the same time she wondered which poison the old lady had used. Bringing it to her lips, -I-'s senses were enveloped with the aroma of the pasture, its steam misting her vision. She meant to ask herself what she was doing but felt it would have to wait until after she'd tasted the tea. It was soothing and made her body feel cool in the breeze of the hot day. Drinking in small sips, she quickly downed the cup while the witch packed a pipe with dried leaves from a possum hair pouch.

As -I- placed the empty cup back on the table, the witch handed her the smoldering pipe—a thin hollowed out tibia with a bowl carved to resemble the form of an owl.

"What was the tea? And what is this?" asked the assassin.

"The tea was clippings from the garden, stored underground through a frost, drying in sugar. The smoke is Simple Weed."

"It makes you simple?"

"Does everything need to be complicated?"

-I- laughed and accepted the pipe and candle with which to spark it. She forsook caution, drew deeply, and woke in the middle of the night, the stars shining overhead. She sat up suddenly, confused, her joints aching from the cold ground she'd slept upon. She staggered to her feet and drew her sword only to find she was completely alone. The starlight was enough to show her she'd lain among the ruins of an old stone building, roof gone and walls three quarters shattered. Grass grew up around the fallen masonry and crickets sang.

She reached her free hand to the back of her neck and found the tiny dart she'd put off to an insect still lodged there. It was instantly clear that she'd been out cold since the moment she'd felt the sting amid the tall grass and all else had been a dream.

She called for her horse and it approached from the pasture. Mounting it, she rode fiercely toward Camiar, and within the first mile realized the witch in the dream was her future-self. It was then she decided to assassinate all in the secret council of the Alliance of the Back of the Hand.

And she did just that. Five fat, miserable old men. She stalked them and dispatched them without remorse. Each of the four remaining after the first councilor was found, his head stuffed in his hind quarters, hired their own small army of body guards and assassins, but -I- cut through all of them. It was a time known to those in the know as the 'Hemorrhage,' for there was a great bleeding although none of the blood seeped into public view. She killed the councilors and their minions, quietly, secretly, each assassination merely a whisper. She killed the head of the Alliance, the so called 'middle finger of the Back of the Hand,' so exquisitely that it took him an hour to realize he was dead before dropping over. And when the last was opened like a mackerel to let the insides become the outside, she rode out of Camiar and lost herself in the Sussuro Mountains.

She ate what hermits eat, locust and honey, weeds and flowers, fruit and fish. She hunted with her sword, facing off against mountain goats, bears, wild cats, badgers. Those she assassinated for the Alliance rarely had a chance to fight back, but these creatures were cunning and fast and fought to the death every time. Her style of engagement became more calculated than ever, seeing that the fierceness in creatures was a mask of fear. While they pounced, she analyzed and then in the last instant struck with accuracy—one thrust of the blade to let the fear out.

Her dagger trimmed the hide from the meat, which she wrapped in an animal skin and dragged back to her cave. There she had fire and fresh clothes she stole on raids of Camiar's clothes lines. At night she read her only book, *The Consolation of the Constellations,* by the light of a lantern that cast a silhouette of an ibis on the wall of the cave. When reading wouldn't do, she worked through her imagination to create a thought form servant like the one mentioned by her dream witch.

When she finally climbed into her sleeping bag nestled upon willow branches, let the fire burn low, and closed her eyes, she always wondered who it was who'd cast the dart that day she'd gone to kill 'the witch'. She wondered if there'd ever been such a sorceress as the crone of Aer or if the whole thing had been an ambush. Since she wasn't killed, she believed that perhaps a larger spell had been cast that might strike a blow against the Alliance and remove her deadly art from the covert war between the powerful and the people. The longer she stayed away from Camiar, the more she considered that dart an act of kindness.

In spring of her second year in the mountains, while chasing down a stag, she followed the creature into a place she'd never been before. It led her down a canyon as wide as an alley to the floor of a gorge. There, things opened up to a vast mudflat shadowed by 300 foot vertical walls of granite. She looked up and saw the blue sky over the rim of the cliffs and the sight of it made her cold. In an instant, she felt that the place was haunted and she turned to flee.

It was then that she noticed the bodies, lying here and there, dressed in finery, decomposing in the mud. They were badly broken, limbs in odd twisted positions, obviously having fallen from the cliffs.

Seeing the manner in which the corpses were dressed, she remembered from her days with the Alliance having heard of a place in the mountains where people were coaxed to commit suicide by leaping to their deaths. The natural setting of the gorge was staggeringly beautiful, and so the secret council gave some of their victims the choice—either -I- could come for them or they could willingly take the plunge at Churnington's Gorge surrounded by nature and with a modicum of dignity. When she realized who the dead were, she rifled their pockets and took the mink coat of a recent arrival. Her fear of spirits was strong every second she delayed to pillage them, and eventually she left behind a string of pearls she easily could have had and ran, heart pounding, back through the narrow canyon.

That night, lying in the cave, the fire burning low, -I- remembered looking up to the cliffs and seeing that sliver of blue sky. With that image in mind, she had an idea that wealthy people about to jump might leave something behind for the world to remember them by. She daydreamed a large man in a violet suit, brandishing a cane, leaving behind a short stack of books before stepping over the side, and realized she would go there, to the top of the gorge, and see what treasures could be found.

The journey was arduous, the trail leading over a mountain and then a descent to the plateau that ended at Churnington's. What she found at the edge of the cliff was a small boy, sitting, staring out at the afternoon sun. In his pocket, she found a note that read, "I am Ismet Toler." She judged him to be three years old. When she leaned down to him and reached out her hand, he took it. "Come," she said, and led him back to the cave where she raised him.

Little is known about Toler's younger years. Although there are many opinions about what kind of mother -I- made for the boy, or what kinds of qualities he'd carried over from the poor soul who'd chosen to leap to his doom, there exists no proof for any of it. The only verifiable record from this time was a letter written by a sixteen year old Toler to himself about his training in swordsmanship. There were cadavers dragged from the gorge and strapped to the trunks of trees or hung by a rope from a branch—life-like dummies on which one could practice the precise arc and velocity necessary to slice the heel tendon of a large man. There was dance. There were acrobatics and contemplation. About sparring with -I-, he confessed to himself, he couldn't conceive of victory.

The only other verifiable incident from Toler's youth was related to me by Lady Etmisler, who had heard it from the Coral Heart, himself, at a banquet they'd both attended in the palace at Camiar. He told her that when he became masterful with the sword, -I- told him that he'd reached the second of three levels of development. She told him to leave the cave and go out in the world and ply his trade. He wanted to know when his new training would begin, and she told him, "In five years, you can return to me if by then you've renounced the sword. We can only continue if you forsake it."

That night she told him the story of how she came

to the mountains and discovered him on the ledge at Churnington's Gorge. In the morning, he kissed her goodbye, and she told him that at the end of five years, she would send a thought form servant to him to ask if he'd renounced the sword and was returning. He nodded as he walked away, his sword upon his back. In the valley of the known world, he soon found employment as a bodyguard to a corrupt bishop who was often the target of assassination attempts. From there his reputation as a swordsman grew. He moved on to work as a mercenary and fought for the side that paid the most in any conflict, often changing sides in mid-battle for the promise of better. By his fourth year away from the mountains, Ismet Toler was a name to be reckoned with.

But as that fourth year drew to a close, after proving the effectiveness of his blade, he felt he'd had enough of slaughter. The disfigurement of his victims' bodies, the blood and severed flesh, had become nauseating to him. It was all too much of the same gore, and he felt a need to move on to the next level. His diary from this time proves he was on the verge of renouncing the sword and returning to -I-. For the remaining months of the year, he decided to leave his position, training assassins for the Igridot royalty, and head for Camiar, where he would rent rooms, live off the spoils of his killing, and wait for -I-'s servant to appear.

In that brief space of days that he travelled north on the road to Camiar, Fate in all its bad timing and low humor, stepped in, and he somewhere, somehow, acquired the Coral Heart, the blade, whose magical properties would eventually make him a legend. Toler swore to never reveal how he came by it, and so this crucial juncture in the story is blank. I constantly comb the valley of the known world for clues to those few days he spent retreating along that road, and have found nothing. I could spin a fanciful tale, but instead, I merely direct you to where the trail of known fact resumes.

By the time Toler entered the city, he'd already turned to red coral a band of highwaymen who'd foolishly tried to rob him and take his horse. It was the trio of palace guard, though, who confronted him in the market place at Camiar and wound up red statues of their former selves that caused the trouble. He knew he would have to flee. Learning the feel of the sword, he was eager to use it, but he'd not yet mastered its extra weight, or reckoned the sharpness or balance to the point where he could defeat the entirety of the royal guard of the palace of Camiar. He left the city by night as door to door torchlight searches for him were being conducted. There had been witnesses.

Two days later, he arrived in a village, a hundred miles away, separated from Camiar by the Forest of Sans. He chose Twyse as his hideout as it was off the main trails that linked the palaces of the realm. If the snowy, sleepy place had any reputation it was as a home for hunters who stalked the forests that lay just beyond. The furs and skins of Twyse were renowned among the royalty, but its inhabitants cared little for news from outside its borders and would have cheered a tale of the demise of three of the royal guard of Camiar. Toler had stayed there once before and came to know the people as that rare stock who could mind their own business.

He paid handsomely for the use of a barn at the

edge of the village with a fireplace and a loft to sleep in, and paid extra for the owner to keep his mouth shut. Then once the great wooden doors were secured, he unwrapped the Coral Heart, which he'd hidden beneath an extra cloak, and began a regimen of daily practice. His diary attests that every hour he felt his ability with the sword growing. As he wrote, 'The weapon has a personality and if I'm not mistaken a will, which I am learning to merge with mine.'

At night, after a full day of training, Toler would go to The Sackful, the town's one inn, sit in a dark corner, drinking honeycomb rye, and contemplate what he would tell -I-'s mysterious servant when it materialized. Only days earlier, he'd planned to renounce the sword, but now he meant to tell her through her messenger of the nature of the enchanted weapon and how it was changing him. He wanted to tell her that it took the art of the blade to a new level, one he wished to explore. He'd beg her for a reply in which she would tell him her thoughts about his decision.

The days passed in Twyse, overcast but with no visits from the royal guard or news of local manhunts. Toler continued his exercises and imaginary battles and now had begun to move around the entire expanse of the barn in a lunatic dance that made even him doubt his sanity at times. Still, it was exciting and he'd burst out laughing when the sword would show him something new. Now when he held the coral heart of the grip, he felt a pulsing in his palm that matched the beating of his heart. As Toler reminds us in a diary entry, all he wrote for that particular day—'This sword has slain monsters.'

As his confidence grew through his daily practice, he became bolder at night as well, conversing and drinking with the people of the village at The Sackful. They told him of their hunting and he recounted some of his exploits as a mercenary, failing, of course, to mention his name. The moment that marked a monumental transition in the life of Ismet Toler was the night, before leaving for the inn, that he removed his old sword from its sheath and replaced it with the Coral Heart. From the moment it hung at his side, he felt a great sense of calm and a new shrewd reserve, an intuitive calculation.

That night he drank more than his fill and revealed too much about himself. Halfway into the evening, while the inn crowd was listening to a young girl sing a hunter's hymn, he realized that all his new found energy and personality, his reserve was as a result of his yearning to use the sword again in a battle. The charm of practice had just about reached its limits and he was eager for the fray. To build the energy, he decided to hold off using the Coral Heart for another two weeks, and then if the occasion arose, or he were to coax one into happening, he would draw the weapon and turn the world red.

That night, soon after he'd made his decision to continue to lay low, the chatter of The Sackful died down for an instant and the patrons were able to hear a horse approaching on the frozen road. All eyes glanced at the door, including Toler's. A moment passed and then a hooded figure strode in dressed warmly against the winter night—gloves and leggings, a thick cloak. The swordsman noticed first, of course, the stranger's sword hilt, which appeared to be made of clear crystal. The man strode to the bar, and the inn crowd, out of a sense of rural politeness, tried to avert their glances. They were soon drawn back to the figure, though, when the inn keeper, after inquiring if the stranger would have a cup of holly beer, gasped aloud.

What he alone was seeing, all beheld a moment later, when the man who'd just arrived drew back his hood—a face and neck and even hair of a deep red hue. Toler went weak where he sat, realizing from the smooth, shiny consistency of that face, that the fellow was made of red coral. He wondered if this was one of his recent victims having chased him down for revenge. But there was nothing in the legend of he Coral Heart to suggest that its prey returned to life as breathing statues.

"I want whiskey," said the stranger and although he looked to be made of polished coral his mouth moved pliantly and his lips slipped into a smile without cracking his face. He pulled off his gloves, and yes, his fingers and palms too were red coral and flexed easily, although when he set one down upon the bar there was a sound as if he'd dropped a rock. He lifted off his cloak and set it on a chair. None were prepared for a statue come to life.

Toler, like the rest of his Sackful compatriots couldn't move, so stunned were they at the sight. "What manner of creature are you?" asked the innkeeper, backing away.

"My name is Thybault, and I, like you, am a man, of course."

"How'd you come by that color?" asked one of the more brazen patrons, lifting the hatchet from a loop in his belt. "That's the color of the devil."

"The devil? You're an idiot," said Thybault.

The hunter with the axe stood, his weapon now firmly in his grip. "An idiot I may be," he said, "but at least I know god never made a man out of red stone." This said, two of his fellow hunters rose behind him.

"Coral," said the red man.

Toler would later recount in his diary that it was at this moment that he realized the stranger had come for him. He cautiously moved his cloak up to cover the hilt of the Coral Heart. A tightness in his chest told him not to get involved in what was about to happen. The anticipation of battle in the room was palpable. The hunters slowly advanced toward Thybault, who turned to the innkeeper and said, "Where's my drink?"

While he was looking away, they lunged. When they saw the speed with which he drew his sword, it was visible in their faces that they knew they'd made a mistake. The lead hunter raised the hatchet high, but the crystal sword had already punctured his throat, and in an eyeblink later, he disintegrated into salt that showered down into a pile on the wooden floor. There were screams of fear and wonder from the patrons. The two other hunters' eyes were wide. The shock made them living statues as Thybault became a statue alive, spinning into a crouch and running one through, exploding him into salt. Then an upward motion and the crystal blade buried itself in the underside of the third man's chin. Again, it rained salt onto which fell the empty garments.

The innkeeper put Thybault's drink on the bar. There was silence as the coral man returned his glistening sword to its sheath and lifted his whiskey. The only one to move was a young woman who, getting to her knees, gathered in her apron the salt that had been the hunters. Toler was frightened and he hated the feeling. He'd trained for weeks to reach the condition he was in, and the first instance where he might have tried out the Coral Heart, fate threw at him an enemy who was a superior swordsman and made of red coral. He knew it could only be magic.

Thybault finished his drink and smashed the clay cup on the floor. He turned and stared out at the patrons cowered into the corners of the inn. The candles' glow against his polished complexion set him in a bright red haze. He put on his left glove. "If anyone knows of a man, Ismet Toler, tell him I challenge him to a duel out in this latrine of a street tomorrow morning when the church bell chimes. Every day he doesn't meet me, I'll turn another three of you to salt. We'll start with the children." He put on his other glove, wrapped his cloak around him, lifted his hood, and was gone. In the silence that followed, they heard his horse, which must have been massive from the percussion of its hoof beats, moving away into the sound of the winter wind.

Someone cursed, and then the inn erupted into a den of chatter. Toler was so scared he could barely move. Still, he managed to stand and slowly make his way to the door. He didn't want to run, which would, although they didn't know his name, identify him as Ismet Toler. When he neared the entrance, he turned around and shuffled backward, a little at a time, until he was free of the place. The cold air helped him to think, and he realized that it wouldn't be long before the people of Twyse gave him up to the crystal sword. As he ran toward the barn, he made the decision to ride out that night, take to the forest and escape.

In his diary entry that was made apparently just before setting out on horseback, he wrote, 'Something powerful is after me. I'm running away.' Then he fled into the night forest, stopping and listening every now and then to make sure Thybault and his giant horse weren't following. There was no moon and the sky was overcast. Toler stayed off the trails and that made the journey slow and difficult. The temperature dropped well below freezing and before he was even an hour into his escape, it began to snow. Still, he kept moving forward, but for every few yards he'd cover the white wind pushed harder against him. By the end of another hour, he was sure he'd freeze—a statue in a saddle.

An hour further on and the snow was so blinding, he was sure they'd been traveling in circles for the last five miles. His hands were so cold, he was losing his grip on the reins; his face was all but numb. The incessant pummeling of his eyes by the small hard flakes made him ride with them closed, and what he saw behind the lids was more snow driving down within his mind. In his confusion he mistook the sound of the wind for that of a children's choir, and it made him recall Thybault threatening, "We'll start with the children." The only thought that stayed fixed in his mind was that he was a coward.

It came to him at one point in the storm that the horse was no longer moving. He looked up into the squall to see what had happened and felt a pair of hands grasp his arm. Their touch was so wonderfully warm. He squinted against the snow and saw a small form in a black cloak standing beside his horse, reaching up to him. "Come with me," said a female voice. Ice cracked off him as he climbed down. He turned back to the animal to see if it was still alive. "Don't worry, your mount will be fine." Somehow he heard her voice clearly beneath the howl of the wind. She pulled him gently by the arm and he followed.

A few minutes later they entered a cottage built beneath giant pines whose boughs blocked some of the blizzard. He groaned slightly when he heard the door close behind him and felt the warmth of a fire. "You saved me," he said finally, turning to his host. The young woman had already removed her cloak and was hanging it on a peg near the door. When she looked up and smiled, he knew he'd seen her before. "Where do I know you from?" he asked, his hand dropping to the coral hilt.

"I was at the inn tonight when the red man came," she said.

"Ahh," said Toler. "I saw you gather up the remains of the hunters he, what would you call it, killed?"

"Yes."

"How did you find me in the storm? How did you know I was out there?"

"Do you know who I am?" she said.

Toler began to sweat. He shook his head and gripped his sword. "Are you my mother's servant?"

The young woman laughed. "Perish the thought. I'm the crone of Aer."

"The crone of Aer?" said Toler, knowing he'd heard the title before. "Where's Aer?"

"At the end of the valley of the known world," she said.

"You don't look like a crone," he told her.

"To each her crone," she said.

"And so I'm to assume you sent this hellish swordsman after me? Made him of coral so as to cancel the magic of my weapon?"

"That monstrosity isn't mine," she said. "I want to help you defeat it."

"There's not going to be a battle," said Toler. "I'm fleeing for my life. I'm not prepared to meet such an opponent."

"Because he has an advantage like the one your sword, in any other duel, would give to you?"

"Precisely," he said.

"You will fight him," she said.

"I can't."

"I've made you something that will help." She walked past him and the glow of the fireplace into the shadows of the cottage.

Toler sweated profusely; the so recently welcomed warmth was now oppressive. He didn't trust anything. A sword that turns opponents to coral, a red coral man with a crystal sword that turns opponents to salt, and a witch in a cottage in the middle of a blizzard. "Wake up," he whispered to himself, and then the crone of Aer returned, holding a large goose egg out toward him. He took a step back from this new strangeness.

"This egg holds your salvation in a duel with Thybault. Do you remember the salt I gathered at the inn?"

"Yes."

"I mixed it with green vitriol and derived the spirits of salt. They're here in the egg. Merely crack this in the face of Thybault and you will have gained back the advantage."

"What will happen?"

"The spirits will be released."

"I'm going back into the storm," he told her. "I don't trust you. I remember the story my mother told me about you."

"Your mother, who was sent to assassinate me? That demon we saw at the inn tonight, that wasn't my doing."

Toler moved toward the door. His hand touched the knob and he felt a sudden sting at the back of his neck. He tottered for a spell and then fell into the heat of the cottage. The crone spoke directly into his ear. "It's your mother's servant."

He woke in the street, the Coral Heart drawn and in his hand, a crowd surrounding him. He heard the church bells and in a second realized he was back in Twyse. He pulled himself up off the frozen mud and the crowd retreated a few steps. Freezing to the point of shivering and totally confused, he turned to look for an escape from the people, and saw Thybault charging, the crystal blade above his head. He wore no shirt or shoes, the cold meant nothing to him.

Toler crouched and brought his weapon up to block the downward chop of the crystal blade. The crystal clanged off the metal of his weapon, hard as blade steel. He absorbed the blow and rolled away, two somersaults backward and then into a standing position. As he lifted the Coral Heart in defense, he felt the beat of the pulse in his palm. His heart regulated it and regulated the sword. The training he'd done was paying off. Thybault came after him, swinging wildly, massively, as if to cut Toler in half. The red man's blade caught a bystander on the earlobe and made her a cloud of salt. The sight of

211

it distracted the Coral Heart and it was everything he could do to gather in his wonder and counter a thrust of the crystal death.

The duel became fierce, a crazy clash of swords amid the thronging crowd. The pair moved around the street, attacking and defending. At one point, Toler could have sworn that he'd been cut by Thybault. In fact he stopped to look along his side where his shirt was ripped.

"Don't you get it," said the red man. "You'll know when I cut you because you'll be a pile of salt." With this, Toler's opponent punched him in the mouth, those polished coral knuckles like a hammer, and sent him stumbling backward into the crowd. Afraid to be caught by an errant blade from the red man, the crowd retreated, and let their defender fall on his back in the street.

Again, Thybault advanced, this time more deliberately, as if confident he could finish the duel at will. Someone behind Toler helped him to his feet. As he regained his stance, he felt something smooth slip into his free hand. It could have been a stone by its size but it lacked the weight. He cantered to the left and began circling Thybault. The red man swung, every time just a second behind the moving target. When Toler stopped abruptly, Thybault kept turning and swinging, and this gave the Coral Heart a chance to look down at the object he held; the crone's goose egg.

He got in two good slashes to the red man's neck, but his blade had little effect upon the coral. Tiny slivers chipped away, leaving barely visible creases. One thing he was sure of was that the longer he could stay alive the better his chances were.

The red man, carrying and swinging the crushing weight of red coral arms, was growing winded. He redoubled his efforts to finish off Toler and came with a barrage of lunges and half fades that pressed the youth back nearly to the wall of the inn. Thybault then executed an empty fade and instead of retreating, lunged with his foot drawn up. He caught Toler in the chest with a kick and slammed him against the wall, knocking the air out of him. He slid down to a sitting position. The Coral Heart had sprung free from Toler's grasp, and the crystal sword advanced, slashing the air.

Thybault stood now above his prey, leering down. The crowd cheered, shifting allegiance upon seeing that Toler was doomed and fearing reprisals from the apparent victor for having initially cheered against him. The red man lifted the gleaming blade into the air for the final blow, and it was here that Toler threw the egg that was still in his hand. It hit his opponent in the face and cracked. Something wet inside spilled across the coral man's visage. He laughed at Toler's desperate attempt at defense, and the crowd joined him.

Then Thybault's face began to smoke and fizz and a chunk of his chin slid off. The coral man's laughter turned to screams, and the crowd, not knowing how to react, screamed as well. Toler gathered his wits and rolled to where the Coral Heart lay. As he sprang up with his weapon in his grip, Thybault dropped the crystal sword and clawed at his face, more slivers and chunks bubbling pink and fizzing away, coming loose. The Coral Heart didn't rely on the magical properties of his sword but just its strong steel blade, and with a mighty arcing swing, the air singing against the blood groove, he took off his opponents already rotted head. It fell on the ground smoking. A moment later the massive weight of the coral body tipped over and smashed to pieces in the frozen street. The crowd cheered for Toler.

Toler stared at the smoldering face and, in awe, noticed the lips moving. He got down on his knees and put his ear to them. To his astonishment, the sound that came forth was his mother's, -I-'s, voice. "You have now ascended to the second level," she said. "I thought I was to renounce the sword," whispered Toler. "Don't be a fool," were her last words. Then the crowd swarmed him and took him on their shoulders into the inn to celebrate his victory.

Late that night, when he returned to the barn to prepare his things for a journey back to Camiar in the morning, the crone of Aer was waiting for him. She stepped out of the shadows and her sudden presence made him draw the Coral Heart.

"I noticed Thybault's crystal sword disappeared soon after the duel," he said to her.

"I took it and hid it away. No one will find it. You now have no equal."

"I don't understand my mother's creation."

"She was testing you. She may live in a cave in the mountains, but in her heart she'll always be an assassin."

"But didn't you put a spell on her and change her?"

"That was all just a dream she had, twice deluding herself. You can create incredible, deadly, thought form servants and raise a child while surviving in the mountains, but you can't change what's in your heart."

"So you helped me because she once intended to kill you?"

"From what I saw today," said the crone, "it looks like she intended to kill you as well."

"You said no one else knows where the crystal sword is?" asked Toler.

It was only hours after he'd left the village, riding on a main trail through the Forest of Sans, that the owner of the barn Toler had stayed in found the red coral statue of a young woman with long hair. The man was surprised and perplexed by it for a few years until news of the hard red slaughter reached even Twyse. Upon learning of the Coral Heart, he told his daughter how the ancients once believed that the planet Mars was made of red coral.

FOREVER PEOPLE
ROBERT V S REDICK

WHEN MAJKA STEPPED out through the kitchen door at dusk she found a huge white weasel in the garden. Brazen, it locked eyes with her: a rare *chelu*, a ghost weasel, halfway between the garden wall and the little ramp by which the chickens entered the barn. Majka hissed. The *chelu* answered with a growl. The animal was nearly the size of a wolverine.

The door stood open behind her. From within came the eager *thok thok* of her mother-in-law's knife as she battled a turnip, then a chord from the mandolin her son was learning to play. They had borrowed the instrument from a neighbor; it was scratched and worn, and the neck felt slightly loose, but the family treated it like the relic of a saint. It had changed their evenings, brought life to those shadow-swamped rooms.

Majka closed the door. She would face the *chelu* with the axe from the wood-splitting stump. Never taking her eyes from the creature, she backed along the side of the whitewashed house. A fierce wind was rising. The warmth of the day was ebbing fast.

She had guessed that a predator was about. The chickens had gone early to roost, and Bishkin, the family's smoke-gray cat, had slipped upstairs after his plate of buttermilk instead of rambling through the village or the ravine. Of course what they needed was a dog. Just days ago she had worked the village, opening her lean little purse. Sell me that mongrel, that runt in the corner, that toothless bitch. Any goddamned dog. She'd come back with nothing. They'd wanted twice what she could pay.

And now the axe was gone. Beside the stump lay only the small spade they used to bury ashes from the stove. Majka snatched it up and advanced on the *chelu*. The weasel only narrowed its eyes.

Suddenly furious, Majka charged, brandishing the spade like a madwoman.

"You want this, thief? You want me to split you in half?"

The creature bared its perfect fangs—and then thought better of the confrontation, and dashed away across the yard. In a white blur it flowed to the top of the garden wall. Looking back over its shoulder, it favored her with a different sort of noise: an odd, almost sympathetic keening. Then it sprang away towards the ravine.

Majka glanced quickly over her shoulder: the kitchen door remained closed. That was something. No one else knew the animal had appeared.

A gust of wind blasted the garden; the leaves of the withered sunflowers rasped together, gossiping women in a bread line. Feel that cold, now. Look at that sky full of bruises and rage. She knew this sort of weather: it had roared in from the northeast every autumn of her thirty-three years, scouring the last whiff of summer from the high country, sealing the villagers in their shacks.

Majka stomped into the barn. *Chelus* were horribly unlucky. Even to glimpse one in the forest could prompt certain old hunters to call it a day. She couldn't imagine what they'd make of a *chelu* in the garden. There were stories—

But damn the stories; it was after her birds. She counted quickly: fourteen laying hens drowsing in the rafters, three speckled geese. These and nine rabbits were all the life remaining in that barn that had once boasted hogs, goats, dairy cows, a draft horse with a braided mane. They were not enough for the coming winter, but she would make do, make them last, along with the tubers in the cellar and the beans and amaranth she would buy at week's end. No one under her roof would starve. But what if she hadn't stepped outside? If she had stayed in the kitchen for pleasure's sake, listening to her son's lovely tune?

She looked around for the axe but did not find it. She crouched before the chickens' nesting crates and found an egg. Beside the crates, the grimy rug where her husband's dog had slept for years. After his death the big animal had spent a fortnight whining and watching the road, then descended purposefully into the ravine and not returned.

"Pussy Willow."

Majka leaped up, nearly stumbling as she did so. "God *damn* you," she said.

Pankolo, the horse breeder, stood laughing in the doorway, his beefy shoulders twitching up and down. The wind tossed his stringy hair forward to tangle in his beard. He pointed at Majka's hand.

"There's a waste."

She had cracked the egg in her fist. She wanted to hurl it at Pankolo, but that would only make him laugh the louder. The big man stepped into the barn and placed a small package on the chicken crates. Majka threw the egg into the yard.

"What in the stinking Pits do you want?"

"Ain't you nice," he said. "I brought you a sugar loaf."

Majka sniffed. "Baked it yourself, did you? Or was it another present from Slager's girl?"

Pankolo just stood there grinning, and Majka realized that he thought she was jealous. They had been lovers once. Her husband had caught them in this very barn, not even undressed yet, not even touching. After a moment when no one could think of what to say, Pankolo had stepped over to her husband and lifted him from the ground by his shirt. He slept with Majka, he declared, and would go on sleeping with her whenever he liked. "And you, my little scholar: just keep to them rocks."

Dangling like a sad marionette, her husband had looked down at Majka. He was a scholar; the fact marked him indelibly, as did the fact that he had come here from the lowlands: two unpardonable sins. Majka had stepped forward and touched Pankolo's elbow, and the big man had shrugged and dropped her husband on his feet. Yet that calming touch had nonetheless ended her marriage. Her husband might have forgiven her for sleeping with Pankolo—he knew his own shortcomings—but that gesture of intimacy burned like a brand.

"If you came for rabbits, you're a month early; they're too small to skin."

Pankolo chuckled. "Ain't that a shame."

He liked to pretend it wasn't over. He brought food, too, sometimes; food he could well afford. He sold twenty or more foals a year, and the occasional full-grown stallion. He was the only man in the village with something to sell.

Which meant that it was not over, entirely. He entered the barn and pulled her near. Majka sighed, put her egg-sticky hand into his trousers, closing her mind to the smell of horse dander and beer. She moved quickly, before he could object, although it meant the brute would only leave her gasping, unsatisfied, not well fucking served like him. Majka's son never asked for second helpings, but he cleaned his plate like a cat. Sometimes, if the boy stepped away from the table, Majka or his grandmother would scrape their food onto his plate.

"Get them shucks off," said Pankolo. "Get 'em down to your knees."

"It's too cold."

She worked faster still. He groaned and groped and then was finished, and Majka bit her lips in frustration. She had sworn to herself never to ask the least favor of this man. She had never liked him. It was a very small town.

"Pussy Willow—"

"Don't fucking call me that."

Pankolo glared. "You got nothing but snarls for me today. Ain't we friends at least?"

Majka closed her eyes. They were not friends. "I saw a *chelu*," she said.

The man froze, then took his hand from beneath her shirt. When he spoke his voice had changed. "What were you doing in the woods, then?"

"Not in the woods. It was here, in the garden. It was after the birds, I expect."

Pankolo rubbed his hands together. "That's bad, ain't it? You ought to hire one of them Shyram witches, Majka. Get yourself a house cleansing."

"A cleansing. You believe in that old fluff?"

"Not... for certain." But he was retreating, buttoning his pants. Majka smirked, guided his hand back to her breast.

"Thought you wanted to do it properly. Or is once all you're good for these days?"

"Too cold. You were right."

"Not if we're quick about it."

"Let go, Majka."

She put her head back and laughed. "You're scared. Of a weasel. If only the lads could see you now. Better yet, Slager's girl—"

Pankolo snatched his hand away and slapped her. Majka staggered, astonished. The birds screeched; the rabbits slammed against the walls of their cages. Pankolo hovered in the doorway.

"Slager's girl," he said, hovering there. "Tabitha. That's right. I don't need your old cunt no more, do I?"

"Get off my land."

"It's you who need *me*. To keep your brat from starving. Does he know how you pay for them cakes?"

Majka wiped blood from her lip. "No," she said, "but you do, don't you? You know how I take care of my boy."

Pankolo's face froze; then he turned on his heel and fled. A moment later she heard the gate slam shut. Majka stood in the dark, staunching her lip on the sleeve of her blouse. She put a hand on the sugar loaf; it was still vaguely warm.

THE MANDOLIN HAD fallen silent. Majka swept into the kitchen, already shouting at her son, "You go find that splitting axe! I've told you fifty times, never leave things—"

She broke off. Her son and mother-in-law were staring at the open front door. A tall man, a stranger, stood on the threshold, one hand raised as if to knock.

"Forgive me," he said, "the door opened at a touch."

It was true that the latch was failing; for some weeks they had relied on a sliding bolt to keep the door closed in windstorms. The stranger removed his hat. Then he bowed and pressed fingertips to forehead: an old and very humble gesture of greeting, rarely seen in those hills. He was middle-aged but very strongly built. And his skin: so pale. The villagers had skin like dark olives; this man was clotted cream.

"Who are you? What do you want?" Majka demanded.

The stranger turned his eyes in her direction: ice-blue eyes, unblinking.

"I've walked all day," he said simply.

The thing to do was to invite him in. The only thing. He bore no weapon, unless a knife were stashed somewhere in that coat of tattered wool. He looked prepared to stand there forever, icicle-straight, the fierce wind gusting about his ankles. Majka couldn't breathe. The other two might as well have been stone.

"Why are you standing there?" she cried at last. "Come in, sit down. Udi, God's love, why don't you bolt that door?"

The man stepped into the parlor—that was what they called it, the parlor, although it was the only room on the first floor beside the kitchen. It had a table, three wretched chairs, a woodstove shaped like a fat man sitting cross-legged, a coat rack, a butter churn rendered useless when the last cow was sold.

The room seemed to shrink around the newcomer. Majka's son moved towards him sidelong, on unwilling feet. At last he darted around the man and shot the bolt home.

Majka felt ashamed of their behavior. "Pour him some wine, *tata*," she shouted at her mother-in-law. "Udi, bring logs, if you've split any that is." To the stranger, Majka said, "We'll build a fire in no time. You'll be wanting some bread and soup. They didn't feed you in Shyram, then? Of course not, they don't help anyone; if Saint Jal herself came and asked for a sip of water—"

She was babbling. She stopped. With a lurch she dragged a chair to face the lifeless woodstove. "Come and sit." Brisk now; what had she been thinking? She'd be dead before she turn a man away into a storm.

But he was too pale. Majka had seen his like only three or four times in her life. He was from the capital, or some distant country. No one ever came from such lands to the village, this place of wind and nothing, this clutch of sixty houses strung out along a gorge.

Unless they came for the ruins. The thought made Majka break a precious match.

The man crossed the room slowly. He held his hat against his chest like a peasant in the house of a lord, but there was nothing of the peasant in his bearing. He lowered himself into the chair.

"Don't go to any trouble," he said.

Majka was crouched almost at his knees, trying to light the tinder at the back of the stove. The man smelled of earth and moss and wind-dried sweat; there were small brown burrs on his trousers. From the corner of her eye she saw the hand he rested on his knee: a powerful hand, tough and sinewy, a harness-leather hand.

He moved his chair to give her room. There was nothing wrong with him. She was losing her dignity, and without it everything else would slip through her fingers.

The tinder caught. Majka blew gently, added twigs as though feeding a baby. The blue eyes studied her. She closed the iron door and stood.

"This is Chamsarat Spire?" asked the newcomer.

"Chamsarat Village," said Majka. "The Spire's just a heap of rubble, further up the hill. There's nothing but ruins here. The fortress was destroyed four hundred years ago they say. The tower survived, but twenty years ago it collapsed as well—"

"There was an earthquake," cried her son from where he stood by the cellar door, so excited he was all but dancing in place. His grandmother, suddenly restored to life, turned on him and shouted "Logs!"

"It's true," said Majka, as Udi fled. "There's nothing left here but stones. I hope you didn't come all this way to see the tower."

She put the soup kettle on the stove: it would have to stretch to four tonight, and this man looked as though he could empty the kettle at a draught. Once more, accidentally no doubt, she found herself meeting his gaze.

"I didn't come for the tower," he said.

"That's good." Majka considered laughing at her own remark, but what if her mother-in-law joined in, with her raven's cackle? The man was still looking at her; Majka felt her composure about to dissolve.

"You're welcome to ride out this storm with us," she said, astonishing herself. "We've a spare bolster. You can sleep here right here by the stove."

Her mother-in-law was gaping. The man looked down at the hat on his knee. After a long pause, he said, "I might just. You're very kind. It's a long road I'm on."

Majka stared hard at her mother-in-law, who bethought herself and fetched the wine. Majka poured him a generous measure. "Where are you bound, then?" she asked.

"Where God wills."

And mind your own business, woman. She was about to turn away when the man glanced at her sidelong.

"God, or the Proconsul, whoever remembers us first. Isn't that what they say in these hills?"

This time Majka didn't meet his eye. They did indeed have such a saying. Neither the Prince of Heaven nor the leader of the Republic was much loved in Chamsarat.

But why had he mentioned the Proconsul? They were six hundred miles from the capital. The village stood in a distant corner of a neglected province on a road like a long bad dream. Even the local ministers rarely bothered with the climb.

"We say the same as everyone," she answered lamely. "A republic is a fine and fragile thing."

"Yes," said the stranger, lifting the wine to his lips.

"We have the vote here," said her mother-in-law, as though confessing some shame.

The man turned in his chair to look at her. Majka tried to smile and achieved a grimace.

"The vote. She means that every few years they send a soldier and a mule, and an iron box with a padlock. He shows up unannounced and sets the box on a chair in the tavern."

And drinks all day. And notes the color of the ballot slip in every hand. And bears the box away in the morning with a smirk, and a coin or two for the girl whose favors he's enjoyed.

"And you vote your conscience."

It was not a question, or an order, or even a jibe. It was merely a statement. The man spoke as though saddened by his own remark. And for some reason his words sparked a terrible idea in Majka's mind: that she stank. The room was close and the man could smell her unwashed skin, smell the barn and the broken egg, smell Pankolo.

She excused herself, reddening. She snatched up the wash pail and a cake of soap and fled through the back door again.

Crouched by the rain barrel, she scrubbed to her elbows. The cold was agony, but also a relief, like putting her head back to scream. Udi, laden with firewood, staggered out of the barn.

"I can't find the axe, mama."

"Well what in the Nine Pits did you do with it?"

"Nothing, I think."

"Nothing you think! Take the wood inside. Then go

back with a lamp and search properly. And wear your coat, you little fool! If you catch a chill I'll slap you."

Udi looked at her in horror.

"Oh stop that, boy. I wouldn't really."

"I don't want him to be here, mama."

"Saints above! What's the matter with us all? Can't we be decent to a soul in need? What in the Pits are you afraid of? I've told you about white men."

"In the capital. Is he from the capital?"

"Maybe. They come from other places, too."

"What's he here for?"

The soap leaped like a fish from Majka's hands. "That's his business," she snapped. "Yours is to be gracious. Only peasants lose their heads at the sight of a foreigner. We're not peasants, Udi."

He blinked at her over his armful of logs.

THE SOUP WAS delicious. The man sipped his portion slowly, making it last. The room warmed. Majka all but shoved her mother-in-law into a chair beside the stranger. Udi stood behind his grandmother's chair, spellbound. Majka herself could not dream of sitting still, invented tasks to take her endlessly from parlor to kitchen and back again. Dusting under the table. A small rug tossed over the crack in the floorboards. The lamp in the window for a husband dead not quite a year.

Suddenly the man, wonder of wonders, spoke to them unprompted. "I thought I might go and see the Thrandaal, beyond the mountains. They say the valleys there are lush, and the rivers clean."

That was it: he was running. Majka could have laughed with relief. The man needed to get out of the country, and you could do that here, you could climb from these hills into the mountains, cross the border into the Thrandaal, and pass unchallenged into that empty land. That was why he had looked at her so oddly when he mentioned the Proconsul.

"But I've waited too long, you see," the man continued. "Down here you've had rains; up in the peaks it will be snow. I don't mind a little snow, but I do mind dying in it. I've waited too long."

He looked again at his hat. Majka felt dizzied: what in the Pits was he trying to tell them? Could he possibly mean to spend the winter in Chamsarat? To spend it under her roof?

The thought was rending. She couldn't feed this man. Did he have money, would he offer to pay? And who would she be harboring? Would his enemies track him here? No, he couldn't stay. Not in this household, twenty feet from her son. Not if he filled the barn with cattle and their pockets with gold. Not even if he fancied her, if there was kindness in those hands.

"What's your name?" her son asked quietly.

"Wren."

"Like the bird?"

The stranger glanced at the boy. Ever so slightly, he smiled. "They teased me when I was your age. Flap your wings, Wrenny Boy. Fly away home."

Udi glanced at Majka, seeking permission to grin. Majka felt herself blushing once more and rose to stir the soup.

She cleared her throat. "Well, Mr. Wren—"

Sudden terror. Broken glass, her mother-in-law screaming, a dark object landing on the rug. The storm suddenly loud through the shattered window. Udi clung to her, his nails biting her wrist.

"It's a horseshoe, mama. Someone threw a horseshoe at our house."

But Majka was gazing at the stranger. He was flat against the wall of the parlor, twelve feet from the woodstove. This man named for a bird had moved like a snake, faster than the eye could follow. He had slipped one hand into his coat, reaching for something beneath his left underarm.

He had a knife after all.

Through the broken window, a man's voice, loud and derisive: "Majka! What'll you do in a month's time, eh? When the snow lies deep and you're hungry?"

"That's Pankolo," said her son, his voice trembling. The stranger shot a hard glance at Udi.

"You can come to the back door," shouted Pankolo. "There's a little dish Tabitha puts out for the cats. You can bend down and lick, you hear me? You and your boy."

The stranger moved to the window, looked out through the shattered pane.

"Never mind him," said Majka. "He's a drunken fool. Get the broom, Udi."

Her son did not seem to hear her. "Pankolo," said Wren. "Is that short for Panarikolos? Is your drunken fool Panarikolos Rabak?"

Majka froze. Wren turned from the window and studied her, waiting.

"Yes, that's him," said her mother-in-law.

Majka winced; the old woman's voice was caustic. She had never said a word about Pankolo, but she knew.

"Tata—"

"It's a large family, the Rabaks, though most

of them have ended up in Shyram. They were respectable once."

Majka couldn't look at her. "I'll make him pay for that window," she said.

"Will you?" muttered the old woman, nudging the horseshoe with a slipper. "I'm sure I don't want to know how."

The stranger walked to the front door and opened it wide. Cold wind flooded the parlor; the rain lashed him in the face. There he paused, and Majka took a step towards him, not knowing why. The man glanced up at her fiercely, then closed the door behind him and was gone.

SHE CUT A square of canvas and nailed it over the broken pane. They rebolted the front door and fastened the chain lock on the door in the kitchen. Udi asked if the man was going to fight Pankolo, and she told him yes, probably. When he asked if one of them would be killed she sent him upstairs to pray.

The wind grew fiercer. Majka took a lamp into her bedroom and gazed mutely at a trio of crude earthenware saints on her dresser. Behind them stood a little congregation of lead and glass bottles: half-empty salves, rancid skin creams, a bottle the size of her little finger that contained the ghost of a perfume and the memory of the night Udi was conceived. No one would ever hurt him. There was no logic left to her but that.

Her fingers crept to the bottle with the tooth. As always the little lead vessel was extremely hot. She lifted it gingerly. No reason to open it, now or ever. There was nothing inside but sesame oil and a fragment of bone.

"A finger bone, I think," her husband had said. "You keep it, Majka; remember that it's something to be proud of. And perhaps it will bring good luck."

She walked to the window overlooking the ravine. Four years since she'd made the descent. Four years since that river stopped giving and decided to take. She held the bottle in her fist until she could no longer stand the heat, then wrestled open the window and hurled the bottle into the night. She let the rain cool her throbbing hand. She was done with luck.

Returning to the dresser, she opened the bottom drawer, slid a hand beneath her petticoats and drew out a machete. She removed its sheath and ran her fingers up the blade until they met with a dry spot of blood. Something else to be proud of. She tested the weight of the machete in her hand.

Then she heard it: the clop of hooves on the muddy street. She left the sheath in the dresser and hurried downstairs, where she looked around the empty rooms in desperation. At last she rushed to the cellar door. With great care she propped the machete on the first stair, handle against the wall. There came a knock on the door of the kitchen.

Majka closed the cellar door. She had to compose herself. When the knock was repeated she walked to the kitchen door and opened it as far as the chain would allow.

Wren stood there, drenched. He'd gone out without his hat. One of Pankolo's better horses stood steaming behind him.

"He subtracted six cockles from the price of the stallion. For your window, of course."

The stranger reached through the gap, and Majka let him pour the heavy coins into her hand. Six gold cockles. Twenty times what she needed for the window. "You bought a horse from Pankolo? Just like that?"

She might have been asking if he had walked on water. But what was odd about it? He needed a horse, he bought one. And if his hand was shaking a little, what did that mean?

"Your friend said you might have room in the barn."

"He's not my friend. And you. You looked like something drowned."

He brought his face close to the gap. "The prospect grows more likely by the minute," he said.

No smile, but a wryness to his look. Majka found herself laughing. She grabbed her overcoat and unchained the door and stepped out into the rain.

PAST MIDNIGHT. THE mandolin sang softly in her son's gifted hands. Udi smiled as he played; Majka rarely let him stay up late. The room was dark: she had lowered the flame on the oil lamp as far as she could without snuffing it altogether.

Her mother-in-law had retired. Bishkin purred at Udi's feet. Wren had changed into her husband's clothes, although the dead man's shirt would scarcely button across his chest. He still had his cup of wine; she had never seen a man drink so slowly. Majka herself had taken a cup, her first in several years.

The music affected Wren. The line of his mouth softened, and the wariness left his eyes. He paced the house, listening with great intensity and turning often to glance at Udi, and sometimes at Majka herself. They had spoken no more of what was to come.

Majka tensed each time he drew close. She felt him pause behind her chair. In her bedroom she had rummaged through her old crates and foot-lockers, at last finding a warm shirt and pair of trousers. She had turned, and there he was in her room, watching her, glistening with rain.

"I'll undress now, if you don't mind."

She had placed the folded clothes on the bed and stepped into the hall. When she returned a moment later with a towel he was already removing his shirt. He grew still, noticing her gaze. She put down the towel and turned quickly away.

I was only looking for his knife.

Udi finished his tune. Wren stopped his pacing and nodded his approval.

"You're a fine player already," he said. "Do you have a profession in mind, boy?"

Her son averted his eyes. "Stone," he mumbled.

"Stone?"

"Walls and such. My mother's teaching me; she's better than anyone. She built our garden wall."

"There's no demand for it," said Majka. "He can't make a living from stonework in Chamsarat. But then what could he make a living from?"

She wished she hadn't spoken, for she knew the answer too well. He could have made a living from horse breeding. Pankolo had offered, several times, that spring when she first let him bed her. Majka had never raised the issue since.

"You must keep up with the music, come what may," said Wren, seating himself again by the stove. "Will you play us one more tonight?"

Udi shrugged. Then, shyly, he began the first tune the mandolin's owner had taught him. The melody was simple, haunting. Majka glanced at Wren and found him sitting oddly still.

When he finished, Udi rested the mandolin on his knees. "There's words, but I never learned them," he said.

"Many words," said Wren. "It is a balladeer's standard, known all across the Republic. I have heard the tale of Niseta the Beautiful set to that music. Niseta, who waited years for her lover's return, knowing he still lived because he entered her dreams every new moon, and lay with her to sunrise, and she woke drenched with love."

Udi squirmed in his chair. "The one I heard was about a goat."

Majka lifted the wine jug, reached casually to take Wren's cup from his hand. Casually! There was nothing casual about it. She let her fingers graze his own and the breath went out of her. She was not a selfish person; no one could accuse her of that. She filled the cup and pressed it back into his hand. *Give me this night, God of mine. One night only. Let him stay.*

"I have heard a much longer lyric as well," said Wren. "It tells of an ancient clan who called themselves *Ve'saqra,* which means the Forever People."

Majka froze.

"They were few in number but very proud," the man continued. "Absurdly proud, one might say. They told themselves that their clan would never perish from the earth. But they failed to notice the earth changing around them. They were a woodland folk—warriors, hunters, trappers. They did not understand cities, or that a man could build armies from the peasants who came to cities like moths to a blaze. And they laughed when a certain warlord decreed that he was God's will incarnate, and would rule over them."

"Time you slept, Udi," said Majka.

"*Incarnate?*" said her son.

"God's will made flesh," said Wren. "And it is true that heaven seemed to favor his soldiers. They conquered all the lowlands, from the Ilidron Coves to the pine barrens of the north. But the Forever People would not yield. They had strong men and swift horses, and above all they did not fear him. We are conquered first through fear, boy. I hope you will never forget that."

"Did they fight?" asked Udi.

"Oh, yes."

"And beat him in the end?"

Wren shook his head. "They lost their land, village by village. Half their men were slain, and the whole clan driven into exile. But even in exile they resisted. They seized an old castle and began to repair it, stone by stone. And the warlord ignored them. 'Let them rot in those hills,' he declared. And so within their rebuilt walls the *Ve'saqra* knew some years of peace. It was doomed from the start, however. The warlord had turned his back on them, yes, but only because he had developed a new fascination."

Majka brought the jug down on the stove with a smack; droplets of wine flew and hissed. Udi did not even glance at her. "What fascination?" he asked.

"Sorcery," said Wren. "He became the patron of conjurors, necromancers, priests of the Night Gods. He gathered them to his court, plied them with gifts, granted them titles and estates. Year by year they claimed more of his attention, and more of his gold.

"One day he found the royal coffers empty. Having already squeezed his own people dry, he sent a messenger to the hills where the *Ve'saqra* lived, demanding a tribute of men and gold. The man was met with jeers. If the wolf in his prime had not killed them, they said, why should they tremble if he crawls from his cave a last time, toothless and feeble, to howl at the moon? And to underscore the point they took the scroll case with the royal demands away from the messenger and stuffed it with horse dung, then sealed it and sent it back to the king."

Udi's jaw hung open. For a moment he struggled with himself; then he collapsed in laughter, shrill boyish peals. Majka gripped her chair. Horror had pounced on her again.

"Udi, to bed. We're done with stories for tonight."

"But the story's *not* done," cried Udi, instantly contained. "Let him finish, Mama. Then I'll go."

They bickered. Majka started counting to three. Udi whined as though his life depended on hearing the end of the tale, and in her fear Majka found herself imagining that it might be so. That, or the reverse.

"Get marching!"

"No!"

She pointed at the mandolin, "I'll send your plaything back tomorrow. Just try me, you little runt."

Tears sprang to Udi's eyes. Majka swore, crossed her arms, turned away from the man and child. She was trembling; they would notice. She surrendered with a wave.

Wren looked down into his cup. "I've done wrong," he said. "Forgive me."

"Not fucking likely."

"It's just a *story*, Mama," said Udi. "What happened? What did the king say to the people?"

The stranger shook his head. "Nothing."

"You're lying," said Udi, forgetting himself entirely.

"No, I'm not," said Wren. "The king sent no word to the Forever People. He called instead for his sorcerers, and told them it was time to prove their loyalty. And the sorcerers locked themselves in a tower for five days and nights, and a blood-red glow lit the tower windows. When it was done a great shriek went up from the tower, and half the sorcerers went mad and never recovered. But the curse was cast, and it fell upon the *Ve'saqra* and heated their bones like irons in the forge, and all eight thousand were scalded to death from within."

Silence. Udi looked at Majka. She could find no face for him but rage.

"Is it true, Mama?"

She couldn't speak. The man looked at Udi with a strange intensity.

"It is a legend, boy. Legends are never simply true or false. The *Ve'saqra* were real; there are ruins to prove it. And the warlord: he was very real. His descendants are men of power in our Republic today."

Udi frowned. "But the curse wasn't real."

The stranger cocked his head slightly to one side.

"I misspoke in one regard. There were survivors. It seems the curse glanced off certain houses, just as a whirlwind may tear fifty homes to pieces and leave the fifty-first untouched. In the case of the *Ve'saqra*, about a hundred souls were spared."

"Why?"

"I've just said I don't know, Udi. No one does. It was four hundred years ago."

"What did they do with the bodies?"

Majka looked at her son, appalled. The fascination in his voice.

"What indeed?" said Wren. "The bones went on burning, like white-hot coals. What does one do with such relics? And what if they go on blazing for centuries, reminders of infamy, proofs of an unthinkable crime?"

Majka seized Udi's chin and turned it. Udi winced at her brutal grip, but one glance ended his whining: Majka's face left him terrified. He rose and whispered goodnight.

A log cracked in the woodstove. The stranger sat like a statue, or a corpse. Majka listened to Udi's feet ascending the stairs, the groan of the top step, the squeak of his bedroom door. Finally the latch clicked shut.

"I was sent here to kill you."

Her mind seized. *Don't look towards the cellar. Don't leap up or he'll move like a snake again. Don't laugh or scream or weep. Stay alive, stay alive.*

"You can spare us," she whispered. "Just take what you want, and go."

"Take your name? Your ancestry?"

"But there's some mistake," she said. "We haven't done anything. What could Udi have done?"

The man shook his head. "Not this household. This village. First the people, then the crops, then the ancient bones you've scattered or concealed. And in

the springtime, the very ruins of Chamsarat, stone
by stone. By next summer it will all be gone."

"You knew Pankolo's name."

"From traders in Shyram. He's the big man in town,
they said. The one with all the horses. I had to see to
those horses."

Majka shuddered, recalling the tremor in his hand.

"They gave me your name as well. Majka, the
savage one. You're a little bit famous."

"They don't know anything, they're dullards like
Pankolo."

"They know that you chopped a man to bits with
a machete."

"He climbed in Udi's window," she said. "A baby,
not old enough to walk. You make it sound as though
I *liked* it."

"Did you?"

"He was touching Udi. He was drooling."

The stranger closed his eyes. What if she just walked
to the cellar and took out the machete? Or screamed?
Udi could jump from that same window, run away
into the night.

"You're not alone, are you?"

"Of course I'm not alone."

"You don't have to do this. You're a human being."

"Oh no," he said, "not for ages."

She should get up now. Stand up, walk to the cellar.
She felt as if her legs were missing. As if by some
nightmare procedure they had been removed.

"You starvelings," said Wren. "You beggars with
your rags and rotten teeth: you're what's left of the
Forever People. A sad end to the story, isn't it? But
you're still an inconvenience to my master. This is an
election year, after all."

He sighed and leaned forward, resting elbows on knees. "He's quite the ambitious man. He would make a modern country of us, do away with old factions and beliefs. But he can do nothing without votes. Tell me, Majka: who would vote for a man whose forefathers scalded eight thousand peasants to death? No one, in fact. So the legend must be disproved, the evidence effaced. The work began years ago: my master's grandfather arranged for the disappearance of certain history books, and their authors. That was good enough for a time. But a would-be Proconsul attracts far closer scrutiny. It was his wife who put her foot down. Rub out the stain, she said."

"The stain."

"Chamsarat Village. You."

He drew a weary hand across his face. Something in the gesture freed Majka to rise and move towards the cellar. Weak with fear, dragging her feet like a whore at sunrise. She had wanted him to fuck her. She had prayed for it. Her first prayer in ever so long.

"They also told me you were kind-hearted," said Wren.

She turned away from him, leaned her cheek against the cellar door. "Anything else?" she asked.

"Well, yes," he said. "Drunks talk."

He was approaching. She rested her hand on the doorknob, exhaled, tried to make her face serene. Udi would get away somehow. Others would die but not her son. He would cross the ravine and flee into the Thrandaal and become a prince of the forest, wed some Thrandaal girl, found a new clan, die surrounded by family in a mansion of logs.

All at once she felt the warmth of him, the clothes that still smelled of her husband, his breath in her ear. The cellar stairs would be in shadow, black as pitch. She would just lean forward a little, as though groping for the wall. A reverse grip on the weapon. A backwards thrust.

Her left hand felt the touch of his fingers.

"They told me you were beautiful."

"And wanton?"

His fingers released her. "Yes, but they lied. That was their envy speaking. I'm a good judge of such things."

She turned the doorknob.

"Take me first."

"Nonsense," he said.

"In the cellar, where Udi won't hear. I want it once more before I die."

"You want no such thing. And I, even less."

She reached back to fondle him: there was proof of his lie. Then she bit down on the wailing in her soul and pushed open the door and slid her hand along the wall.

Nothing.

She lurched down a step, groping wildly. "Your machete is at the bottom of the stairs," he said. "Don't go for it, please."

She whirled, snarling. Time to kill, she was the savage one, she still had hands and teeth.

And then her legs simply buckled and she dropped on the stairs. To fight this man was to die and save no one. Tear-blinded, she pawed at his feet. Babbling, apologizing, begging him to let Udi go.

"It was a fine idea, the machete," he said. "I hid your axe, of course, but I could do nothing about a weapon already in the house. And when you went to fetch these clothes I had only a moment. I might have overlooked the cellar, distracted as I was by your charms."

Mockery. She couldn't care less. She pressed her head against his leg. Fighting not to howl, scared witless at the thought of Udi waking and rushing from his bedroom.

He crouched down, placed a rough hand on her cheek.

"You must try to understand."

"Go rot in the Pits."

"One day, no doubt," he said. "But tonight there's still work to be done. And you must help me."

"Help you kill us?"

"No, Majka. Help me stop that man, and his long line of bloodsuckers. Help me ruin them for good. I've thought about it for years. Now at last it can be done."

He was a lunatic and no more. This was all much simpler than she'd supposed. "You should rest a little," she said. "Sit down, there's still soup in the kitchen, or I could bring you some—"

He pulled her roughly to her feet. "You'll bring me those bones."

"Bones?"

"The bones of the *Ve'saqra*, woman. Haven't you been listening? My master is a beast and the descendant of beasts, but he could win. The family has been washing out stains for generations, now, and their work is almost done. Only proof of the massacre will stop him. Can you give it to me?"

She felt her own words doom her, but she spoke

them all the same: "I can't. I never would anyway. You're his—dog."

Once again the man grew still.

"It's worse than that. I'm one of his bastard sons. My mother washed linens on his estate: she probably washed her own blood from the sheets, after he dragged her to his room. His spymaster took me from her when I was half Udi's age, and when that old killer died I inherited the job. And I've done my share of killing. Three senators. Four heads of rival families. Never fear, I'll spend eternity in the Pits."

He was sweating, his gaze naked at last.

"There was a time before it started. A few mornings in our shack in the servants' ghetto. My mother brought apple cores back from his kitchen. They were delicious, if you chopped them fine."

She couldn't help him, or kill him. She did not know which of the two she should want. Perhaps they were one and the same.

"The bones are the only proof," he said. "Where are they, Majka? You can't have lived here your whole life and not know."

She couldn't speak. Udi's life, the lives of all the villagers, caught in her throat.

"*Where?*" he demanded.

"They're lost," she said at last. "Graverobbers. It's been four hundred years."

"Graverobbers made off with bones that scald at a touch?"

"People will buy anything," she said. "And there are ways of carrying them—"

Wren's eyes narrowed. Majka stammered: "I mean, couldn't you? If there were any? In pails of water, or—"

"Across the hayfield," he interrupted, "in that ruin of a barn, six men await my signal, Majka. Chewing mutton, sharpening their spears."

"Just six?"

"Six is quite enough. You have no fighters here to resist them. And they are terrible, terrible men."

"Send them away!" Majka forced herself to lean against him, touch his face with her fingertips. "Do it, please do it, send them off, just make up a story—"

"They would never dare return to our master with the job undone."

"The job! Killing us, slaughtering us like a village of pigs."

He broke away from her, walked back to the stove. Crouching, he opened the iron door and warmed his hands.

"They will not be turned," he said, "and if I do not return by daybreak they will strike without me. They are too strong for Chamsarat, even if you faced them together. But with Shyram's aid things might be different. There I saw at least twenty young men."

"Yes," she said. "Half of them are Pankolo's cousins."

"That is why I sent him there."

"You *what*?"

"On his fastest horse. I told him the village would be dead by morning, if he did not bring aid. When he returns I shall fight beside them, and we will win."

A lunatic. Majka put her face in her hands. "Pankolo," she said, "will never show his face in Chamsarat again."

"You don't know that. For all of us there is a path beyond fear. Majka, where are the bones of your ancestors?"

He waited, still crouching, one side of his face gold in the firelight, the other a featureless shadow. For a long moment she stood leaning against the wall by the cellar door. Then she stood straight and crossed the parlour and lifted her coat.

THE DESCENT INTO the ravine was slippery and black. Wren carried the ash bucket and a pair of iron tongs, Majka the oil lamp. When the storm defeated the little flame she crept forward like a blind woman, trusting feet and fingertips. She had used this trail all her life, until four years ago.

The bottom of the ravine was a maze of boulders and underbrush and gnarled pines. They crept upstream until the gorge narrowed and the river lapped the feet of the cliffs. Majka told him to remove his boots. "From here we wade upstream."

"Good God."

"Never mind the cold," she said. "You won't be feeling it long."

They wallowed and stumbled among the high black stones. While it lasted the cold was a torture, animals gnawing their flesh. But soon she felt the familiar weakening of those teeth. The river became chilly, then merely cool. "I hear a waterfall," said Wren.

She could see now, just barely: the clouds were unbroken, but had thinned enough to glaze the river's surface with an eggwash of moonlight. There were the falls, broad and snaggletoothed. And there were the three squat boulders, hunkering together by the cliffside. Majka flailed across the river. She squeezed into a narrow gap between the two nearest boulders, and sighed. Before her stretched a narrow, crescent-shaped pool. The water flowing from it was almost hot.

She clawed her way onto the ledge she remembered, then reached back and took the bucket and tongs from Wren. He floundered onto the ledge. Majka could barely see the man; he was a breathing blackness at her side.

"Gods of death," he said. "It's all true. It happened. Eight thousand souls."

"My husband found the pool," she said. "He was a very clever man. Grave robbers still waste time in the ruins, but they were picked clean before I was born. My husband knew better. He guessed what our ancestors did with the bones."

"Into the river, eh? Where they'd draw no more attention."

"And start no more fires," said Majka. "They were thrown from the old battlements, miles upstream. Of course they were mostly smashed to bits and washed away. But not here. The pool's too deep. Whatever washes in here sinks to the bottom and stays."

"You've been back since he died?"

She nodded. "This end's a bit shallower. I used to sink straight down and dig with my toes and find coins—gold coins; they washed down here too. But they're gone now."

"Why don't you try the deep end?"

"Because I can't swim, that's why. And it's a death trap. The current tries to suck you down under those rocks. If it does, you're finished. Horses couldn't pull you out."

A weird sound came from above them. Feral, pitiful, pliant: it was the *chelu*, somewhere in the brush atop the cliff. Wren's shadow moved. He was kneeling, removing her husband's shirt.

"Don't worry," he said, "I'm a very good swimmer."

"So was he."

In the darkness she felt him study her once more. Then his wet lips brushed her forehead: not an accident, nor quite a kiss. She placed a hand on his thigh, but he drew it away and took up the iron tongs. She saw him stand and begin to creep along the ledge.

A minor miracle, then, the gray veil of the clouds torn away, and there he was in the moonlight, naked, pale gold, and Majka scrambled to her feet as he dived. For a moment he vanished, but then she had him once more, pulling for the depths, a trick of the water making him look small and fragile-limbed and anxious as a child.

SPONDA THE SUET GIRL AND THE SECRET OF THE FRENCH PEARL

ELLEN KLAGES

TIMES WERE LEAN. The capital had been under siege for months and supplies were running low. In the provinces, drought and disease had decimated the herds and parched the fields at the height of the summer growth. Food prices had soared, and little was available, even on the clandestine market, which was bad news indeed for a scrawny thief called Natto.

He stood at the counter of a tavern by the wharves one afternoon, nursing a tankard of sour ale and hoping to glean a lead that might put some coins in his rattling purse. Natto was not overly particular about where his profits came from, as long as they came steady and often, which they had not, recently.

"It's called the French Pearl," a man named Petin said from one of the tables. "The emperor has offered a prize of a thousand royals for the man who discovers its secret and delivers it to him. A thousand royals!" He slapped his hand onto the battered wood for emphasis.

Natto's mouth twitched. Petin was no friend of

his, nor was his companion Masquiat. They would not speak if they noticed his attention. He brought out his little knife and began to dig at his filthy nails, feigning disinterest as he listened.

"All that for a pearl?" Masquiat asked.

"Not just any pearl. Some say it has the power of everlasting life." He looked over to the counter, smiled, then signaled for another cup of dark wine. "But its secret is hidden in a wizard's lair." He shook his head and drank.

"I see," said Masquiat. "And how do you come to know this?"

"Three nights ago I made the acquaintance of a man, a tax collector, who had been traveling for a fortnight. Twitchy fellow, always scratching at one part or another. He was forced by weather to spend the night in a wretched village at the back of beyond, and saw the wizard himself."

"He told *you*?"

"After a fashion. He was not used to strong drink. A small investment on my part loosened his tongue." Petin shrugged. "After he'd had a few, I relieved him of his purse, and was quickly repaid."

"Where is he now? Describing your ugly face to the authorities?"

"No. Sadly, late that evening, he lost his footing out on the docks. But not before he drew me a map." Petin opened his coat, allowing a glimpse of ragged paper.

"Then why are you not gone in search of this so-called treasure?"

"What, do battle with a wizard? I have a bad leg." Petin laughed. "And I like it here just fine. But wine does not come cheap. This map will bring a pretty penny when I find a fellow with a few pieces of silver who fancies himself an adventure."

"True," Masquiat said. "But where will you find such a man?"

"I have prospects. Tomorrow I'm meeting—"

"How much?" Natto said, standing.

Petin looked up. "I don't barter with scum like you."

Natto laid his hand on his knife. "How much?"

"More than your purse has seen in years."

"How much?"

There was silence, the sort that made a few men reach for their weapons. Finally Petin smiled. It was not a friendly smile. "Ten silver crowns. Take it or leave it."

Natto had the money, but only just. Still, ten crowns against a prize of a thousand royals? He would be a fool not to take *that* wager. "Done," he said. He dug the coins out and laid them, one by one, onto the wood.

Petin picked the first up and bit it to be sure, then reached into his coat and took out the map. "It is yours."

The paper was rough, and the map was crude, but Natto recognized the capital and its bay and the steep mountain ridges surrounding it. One road wound up and through them, a jagged line that ended at a labeled **X**. "Fossepuante?"

At the sound of that name, Masquiat quickly made the sign of warding. He stared at Petin, who laughed.

"Ah, now even you see why *I* was in no hurry to make the journey." Petin quickly scooped the coins from the table and jabbed his knife into the wood. "I would wish you good luck," he said, waving a hand, dismissing Natto, "but in times like these, one hates to waste a wish."

THE WHITEWASHED ROOM of the outbuilding behind the inn was small and extremely tidy, two walls lined with shelves of jars and bottles containing powders and tinctures of a hundred hues and consistencies, all neatly labeled. A wide table ran the full length of a third wall. At one end stood a row of brown crocks filled with a pale opalescent substance. At the other, next to a stack of leather-bound books, paper flags sticking out from a dozen pages, a chemist's apparatus consisting of flame and stand and beaker bubbled with a smell faintly reminiscent of a Sunday roast.

Standing at the center of the table a trim, bespectacled young woman in a linen smock, her dark hair pulled back into a tail, took up a knife and a thick block of suet and minced the brittle beef fat into a small pile. She weighed the shreds, made a notation in a lined journal, and added the mass to the beaker, stirring it with a glass rod. She was reaching for a jar marked 'Potash' when a knock came at the door.

"Anna?"

"Who's there?" she called.

"Just me, Sponda."

"Oh. Come in, come in."

A red-haired girl entered the room.

"This is a nice surprise," the chemist said, kissing her on the cheek. "I didn't think I'd see you until supper."

"I wanted to bring this back, before it got mixed up with my kitchen spices." She set down a jar marked 'Dried Rosehips'. "It worked like a charm. That so-called tax-collector only stayed one night."

"A bed full of itching powder will do that." Anna replaced the jar on its proper shelf.

"Do you really think he was here to steal your—?" She glanced at the row of crocks.

"The emperor is offering a thousand crowns as a prize, Sponda. That's temptation enough."

"I suppose. How's it coming?"

"I made a new batch this morning, and added both lime and potash. That helped the texture. It's creamy as butter, and spreads as smooth."

"But—?"

"But the flavor still isn't right. Nor the color. Too white. This morning I boiled some carrots. Once the paste dries, I'll grind it into powder. A pinch should make the spread yellow enough for a proper presentation."

Sponda stuck a finger into one of the crocks and licked off a bit of the creamy substance. "It doesn't taste *bad*," she said. "Makes me think of a farm, wholesome and fresh. But I don't think I'd care for it on my morning toast."

"I know. And it's that last bit of caring that's going to get us the prize, if I can figure it out before anyone else does." She smiled. "The first man-made, edible fat. Cheap, plentiful, and will last for *weeks* without going rancid. Imagine what that will mean for the poor, not to mention the navy, which I think is the emperor's first concern."

Sponda licked her finger again. "It does need a little something."

"I know, and I've got a few ideas. We're getting close." Anna smiled. "But it won't get done if I stand here talking."

"I'll leave you to your experiments." Sponda went to the door, stopped, and blew a kiss. "Supper's at six. Raisin clootie for dessert."

NATTO WAS UNCERTAIN of his purchase; Petin could not be trusted. But having spent the silver, he readied himself for a journey. He stole a full wineskin and a loaf of bread, and bedecked his coat with a handful of rude charms and amulets in case there *was* a wizard.

He made further enquiries about the village, Fossepuante, and was not reassured when, a number of times, the response was widened eyes and the sign of warding. But he had been able to discover that there was an inn. Not the finest lodgings, although one man said that his supper had been the most delicious suet pudding he had ever eaten.

This was the first good news Natto had gotten since he bought the map. He fancied himself a gourmet—although glutton would be closer—and nothing delighted him more than a good pudding.

Putting that thought ahead of any others, he set out from the capital on a crisp autumn morning. Once he passed the army checkpoints that ringed the city he had the road to himself. It narrowed as it climbed, the sound of his horse's hooves muffled by a carpet of fallen leaves, scarlet and golden and copper. The trail had not been much traveled; few had business in the region beyond the cliffs, which was populated more by cattle than people.

From the summit, the land spread out before him, vast grazing plains mottled by rocky outcrops. The once-green fields had been parched to pale straw, the streams mere trickles. Late in the afternoon on the second day of his travels, saddle-sore and weary, he was glad to see a thin plume of smoke on the horizon. Fossepuante.

He rode for another hour and was close enough to see the outlines of low stone buildings when the smell hit him. The putrid emanations made his eyes water and his gorge rise, filling his throat with the sour remnants of his midday meal.

What foul protection had the wizard devised to guard his treasure? Natto touched the amulet on the collar of his rough wool coat and muttered an oath under his breath. He yanked on the reins and forced his horse to advance in the direction of the village.

The stench grew stronger with every step. Natto pulled his neckerchief up over his nose, the odors of tobacco and wine and sweat masking, for the moment, all other smells. That moment did not last long.

By the time he reached the first outbuilding, the horse was flagging and Natto imagined that his own face was the tint of a greenish putty. His stomach roiled, and for the first time he could remember, even the idea of ale was repellent.

Fossepuante consisted of a single muddy street bordered by a handful of stone buildings, half-timbered and thatched. The sign on the two-storey inn said 'The Pond and Clootie' in faded gold letters. Next to it was a stable. The horse whinnied at the oddly welcome odor of manure.

At a distance of some hundred yards was a large

barn surrounded by wooden fencing. Scores of animals lay in heaps amid swarms of flies; above them hung a dreadful cloud of grayish vapor.

The wizard was clever, Natto thought. Unless one *knew*, this would seem an unlikely hiding place for a valuable jewel.

He dismounted and thought for a moment. He had no plan but to rely on the fortunate opportunities upon which thieves thrive. He would arrange a bed for the night, and a meal, then insinuate himself among the locals. The pearl was bound to be a topic of conversation, and when ale loosened some tongues, information would be revealed.

He tied his horse and entered the inn.

The interior was close and dim, but the air smelled more of spice and ale and smoky peat than it did a charnel house, for which Natto was grateful. He lowered his neckerchief and breathed deeply.

To his right, a narrow staircase rose up into silent darkness. Three wooden tables sat to his left, each with an unlit candle. They formed a half-circle in front of a soot-stained hearth, coals glowing. Before him lay a long counter topped with varnished wood; behind it shelves held an array of tankards and pottery mugs and a few cork-stoppered bottles.

At the far end, an open doorway admitted the sounds of clanking pots and the sizzle of meat. He waited for a minute, then two, and finally rapped his knuckles on the countertop.

"Just a tick," said a woman's voice. "I'll get this off the fire and be right there."

He heard another sizzle, then a loud hiss and watched a wisp of fragrant steam wander out and disappear among the rafters.

A moment later a red-haired, red-faced young woman filled the doorway, wiping her hands on an apron. She wore a blue smock and a pair of heavy woolen trousers, her hair tied back in a kerchief. She was, to put it politely, a *sturdy* lass, fully as tall as Natto himself, and half again as broad.

"I'm afraid you'll have to wait till morning to unload your wagon," she said, shaking her head, but smiling. "My Da's just now banked down the fires."

Natto inclined his head in what might, in such a rustic place, pass for a bow. "That would be unwelcome news indeed, if I had a wagon."

The woman's smile faltered. "Everyone comes here has a wagon or a cart. How else would you carry your stock?"

"A horse with saddlebags is quite enough for me."

"In your saddlebags?" She wrinkled her nose. "First I've heard of that. What parts are you selling, then?"

Parts? Natto was unsure how to answer. "Depends on what parts you're buying." He smiled, his most unctuous and charming smile, reserved for the ladies.

"Whatever doesn't go into the pot." She stared at him. "You're not in the trade, are you?"

"What trade is that?"

She nodded, as if she had been given the answer to a question Natto had not heard asked. "Ah, you poor man. No wagon and no nose?" She pointed to the outer door. "Most can smell the plant from miles away."

"Oh," Natto said. "That. Yes, I did notice a change in the—air—as I rode in." He touched his neckerchief. "What is it?"

"Da's the renderer. Boils down what's left after the butcher's taken his cuts. Bones, skin, gristle, fat." She put her hands on her hips. "Any of that in your saddlebags?"

"No, I'm not in that line of work."

"I see. And what *is* your line?"

"Tax collector." It was the first thing that came to mind. A traveler's occupation, and it should put an end to any further inquiries, tax collectors not being the most popular fellows. "I'm on my way back to the capital. I saw your sign, and hoped you'd have a room for the night."

"Fancy that. And where might you be coming from, if you don't mind me asking?"

"I set out this morning from—" and here Natto stopped, because he had very little knowledge of the provinces.

She looked at him for a moment, then said, as if it were amusing, "Maulde?"

"Yes," Natto said quickly. "Maulde. Charming place."

The girl's mouth twitched in what Natto thought was a most unbecoming way. "Isn't it just," she said.

"Do you have a room?" he asked after a moment of awkward silence.

"I will in about half an hour. I'll need to go up and change the linens." She pointed to one of the tables. "Sit there and have a pint while I tidy up. Ale and supper's included with the tariff. May I ask your name, sir?"

Natto thought as quickly as he was able. "George," he said. "George, uh, Petin!" *There.* Now if any trouble followed him to the capital, Petin would be the one pursued.

"Very good, Mr. Petin. I have a nice front room."
She named a price that was, nearly to the copper,
what his purse contained. It was not a princely
sum—he'd paid more for a single meal, when he was
flush—but his circumstances had been drastically
reduced by the purchase of the map.

He nodded, laying his coins on the counter as she
drew a pint from the barrel and set it on the nearest
table. She put the coins in a wooden box.

"What's on offer tonight?" he asked.

"I've got a lovely pud coming off the hob in about
two hours. Pearl barley, mutton, and mince."

Natto's mouth watered.

SPONDA RAPPED ON the outbuilding door. "It's me."

"Come in." Anna wiped her hands on a stained
towel. She saw Sponda's face and frowned. "What's
wrong?"

"Another stranger. Says *he's* a tax collector, too,
just like the first."

"Did he say anything else suspicious?"

"No, but when I asked where he'd ridden from, he
didn't seem to know. I suggested Maulde and he was
quick to agree."

"Maulde? That's two hundred leagues from here!"

"I know," Sponda said. "Once he failed that first
test, I did what you said, if another came. I told him
there'd be pearl barley in the pud, and I saw his eyes
go wide for just a moment."

"If he startles at the word *pearl*, he could be from
Mége-Mouriés laboratory, snooping around to see if
I've made any progress."

"He doesn't really look the chemist type, but I

think you're right. It's been an age since we've had two guests in a week, and neither one of them a rag and bone man with reason to stop here."

"True. But that may be good news."

"*Why?*"

"Well, if the prize had been claimed, there'd be no need to send spies around to snoop, would there?"

"I suppose not. I gave the one we have a pint of ale and told him I needed to make the bed, then took the back stairs here. Thought you ought to know."

Anna sighed. "Take the rosehips." She pulled the jar from the shelf.

Sponda nodded. "Should I set a place for you at supper?"

"No. Save me a slice. I'll eat it cold later. I think it's best that this stranger doesn't meet me yet. But listen closely to what he says. See if you can find out what he's up to."

"I will. I told him ale comes with the room, so I'll make sure he gets full value." Sponda slipped the jar into her apron. "What if he keeps on, though?"

Anna looked around the room and laughed. "I'm a trained apothecary. And I had three brothers. I'm a wizard at concocting any number of unpleasant surprises." Her face took on a curious look. "And I just had an idea."

"What?"

"I'll tell you later, once I work it out. We're too close to claiming the prize for *anything* to get in our way."

THE SMALL UPSTAIRS room faced the road. It had a washstand with a pitcher and a chamber pot, and a narrow bed covered in a quilt that smelled like roses. Natto combed the road dust out of his beard and put on his other shirt, to make a good impression with the locals. He descended the stairs at dusk. The air now smelled of spiced meat and tobacco, and at one of the tables sat a large, ruddy man with a pipe in his mouth and his ham of a fist wrapped around a tankard.

He looked up at the sound of footsteps. "Hello, hello!" he called. "I'm Ian Cubbins. You must be the tax-man." He indicated the chair across from his with a wave of his pipestem. He called to the kitchen, "Sponda! Ale for our guest!"

The red-haired woman came out and drew a pint for Natto. "The room to your liking, Mr. Petin?"

"It's fine."

"Supper in an hour." She put his ale down and returned to the kitchen.

The man puffed on his pipe. "Do you like steamed pudding?"

"I do. It's a favorite of mine," Natto said, telling the truth for once.

"Then you're in for a treat. My daughter's won ribbons at the fair for her puddings." He lowered his voice. "It's the suet that does it. Fresh from the plant, every day."

"I see." Natto's ale caught in his throat. He liked a good suet pudding as much as any man, but until now had not really considered its origins. "You make a lot of it?"

"Aye. Hoof disease hasn't hurt *my* business none." He smiled, showing a few more teeth than Natto had expected. "You know what they say, 'all's not butter that comes from the cow.'"

"Um. Yes. You've been doing this a long time?"

"Since I was a lad. Learned from my Da, and he from his on back to—" he waggled his pipe at the uncountable years. "Yourself?"

"I'm in—revenue," Natto said. Another semblance of truth. He took money in, but not for the benefit of the government.

"Never was much with figures, me. My Sponda keeps track of the accounts, since her Ma passed." He ducked his head in a moment of remembrance then took a long and hearty swig of ale. "Ready for another?" he asked.

"Can't say that I'd mind." Natto drained his mug.

Ian was a friendly host, although his conversation ran mostly to the weather and odd facts about cattle, neither of which interested Natto. But the ruddy man saw to it that their mugs stayed full. Natto felt a familiar and pleasant glow by the time Sponda brought out their supper.

"Here you go," she said, setting the platter down. It held a golden-brown mound nearly the size of a man's head, giving off a wonderful savory steam.

Ian cut into the crust, and the gravied meat and grain spilled out, redolent of onions. He placed a generous portion onto Natto's plate. "There now. Tell me if that isn't the finest pudding you've ever had."

Natto would have replied, but his mouth was already full. He nodded enthusiastically, and a few minutes later, asked for another helping of both pudding and ale.

When he was sated, Natto sat back in his chair. Sponda cleared the table, refilling his ale once again.

"Da?" she asked.

"No more for me," her father said. "I'm off to bed. Dawn comes early." He patted her cheek and went upstairs.

Sponda filled a mug for herself. "You liked the pudding, then?"

"It was magnificent. What's your secret?"

"Well, suet and tallow *are* our bread and butter," she answered. "Though I suppose few in the capital have had butter since the troubles began."

"True enough. It's gotten too dear for the likes of me."

"We get a bit, now and then, from farmers who still have herds, but even here it's become scarce." She looked thoughtfully at him, then nodded to herself. "Da says he doesn't miss it much," she continued. "Says he's more of a greaves and drippings man."

"They have their place," Natto agreed. He took another pull on his ale. "You should move to the capital. A cook like you would be in high demand."

"Perhaps I will, some day," she said with a hint of a smile. "Now, tell me about your journeys. We don't get many visitors, and it must be so interesting, traveling all over, in search of—" She paused to wipe an errant crumb from the table. "I'm sorry, I've forgotten what it is you said you're after."

Natto's ale-fuzzed brain almost blurted, "The French Pearl." He stopped himself, but could think of nothing else and "Hidden treasure," was what came out of his mouth.

"Treasure? Really?"

"Well, in a manner of speaking." He tried to recover. "That is to say, assets that have not been properly reported, or—" He gathered what were left of his wits. "—uncollected revenues. Very important, especially in times like these."

"Silly me," Sponda shook her head. "Here I was thinking you meant chests full of pearls and jewels and gold coins."

Natto almost spilled his ale. Was this the opportunity he had been waiting for? "Those would certainly be of interest to—to my superiors. As an innkeeper, you must hear all sorts of stories. If they turn out to be of use, there might be a generous reward."

"I see." She stood still for a moment, then smiled as if she had just remembered something. "You know, there is an odd fellow on the outskirts of town, and there are rumors—"

"Yes, yes. What sort of rumors?" Natto sat up eagerly.

"Well, I don't like to gossip," she said. "But he's rather secretive about what he does in his cottage. Strange lights and eerie noises, all times of the day and night." She leaned toward him and lowered her voice. "Some say he's a wizard."

"Really?"

"Some say."

"Where is this cottage?"

"I'll show you, after breakfast." Sponda looked back at the kitchen. "But now, I'm afraid, I've got the washing up to do and a few things to prepare before morning."

"Then I will say goodnight," Natto drained his ale and stood on his second attempt.

"I hope you sleep well," Sponda said, and again her mouth twitched. It was most unbecoming.

ANNA CAME INTO the kitchen as Sponda was drying the last of the plates. She put her arms around the innkeeper and kissed the back of her neck. "How was supper?"

"The pud came out well. Yours is on the table, under the cloth."

"And the stranger?" She sat down and picked up a fork.

Sponda made a face. "He's not a spy. Just a common thief."

Anna raised an eyebrow, her mouth full.

"While I was out talking to you he opened the cash box. Nicked back what he'd paid me, and three coppers besides."

"Ah." She swallowed. "I'm a little relieved, though. Why do you think he's *here*?"

"It wasn't just chance. He's looking for something. Every time I said the word *pearl*, he jumped out of his britches."

"Really." Anna sat quiet for a minute, then smiled. "In that case, I think we ought to give him one."

NATTO SPENT A restless night. He was up several times to relieve himself, not uncommon after an evening of drinking, and every time he crawled back into bed, his bare legs itched like the devil. Chafed from two days of riding? He was miserable, and thoughts of the mysterious wizard flittered through his head as he tossed and turned.

At first light he heard the father rise and lumber down the stairs in his hobnailed boots. Natto buried his pounding head in the pillow and tried vainly to fall asleep, but gave up after another hour. He used the chamber pot again—it had become rather full—and put on his trousers. Downstairs, breakfast was laid out on the counter: tea and oatcakes with jam. They were plain fare, hearty and filling, and he had two helpings.

He hadn't seen the red-haired woman, so when he'd finished, he picked up his plate and cup and took them to the doorway. "Lady?" he called.

He heard the noise of a door shutting at the back of the kitchen, and a moment later she appeared, pulling off a heavy cloak. "Sorry," she said. "I was out back, um, checking to see if the hen was laying." She saw the dishes in his hands. "Here, let me take those for you."

"Can you show me the odd fellow's house?"

"What? Oh, yes, him." She glanced toward the back door, then hung her cloak on a hook. "Give me fifteen minutes to put away the breakfast things." She gestured to a skillet and a mixing bowl. "Did you pass a pleasant night?"

"Not really," Natto said. "A lot on my mind, I guess. My duties and all."

"Sorry to hear that. Care for a fresh cup of tea?"

"Thank you, no." He rubbed his temples, which throbbed from lack of sleep and what his acquaintances called ale-head. Perhaps a hair of the dog that bit him? It was still part of the tariff, even if the coins hadn't stayed in the till. Stupid cow hadn't noticed. "I don't suppose it's too early for a pint?"

She smiled. "My Da's been known to breakfast on it himself. I've just washed up the tankards. Go and have a sit. I'll bring you one."

Natto went out and stretched his legs in front of the fire, and in another minute he had a drink in front of him.

"By the time you're done with that, I'll have the

kitchen tidy, and we'll take a walk outside," Sponda said.

The first ale of the day always seemed to have a special tang to it, Natto thought. And it was just what he needed. By the time Sponda came out of the kitchen, fastening her cloak, he felt ready to take on the world again.

"There's a nip in the air," she said. "You'll be wanting your coat."

And the amulets on it, Natto thought, if the rumors turned out to be true. He climbed the stairs, and once in his room started to unbutton himself, but the chamber pot was far too full. He put the lid on and shrugged into his coat.

"Pardon me," he said from mid-stairs, "But the—um—pot—upstairs is a wee bit full and I'm afraid I need to—" He felt his face turn red.

"I'm a country girl. I understand," she said. "I'll empty it when I get back. In the meanwhile, you can use the stables. Aim for the straw, if you please."

Natto mumbled his thanks and went outside. The smell of the rendering plant hit him like a blow. He felt the oatcakes stir. He pulled his neckerchief up, and went to the stables. When he came out, Sponda stood bareheaded in the middle of the street, looking down the road, her hand up as if she'd been waving. But she merely tucked an errant strand of hair back into her braid.

"Better?" she asked.

"Much," he said, his voice muffled by the cloth over his mouth. "How do you stand the smell?"

"I've lived here my whole life. You'd get used to it, after a time."

Natto found that highly unlikely.

They walked down the road until Sponda stopped and pointed to a building twenty yards on the other side. "See that smoking chimney? That's his cottage. Name's An—drew. Andrew Barnes."

"Thank you," Natto said. He squared his shoulders. "I think I can take it from here."

"Of course. You have your duties." She nodded, then walked back in the direction of the inn.

He waited until she was gone, then crossed to the same side of the road as the cottage so that his approach could not be seen from its windows, feeling rather clever for thinking of that. He slunk along a rail fence until he reached the one-story hovel. Its yard was bare mud, strewn with rocks. A bundle of feathers was nailed to the front door.

His knees trembled as he eased around the corner and peered in a grimy side window. He saw a small room, barely furnished with a single chair and a table in front of the hearth, where a low fire burned. The only other light came from a candle at the center of the table. Around the base of the candlestick lay an array of small objects—a key, a bone, a few coins, a black box, a bundle of herbs.

Natto drew in his breath. Wizard's goods, if ever he'd seen them. Beside the table, standing in shadow, was a bespectacled man, slender as a girl, with a thick mustache, his hair in a dark tail, as had been the fashion in the capital a few years back. He wore a long purple robe with a matching skullcap. As Natto watched, he picked up the bone, muttered some low words, then replaced it in a different position.

Clutching the amulet on his coat, Natto felt the hair on his arms and the back of his neck prickle with fear. He held his ground and watched as the wizard practiced his arcane rites.

After what seemed like an endless time, the wizard picked up the square black box, half the size of a man's fist. He muttered some incomprehensible syllables, then slowly opened it and removed a velvet pouch. He undid the drawstrings, muttering incessantly, and tipped its contents into his hand.

It was a pearl, a magnificent jewel, fully as large as a gooseberry.

Natto gasped, and quickly put his hand over his mouth, lest his position be revealed. He drew his head back a few inches.

But the wizard had not heard. He stood for several minutes, tipping his palm toward the candlelight, rolling the sphere so that its color shifted with each movement—white, then silver, lavender, pink, pale green, white again—as if he had captured a rainbow, transformed again and again in the flickering light. Finally, with a small sigh, the wizard replaced the pearl in the velvet bag, and the bag into its box.

He looked around the room, his glance passing over the window without pause, then stepped over to the hearth. He set the box on the mantel and slowly tugged loose a brick waist-high on the right side. Behind it was a dark opening, into which he put the box, muttering all the while. He replaced the brick, returning the hearth to its original appearance.

Stepping back to the table, he reached into a pocket, and in one fluid motion tossed a handful of sparkling powder toward the candle flame. The room filled with a blinding, blood-red flash.

Natto jumped back, sightless for a moment.

When the spots in his vision had cleared, he peered into the tiny room again.

The table was bare. The wizard was gone.

Was he? Natto waited for a minute, five, ten, then broke into a jig. He had done it! He had found the pearl! In two days' time, he would be a wealthy man. He walked cautiously around the cottage, nerves quivering, but the yard was also empty. He circled one more time, to be absolutely sure, then put a hand on the latch.

Nothing happened. His hand didn't tingle, there was no fire, no demons. He went inside. The room was dim, lit only by the coals, but it smelled like sulfur. He made the sign of warding and touched the amulet, kissing his fingers and murmuring the only prayer he knew. Then he walked to the hearth and ran his hands down the bricks on the right side.

It took him a few tries to find the loose one; he pulled it out with a grating sound, loud as a trumpet to his own ears. He stood motionless for a full minute before daring to reach into the hole, but encountered only the smooth leather of the box. He opened it, felt the round weight of the velvet bag, and tipped the pearl into his hand.

Even more beautiful up close. He gazed at it for a moment, then roused himself. There would be plenty of time for admiring once he was away from this wretched village. He replaced the pearl and bag and slipped the box into the pocket of his coat.

It took all his will to stop himself from whistling on the way back to the inn. Even the stench from the rendering plant seemed less odious.

Sponda was behind the counter, a ledger and an inkwell in front of her. She looked up from her accounting. "Were you successful?" she asked, smiling. "Did you find treasure?"

"What?" Natto nearly jumped out of his boots, then remembered his presumed errand. "Alas, no. The man is an eccentric, to be sure, but there was nothing to collect, tax-wise."

"Sorry," she said. "I seem to have sent you on a fool's errand."

"It is a frequent part of my job. I'll be heading back to the capital as soon as I gather up my things." He turned toward the stairs.

"Wait," she said. She put down her pen. "The least I can do is wrap up some bread and cheese for your journey. Perhaps one last ale—for the road?"

It *was* a long ride, and his wineskin was nearly empty. "Thank you. That's very kind." He sat at one of the tables.

She fussed a bit with the tap, then set the tankard onto the wood in front of him. "I'll make you up a lunch." She went into the kitchen.

WHEN SHE HEARD the door open, Anna looked up from the chest in the corner of her laboratory. She folded her academic robes—the purple of St. Zatar's—and replaced the horsehair mustache in the box with her other disguises. Her family had been fond of theatricals, and although St. Zatar's now admitted women, there were traditionalists who disapproved, and she had often found it easier to navigate the campus as a gentleman scholar. She closed the lid of the chest and turned around. "Did he fall for it?"

"Hook, line, and sinker," Sponda said, laughing. "What *was* the thing he found?"

"Just a sphere of camphor, dipped in a few coats of *essence d'orient.*" She saw the blank look on her lover's face. "It's a mixture of carp scales and varnish." She pointed to a piece of linen spotted with lustrous patches that shone like a rainbow. "Wouldn't fool a jeweler for a moment, but *he* was delighted."

"How do you know?"

"I stayed to watch. Once the flash powder hit the candle I had plenty of time to scamper up to the loft and hide."

"You're the most clever girl I've ever known." Sponda gave her a hug. "He's headed back to the capital. When he tries to fob off that 'pearl,' he'll get his comeuppance."

"But we won't get to see it. Where's the fun in that?"

Sponda stared. "You're up to something."

"I am. You put the powder in his ale this morning?"

"I did."

"Then it will be an interesting afternoon," Anna said. "What are you making for supper?"

"Biscuits and drippings."

"I do love your biscuits."

"It's the buttermilk," Sponda nodded. "It makes them sing in your mouth without you putting a name to any particular flavor."

Anna stared at her. "That's it!" She jumped up and began jotting notes into her journal. "That's exactly what my spread lacks. Buttermilk will add a creamery flavor, it will keep for ages, it can't go rancid—" she threw down her pen and flung her arms around Sponda. "Now who's the clever one? I'm going to make a new batch this afternoon. We'll try it at supper, and if it passes the taste test, *we'll* be on our way to the capital!"

They capered around the room for a minute in a most unscientific way.

Anna finally stepped back. "I must get back to work. But when your Da comes in, send him back here. He'll play along, won't he?"

"Da loves a good prank as much as anyone."

"Good." Anna turned to her well-stocked shelves and handed Sponda a metal canister.

"What does *this* one do?"

With a wicked grin, Anna told her.

WHEN NATTO HAD finished his ale he went up to his room. As he lifted his rucksack, the two pints he'd consumed that morning began to vie for his attention, too urgently to make it to the stables. He looked down and saw the empty chamber pot, back under the washstand.

With a sigh of relief, Natto opened his fly and aimed at the pot, closing his eyes for a moment as the pressure inside him was released in a long and satisfying stream. He shook himself off and opened his eyes to do up the buttons of his trousers, then shrieked in surprise.

His piss was blue.

He began to shake. It had been too easy, getting the pearl. He should have known there'd be a spell. He grimaced as he looked down at himself, but saw no difference on the outside.

"Is something wrong?" Sponda called from the bottom of the stairs.

"Yes!" Natto cried.

"I'll be right up."

"No!" He stared at his open fly. "I'll come down." He did up his buttons, then put the lid on the chamber pot and took it downstairs.

"Is there a problem with the pot?" Sponda asked. "I just cleaned it."

"I know, but—" And here Natto stopped cold, because although he was not a man of courtly manners, there were some things that weren't proper conversation with a woman, even if she was just the renderer's daughter, and—"Hell," he said. "Look."

She took off the lid. "Oh dear. Not again."

"Again?"

"More than once." She tilted her head and looked at him. "When you were at the wizard's house, you didn't eat or drink anything, did you?"

"No, nothing."

"Hmm. Touch anything, other than the seat of a chair?"

"Well, I might have—"

"That's it, then. He's got protections everywhere. He whisks them off when he knows there'll be company, but you took him by surprise."

"Will it go away?"

"Usually does. Unless—" She stopped and lowered her eyes. "I don't mean to be bold, Mr. Petin, but did you notice any other changes in your—your manhood?"

Natto shook his head. "No. And I did look."

"Well, *that's* good. One poor fellow had his turn black on him. Within a day it had shriveled like an old carrot. Nothing the doctor could do, by then." She took the pot and set it on the floor, replacing the lid. "'Course he deserved it. He was a black-handed thief. And a *stupid* thief, if you ask me, stealing from a wizard."

"Only a fool," Natto said in a small voice. He felt the blood drain from his face and barely made it to one of the tables before he sat down with a thump. "Might I have another ale? It was, as you can imagine, a bit of a shock, seeing..." He stared at the pot as his voice trailed off.

"Of course. Best thing for it. The more you drink, the faster you'll get rid of it." She went behind the counter and busied herself with the tap. "Oops. I'm sloppy this morning." She held the tankard up by its rim and wiped it off with a rag, removing the cloth with a flourish when she set the ale down. "That ought to help."

"Thank you." Natto gripped the mug in both hands and downed half of it in one mighty gulp. "I'll finish this and be on my way."

Sponda shook her head. "You can't ride, not in your condition."

"Really, I must return to the capital." Natto felt as if the box in his coat pocket were burning a hole through the wool. "Urgent business."

"What if complications set in, out there—?" she gestured toward the window and the desolate country beyond.

"Hmm. Perhaps one more night might be prudent. The same tariff?"

"Three coppers more," Sponda said. "It's the week-end."

"Oh." He withdrew his purse and counted out all the coins from the day before.

Sponda glanced at the cash box, then put the coins into the pocket of her apron and smiled. "I'll even make another pudding. Dessert, this time. Let me see, how about spotted dick? Oh, dear. Perhaps not tonight." She thought for a moment. "I know. I'll make you a Pond. It's my Da's favorite."

"Sounds delicious." Natto drained his ale. "I think I'll have a little lie-down." He bent to pick up the chamber pot, but she held up her hand.

"I'll rinse it and bring it to you. Only way to tell if the ale is doing its job is to start afresh." She refilled his tankard, wiping it off with the same cloth before pushing it into his hands. "There. Take that up with you."

Natto did. He drank it sitting on the edge of the bed until she brought the pot. Once she was safely downstairs, he took off his pants and, handling himself gingerly, produced a steady blue stream. He looked down. *That* was still its original color, at least. He bit back a moan and crawled under the covers.

He tossed and turned for a while, bare legs itching again, but had had so little sleep the night before that he eventually fell into a fitful slumber, full of disquieting dreams. When he woke, late afternoon light slanted through his window. Cooking smells wafted up from the kitchen, and his stomach growled. The growling set off another urge, and he stood, stretching. Standing over the chamber pot in his loose shirt, he reached down and gripped his—

Natto screamed.

It was black. So were his hands.

He stood in panic for a moment, then felt a warm dribble run down his leg. Blue.

He began to weep.

Eventually he dressed and trudged downstairs.

"Well, well. You're still with us, then?" Ian called from his table by the fire. He had a mug and a basket of roasted chestnuts, the floor littered with papery skins.

"I'm not on my way home, if that's what you mean." Natto pointed to the tap. "May I?"

"Help yourself. Sponda's up to her elbows in flour, and I'm not of a mind to move."

Natto drew a mug of ale and perched on the very edge of his chair. "Is there a doctor nearby?"

"Why, are you ill?"

Without a word, Natto held out his hands, the palms and fingers stained black.

"I see." Ian stared, then cleared his throat. "Is it only the hands, lad?"

Natto shook his head.

"Your johnson too?"

When Natto nodded, the older man huffed. "You *do* need a doctor, and soon." He clasped Natto's shoulder. "But you're in luck. He's already on his way. Coming after supper to take a look at my aching foot." He tapped his boot on the floor. "It's just a touch of the gout, but Sponda worries."

Natto drank his ale. "Does your doctor have any experience with my—problem?"

"Aye. More than most." He smiled and reached for a chestnut.

It was only the two of them for supper. Sponda stayed in the kitchen, seeing to the pudding. Natto didn't think he had an appetite, but the biscuits were light and flaky and the drippings rich, and he found himself mopping his plate.

"Save some room. Sponda's Pond is the queen of puddings." Ian lit his pipe.

"I look forward to it." Natto excused himself and went upstairs. He had been drinking steadily, which made his predicament seem somewhat foggy and distant, but every twenty minutes he was jarred back to his desperate reality. Ian was sympathetic and tried to keep his spirits up by telling stories of a life in rendering, which had to do with unidentifiable lumps, and why you shouldn't confuse soap and candle tallow. Natto listened numbly, released by a knock at the door.

"There's the doctor now," Ian said and went to let him in.

The doctor was a tall, thin man with spectacles and a van Dyke beard. His graying hair was pulled back into a tail. He wore a suit of brown worsted and carried a black leather bag. "Ian, good to see you!" he said in a reedy voice.

"Doctor Reynard. Good of you to come. You're just in time for dessert. Sponda's made a Pond."

"Excellent. No one makes it better than she." He set his bag on one of the empty tables.

"It's done!" Sponda called from the kitchen. She came out bearing a platter on which sat a caramel hummock, the top sunken, the crust glazed and crackling along the edges. The steam smelled like a summer's day.

"That," Ian said proudly, "is our Pond." He picked up a knife and a large spoon. "Watch close now. This is the best part." He sliced into the pudding, revealing a whole lemon in the center and releasing a glorious oozing stream of golden syrup. It flowed until it had formed a pool of rich sauce that filled the platter like a moat. "See?" he said. "Now it's an island in its own pond. Doctor?"

"Please."

Ian cut a generous slice and ladled the sauce over it.

"George?"

"What? Oh, yes, thank you."

When everyone had been served, Sponda said. "What do you think, Da?"

"The crust is splendid—our good suet—and oh, my dear, the sauce! Lemon and sugar and sweet butter. It may be the best you've ever made."

Sponda clapped her hands in delight. "Do you really think so?"

Natto dug in eagerly. "Oh my god," he said, true reverence in his voice. "This is—this is—it's spectacular."

The doctor took a bite. "Is that butter I taste?"

"What else could it be?" Sponda laughed.

"I thought you said it was scarce." Natto scraped his fork through the last of his sauce.

"It is," Sponda replied with that odd, twitching smile. "But we make do."

"You do, indeed," said the doctor. He smiled at her, then pushed his empty plate aside. "Now, Ian, about that foot?"

Natto sat patiently while Ian's foot was examined. It didn't *look* any different than an ordinary foot. Dirtier, maybe. But the doctor tutted and poked, then dug into his bag for a jar of salve.

"Thanks. What do I owe you?"

"Let me see, with the salve, it's," he tapped a finger on his beard. "Twenty silver crowns."

"I have it right here." Ian pulled a cloth bag from his pocket.

"Twenty crowns!" Natto blurted.

"That's the usual rate," the doctor said. "I see that you're surprised. I imagine a doctor's visit is much, much more in the capital."

Natto had no idea. He'd never been to a doctor in his life. And a good thing, too. It cost a bloody fortune.

"George has a bit of a problem, if you don't mind," Ian said.

"Certainly." The doctor turned to Natto. "What's the trouble?"

"I—it—never mind." He would just have to wait until he got to the capital. A doctor's visit might cost more there, but it wouldn't matter. He'd be able to afford it.

"Don't be daft, lad," Ian said. "You need help. You—" he looked at Natto and snapped his fingers. "Ah. I think I understand. Excuse us for a moment." He pointed to the door. "George?"

Natto hesitated, then followed him out into the street, pulling his neckerchief up as he did.

"You get used to it," Ian said. He leaned against the wall of the building and lit his pipe. "Are you short of funds, lad?" he asked in a kindly voice.

"At the moment. I just need to get back to the capital. I'll see my own doctor there," he lied.

"You won't make to sunrise, as fast as that's spreading."

"What!"

Ian shook his head, slowly and sadly. "George, you seem like a good fellow. Let me ask the doctor to put your treatment on my account."

"You'd do that?"

"It's a sorry world when you can't rely on the kindness of strangers."

Foolish old man, Natto thought. "Thank you," he said aloud.

"'Course I'd need some collateral," Ian continued. "We may be country folk, but I wasn't born yesterday."

"What sort?"

"That mare of yours is a fine animal and I could use another horse until the loan's repaid."

"That seems reasonable." Hah. Natto laughed to himself. He'd get the salve or ointment or tincture, whatever it was, and be saddled and gone hours before first light.

"Good. Now what about the rest?"

"Rest? What do you mean?"

"Well, around here, horses aren't so dear. Ten crowns is a good price. But that leaves another ten unaccounted."

Natto's brain raced. What else did he have to offer? He came up empty, just as his bladder reminded him that it was not. He stepped toward the stable. "The ale," he said.

"Oh, me as well. It's the only bad part about drinking, I say."

They did their business over the straw. Ian looked over and sucked air through his teeth in a startled hiss. "Good god, lad. You didn't tell me it was that far along. It's a miracle you're still alive."

Natto heard a squeak come out of his mouth. "It could *kill* me?"

"Aye and it's an ugly, painful way to go." Ian buttoned up. "You *need* what the doctor has." He put an arm around Natto's waist. "Tell you what. Get help, and I'll find a way to let you work off the other ten crowns."

Here? Not on your life, Natto thought, then reconsidered. He had no intention of paying the man back, so it didn't matter if it was ten, twenty, or fifty crowns. As soon as he had the medicine, he'd scamper. It wouldn't be the first time he'd left town owing money. "Yes, thank you. You're very generous."

"Good lad."

The doctor sat alone when they returned. "Sponda's in the kitchen," he said. "It's just as well. She told me what she knows, but it's nothing a woman needs to see."

"I'd like to put George's treatment onto my account," Ian said.

"I can do that." The doctor hesitated. "But, Ian, I must warn you. If Sponda is correct, the curative costs much more than a common gout-salve."

"I understand," Ian said. "I'll do whatever it takes."

Natto moaned. If he got in *too* deep, Ian might come after him. No. He smiled. Ian would come after *Petin*. Natto sat down and held out his hands.

"His johnson, too," Ian added. "Black as night."

"I see," said the doctor. "Blue urine?"

"Yes."

"How long?"

"Just since this morning," Natto said.

"That's good. If you'd waited until tomorrow, there would have been nothing I could do." The doctor opened his bag and took out an amber bottle with a cork stopper, then laid a mortar and pestle on the table. "How much do you know about medicine, Mr. Petin?"

"Not much."

"That's all right. I'll explain it in layman's terms." He clasped his hands behind him. "You see, the four humors of the body are each governed by a particular mineral compound." He stopped and looked at Natto. "Understand?"

"I think so."

"Fine. Now a blood disorder calls for iron. Lungs react to salt, and the stomach and intestines to charcoal. The bladder—and its related organs—respond only to calcium." He paused in his recitation. "Still with me?"

Natto shrugged.

"However, when it comes to a specialized ailment such as your own, the minerals themselves also become more specific. The *only* known cure is a compound of crystallized calcium carbonate, powdered and dissolved in an acetic elixir."

"And you have all that?" Natto asked. His head spun with every word.

"This is the elixir." He held up the amber bottle. "It's a formula of my own devising. Extremely difficult to distil in the proper proportions."

"You're a lucky man," Ian said. "He's one of the few doctors in the realm that keeps a supply on hand."

Natto felt anything but lucky. "What about the other part? The calcium bit?"

"In a separate vial," the doctor said. He rummaged in his bag, pulling out bottles and jars, frowning more and more. "Oh dear," he said. "It appears to have fallen out on the ride here."

"What?" Natto said in a panic. "Then how will you—?"

"I suppose I'll have to improvise." He tapped

his beard again. "It doesn't *need* to be laboratory grade," he muttered. "I suppose any pearl would do."

"Pearl?" Natto's mouth was suddenly dry.

"Yes." He picked up the mortar and pestle. "I crush it in here, then add it to the elixir."

"*Crush?*"

"Crush, pulverize, grind up." The doctor waved his hand. "For *that* component, technique is largely irrelevant." He placed the mortar on the table. "Once you down the mixture, you'll be completely cured in twenty-four hours' time."

"I changed my mind. I'll just wait and see what happens."

"Mr. Petin. Do you not understand the gravity of your condition? Waiting is simply not an option."

Natto sat very still for a long time. Without the pearl, he had nothing. But even he had to admit that nothing was better than dead. With a deep, painful sigh he reached into his coat pocket and—

His pocket was empty. He tried the other one. Empty as well. With a great, gulping sob he laid his head on the table.

"Now, now, lad," Ian said, patting his shoulder. "It's not as bad as that. If you need a pearl to save your life, well, I couldn't look myself in the eye if I just stood by."

Natto raised his head.

"It's been in my family for—for a while now. I was saving it for my Sponda as a wedding present, but—" he smiled. "I think she'll understand." From the pocket of his trousers he pulled out a small black leather box and handed it to the doctor. "Will this do?"

Natto gasped as the man opened the box and rolled the gooseberry-sized pearl out onto his hand. "Perfectly," he said. He dropped it into the mortar with a delicate plink and before Natto could say a word, crushed it into powder with a few deft motions.

"No. No. No." Natto moaned, but it was too late.

The doctor opened the amber bottle and tipped in the powder. The mixture fizzed and bubbled over the glass lip before settling. "There you are," he said. "Drink up."

Natto drank. The vile, acrid liquid burned his throat and when he belched, a few seconds later, it stank of fish and turpentine.

"Have some ale," Ian said. "To wash the taste out. And don't you worry about the pearl. It *was* a family treasure, but I can add it to the rest you owe me." He patted Natto on the shoulder. "Rendering is a fine profession. You'll work your tab off in no time at all."

WHEN THE SOPORIFIC that Anna had added to the elixir had taken effect, and the man who called himself Petin lay snoring and drooling on the table, the others retired to the kitchen.

"I thought that went well," Ian said. "I picked his pocket clean as a whistle. He never felt a thing. 'Course he *was* a bit distracted." He cut himself a slice of Pond. "What was the black stuff?"

"Silver nitrate. Sponda wiped it on his tankard." Anna peeled off her beard, and began to remove the bits of spirit gum beneath. "It's one of my brother Roger's favorite pranks. Invisible until light hits it, then the stain lasts a good long while." She set the metal canister on the table. "I'll leave it with you, in case he needs another dose."

"Does it make the blue, too?"

"No, that's methylene. That you dissolve in his ale." She gave him the jar.

Ian looked at the chemicals, then sighed. "I can't believe you'll be gone in an hour," he said to Sponda.

"We have to take the horses before he wakes up."

"I know, but I'll miss you, girl. Every day."

"Me too, Da." She gave him a long hug. "But I'm not leaving you all alone. Now you'll have an assistant to keep you company."

"What do they say about small favors?" He kissed her cheek. "How long will you be in the capital, do you think?"

"Weeks," Sponda said. "Maybe months. We'll have to see what happens."

"This stuff of yours, you really think it might win the prize?"

"It has every chance," Anna said. "Even you couldn't tell the difference in the Pond tonight."

"That wasn't butter?"

"It was not," she smiled.

"I'll be swoggled. That was really your—" he stopped. "What are you going to call it?"

Anna patted her journal. "I've thought of dozens of possible names. The one I like best is a variation on the Latin word for 'pearl.'"

"Because of the way the suet fat looks when it melts?"

"Exactly. So I'm calling it *margarone*."

"That's a pretty fancy word for fake butter," he said.

Sponda laughed. "You'll get used to it."

SHAGGY DOG BRIDGE: A BLACK COMPANY STORY

GLEN COOK

TO PARAPHRASE A bit player named Rusty, "Shit happens. Sometimes no matter how much you dog-gnaw the bone you don't get it to make no sense, 'specially the who done what why."

So it was with the shaggy dog bridge.

THE GREENS AND grays around and below me had become perilously hypnotic. Then a buccaneer deer fly snagged a big-ass bite just west of my Adam's apple.

I let go the rope to take a swipe. Naturally, I missed the agile little buzzard.

Better lucky than smart, sometimes. My lifeline caught me. I stood on my head on a hundred feet of air while the guys up top lowered away. The dickheads on the stone shelf below grinned but tucked the needle in the trick bag for later.

I lack the born-again haughteur of a cat. No way could I manage a pretense of deliberate intent.

"Hold still." One-Eye smeared something stinky on the bug bite. "That will kill any eggs."

"Admirable caution," I grumbled. We had yet to see the botfly horror in these parts, but the people hunting us would deploy them gleefully if they had some and could get them to bite Black Company guys exclusively.

Eight men crowded the ledge. More would follow me down. At the narrow end Rusty told Robin, "I ain't carrying that dumbass crab catcher out'n here, he gets hisself hurt."

Rusty was a FNG, with us only six months. He had no hope of becoming a Fucking Old Guy. He was an asshole and a bully. His type never prospers with us.

First aid complete, One-Eye faced the view.

"Sure is something. So much green." The Rip. To the left it was a thousand feet more to the bottom. To the right, cliff collapses had choked the canyon partially, so long ago that heavy forest cloaked the fill.

One-Eye gave his filthy black hat a quarter turn, 'To confuse the enemy,' and said, "Something ain't right, Croaker. I smell something gone off."

His wizard's sniffer was why Elmo had brought him along.

BEFORE HUMANITY BEGAN counting time, and maybe before there was any humanity to count it, something weird smacked the living shit out of this end of the world. Maybe a god swung a cosmic cleaver. Maybe some natural force acted up. Whatever, a knife-edge wound slashed the earth for seven hundred miles, across the grain, through mountains and forests, swamps and plains, often more than a thousand feet deep, never more than an eighth of a mile wide.

It drained lakes and shifted rivers. Our side, the west, boasted hundreds of square miles of dense hardwood forest on rounded mountains with deep valleys between. Tough traveling. From what I could see the east side was exactly the same.

We were on the run. Bad people were after us, in no special hurry. We were nuisances. They had bigger fish in the pan, like overrunning the unconquered civilized world. They pushed just hard enough to keep us from wriggling loose.

We had been herded here, to be pinned against the Rip. We would cross only if we abandoned our wagons, animals, equipment, our crippled and sick. First, though, we had to find a way down this side, then up the other.

Rusty belonged to a faction disgruntled because the feeble and dying were sucking up resources that could be better used to keep him chubby.

Whittle said, "I gettin' weak-kneed in the 'membrance, some, but seems like dere was you all graveyard sick jes' las' spring. De buzzards was roostin' on your shoulders." Whittle whittled while he talked. He could lure some peculiar folk art out of plain dead wood.

Robin caught Rusty's wrist. Whittle was not just a master at finding hideous things hidden inside chunks of wood. He was a master at letting out the ugly stuff inside people.

Elmo declaimed, "Gentlemen, save it for our enemies."

We had plenty, including several Taken.

One-Eye went into a trance, for sure smelling something not right.

I exchanged looks with Robin. The boy was

Rusty's favorite victim… and his only excuse for a friend.

Some relationships answer only to their own secret logic.

Robin showed a flash of private pain. He knew there was a pool. How long would Rusty last?

Rusty shook him off.

Whittle rose from his couch of broken granite. "First news you know, you goin' to be blessed to fine out what pain an' sufferin' is all about."

Elmo interposed himself. "That's it. Knock it off."

Whittle leaned around him. "First time you wink loud." He jerked a thumb toward some crows above the far side of the gorge.

One-Eye blurted, "It's all illusion!"

Elmo snapped, "What is?" He was on edge. If we did not find an out soon our next all-Company assembly would happen at the bottom of a shallow mass grave. The Rip left no room to run. Unless…

Elmo was convinced that the 'unless' was his to create.

Escape was sure to be expensive. We would take nothing but personal weapons and what we could carry or wear. It would become pure march or die.

Whisper, the Taken managing the hunters, was enjoying the cat and mouse. We had messed her up for years. But she had us now.

One-Eye, always drowning in showers of self-delusion, suddenly wanted to call shenanigans.

Elmo loomed fierce, as only a natural born first sergeant can. "Talk, runt. Straight. I'm fresh out of patience for witch-man talk-around."

He was displacing his irritation with Rusty, but scapegoating a sorcerer can become a less than profitable exercise.

One-Eye had looked past the moment. He had seen something to make him nervous. "That woods mostly isn't real. It's the most persistent daylight illusion I've ever seen but from up close you can tell." His old black face twisted. He was puzzled.

The troops stayed quiet. Sorcery encountered in strange country never bodes well. It is a definite conversation stopper.

One-Eye scowled at the Rip some more.

Elmo prodded, "Any day now."

"Sometimes even sergeants need to be patient."

Certainly not their nature but this one let a few minutes glide. Then One-Eye sighed, sagged under the weight of the world. "I'm not strong enough to see inside. We have to go look."

Rusty barked, "We ain't out here to go poking sticks in no hornet nests."

Elmo glowered. "That's exactly why we're here, moron. The name says it. Recon. We look. We poke. We find out."

And we might ought to get on with looking for our latest way out.

For centuries the Company has found one. Always.

This was the twentieth-something search but my first. I was 'too valuable' for grunt work. I had invited myself on the sneak and had stayed out of sight till it was too late for Elmo to send me back... and too late for me to admit that I had made a mistake.

The view of the Rip, though, was amazing.

Nervously, the squad helped One-Eye study the landscape. He became fixated on the Rip to our right. We stayed quiet. Nature did not. The crow posse across the way kept getting louder. The birds had a lot to debate. Closer by, buzzing insects scouted our potential as fodder.

One-Eye announced, "I'm going to mess with the old girl's wig and makeup."

"Meaning? Try some plain language."

"All right. What a grouch." He frustrated Elmo by taking time to loose a curse that crisped every bloodsucker within fifty yards. Though selfishly motivated, that did move him a few slots down the communal shit list. "All them five hundred year oaks and ashes and chestnuts, hardly any of them are real."

Elmo cut to it. "Means somebody has something to hide. Saddle up, troops. We're gonna take a peek."

WE WORKED MORE sideways than down. Come mid-afternoon we busted through some thorns and found a fine place to rest, a flat, wide, descending ledge that ran in the direction we were headed.

Super genius Rusty announced, "It's almost like a road."

Even the parliament of crows seemed to go quiet.

One-Eye butchered the silence. "You don't see what you don't expect."

It was obvious once someone said it. This was a road cut into the wall of the Rip. It had been there for ages. It showed signs of use, though not recently.

Elmo split the band. Rusty, Robin, and two others he sent upslope, to find a way back to camp. The rest of us went the other direction.

I got everybody scowling by asking, "Who could be using this? Where could it go?"

Elmo suggested, "How about you shut the fuck

up?" He indicated the caucusing crows. "One of them just asked a dumbass question, too."

'Dumbass' was the Croaker referent of the day.

I am nothing if not unable to take a hint. "One-Eye, you saying all this nature is fake? The bug bites sure feel real."

"Seventy per cent. Just to hide the road."

Elmo signaled a halt.

One tight turn under leaves turning golden had us facing an unexpected phantom bridge. It spanned the Rip where the massive collapses had filled the gap two thirds of the way.

"Nobody do anything till I say it's all right," One-Eye ordered. "Including you, Croaker." He babbled about lethal residual magic, the half-lives of curses, and the magnitude of the sorcery needed to drop the walls of the gorge.

The more I stared the more real that bridge became.

The top hundred feet was a complex of mutually supporting wooden beams perched on two massive stone piers. The taller pier rose two hundred feet from the scree. The worked blocks making it up fit so finely that mortar had not been necessary.

Serious sorcery helped, surely, or time would have taken considerably bigger bites.

One-Eye said, "There are no booby trap spells."

Elmo said, "I don't like it. It's too damned convenient."

I grumbled, "So some villain four hundred years back built a bridge just to lure the Black Company into a trap?"

One-Eye argued, "If it was convenient we would've found it a long time ago. We'd be five hundred miles east of here, now."

Whittle volunteered to go over first. If he found no trouble we would set a cold camp on the other side.

WE MEANT TO give Whittle a forty yard lead, keeping him within bowshot, but at twenty yards he began to fade.

The crows got all raucous again.

"The illusion is old," One-Eye said. "It's getting patchy."

WE FOUND A shack twenty yards beyond the end of the bridge. Inside there was firewood cut for cooking and split for heating, with tinder and kindling. Elmo nixed a fire. Grumble grumble. Mountain nights got chilly, but no need to attract the attention of the people who stored the wood.

It rained enthusiastically all night. The roof leaked only a little.

Come morning Elmo sent three guys back to report. I made myself scarce and deaf so none of them would be me.

Elmo told me later, "You are so lucky you count as an officer. I'd beat you bloody if you were a grunt."

We ate a nasty cold breakfast. One-Eye gave the shack a going-over. All he found was a coin so corroded its provenance could not be determined. Elmo announced, "Now we scout. Croaker, how about you wait here for whoever the lieutenant sends." Phrasing a suggestion but sounding all officious. One-Eye, Whittle, and Zeb the archer nodded.

Selfish bastards. They just wanted to make sure I did not get killed and leave them to self-medicate when they caught the crabs or came up with a dose of the clap.

One-Eye grumbled, "There's that stubborn look, Elmo. He gets that look, somebody is about to come down with the drizzling shits."

"Screw it, then," Elmo said.

I smirked. I got my way, I did, without a word of argument.

WE WALKED A ways. The road was hidden by leaves and brush and faded spells. While you were on it, though, there was no missing it.

Some of the crows stuck with us. They never shut up.

"A secret bridge and a secret road," I mused. "Used, but not much."

"It's old," One-Eye said. "*Way* old."

The world is filthy with old things. Many of them are deadly.

The road did not have that smell.

It was on no modern map. Were it, we would have been long gone.

The road inclined upward for a mile, then began a gentle descent. We encountered our first obstacle after eight or nine miles. Deadwood had clogged a culvert during the night. Run-off had overtopped the road and washed away some fill.

Elmo said, "This won't be hard to fix. Pray there's nothing worse."

The road was wide enough to carry everything we had.

The crows shrieked, scattered. I jumped like somebody had slammed me with a hot iron spike. I squawked, "Spread out! Get down! Get under something and don't move. Don't even breathe."

I took my own advice.

I had just stopped twitching when I heard the scream that had set me off repeated.

It was not audible. It was inside my head, a paean of agony, rage and hatred. It approached unsteadily but should pass to the south.

"Taken!" I breathed. One of the Lady's enslaved sorcerers. Whisper has been after us forever, carrying a bushel of grudges. This airborne sack of pain, grief, and hate, though, was not one I recognized.

Taken are hard to kill. Whisper was harder than most. Yet death is the only escape for the Taken.

Each was once a massively wicked sorcerer who fell prey to the Lady. They never forgot who and what they were but could do little to resist. They were the most damned of the damned.

This latest reeked of aggravated despair and self-loathing.

The scream faded. One-Eye called, "Allee-allee-in-free!"

Elmo observed, "Must be a new one."

One-Eye bobbed his head. That stupid black hat flopped off. I said, "She wasn't hunting."

"She?"

"Felt that way. It don't matter. Taken is Taken. Elmo, we've hiked far enough." I was not used to all this walking. And the farther we went the farther I would have to walk back, uphill all the way.

"We'll stay here. We'll work on the road while we wait."

Whittle reserved his opinion, as did Zeb. One-Eye did not. Elmo paid no attention. One-Eye is always whining about something.

A FEW RIDERS caught up next morning. They said the Company was on the move. The enemy had not yet noticed.

Elmo told the riders to take over fixing the road. He and his crack team would go find the next obstacle.

The dick.

Our corvine escort never rematerialized. We heard nary a caw.

THE MOON WAS near full in a cloudless sky. The screaming Taken passed again, unseen but strongly felt. I could not get back to sleep. I imagined ghosts slinking through the moonlight. I heard things not there sneaking toward me. I had caught more from that Taken than just a scream.

We found another little bridge next morning. It spanned a steep run where the rushing water was barely a yard wide. One rough-hewn replacement plank had not yet begun to gray.

We smelled smoke soon afterward. Lots of smoke, wood and something with a sulfurous note.

I guessed, "There's a village ahead."

Whittle volunteered to scout. Elmo sent One-Eye instead. One-Eye could make himself invisible. He could use birds and animals to spy, given time to prepare them. No breeze stirred a leaf while he was gone, which explained why the smoke hung around.

One-Eye reported. "There are a hundred homesteads scattered around a valley. Motte and timber bailey, in the middle, town around it. Wooden blockhouse where the road leaves the woods. It isn't manned. People are in the fields but they're not working. They're watching the sky."

A FARMING COMMUNITY hidden in the mountains? Sketchy. Whittle guessed, "Dey's maybe bein' religious crazies."

The cleared ground was a mile wide and several long. The road dropped in near the north end. It wandered the open ground beside a modest river. The river had been dammed in three places, creating one large and two small pools. The large one served watermills on either bank, a flour mill and another, its purpose less obvious. As reported, a blockhouse guarded our approach.

Elmo pointed. "There. In the woods. Tailings piles."

He might know. He supposedly ran away from some mines when he was thirteen. But we all lie about who we used to be.

One-Eye was right about the people. They were bothered.

Elmo suggested, "Let's don't let them know we're here."

We kept a rotating one-man watch.

THE MOON WAS full. I had the watch. Whittle would relieve me. Shifting moon shadows had me spooked. I squeaked like a little girl when Whittle got there.

"Gods damn! Do you have to sneak?"

"Yes." Of course he did. The locals had sent four youths to the blockhouse come sunset.

I had eavesdropped and had learned two things. The boys were not alert and I could not understand a word they said.

I whispered, "Other than those kids coming out nothing's... Shit!" The Taken was coming. I sprawled on my belly, bit my lip, wrestled my dread. All that pain and hatred passed directly overhead, fifty feet up, illuminated by the moon.

"Weird," I breathed once it was gone. "I didn't see a carpet, just a lot of flapping cloth." Maybe scarlet cloth. Hard to tell colors by moonlight.

"No carpet," Whittle agreed. Taken use flying carpets.

Petals of cloth whipping in a violent updraft, like leaping black flames, crowned the bailey in the moonlight.

The boys in the blockhouse wailed.

I whispered, "Think they know something they don't like?"

Screaming came from the valley.

"Gots me a 'spicion."

The night puked One-Eye, shaking. He said nothing. Not much needed saying. Something ugly was going on yonder.

The bailey produced what sounded like a god's liquid fart, then violet and darker lightning. We missed some of the show because it was in indigos too dark to see.

"Something awful is happening," I blurted.

Whittle chuckled. "Mought be blessed to spell him quiet."

One-Eye tapped my lips. "Shut the fuck up."

I bobbed my head. I was now inspired. My precious ass's fine health could benefit from an extended silence.

Purple lightning pranced among the rooftops of the town skirting the motte. Something did something weird to something. There was a flash and a roar that left us too deaf to hear one another whine, "What the hell?"

Elmo arrived. Whittle used sign to explain the nothing we knew. Elmo grunted. He waited. We waited. Hearing returned. The boys in the blockhouse caterwauled. The night reeked of Taken rage and despair.

"Overturned anthill over there," Zeb explained. There was just enough light to show it.

The kids from the blockhouse headed home at an uninspired pace.

There was no sign of the Taken.

Elmo looked rough. He had not gotten much sleep. "Damn! There's a thousand people out there. Maybe even two thousand. And half of them got split tails. That's gonna mean trouble."

Few of our not-so-nice brothers had seen a woman lately. Though Elmo did not favor men he did own an abiding conviction of the innate wickedness of women. He *knew* all the ills of the world could be traced to the ear-whisperings of evil-minded females.

I sometimes remind him that his mother was probably a woman. He says that proves his point.

* * *

"WHAT'S THAT?" ZEB asked. "What the hell *is* that?"

'That' was the Taken blossoming atop the bailey.

I was right about the scarlet, only it was a deeper red still, like cardinal. Once the bloody petals settled I could not distinguish her from the other figures on the stronghold's catwalk lookout.

The internal screams had been nominal before the bloom. Now they promised headaches.

A long column of mules began to emerge from the town around the artificial hill. They headed our way.

Elmo decided, "Time to go, troops!"

It was. Oh, it was.

The Taken blossomed again, took to the air. How did the mules endure her?

So. We had a Taken headed west on a road where the Company was strung out for miles, supposedly making a miracle escape.

"We need to warn them," Elmo announced, like that was something only he would realize. "Move faster!" He set a ferocious pace. It was soon evident that the Company doctor could not keep up.

Elmo and I went back a long way. He did not let sentiment hamstring him. "You're still moving faster than she is. Keep plugging." Smug ass saw a teachable moment. Croaker would learn about pushing in where he was neither wanted nor needed.

I dawdled, alone, revisiting my arsenal of obscenities, till I felt the Taken gaining.

SNAPPER'S PATROL PICKED me up. Seven riders with eight horses. Timely. The strain of trying to keep the Taken out had exhausted me.

Her sad history kept leaking over. I had my time as

a prisoner of the Lady to thank. That lovely horror had burrowed never healed channels into my mind. To the grand good fortune of the world she never found anything useful there.

I observed, "Elmo isn't a complete dickhead."

The nearest horseman snorted. Elmo was a sergeant. That made him a dick by definition.

Soon we ran into other Company people. They were not withdrawing. They were preparing hiding places.

The hell? What about the wagons and artillery and animals? Even if you hid up every other trace you would still have the reek of animals and unwashed men hanging in air that would not stir.

I asked. My companions shrugged. Nobody cared but me.

THE SHACK HAD become a clinic. My medicine wagon was cunningly hidden in the woods behind. I had patients waiting, and the lieutenant. He did not care that I was tired and hungry.

"I'm considering lopping off one of your feet so you can't pull this shit. You pick."

"There wasn't anybody who couldn't get along without me..." Dumbass Croaker, arguing with the boss.

"There are now. See me when you're caught up."

Little actually required my attention. Ticks were the big issue. That was an educational matter, really. The same for blisters, common because nobody had decent footwear anymore.

I wrapped up, washed up, went to see the lieutenant for my reaming.

He and his staff were watching limping men

appear over the Rip, on the bridge. This Company flight was no precision manoeuvre.

He will let slide lesser things situationally. His recollection of them is eidetic, however. They ripen. They come back. He looked at me like he was reviewing every indiscretion of mine across the last two decades. "Are the Annals up to date?"

I am Company historian as well as lead physician.

"Up to the day before I went on patrol."

"There's a shitstorm coming. We'll talk job obligation afterward."

"I reckon. We are in a narrow passage. Whisper behind us and this new Taken on the road ahead."

"Not a Taken, Croaker. But definitely new to us."

"Sir?"

"The road."

Oh, the laconic treatment! "What about it?"

"It runs two directions."

"That's kind of in the rules for roads."

That crack brought in a crop of dark looks. Some folks do not appreciate Croaker the Annalist. He has a nasty habit of recording flaws and fuckups as well as triumphs. Plus, as he ages he speaks his mind more.

The lieutenant made a mark in the notebook of his mind. "This road could go back to before the Domination. You went east. We went west. We found a ruined fortress that was the nightmare of someone worse than the Dominator."

So. Once he knew there was a secret bridge and hidden road he went to see where it started.

"The new Taken hails from there?"

"She does. Reminding you, she isn't Taken. Yes. It's only eight miles. It was uglier than that place in Juniper was. Bones everywhere, some of them human."

I was not overwhelmed. Some of that had leaked across from the Taken. "There's more?"

"We found people there, living in squalor you wouldn't believe. Servants, sort of, and livestock in lean times. They don't speak a modern language. We couldn't have communicated without Goblin and Silent." Those two being senior Company wizards.

"Your new Taken is Blind Emon. She *is* blind. She's the slave of something called the Master, which sounds more intimidating in their language. He was human once. He made himself immortal. Now he just lays around and eats, too bloated to move. No one has seen him for ages except Blind Emon. Anyone else gets that close, they end up on the menu."

Ours is an ugly and challenging world.

"So Blind Emon *is* a Taken, just not the Lady's Taken."

Much that had leaked to me from her now made more sense.

"If that's how you want to see it. It doesn't matter. What does is, we need her not to notice us."

Hmm. The hiding off the road now made sense. He wanted Blind Emon's caravan to slide by rather than us falling back toward Whisper.

He said, "You know what you need to do. Go do it."

Blind Emon's mules would not be long arriving. Time to get the clinic hidden inside a glamour.

LIKELY THE BRIDGE and road had been built to connect the settlement and the Master's hangout. I could not imagine why, though.

Everybody hid in the best glamour.

Warning came. The mule train was close. I needed no word of mouth. I felt Blind Emon's pain. I was more sensitive to her than was anyone else. Bless my happy days as a prisoner in the Tower!

This contact was the worst yet. It wormed inside more deeply. I became disoriented and distraught. I suffered fifteen minutes of condensed torment, reliving Blind Emon's Taking.

There had been others like Emon, once. She was the sole survivor of the Master's ancient collision with the Domination. He actually antedated the Domination era. He had repulsed the bilious sorcerer-tyrant known as the Dominator, at the cost of becoming the darkness-bound buried horror that he was now.

Emon had started out as a brilliant mage known for her clever mining of ancient mysteries. She was beautiful, she was young, she was in love... Then she unearthed something foul that had faded to a dreadful rumor and should have been left to fade even further.

Blinding was the first of a thousand atrocities she suffered.

Too much of her torment leaked over. I was so bowels-voiding scared that I was leaking back.

SHE WAS PAST. She had become an intermittently visible scarlet lily blossoming over the improbable bridge. Countless mules and men crossed that dispiritedly, making an art of their absence of enthusiasm. Blind Emon barely kept them moving.

Shit. Toss it in a hot iron skillet and fry it up, shit!

Distracted, I thoughtlessly moved to get a better look at Blind Emon. Now I had a frozen muleteer staring at me, mouth agape.

I froze, too, hoping to disappear into the glamour.

He dropped his mule's lead tether and oozed away, never breaking eye contact and never showing expression. As I began to have trouble keeping him in focus he stepped out briskly toward home. He never said a word to the mule driver behind him.

Him just taking off was as good as doing some yelling. He was too near Blind Emon to exit unnoticed.

Emon was a ruddy shimmer amidst the high foliage of illusory trees when the muleskinner began his heel and toe dance toward home. She solidified as she moved my way.

I tried becoming one with the forest. That worked, some. She failed to pick me out of the mast but she for sure did sense someone who could be touched, mind to mind.

She searched but never pinned me down.

Kill me!

She knew I would hear her.

Kill me, I beg you!

Her dash round the sky turned frantic. My head felt ready to explode. Normal men ground their knuckles into their temples. Mules brayed.

The plea for surcease from pain, *Kill me!* eventually knocked me out.

ELMO AND THE original patrol, with my apprentices, surrounded me. I mumbled, "Shouldn't have tapped that last keg." My head throbbed, worst hangover ever. There was a foul taste in my mouth. "I puked?"

"You did, sir," my apprentice Joro admitted. "In record fashion."

I was dizzy. The dizzy was getting worse.

Elmo added, "You yelled a lot, too, in some language nobody knows."

"That was only for a minute," Joro added. "Then you were out and the thing in the sky shrieked in tongues."

Dizziness morphed into disorientation. I fought to focus. "What about her?"

Elmo said, "She went away. She gave up looking for you."

No. Even unconscious she had left me with news enough to know that she had been summoned by the Master.

The lieutenant appeared. "He going to make it?"

"Yes, sir," Joro replied. "The problem is mostly in his head."

"Always the case with him, isn't it? Move out now, Elmo. Let him get his shit together on the road."

THEY PLANTED ME on a captured mule. The old jenny had been loaded with produce that was in Company bellies now. Other captured mules had carried kegs of salt pork, salt and pepper color granules, or sacks of what looked like copper beads. Elmo thought the beads were ore. Others said it was too light. I felt too lousy to work up a good case of give a shit.

Prisoners had been taken but were almost useless. Nobody understood their turkey gobble.

"What the hell?" I blurted when I realized Elmo was headed across the bridge.

"Super shitstorm about to hit. Our guys will be in it. They need you there."

A fight? I was headed for a fight? Feeling like this?

A lone crow, notably ragged, watched us pass from a perch on the rail of the bridge. It offered no comment.

THE EARTH TREMBLED. My mule shied. She had been skittish for a while, now.

We were two hours west of the bridge, near where our guys were operating. Twice we heard distant horns.

I was lost. Nobody else had a clue, either. Some thought that the lieutenant hoped to engineer a collision between Whisper and the Master. If that happened Whisper would have to consult the Lady, who might recall the Master from back when she was the Dominator's wife. She might want to get in the game herself. All that would cost time. The lieutenant could build a bigger head start.

The road west of the bridge was better hidden. The farther we went the healthier the glamours became. The earth trembled again. There was noise ahead, muted by the forest and the hill we were climbing.

We found a gang of mules and mule drivers hiding beside the road, just short of the crest. They were unarmed and disinclined to resist. They were terrified. I did not blame them. Blind Emon was not happy.

Some heavy-duty shit was shaking beyond that ridge.

I urged my mule forward. I had friends involved. Some might need help.

Came an epic flash. An invisible scythe topped every tree rising above the ridgeline. Whittle observed, "First news you know, de weader be gettin' parlous roun' dese parts."

Rusty did a credible job of managing his fear. This would be his first experience with battlefield sorcery. A little real terror might be just the specific to purge his soul.

We clambered through fallen limbs that had been shredded like cabbage for kraut, reached a tree line, looked out on a bowl-shaped clearing more than a mile across. It had been farmland once but most was going to scrub, now. A natural rock up-thrust centered it. Ruins topped that. They were ugly and, though it sounds ridiculous, they felt abidingly evil... probably because Emon had prejudiced me.

Emon was a roiling storm of cardinal strands above the ruin, filling far more sky than she had over the bridge. Three Taken on flying carpets circled at a respectful distance. A fourth carpet lay mangled in a field, smoldering while someone dragging a damaged leg crawled away.

Imperial soldiers crept toward the downed Taken. Local people were fleeing the invaders.

Elmo nudged me. "Whisper," indicating one of the airborne Taken.

"Where are our guys?" They were nowhere to be seen.

Mule drivers gobbled and pointed.

Some of their gang had reached the ruins before the excitement started.

Elmo said, "We're exposed here. We need to take cover." And that was the moment when ill fortune noticed its opportunity.

Whisper sensed me... for the same reason that Blind Emon had: my one-time exposure to the Lady's Eye.

Meantime, Emon grew inside my head, trying to gain control of my eyes. She knew who I was, now. She could pull on me as strongly as I could read her. She was more powerful here, near the Master.

She riffled through my memories, trying to gain a better handle on a situation for which she and the Master had been preparing for weeks.

Whisper probed. One sniff of Croaker had her convinced that this incident had been crafted by the Company to inconvenience her personally.

I felt both Taken. Blind Emon had a fine read on my emotions. She pilfered random thoughts while depositing disturbing notions. Whisper drifted our way. Meantime men, mules, and that sentinel crow all oozed into concealment. I refused to give up my view completely.

A keg of the sort that had been aboard so many mules flew up out of the ruin. Blind Emon jinked, did something to shift its course and add velocity. Wisps of smoke trailed it. It exploded thirty feet from Whisper. The fireball enveloped her.

Elmo offered up a soft prayer. "Holy shit. That's gotta hurt."

Whisper wobbled out, trailing flames. She headed down toward someplace where she would not have to fall any farther.

"It was stupid to come here," Rusty grumped. "Ain't our fight."

Even Robin glowered at that. Still, the man was close to making a point. He told Elmo, "We should get the hell gone while that bitch is cleaning the crap out of her drawers."

"Right." Elmo stared past where Whisper had hit hard enough to fling smoking chunks of everything but her fifty yards in a dozen directions. A second keg had sailed out of the ruin.

Blind Emon repeated her manoeuvre, her aim direly precise. A Taken distracted by Whisper's calamity took a direct hit, but this keg did not explode. It fell, shattered, ignited belatedly, created a foul gray miasma.

The impact did overturn the Taken's carpet and left that dread entity hanging on desperately with one hand.

My companions were more interested in travel than observing sorcery spectaculars. Rusty poked me with the dull end of a javelin. "What part of we need to get the fuck out of here are you not getting?" He added, sarcastically, "Sir."

Elmo barked foul agreement from the shredded woods. I moved reluctantly. Our crow friend watched from an oak stump, head cocked.

I felt a sudden urge to put distance between me and what was bound to turn uglier than I could imagine. Emon guaranteed it.

I cannot deliver an account of the evil versus evil sorcery duel of the decade. The desire to see the sun rise again quashed the compulsion to watch. But I do have to report that Emon and the Master engaged in an action they had been preparing for since soon after we invaded their forest.

We clotted up getting out of there, our patrol, mules, gobbling foreigners, local refugees, and the troops and wizards the lieutenant had sent to stir the pot before.

* * *

THE MOB KEPT moving, less panicked but jockeying and jostling. Everybody wanted across the bridge. Our wizards tried to nurse information out of the gaunt serfs but they were little help.

The road was about to tilt down into the Rip. There would be no leaving it then. A demand of nature haunted me. I would not last till we crossed the bridge. I flitted into the woods, found a useful log, dropped my trousers, began my business buzzed by flies, plagued by mosquitoes, and watched by a curious crow.

I heard a rustle. I looked down. A rattlesnake looked back, equally surprised. I froze. It coiled but reserved its warning rattle.

The crow made a leap and single flap, took station behind the snake. Its eyes shone oddly golden. One began to glow. The glow expanded into a ball an inch in diameter, a foot, a yard. The rattler decided to take its business elsewhere. It took off at maximum snake speed.

My bowels released, explosively and rankly, as I saw exactly what I dreaded: the Lady in the golden light, sweetly beautiful, the most alluring, lovely evil ever. She had not aged a moment in a decade.

The air all round whispered, "There you are. I was afraid I'd lost you. Come home."

Gods! Temptation, Lady is thy name! Suddenly, treason seemed entirely reasonable. I forgot most of what made me *me*, including recollections of suffering in the Tower. She infiltrated channels into my soul already chafed by Blind Emon, scraping up informational residue left by Emon while she explored.

The Lady was not pleased.

She abandoned me suddenly, no explanation, leaving me convinced that she regretted not being able to linger.

I tried pretending that I was not disappointed. It gets harder to fool myself as I get older.

ONE-EYE ASKED, "You see a ghost?" He was repairing that ugly hat.

"Worse." I told him.

The lieutenant arrived before I finished. He had a special assignment for Elmo's patrol. We had impressed him that much. Goblin got to join us.

Heads together with the boss, Elmo looked less happy by the second. Meantime, the lieutenant's staff cut mules out of the passing mob. Each carried kegs or sacks of coppery beads.

Elmo rejoined us. "Great news. We've been entrusted with cutting the bridge once everybody gets across. And you get to help, Goblin."

That little wizard's toad face twisted up nasty. He had come around just to check on how we were. Elmo thumped him atop the head before he started bitching. "And we get to do it in the dark, using those kegs that go boom when sorcerers toss them around."

One-Eye got all positive, told Goblin, "There'll be plenty of moonlight later." He grinned wickedly.

"Dey's still light now, some," Whittle noted.

"Yeah. I can still see my wife if I squint," Rusty countered, waving his hand in front of his face.

"We got to do it so let's get doing," Elmo said. "No farting around. Whisper's gang shows before we're done, the lieutenant blows it with us still out there."

A true motivator, our Elmo.

He said, "Robin, you head back up to that last straight stretch and keep a lookout. Somebody comes, you get your ass down here fast."

The complaining commenced.

"Did somebody declare this a democracy?"

One-Eye grumbled, "You can rob a soldier of his choices but you can't take his right to bitch."

Goblin giggled.

Elmo told Robin, "Grab your gear and get. And be careful."

Rusty started getting his stuff together, too.

Elmo shook his head, pointed at the bridge.

SO THERE WE were, clambering through the trestlework, operating on guesses based on what we thought we had gotten from the mule people, plus what we saw happen between Blind Emon and the Taken. If it went the lieutenant's way he would look like an improv genius. If not, he could become the fabled Commander Dumbass.

It did not start well.

Rusty fell. He survived only because Elmo had bullied him into wearing a rope safety harness. I dropped a keg, almost fell trying to save it. It rattled around in the rocks below, never breaking up. A keg Goblin was wrestling came apart. Its contents caught fire, sparked by his gear clanking together. For a while we were enveloped by ghastly sulfurous smoke.

There were lesser mishaps too numerous to recount. We accumulated bruises, bloody abrasions, splinters, and mashed fingers. The moon was no help when it rose. We were down in the Rip, under the bridge deck. We did catch a break when a cold breeze rose and dispersed the smoke.

Robin swung over the rail and came down. "Blind Emon is coming." Somewhere, a mule brayed.

Soon we heard chatter and clatter approaching. Blind Emon began to leak over.

Had she won? No. No final winner yet. Whisper and the Taken had gotten mauled, bad. But they had broken the command link between the Master and Emon. A tactical success for them. Emon ran the moment the connection went. No loyalty at all, that gal. She was wiped out, now, barely able to keep up with the people she was trying to protect.

All of the Lady's Taken had suffered grievously.

Emon seemed unaware that the Lady had become interested herself.

The Lady, I was sure, would deal with the Master permanently.

I knew the exact instant that Blind Emon sensed my proximity.

Right away she wanted me to know things. I needed the information. She was hurt bad. She did not expect to see the dawn.

I monkeyed through the trestlework, reported to Elmo. He asked, "You able to communicate?"

"Sort of. She's getting most of my thoughts, now. I think."

"You being a wiseass?"

"No. I feel her emotions. She's excited about being free, down on herself about not being strong enough to refuse to do the evil he made her do, and open about how they planned to use us the way we meant to use them."

"What?"

"They knew we were in the forest from the start. They knew they couldn't avoid a collision with the Taken. There's bad blood from olden times. The mule people serve them, raising most of the food for the people at the ruin. They have been making bang stuff for over a month. They never thought we'd find the road and the bridge. They thought those were hidden too well. They didn't know we had One-Eye in our trick bag."

Elmo muttered something about adding a hundred bricks and chucking that bag into a handy river. Then, "Am I wrong, guessing your new girlfriend wouldn't be running loose if the Lady hadn't been interested?"

I had abandoned all hope of ever clarifying my relationship with the Lady. "Probably."

"So even if Whisper and them are dead and half their troops besides, them that survived will come after us as fast as they can stagger. This shit ain't going near as fast as I hoped. See if you can get her to help."

"How? Doing what?"

"How the fuck do I know? Somehow. Anything. Don't look at me. I'm day labor. I don't get paid to think. I been told that plenty."

A WAY TO make kegs bang bigger slithered into my head. I told Elmo. One-Eye disagreed. "One of them gobble jockeys told me, knock a hole…"

"I got it from Blind Emon. The inventor. We pack those sacks of beads around each keg. She sends a curse and the *Bam!* is way bigger."

Blind Emon was feeling vindictive. She hoped people would be on the bridge when she made her wish. She did not much care who.

One-Eye wanted to use burning rope fuses. I wondered where he would get them. Elmo said, "They'd smell the smoke."

"If we do it like Croaker and his new honey want, we have to start all over to pack the stuff the way she wants."

"Then you better not waste time complaining."

I demonstrated the way Emon wanted the bead sacks installed. "And stop asking why. I just know there'll be more bang."

Later, One-Eye announced, "Time to get quiet. Company is coming."

For sure. The enemy, neither sneaking nor hurrying. They had no one pushing them. Their command authority remained engaged with the Master. Chatter suggested that two Taken were gone forever.

I hoped Whisper was one. She had been a pain in the ass for ages.

The Imperials reached the bridge. In moonlight it seemed ephemeral. It caused a lot of awed chatter. Underneath, there was angry muttering bearing on the name of Blind Emon's new boyfriend.

The Imperials were not looking for us. They had been sent to secure a bridge they had not believed existed. They did mention a bounty that had been offered for me.

Some of my brethren probably wondered how they could collect.

The bridge became crowded. The Lady had sent a lot of men. We kept on working underneath, slowly and quietly, me enduring a drizzle of catty whispers. We would have been long gone if that asshole Croaker had not insisted that the kegs and sacks be rearranged.

Even Elmo had an unhappy remark or seven.

The lieutenant did not blow us up, possibly only because he lacked the means.

WE WERE ABOUT done. Only Whittle, One-Eye, and I were still under the bridge. Clever Goblin had charted a pearl string of potent glamours that could be used to slink off to the forest unnoticed. Whittle was shaving a bit off a last keg so it would fit where Emon wanted it. One-Eye was doing a whole lot of nothing but being disgruntled. I was trying to manage two sacks of beads while trying not to be distracted by Emon nagging me to hurry. The bridge creaked and rattled as a heavy infantry battalion crossed leisurely. Those not troubled by heights paused to gawk at the spectacular moonlit Rip, where exposed granite looked like splotches of silver.

One-Eye muttered, "Marvelous! And now it's raining!"

Whittle was quickest. He cursed so loud a couple guys up top wondered what they had heard. We were, for once, blessed by Whittle's fierce dialect.

What it was, was, those guys were pissing off the bridge to watch the liquid fall. The breeze broke that up and pushed it under the deck.

Naturally, them amusing themselves that way was all my fault.

One-Eye offered to throw me overboard. He did not do so only because he figured I would glom on and take him with me. All the screaming during the fall might alert the Imperials that something was up.

Finished work, we weaseled carefully out of the trestle into a glamour patch just yards from a clutch of officers debating what to do next. A break for supper and sleep was the more popular proposition. The bridge was secure. The old bitch was busy elsewhere. She would never notice.

A crow squawked angrily.

Crows do not, usually, jabber much after nightfall.

I WAS BEHIND some brush, inside a glamour reinforced by Blind Emon. She lurked beside me, like a heap of dirty rags, emotion and agony held in check. Most of Elmo's patrol were close, plus the lieutenant and some henchmen. One-Eye never stopped muttering. He could not let the golden rain go. He would have to take a bath. He had not suffered through one for years. Baths were not healthy. Everyone knew that.

One nocturnal crow nagged on, almost conversationally. Hell! It *was* conversational. One-sided conversational. Listening closely, I could make out most of it.

A generous ass-chewing was in progress. The Lady was not pleased with the day's outcome. She was almost displeased enough to come out her own physical self instead of just relying on a spiritual messenger.

Commanders fell over one another assuring her that a personal visit would be unnecessary.

The lieutenant asked, "What now, Croaker?" He, Elmo, One-Eye, and a dozen others looked at me like the future was mine to design.

Blind Emon sent, *There is only one way.* To her surprise and mine, she had been regaining strength, probably at my expense.

"Huh?" A rejoinder scintillating in its Croakeresqueness.

The conversation between the Imperials and crow drifted our way. I had not paid close attention for several seconds.

"They are here!" the crow insisted. "I smell them!"

"Oh, shit! Get the hell out of here!" I said, having a hard time keeping my voice down. "Run!"

Most of the gawkers had recognized the wisdom of that action already. The lieutenant said, "Whatever the hell the plan is, Croaker, it's time to do it."

"Run."

Then there was just Emon and me, with a hostile horde bearing down and me unable to get my feet to move. Then Blind Emon bloomed.

Petals waving like tentacles, she rose and swept toward our enemies. They produced squeals of awe and fear. Dumbass Croaker got his feet unstuck. He stumbled along after Emon.

Several petals extended. One thirty yards long snapped a fleeing crow from the air with a vicious *crack!* Others snatched at officers' throats.

Get down. Cling to the earth like it is your mother's teat if you want to live.

I did so. That Blind Emon was one smooth talker.

I could still see her and the bridge. She soared over the Rip. Petals reached into the trestlework.

Flash! And then a parade of flashes, with rolling thunder. The middle of the bridge humped up eight feet like the back of a sea serpent surfacing. The rest of the deck rose off its supports. The roar deafened me. I did not hear the screams of the hundreds falling into the gorge.

Nasty smoke masked everything. It swallowed Blind Emon. I never saw her again. She sent no farewells.

In time the breeze pushed the smoke away.

And there stood that gods-be-damned bridge, singed, but... The gods-be-damned deck had dropped back exactly where it was before it flew up. Imperials lighted torches and started checking its stability.

Shee-it! Oh holy fecal fall!

Time to run!

Run, Croaker, run. Run like hell is on your ass, because it is for sure going to be, real soon now, and it will be very, very hungry.

The miracle in this latest miracle escape had just turned out to have a great big old hairy-assed shaggy dog story ending.

THE GHOST MAKERS
ELIZABETH BEAR

THE FACELESS MAN walked out of the desert at sunset, when the gates of the City of Jackals wound ponderously closed on silent machinery. He was the last admitted. His kind were made by Wizards, and went about on Wizards' business. No one interrogated him.

His hooded robe and bronze hide smoked with sun-heat when the priest of Iashti threw water from the sacred rivers over him. Whether it washed away any clinging devils of the deep desert, as it was intended, who could have said? But it did rinse the dust from the featureless oval of his visage so all who stood near could see themselves reflected. Distorted.

He paused within and he lowered the hood of his homespun robes to lie upon his shoulders. The gates made the first sound of their closing, a heavy snap as their steel-shod edges overlapped and latched. Their juncture reflected as a curved line up the mirror of the faceless man's skull. Within the gates, bars as thick as a man glided home. Messaline was sealed, and the date plantations and goats and pomegranates and laborers of the farms and villages beyond her walls were left to their own devices until the lion-sun tinted the horizon again.

Trailing tendrils of steam faded from the faceless man's robe, leaving the air heavy with petrichor— the smell of water in aridity—and the cloth over his armored hide as dry as before. His eyeless mask trained unwaveringly straight ahead, he raised his voice.

"Priest of Iashti." Though he had no mouth, his voice tolled clear and sonorous.

The priest left his aspergillum and came around to face the faceless man, though there was no need. He said, "You already have my blessing, O Gage... of...?"

"I'd rather information than blessings, Child of the Morning," said the Gage. The priest's implied question—to whom he owed his service—the faceless man left unacknowledged. His motionlessness—as if he were a bronze statue someone had draped in a robe and left inexplicably in the center of the market road—was more distressing than if he'd stalked the priest like a cat.

He continued, "Word is that a poet was murdered under the Blue Stone a sennight since."

"Gage?"

The Gage waited.

The priest collected himself. He tugged the tangerine-and-gold dawn-colored robe smooth beneath his pectoral. "It is true. Eight days ago, though—no, now gone nine."

"Which way?"

Wordlessly, the priest pointed to a twisting, smoky arch towering behind dusty tiers of pastel houses. The sunset sprawled across the sky rendered the monument in translucent silhouette, like an enormous, elaborate braid of chalcedony.

The faceless man paused, and finally made a little motion of his featureless head that somehow still gave the impression of ruefully pursed lips and acknowledgement.

"Alms." He tossed gold to the priest.

The priest, no fool, caught it before it could bloody his nose. He waited to bite it until the Gage was gone.

THE GAGE MADE his way through the Temple District, where great prayer-houses consecrated to the four major Messaline deities dominated handfuls of lesser places of worship: those of less successful sects, or of alien gods. Only the temple to the Uthman Scholar-God, fluted pillars twined about with sacred verses rendered in lapis lazuli and pyrite, competed with those four chief temples for splendor.

Even at dusk, these streets teemed. Foot traffic, litter bearers, and the occasional rider and mount— mostly horses, a few camels, a mule, one terror-bird—bustled through the lanes between the torch bearers. There were soldiers and merchants, priests and scholars, a nobleman or woman in a curtained sedan chair with guards crying out *"Make way!"* The temples were arranged around a series of squares, and the squares were occupied by row upon row of market stalls from which rose the aromas of turmeric, coriander, roses, sandalwood, dates, meat sizzling, bread baking, and musty old attics—among other things. The sweet scent of stitched leather and wood-pulp-and-rag paper identified a bookseller as surely as did the banner that drifted above his pavilion.

The faceless man passed them all—and more than half of the people he passed either turned to stare or hurried quickly along their way, eyes fixed on the ground by their shoes. The Gage knew better than to assign any quality of guilt or innocence to these reactions.

He did not stay in the Temple District long. A left-hand street bent around the temple of Kaalha, the goddess of death and mercy—who also wore a mirrored mask, though hers was silver and divided down the center line. The temple had multiple doorways, and seemed formed in the shape of a star. Over the nearest one was inscribed: *In my house there is an end to pain.*

Some distance behind the temple, the stone arch loomed.

At first he walked by stucco houses built cheek to cheek, stained in every shade of orange, red, vermilion. The arches between their entryways spanned the road. But soon the street grew crooked and dark; there were no torch-bearers here. A rat or two was in evidence, scurrying over stones—but rodents went quickly and fearfully here. Once, longer legs and ears flickered like scissors as a slender shadow detached itself from one darkness and glided across the open space to the next: one of the jackals from which Messaline took its epithet. From the darkness where it finished, a crunch and a squeak told of one scurrying at least that ended badly for the scurrier.

In these gutters, garbage reeked, though not too much of it; things that were still useful would be put to use. The people passing along these streets were patch-clothed, dirty-cheeked, lank of unwashed hair. Many wore long knives; a few bore flintlocks. The only unescorted women were those plying a trade, and a few men who loitered in dark doorways or alleys drew back into their lairs as the Gage passed, each footstep ringing dully off the cobbles. He was reminded of tunnel-spiders, and kept walking.

As he drew closer to one base of the Blue Stone, though, he noticed an increase in people walking quickly in the direction opposite his. Though the night sweltered, stored heat radiating back from the stones, they hunched as if cold: heads down and shoulders raised protectively.

Still no-one troubled the faceless man. Messaline knew about Wizards.

Others were not so lucky, or so unmolested.

The Gage came out into the small square that surrounded one foot of the Blue Stone. It rose above him in an interlaced, fractal series of helixes a hundred times the height of a tall man, vanishing into the darkness that drank its color and translucency. The Gage had been walking for long enough that stars now showed through the gaps in the arch's sinuous strands.

The base of the monument separated into a half-dozen pillars where it plunged to earth. Rather than resting upon a plinth or footing, though, it seemed as if each pillar had thrust up through the street like a tree seeking the light—or possibly as if the cobbles of the road had just been paved around them.

Among the shadows between those pillars, a man wearing a skirted coat and wielding a narrow, curved sword fought silently—desperately—valiantly—for his life.

*   *   *

THE COMBAT HAD every appearance of an ambush—five on one, though that one was the superior swordsman and tactician. These were advantages that did not always affect the eventual result when surrounded and outnumbered, but the man in the skirted coat was making the most of them. His narrow torso twisted like a charmed snake as he dodged blows too numerous to deflect. He might have been an answer to any three of his opponents. But as it was, he was left whirling and weaving, leaping and ducking, parrying for his life. The harsh music of steel rang from the tight walls of surrounding rowhouses. His breathing was a rasp audible from across the square. He used the footings of the monument to good advantage, dodging between them, keeping them at his back, forcing his enemies to coordinate their movements over uneven cobblestones.

The Gage paused to assess.

The lone man's skirts whirled wide as he caught a narrower, looping strand of the Blue Stone in his off hand and used it as a handle to swing around, parrying one opponent with his sword hand while landing a kick in the chest of another. The kicked man staggered back, arms pinwheeling. One of his allies stepped under his blade and came on, hoping to catch the lone man off-balance.

The footpad—if that's what he was—huffed in pain as he ran into the Gage's outstretched arm. His eyes widened; he jerked back and reflexively brought his scimitar down. It glanced off the Gage's shoulder, parting his much-patched garment and leaving a bright line.

The Gage picked him up by the jaw, one-handed, and bashed his brains out against the Blue Stone.

The man in the skirted coat ran another through between the ribs. The remaining three hesitated, exchanging glances. One snapped a command; they vanished into the night like rain into a fallow field, leaving only the sound of their footsteps. The man in the skirted coat seemed as if he might give chase, but his sword was wedged. He stood on the chest of the man he had killed and twisted his long, slightly curved blade to free it. It had wedged in his victim's spine. A hiss of air escaping a punctured lung followed as he slid it free.

Warily, he turned to the Gage. The Gage did not face him. The man in the skirted coat did not bother to walk around to face the Gage.

"Thank…"

Above them, the Blue Stone began to glow, with a grey light that faded up from nothingness and illuminated the scene: glints off the Gage's bronze body, the saturated blood-red of the lone man's coat, the frayed threads of its embroidery worn almost flat on the lapels.

"What the—?"

"Blood," the Gage said, prodding the brained body with his toe. "The Blue Stone accepts our sacrifice." He gestured to the lone man's prick-your-finger coat. "You're a Dead Man."

Dead Men were the sworn, sacred guards of the Caliphs who ruled north and east of Messaline, across the breadth of the sea.

"Not anymore," the Dead Man said. Fastidiously, he crouched and scrubbed his sword on a corpse's hem. "Not professionally. And not literally, thanks to you. By which I mean, 'Thank you.'"

The faceless man shrugged. "It didn't look like a fair fight."

"In this world, O my brother, is there such a thing as a fair fight? When one man is bestowed by the gods with superior talent, by station with superior training, by luck with superior experience?"

"I'd call that the opposite of luck," said the faceless man.

The Dead Man shrugged. "Pardon my forwardness; a true discourtesy, when directed at one who has done me a very great favor solely out of the goodness of his heart—"

"I have no heart."

"—but you are what they call a Faceless Man?"

"We prefer the term Gage. And while we're being rude, I had heard your kind don't leave the Caliph's service."

"The Caliph's service left me. A new Caliph's posterior warms the dais in Asitaneh. I've heard *your* kind die with the Wizard that made you."

The Gage shrugged. "I've something to do before I lie down and let the scavengers have me."

"Well, you have come to the City of Jackals now."

"You talk a lot for a dead man."

The Dead Man laughed. He sheathed his sword and thrust the scabbard through his sash. More worn embroidery showed that to be its place of custom.

"Why were they trying to kill you?"

The Dead Man had aquiline features and eagle-eyes to go with it, a trim goatee and a sandalwood-skinned face framed by shoulder-length ringlets, expensively oiled. Slowly, he drew a crimson veil across his nose and mouth. "I expected an ambush."

Neither one of them made any pretense that that was, exactly, an answer.

The Gage reached out curiously and touched the glowing stone. "Then I'm pleased to see that your expectation was rewarded."

"You discern much." The Dead Man snorted and stood. "May I know the name of the one who aided me?"

"My kind have no names."

"Do you propose then that there is no difference between you? You all have the same skills? The same thoughts?"

The Gage turned to him, and the Dead Man saw his own expression reflected, distorted in that curved bronze mirror. It never even shivered when he spoke. "So we are told."

The Dead Man shrugged. "So also are we. Were we. When I was a part of something bigger. But now I am alone, and my name is Serhan."

The Gage said, "You can call me Gage."

He turned away, though he did not need to. He tilted his featureless head back to look up.

"What's this thing?" The Gage's gesture followed the whole curve of the Blue Stone, revealed now as the light their murders had engendered rose along it like tendrils of crawling foxfire.

"It is old; it is anyone's guess what good it once was. There used to be a road under it, before they built the houses. A triumphal arch, maybe?"

"Hell of a place for a war monument."

The Dead Man's veil puffed out as he smothered a laugh. "The neighborhood was better once."

"Surprised they didn't pull it down for building material."

"Many have tried," the Dead Man said. "It does not pull down."

"Huh," said the Gage. He prodded the brained man again. "Any idea why they attacked you?"

"Opportunity? Or perhaps to do with the crime I have been investigating. That seems more likely."

"Crime?"

Reluctantly, the Dead Man answered, "Murder."

"Oh," said the Gage. "The poet?"

"I wonder if it might have been related to this." The Dead Man's hand described the arc of light across the sky. The glow washed the stars away. "Maybe he was a sacrifice to whatever old power inhabits... this."

"I doubt it," said the Gage. "I know something about the killer."

"You seek justice in this matter too?"

The Gage shrugged. "After a fashion."

The Dead Man stared. The Gage did not move. "Well," said the Dead Man at last. "Let us then obtain wine."

THEY CHOSE A tavern on the other side of the block that faced on the Blue Stone, where its unnerving light did not wash in through the high narrow windows. The floor was gritty with sand spread to sop up spilled wine, and the air was thick with its vinegar sourness. The Dead Man tested the first step carefully, until he determined that what lay under the sand was flagstone. As they settled themselves—the Dead Man with his back to the wall, the Gage with his back to the room— the Gage said, "Did it do that when the poet died?"

"His name was Anah."

"Did it do that when Anah died?"

The Dead Man raised one hand in summons to the serving girl. "It seems to like blood."

"And yet we don't know what they built it for."

"Or who built it," the Dead Man said. "But you believe those things do not matter."

The girl who brought them wine was young, her blue-black hair in a wrist-thick braid of seven strands. The plait hung down her back in a spiral, twisted like the Blue Stone. She took the Dead Man's copper and withdrew.

The Dead Man said, "I always wondered how your sort sustained yourselves."

In answer, the Gage cupped his bronze fingers loosely around the stem of the cup and let them lie on the table.

"I was hired by the poet's... by Anah's lover." The Dead Man lifted his cup and swirled it. Fumes rose from the warmed wine. He lifted his veil and touched his mouth to the rim. The wine was raw, rough stuff, more fruit than alcohol.

The Gage said, "We seek the same villain."

"I am afraid I cannot relinquish my interest in the case. I... need the money." The Dead Man lifted his veil to drink again. The edge lapped wine and grew stained.

The Gage might have been regarding him. He might have been staring at the wall behind his head. Slowly, he passed a brazen hand over the table. It left behind a scaled track of silver. "I will pay you as well as your other client. And I will help you bring her the Wizard's head."

"*Wizard!*"

The Gage shrugged.

"You think you know who it is that I hunt."

"Oh yes," the Gage said. Scratched silver glittered dully on the table. "I can tell you that."

The Dead Man regarded his cup, and the Gage regarded... whatever it was.

Finally, the Gage broke the impasse to say, "Would you rather go after a Wizard alone, or in company?"

Under his veil, the Dead Man nibbled a thumbnail. "Which Wizard?"

"Attar the Enchanter. Do you know where to find him?"

"Everyone in Messaline knows where to find a Wizard. Or, belike, how to avoid him." The Dead Man tapped the nearest coin. "Why would he kill a *poet*? Gut him? In a public square?"

"He's a ghost-maker," the Gage said. "He kills for the pleasure it affords him. He kills artists, in particular. He likes to own them. To possess their creativity."

"Huh," said the Dead Man. "Anah was not the first, then."

"Ghost-makers... some people say they're soulless themselves. That they're empty, and so they drink the souls of the dead. And they're always hungry for another."

"People say a lot of shit," the Dead Man said.

"When I heard the manner of the poet's death, and that Attar was in Messaline..." The Gage shrugged. "I came at once. To catch up with him before he moves on again."

"You have not come about Anah in particular."

"I'm here *for* Anah. And the other Anahs. Future and past."

"I see," said the Dead Man.

His hand passed across the table. When it vanished, no silver remained. "Is it true that darkness cannot cloud your vision?"

"I can see," said the faceless man. "In dark or day, whether I turn my head aside or no. What has no eyes cannot be blinded."

"That must be awful," the Dead Man said.

The lamplight flickered against the side of the Gage's mask.

"So," said the Gage, motionless. "When the Caliph's service left you, you chose a mercenary life?"

"Not mercenary," the Dead Man said. "I have had sufficient of soldiering. I'm a hired investigator."

"An... investigator."

The corners of the Dead Man's eyes folded into eagle-tracks. "We have a legacy of detective stories in the Caliphate. Tales of clever men, and of one who is cleverer. They are mostly told by women."

"Aren't *most* of your storytellers women?"

The Dead Man moved to drink and found his cup empty. "They *are* the living embodiment of the Scholar-God."

"And you keep them in cages."

"We keep God in temples. Is that so different?"

After a while, the Dead Man said, "You have some plan for fighting a Wizard? A Wizard who... killed your maker?"

"My maker was Cog the Deviser. That's not how she died. But I thought perhaps a priest of Kaalha would know what to do about a ghost-maker."

"Ask the Death God. You are a clever automaton."

The Gage shrugged.

"If you won't drink that, I will."

"Drink it?" the Gage asked. He drew his hands back from where they had embraced the foot of his cup.

The Dead Man reached across the table, eyebrows questioning, and waited until the Gage gestured him in to tilt the cup and peer inside.

If there had been wine within, it was gone.

WHEN THE LION-SUN of Messaline rose, haloed in its mane, the Gage and the Dead Man were waiting below the lintel inscribed, *In my house there is an end to pain.* The door stood open, admitting the transient chill of a desert morning. No one barred the way. But no one had come to admit them, either.

"We should go in?" the Dead Man said.

"After you," said the Gage.

The Dead Man huffed, but stepped forward, the Gage following with silent precision. His joints made no more sound than the massive gears of the gates of Messaline. Wizards, when they chose to wreak, wrought well.

Beyond the doorway lay a white marble hall, shadowed and cool. Within the hall, a masked figure enveloped in undyed linen robes stood, hands folded into sleeves. The mask was silver, featureless, divided by a line—a join—down the center. The robe was long enough to puddle on the floor.

Behind the mask, one side of the priest's face would be pitted, furrowed: acid-burned. And one side would be untouched, in homage—in sacrifice—to the masked goddess they served, whose face was the heavy, half-scarred moon of Messaline. The

Gage and the Dead Man drew up, two concealed faces regarding one.

Unless the figure was a statue.

But then the head lifted. Hands emerged from the sleeves—long and dark, elegant, with nails sliced short for labor. The voice that spoke was fluting, feminine.

"Welcome to the House of Mercy," the priestess said. "All must come to Kaalha of the Ruins in the end. Why do you seek her prematurely?"

They hesitated for a moment, but then the Dead Man stepped forward. "We seek her blessing. And perhaps her aid, Child of the Night."

By her voice, perhaps her mirrors hid a smile. "A pair of excommunicates. Wolf's-heads, are you not? Masterless ones?"

The supplicants held their silence, or perhaps neither one of them knew how to answer.

When the priestess turned to the Gage, their visages reflected one another—reflected distorted reflections—endlessly. "What have you to live for?"

"Duty, art, and love."

"You? A Faceless Man?"

The Gage shrugged. "We prefer the term Gage."

"So," she said. She turned to the Dead Man. "What have *you* to live for?"

"Me? I am dead already."

"Then you are the Goddess's already, and need no further blessing of her."

The Dead Man bit his lip and hid the hand that would have made the Sign of the Pen. "Nevertheless... my friend believes we need her help. Perhaps we can explain to the Eidolon?"

"Walk with me," said the priestess.

Further along the corridor, the walls were mirrored. The priestess strode beside them, the front of her robe gathered in her hands. The mirrors were faintly distorted, whether by design or flaw, and they reflected the priestess, the Gage, and the Dead Man as warped caricatures—rippled, attenuated, bulged into near-spheres. Especially in conjunction with the mirrored masks, the reflections within reflections were dizzying.

When they left the corridor of mirrors and entered the large open atrium into which it emptied, the priestess was gone. The Dead Man whirled, his hand on the hilt of his sword, his battered red coat swinging wide to display all the stains and shiny patches the folds of its skirts hid.

"Ysmat Her Word," he swore. "I hate these heathen magics. Did you see her go? You see everything."

The Gage walked straight ahead and did not stop until he reached the middle of the short side of the atrium. "I did not see that."

"A heathen magic you seek, Dead Man." A masked priestess spoke from atop the dais at the other end of the long room.

It was unclear whether this priestess was the same one. Her voice was identical, or nearly so. But she seemed taller and she walked with a limp. Of course, it would be easy to twist an ankle in that trailing raiment, and the click of wooden pattens as she descended the stair said the truth of her height was a subject for conjecture.

She came to them through shafts of sunlight angled from high windows, stray gleams catching on her featureless visage.

"Forgive me." The Dead Man inclined his head and dropped one knee before her. "I spoke in haste. I meant no disrespect, Child of the Moon."

"Rise," said the priestess. "If Kaalha of the Ruins wants you humbled, she will lay you low. The Merciful One has no need of playacted obeisance."

She offered a hand. It was gloved, silk pulled unevenly over long fingers. She lifted the Dead Man to his feet. She was strong. She squeezed his fingers briefly, like a mother reassuring a child, and let her grip fall. She withdrew a few steps. "Explain to me your problem, masterless ones."

"Are you the Eidolon?" the Gage asked.

"She will hear what you speak to me."

The Gage nodded—a movement as calculated and intentional as if he had spoken aloud. He said, "We seek justice for the poet Anah, mutilated and murdered nine—now ten—days past at the Blue Stone. We seek justice also for the wood-sculptor Abbas, similarly mutilated and murdered in his village of Bajishe, and for uncounted other victims of this same murderer."

The priestess stood motionless, her hands hanging beside her and spread slightly as if to receive a gift. "For vengeance, you wish the blessing of Rakasha," she said. "For justice, seek Vajhir the warrior. Not the Queen the of Cold Moon."

"I do not seek vengeance," said the Gage.

"Really?"

"No." It was an open question which of them was more immovable. More unmoving. "I seek mercy for all those this murderer, this ghost-maker, may yet torture and kill. I seek Kaalha's benediction on those who will come to her eventually, one way or another, if their ghosts are freed. As you say: the Goddess of Death does not need to hurry."

The priestess's oval mask tilted. On her pattens, she was taller than both supplicants.

The Gage inclined his head.

"A ghost-maker, you say."

"A soulless killer. A Wizard. One who murders for the joy of it. Young men, men in their prime. Men with great gifts and great... beauty."

Surely that could not have been a catch of breath, a concealed sob. What has no eyes cannot cry.

The Gage continued, "We cannot face a Wizard without help. Your help. Please tell us, Child of the Moon: what do you do against a killer with no soul?"

Her laughter broke the stillness that followed— but it was sweet laughter, glass bells, not sardonic cruelty. She stepped down from her pattens and now both men topped her by a head. She left them lying on the flagstones, one tipped on its side, and came close. She still limped, though.

"Let me tell you a secret, one mask to another." She leaned close and whispered. Their mirrored visages reflected one another into infinity, bronze and silver echoing. When she drew back, the Gage's head swiveled in place and tilted to acknowledge her.

She extended a hand to the Dead Man, something folded in her fist. He offered his palm. She laid an amethyst globe, cloudy with flaws and fracture, in the hollow. "Do you know what that is?"

"I've seen it done," said the Gage. "My mistress used one to create me."

The priestess nodded. "Go with Kaalha's blessing. Yours is a mission of mercy, masterless ones."

She turned to go. Her slippered feet padded on stone. She left the pattens lying. She was nearly to the dais again when the Dead Man called out after her—

"Wait!"

She paused and turned.

"Why would you help us?" the Dead Man asked.

"Masterless ones?" She touched her mask with both hands, fingertips flat to mirrored cheeks. The Dead Man shuddered at the prospect of her face revealed, but she lifted them empty again. She touched two fingers to her mask and brushed away as if blowing a kiss, then let her arms fall. Her sleeves covered her gloved hands.

The priestess said, "She is also the Goddess of Orphans. Masterless Man."

THE DEAD MAN started to slip the amethyst sphere into his sash opposite the sword as he and the Gage threaded through the crowd back to the Street of Temples. Before he had quite secured it, though, he paused and drew it forth again, holding it up to catch the sunlight along its smoky, icy flaws and planes.

"You know what this is for?"

"Give it here."

Reluctantly, the Dead Man did so. The Gage made it vanish into his robe.

"If you know how to use that, and it's important, it might be for the best if you demonstrated for me."

"You have a point," the Gage said, and—shielded in the rush of the crowd—he did so. Then he made it vanish again and said, "Well. Lead me to the lair of Attar."

"This way."

They walked. The Gage dropped his cowl, improving the speed of their passage. The Dead Man lowered his voice. "Tell me what you know about Messaline Wizards. I am more experienced with the Uthman sort. Who are rather different."

"Cog used to say that a Wizard was a manifestation of the true desires, the true obsessions of an age. That they were the essence of a time refined, like opium drawn from poppy juice."

"That's pretty. Does it mean anything?"

The Gage shrugged. "I took service with Cog because she was Attar's enemy."

"Gages have lives before their service. Of course they do."

"It's just that you never think of it."

The Dead Man shrugged.

"And Dead Men don't have prior lives."

"None worth speaking of." Dead Men were raised to their service, orphans who would otherwise beg, whore, starve, and steal. The Caliph gave them everything—home, family, wives. Educated their children. They were said to be the most loyal guards the world knew. "We have no purpose but to guard our Caliph."

"Huh," said the Gage. "I guess you'd better find one."

The Dead Man directed them down a side street in a neighborhood that lined the left bank of the river Dijlè. A narrow paved path separated the facades of houses from the stone-lined canal. In this dry season, the water ran far down in the channel.

The Gage said, "I told you I chose service with Cog because she was Attar's enemy. Attar took something that was important to me."

"Something? Or someone?"

The Gage was silent.

The Dead Man said, "You said Attar kills artists. Young men."

The Gage was silent.

"Your beloved? This Abbas, have I guessed correctly?"

"Are you shocked?"

The Dead Man shrugged. "You would burn for it in Asmaracanda."

"You can burn for crossing the street incorrectly in Asmaracanda."

"This is truth." The Dead Man drew his sword, inspected the faintly nicked, razor-stropped edge. "Were you an artist too?"

"I was."

"Well," the Dead Man said. "That's different, then."

BEFORE THE HOUSE of Attar the Enchanter, the Dead Man paused and tested the door; it was locked and barred so soundly it didn't rattle. "This is his den."

"He owns this?" the Gage said.

"Rents it," the Dead Man answered. He reached up with his off hand and lowered his veil. His sword slid from its scabbard almost noiselessly. "How much magic are you expecting?"

"He's a ghost-maker," the Gage said. "He travels from murder to murder. He might not have a full workshop here. He'll have mechanicals."

"Mechanicals?"

"Things like me."

"*Won*derful." He glanced up at the windows of the second and third stories. "Are we climbing in?"

"I don't climb." The Gage took hold of the door knob and effortlessly tore it off the door. "Follow me."

THE GAGE'S FOOTSTEPS were silent, but that couldn't stop the boards of the joisted floor from creaking under his armored weight. "I hate houses with cellars," he said. "Always afraid I'm going to fall through."

"That will only improve once we achieve the second story," the Dead Man answered. His head turned ceaselessly, scanning every dark corner of what appeared to be a perfectly ordinary, perfectly pleasant reception room—unlighted brass lamps, inlaid cupboards, embroidered cushions, tapestry chairs, and thick rugs stacked several high over the indigo-patterned interlocking star-and-cross tiles of that creaking floor. Being on the ground floor, it was windowless.

"We're alone down here," said the Gage.

The staircase ascended at the back of the room, made of palm wood darkened with perfumed oils and dressed with a scarlet runner. The Gage moved toward it like a stalking tiger, weight and fluidity in perfect tension. The Dead Man paced him.

They ascended side by side. Light from the windows above reflected down. It shone on the sweat on the Dead Man's bared face, on the length of his bared blade, on the bronze of the Gage's head and the scratched metal that gleamed through the unpatched rent at his shoulder.

The Gage was taller than the Dead Man. His head cleared the landing first. Immediately, he snapped—"Close your eyes!"

The Dead Man obeyed. He cast his off hand across them as well, for extra protection. Still the light that flared was blinding.

The Gage might walk like a cat, but when he ran, the whole house shook. The creak of the floorboards was replaced by thuds and cracks, rising to a crescendo of jangling metal and shattering glass. The light died; a male voice called out an incantation. The Dead Man opened his eyes.

Trying to focus through swimming, rough-bordered blind spots, the Dead Man saw the Gage surrounded by twisted metal and what might be the remains of a series of lenses. Beyond the faceless man and the wreckage, a second man—broad-shouldered, shirtless above the waist of his pantaloons, of middle years by the salt in his beard but still fit—raised a flared tube in his hands and directed it at the Gage.

Wood splintered as the Gage reared back, struggling to move. The wreckage constrained him, though feebly, and his foot had broken through the floor. He was trapped.

With his off hand, the Dead Man snatched up the nearest object—a shelf laden with bric-a-brac—and hurled it at the Wizard's head. The tube—some sort of blunderbuss—exploded with a roar that added flash-deafness to the flash-blindness that already afflicted the Dead Man. Gouts of smoke and sparks erupted from the flare—

—the wall beside the Gage exploded outward.

"Well," he said. "That won't endear us to the neighbors."

The Dead Man heard nothing but the ringing in his ears. He leaped onto the seat of a Song-style ox-yoke chair, felt the edge of the back beneath his toe

345

and rode it down. His sword descended with the force of his controlled fall, a blow that should have split the Wizard's collarbone.

His arm stopped in mid-move, as if he had slammed it into the top of a stone wall. He jerked it back, but the pincers of the steam-bubbling crab-creature that grabbed it only tightened, and it was all he could do to hold onto his sword as his fingers numbed.

Wood shattered and metal rent as the Gage freed his foot and shredded the remains of the contraption that had nearly blinded the Dead Man. He swung a massive fist at the Wizard but the Wizard rolled aside and parried with the blunderbuss. Sparks shimmered. Metal crunched.

The Wizard barked something incomprehensible, and a shadow moved from the corner of the room. The Gage spun to engage it.

The Dead Man planted his feet, caught the elbow of his sword hand in his off hand, and lifted hard against the pain. The crab-thing scrabbled at the rug, hooked feet snagging and lifting, but he'd stolen its leverage. Grunting, he twisted from the hips and swung.

Carpet and all, the crab-thing smashed against the Wizard just as he was regaining his feet. There was a whistle of steam escaping and the Wizard shouted, jerking away. The crab-thing's pincer ripped free of the Dead Man's arm, taking cloth and a measure of flesh along with it.

The thing from the corner was obviously half-completed. Bits of bear- and cow-hide had been stitched together patchwork fashion over its armature. Claws as long as the Dead Man's sword protruded from the shaggy paw on its right side;

on the left they gleamed on bare armature. Its head turned, tracking. A hairy foot shuffled forward.

The Gage went to meet it, and there was a sound like mountains taking a sharp dislike to one another. Dust rattled from the walls. More bric-a-brac tumbled from the shelf-lined walls. In the street or in a neighboring house, someone screamed.

The Dead Man stepped over the hissing, clicking remains of the crab-thing and leveled his sword at the throat of the Wizard Attar.

"Stop that thing."

The Wizard, his face boiled red along one cheek, one eye closed and weeping, laughed out loud. "Because I fear your sword?"

He grabbed the blade right-handed, across the top, and pushed it down as he lunged onto the blade, ramming the sword through his chest. Blood and air bubbled around the blade. The Wizard did not stop laughing, though his laughter took on a... simmering quality.

Recoiling, the Dead Man let go of his sword.

Meanwhile, the wheezing armature lifted the Gage into the air and slammed him against the ceiling. Plaster and stucco-dust reinforced the smoky air.

"You call yourself a Dead Man!" Attar ripped the sword from his breast and hurled it aside. "This is what a dead man looks like." He thumped his chest, then reached behind himself to an undestroyed rack and lifted another metal object, long and thin.

The Dead Man swung an arc before him, probing carefully for footing amid the rubble on the floor. Attar sidled and sidestepped, giving no advantage. And Attar had his back to the wall.

The Gage and the half-made thing slammed to the floor, rolling in a bear hug. Joists cracked again and the floor settled, canting crazily. Neither the Gage nor the half-made thing made any sound but the thud of metal on metal, like smith's hammerblows, and the creak of straining gears and springs.

"I have no soul," said Attar. "I am a ghost-maker. Can your blade hurt me? All the lives I have taken, all the art I have claimed—all reside in me!"

Already, the burns on his face were smoothing. The bubbles of blood no longer rose from the cut in his chest. The Dead Man let his knees bend, his weight ground. Attar's groping left hand found and raised a mallet. His right hand aimed the slender rod.

"ENOUGH!" boomed the Gage. A fist thudded into his face; he caught the half-made thing's arm and used its own momentum to slam it to the ground.

The rod detonated; the Dead Man twisted to one side. Razors whisked his face and shaved a nick into his ear. Blood welled hotly as the spear embedded itself in the wall.

With an almighty crunch, the Gage rose from the remains of the half-made thing, its skull dangling from his hand. He was dented and disheveled, his robe torn away so the round machined joints of knees and elbows, the smooth segmented body, were plainly visible.

He tossed the wreckage of the half-made thing's head at Attar, who laughed and knocked it aside with the hammer. He swung it in lazy loops, one-handed, tossed it to the other. "Come on, faceless man. What one Wizard makes, another can take apart."

The Gage stopped where he stood. He planted his

feet on the sagging floor. He turned his head and looked directly at the Dead Man.

The Dead Man caught the amethyst sphere when the Gage tossed it to him.

"A soul catcher? Did you not hear me say I am soulless? That priest's bauble can do me no harm."

"Well," said the Gage. "Then you won't object to us trying."

He stepped forward, walking up the slope of the broken floor. He swung his fist; Attar parried with the hammer as if the blow had no force behind it at all. The Gage shook his fist and blew across it. There was a dent across his knuckles now.

"Try harder," the Wizard said.

He kept his back to the corner, his hammer dancing between his hands. The Gage reached in, was deflected. Reached again. "It's not lack of a soul that makes you a monster. That, beast, is your humanity."

The Wizard laughed. "Poor thing. Have you been chasing me for Cog's sake all these months?"

"Not for Cog's sake." The Gage almost sounded as if he smiled. "And I have been hunting you for years. I was a potter; my lover was a sculptor. Do you even remember him? Or are the lives you take, the worlds of brilliance you destroy, so quickly forgotten?"

The Wizard's eyes narrowed, his head tipping as if in concentration. "I might recall."

Again the Gage struck. Again, the Wizard parried. His lips pursed as if to whistle and a shimmer crossed his face. A different visage appeared in its wake: curly-haired, darker-complected. Young and handsome, in an unexceptional sort of way. "This one? What *was* the name? Does it make you glad to see his face one last time, before I take you too? Though your art was not much, as I recall—but what can you expect of—"

The Gage lunged forward, a sharp blow of the Wizard's hammer snapping his arm into his head. The force knocked his upper body aside. But he took the blow, and the one that followed, and kept coming. He closed the gap.

He caught Attar's hammer hand and bent it back until the bones of his arm parted with a wet, wrenching sound.

"His name was Abbas!"

The Wizard gasped and went to his knees. With a hard sidearm swing, the Dead Man stepped in and smashed the amethyst sphere against his head, and pressed it there.

It burst in his opening hand, a shower of violet glitter. Particles swirled in the air, ran in the Wizard's open mouth, his nostrils and ears, swarmed his eyes until they stared blank and lavender.

When the Dead Man closed his hand again, with a vortex of shimmer the sphere re-coalesced.

Blank-faced, Attar slumped onto his left side, dangling from his shattered arm. The Gage opened his hand and let the body fall. "He's not dead. Just really soulless now."

"As soon as I find my sword I'll repair that oversight," the Dead Man said. He held out the amethyst. Blood streaked down his cheek, dripped hot from his ear.

"Keep it." The Gage looked down at his naked armature. "I seem to have left my pockets on the floor."

While the Dead Man found his blade, the Gage picked his way around the borders of the broken floor. He moved from shelf to shelf, lifting up sculptures, books of poetry, pottery vases—and reverentially, one at a time, crushing them with his dented hands.

Wiping blood from his sword, the Dead Man watched him work. "You want some help with that?"

The Gage shook his head.

"That's how you knew he didn't live downstairs."

"Hmm?"

"No art."

The Gage shrugged.

"You looking for something in particular?"

"Yes." The Gage's big hand enfolded a small object. He held it for a moment, cradled to his breast, and bowed his scratched mirror over it. Then he pressed his hands together and twisted, and when he pulled them apart, a scatter of wood shreds sprinkled the floor. "Go free, love."

When he looked up again, the Dead Man was still staring out the window. "Help me break the rest of these? So the artists can rest?"

"Also so our friend here doesn't grow his head back? Soul or no soul?"

"Yeah," the Gage answered. "That too."

OUTSIDE, THE DEAD Man fixed his veil and pushed his dangling sleeve up his arm, examining the strained threads and tears.

"Come on," the Gage said. "I'll buy you a new coat."

"But I like this one."

"Then let's go to a bar."

This one had better wine and cleaner clientele. As a result, they and the servers both gave the Dead Man and the Gage a wider berth, and the Dead Man kept having to go up to the bar.

"Well," said the Dead Man. "Another mystery solved. By a clever man among clever men."

"And you are no doubt the cleverest."

The Dead Man shrugged. "I had help. I don't suppose you'd consider a partnership?"

The Gage interlaced his hands around the foot of his cup. After a while, he said, "Serhan."

"Yes, Gage?"

"My name was Khatijah."

Over his veil, the Dead Man's eyes did not widen. Instead he nodded with satisfaction, as if he had won some bet with himself. "You're a woman."

"I was," said the Gage. "Now I'm a Gage."

"It's supposed to be a selling point, isn't it? Become a Faceless Man and never be uncertain, abandoned, forsaken again."

"You sound like you've given it some thought."

The Dead Man regarded the Gage. The Gage tilted his featureless head down, giving the impression that he regarded the stem of his cup and the tops of his metal hands.

"And yet here you are," the Dead Man said.

"And yet here I am." The Gage shrugged.

"Stop that constant shrugging," the Dead Man said.

"When you do," said the Gage.

ONE LAST, GREAT ADVENTURE

ELLEN KUSHNER & YSABEAU S. WILCE

THE HERO IS fashionably late to the ball. He saunters through the ballroom doors, shrugging off the footman's offer to divest him of velvet cloak and magnificently feathered hat. At the top of the stairs, he pauses, surveys the throngs below him, one negligent hand propped on his sword pommel, the other propped on the curve of his hip. He is smiling, as well a hero should.

Although the Hero needs no introduction, the steward introduces him anyway, bellowing over the vigorous music, the vigorous conversation. Those party-goers who arrived unfashionably on time turn away from the music, away from the conversation, and begin to applaud. Who would not applaud such a man, who slew the Lamia of Jengti in single combat, who turned back the invading hordes of Xana, and who, during the bloating sickness, crossed the Ice Ocean to bring back medicine for the city? The people of the City State Asteria love him. He has just returned from a three month campaign up in the highlands, helping their ally, the Sarifather of Irk, rid his kingdom of a pesky dragon, and he's been missed.

The Hero is a mercenary, but he's *their* mercenary.

The ball is not in the Hero's honor, but that does not stop him from being mobbed by well-wishers as he comes down the sweeping staircase. They shake his hand, and pat his back, and ask him to dance, and offer him drinks, all of which he waves away with a good natured laugh. By inches, he makes his way to the dais, where sits the Elector of Asteria, watching the hubbub with a fond eye.

The Hero kisses the Elector's hand, and is warmly received in return. After he extends his well-wishes on her birthday, he is swept away by the Elector's Heir to the roulette table, where he puts his fabulous luck to work at winning a large sum of gold. Later he charms the crowd with a vigorous horn-pipe solo, orates a touching toast to the birthday girl, and quickly dispatches a kettle-snake that somehow managed to crawl in through an open door and help itself to the oyster bar.

Later still, when the ball is called closed by the steward, and the rest of the guests have been stuffed, drunken and exhausted, into their carriages, the Hero slips through the darkened hallways of the Elector's palace, evading the drowsy guards, and climbs the one hundred and fifty steps to the top of the Star Tower. He arrives at the top, puffing and a bit winded, for the steps are steep and very narrow. But the Elector is waiting for him inside, and she doesn't mind that he's a bit sweaty, not at all.

Even later, they lie wrapped in fur blankets, before the fire, and look upward, through the glass ceiling at the star-studded sky. The moon has long since set, but to the south, the darkness is slightly washed with green. The comet will be rising soon.

"I'm getting old," the Hero says with a sigh. "Once this time of night would have felt too early. Now it feels too late."

"Oh, tut," says the Elector, who is older than the Hero by at least fifteen years, and still feels in her prime. Their exertions reopened the dragon scratch on the Hero's thigh, and they are both now liberally streaked with blood, but neither feels like leaving their cocoon to attend to the mess. Their limbs are entangled in the most perfect comfort, and because of the glass above, the room is cold.

"I should retire," the Hero says, yawning. "I'm thinking of retiring, actually."

"And what would you do then, I wonder? Take up knitting?" The Elector toys with the scar on his shoulder, received years ago in a fight with an egregore.

"You don't know how it is, darling," he complains. "People trying to kill you all the time, facing death, pretending you don't care—"

"No, I don't know about any of that," the Elector answers. She has weathered six assassination attempts, given birth to three children, and faced down two coups, all with a smile on her face. But that's not heroic, that's just life.

"I think about it... stopping. Sleeping late in the morning, not being responsible for anyone's well-being. But then I think: What's my legacy? What will I have left behind? What will they sing of in the evenings when I'm gone, and the next hero's come in to slay nameless beasts with his well-named sword...? And I think to myself: one last adventure.

One last great adventure to go out on... And then I can buy a small house in the country and grow fat on apple dumplings."

"Well if that's really what you want, I may be able to help." The Elector slithers from the fur blankets, goes to her desk, pawing through the mess. "Are you familiar with Illyria?"

"It's west, somewhere, isn't it?"

The Elector has found what she was looking for, and now she turns back to the Hero. The comet has risen fully now, flooding the room with green light, turning her long gray hair silvery, turn the dried blood on her stomach and thighs emerald. "Far west. It's a small country, not much to commend it. Some decent rubies. A few songs. And this."

He catches the chain she lobs at him. The pendant hits him square on the chest. He holds it up, sees a dangling gold locket set with a circle of tiny rubies. Inside is a gorgeously rendered portrait of a small pair of bare feet. The feet are young and soft, fragile looking. They are feet that have never walked a mile, or climbed a fence, or worn an ill-fitting shoe.

"Is this a joke?" the Hero asks. He is finding these small feet strangely stirring. They look so defenseless. The toes remind him of little pearls.

"Illyria is a hilly country. They like feet there. Their poets say the feet are the root of the soul. Or something." She fusses with some papers, not looking at him. "And besides, some people find feet to be very erotic."

"Some do." Now he too rises from the fur blankets, to fill his jorum with wine poured from the clay jug warming on the hob. He tosses the wine back, and begins to dress. "But what should I do in Illyria?"

"Along with feet, what Illyria is rich in, is monsters. Strange, complicated, hard-to-kill ones. One monster in particular is causing the King of Illyria a lot of consternation. He has sent out a diplomatic circular seeking a hero to slay this monster."

"Has he no heroes of his own?"

"Apparently not. But he does have a daughter with beautiful feet."

"What is wrong with this princess that she cannot slay her own monster?"

"Not everyone is so enamored of swordplay, my love. And anyway, in Illyria they prefer their ladies to be delicate and decorative." The Elector returns to the snug nest of blankets, watches the Hero as he sits in a chair, pulls on one boot.

He says casually, "You mentioned songs. Is there, perhaps a song in which a hero slays a monster and wins the hand of the princess, and the rights to a kingdom rich in rubies?"

"Now, as to that, you must ask your jongleur. My acquaintance with their legends and art forms extends only as far as that embassy ball I attended, in which feet were greatly celebrated in art and song, but woefully trampled in dance." The Elector arches one of her own elegant feet, and lays it in his lap. He massages it idly with his large and capable hands. "But I imagine the standard rules apply."

"It's a long time," he says with a roguish grin, "since I was a foot soldier."

THE HERO HAD started small, the third son of a highborn family in a country far to the north, which he has never cared to name. In that country's tradition, the third son is the steward of the land, but the Hero did not care to be a steward. His personality was charmingly amoral, and his inclinations were towards flamboyant actions. But those qualities were reserved for the first son, with maybe a bit left over for the second. The third son was to be sober and attentive to the family's extensive holdings, from which derived most of the family's income and influence. He saw no heroics in pumpkins or wheat, so he left, leaving behind his family name, taking with him only his ambitions.

He went south, joined the Elector's army as a private, and rose through the ranks to captain. He fought in her name as she expanded her territories, and in this fighting he made his own name as one who was reckless and bold, who was fair in battle, would honor the terms of a surrender, and who led from in front, not from behind. Then, bored with discipline and taking orders, he resigned his commission, and put together a small hand-picked crew of toughs and renegades, men who would fight to the death for the right price. Together, they embarked upon a glittering career as mercenaries, and with each campaign their fame grew.

But now, almost thirty years later, the Hero is ready to put his sword down. The knee he broke when a wyvern fell on it aches when it rains. The lung-full of dragon smoke he sucked in fifteen years ago still makes him wheeze. He has lost a toe to a shark-shifter, broken his nose in a battle with a catoblepas, and still has nightmares about being trapped for a week in a troll's nest. His horse seems taller and the ground harder and field rations harder to digest. Wedding a sweet young princess and settling down to rule a small but rich kingdom sounds to him like an excellent retirement plan.

And so the next day finds him waiting for the Illyrian envoy in one of the Elector's lesser receiving rooms. He's wearing his best doublet, his best trunk hose, his best sleeves. Golden earrings gleam against his dark skin. His black hair is caught in a gold clasp. He doesn't look at all like a hard-bitten mercenary. He looks like a prince.

"What if she's an idiot?" Reynard says.

Typically, Reynard has not bothered to dress up. He wears the same tattered rusty red robe whenever, what-ever. Since it's never in style, it's never out of style either. Unlike heroes, jongleurs of his caliber have no reason to try to impress with their clothes. When he sings or tells his tales, most people close their eyes to listen harder. Now, Reynard quits his pacing and perches on the velvet settee, hands clasped in his lap.

"As long as the princess is rich, I don't care." The Hero helps himself to a sugar plum. Since he's in constant fighting trim, he never has to watch his waistline.

"Perhaps they are her best feature." Reynard waves the dish away; he doesn't fight. He's been with the Hero ever since the Hero rescued him from a nasty trap he was caught in up in the Refusian Mountains. Like the Hero, he, too, has no place of origin, not that he'll admit to. He knows the songs and stories of many lands, and plenty of good riddles, too.

He says: "What if she's a scold?"

"Let her scold! My hearing is half shot already. Is my buckler on straight?"

"You look perfect and you know it," Reynard says. "What if she's an idiot and a scold and ugly besides?"

"Why then," the Hero says fondly, "I still have you."

Reynard snuggles up to him, and when the Illyrian envoy enters the room, he sees only a handsome dark man with a fox tucked under his arm. The Hero is feeding it sugarplums.

"How much farther is it to the palace?" the Hero asks. He tries to ask casually, aware that even so he risks sounding like a child on the road to granny's. He is game but disgruntled; he's no longer used to not being the one in charge of an expedition. They've been on the road for three weeks, with various modes of transportation: a ship down the coast, barges up river, and now horse-back. And yet, they don't seem any closer to arriving.

Illyria is a much drier land than he had expected. And a redder one, besides. Each day seems hotter, and they left the last tree behind two days ago. Now it's red rocks and cactus, and, at the watering holes, the occasional scrubby thornbush. The only green is a green by courtesy; at home, he would have called it gray. But things are different, here. The sky above is as blue as well-tempered steel.

"Surely that third river was the last one we had to cross?" The 'river' had had no water in it. If the Envoy hadn't identified it as a river, the Hero would have thought it just another wash. The desert was criss-crossed with washes, proof that some day it would rain. But not today.

From the back of his grey gelding, the muffled Envoy sighs and answers, "I'm afraid the map is a bit of a muddle."

"You're *afraid*?" The snappish redhead who rides at the Hero's side turns his head to the Envoy, lightning quick. When he isn't singing or telling stories, nothing but quips and pleasantries ever fall from his lips. It annoys the Envoy no end. "My dear sir," continues the redhead, closing in for the punchline; "if *you're* afraid, imagine how the rest of us feel."

"Reynard." The Hero holds up his hand, and the jongleur stills, as if by magic.

"I only meant," the Envoy says with forced patience, "that things are not exactly what they seem. On the map. We are not used to describing things as if we see them from above. Our maps, the ones our people use, are drawn from the foot's eye view. Foreigners find them incomprehensible."

"A map in translation," the Hero says. "I see."

"But we must arrive before dark," the Envoy intones ominously, and the Hero does not need to ask why.

He betrays no disappointment when they come to the palace. After all, it's not as though he'd been shown a picture of *it* surrounded by rubies. Nobody said it would be huge and splendid. And it's not. Just a long building, melting into the hilltop it sits upon. Made of dried mud, painted a faded blue, with a red tile roof. They cross a moat full of prickly pear cactus, pass through a fence made of tall ocotillo spines. A simple house, but well-fortified.

And the forbidding mud walls hold a secret: a courtyard brilliant with purple and red bougainvillea, fragrant with fruit trees: oranges, lemons, fat red pomegranates. A stone fountain burbles refreshingly in the center of the courtyard. Above, the second floor balcony is lined with people, silently watching their arrival.

"Oh, good," says Reynard; "I love an audience." But he dismounts wearily, and says nothing more.

Before the Hero can follow suit, he is approached by a big man draped in a molting bear-skin, holding a stirrup-cup. The man does not speak any tongue the Hero is familiar with from his travels, but the ever-serviceable Envoy translates as the Hero is enthusiastically greeted with the cup and, once he has drunk and dismounted, an embrace. He still hasn't figured out who the man is—could be the King, or the chief of security, for all he knows—but it doesn't matter for now. Plenty of time tonight for reccy work. There will be a feast. There always is.

The welcome cup is promising, though; it implies brief hospitality, followed by a rest. He's exhausted, and glad to be led to a hot bath. Once, he could ride all day and feast all night. Now he looks forward to his bed.

But first, as he predicted: the feast. The food is simple but ample. It's not like anything he's tasted before—everything is fiery hot, or seems to involve maize in one form or another—but he guesses he'll get used to it in time. There's plenty of cool, fizzy ale to put the fire out.

Reynard's songs are well-received, even if the words are not understood. Reynard is well-versed in many languages and probably can speak this one, too, but he likes to lead with his best material. And not to reveal all he knows.

The bear-skin man does turn out to be the King. No crown, but a very impressive jade earring. You'd think he'd have broken out the rubies tonight, but nothing doing. He grins a lot, and slaps the Hero on the shoulder, his bad shoulder, alas. But he grins back; no need to get on the wrong side of his prospective father-in-law.

The Princess does not appear until the sweet is served; in fact, there are no other women at the feast at all. The Hero, used to the casual egalitarianism of the Elector's court, finds that somewhat jarring. The Princess turns out to be a small, nervous girl, her hair in elaborate braids. No rubies there, either, though some nice enameled hairpins. She wears heavily-embroidered red velvet slippers on her feet, which are larger than the portrait made them appear. Maybe it's the embroidery.

All in all, not what the Hero had hoped for, but it could have been much, much worse, so he will not complain. The Princess pours him tea with shaking hands, and smiles tremulously when he drinks it. It's over-brewed, bitter and skunky, but he smiles his thanks. Heroes must operate heroically on many levels.

Eventually, the Hero brings up the Monster himself. He's been waiting for the King to mention it, but the King seems to have forgotten why he's there. Unaccountably nervous, the King. Probing questions receive vague answers.

Where can the Monster be found? In the hills, somewhere. Or possibly the sky. What does it look like? Big. How big? Bigger, apparently, than a man flapping his arms in a terrifying manner. It flies, then? Maybe. Unless it doesn't. It has claws, or possibly extra sets of hands, or talons.

"It can take many forms, this monster," the Envoy explains. "It is devious. Cunning."

The Hero smiles to himself. He doesn't care what form it takes, or if it's devious, cunning, or smells like a poopy diaper and can sing five-part madrigals with itself. He's never met a monster he couldn't kill. He'll kill this one, too. And then he will claim his reward and be done with heroics for good.

The Envoy communicates this to the King, prettying up the sentiment, of course. They agree he will go monster hunting in the morning. Even if they don't actually find it then, he can get the lay of the land, and show off a little to give them confidence.

The Hero doesn't care that the palace is small, or the country clearly not rich. As long as the bed is soft, he'll be happy.

It is.

THE HERO WAKES in the soft bed to utter darkness and the susurrus of movement. Slowly he moves his hand, touches the warm steel that lies by his left side. He'd gone to sleep with the curled bulk of Reynard pressed against his right side. That pressure is now gone, but not surprisingly. At night, Reynard has a tendency to wander. He listens to the darkness, hears nothing more. But he knows he is not alone. He waits for the danger to declare itself, and declare it does, with the strike of a flint. A spark leaps, and then lights a small oil lamp, flaring green eyes.

"By the spotted god, I almost killed you," the Hero complains. "Why did you not declare yourself?"

"I found the Princess," the jongleur says, instead of answering.

The Hero sits up in astonishment.

"What do you mean?"

"The Princess. They've got her locked up in a storeroom. Not the girl from the feast. The real Princess."

"That wasn't the real Princess?"

"No. I'm sure of it. I recognized her feet."

"Why is she locked up in a storeroom?"

"I don't know. I think we should leave. Get out of here while we can. I don't like the smell of any of this."

The Hero is painfully aware that when Reynard doesn't like the smell of something, it's usually because that something stinks. But the soft bed... and the comfortable manor house... and his retirement. They are hundreds of leagues away from Asteria, and he has exactly three hundred dromas in his purse, five hundred more buried in a cave in the Pachego Mountains, and seventy-nine the Lord of Ravensgill owes him from a long night of euchre. That's not enough to retire on.

And how can he return to the Elector, and tell her it did not work out? That he ran?

Plus he'd really like to know why the real Princess is tied up in the cellar, and a false princess was presented to him.

THE HERO'S DIM light plays off the storeroom's crock-lined walls. A ham hanging from the ceiling almost cracks him in the head. If you can say nothing else about the King, he is well prepared for winter. Or a long siege. Reynard trots before him, leading the way. He would prefer to run, but he understands that a hero has his honor.

They come to a halt in front of a brass-bound door.

Reynard pauses to sniff the crack at the bottom appreciatively. "The stillroom," he explains. "They've got a great vinegar mother starter. Pickles must be amazing."

Reynard will have been in the room already, to bring back word of the Princess's feet; but now he just stands there. It is the Hero's place to open the door to the Rescue.

Still, a hero knows better than to rush into what could be a trap. On the other side of the stillroom door, the Hero holds the light low, not to reveal himself. In the corner, propped up against a giant clay pickle jar, is a sad tangle of clothes from which stick out two very dirty bare feet. The Hero recognizes them instantly. He has looked at their portrait a hundred times. He is wearing it around his neck now.

Still, he approaches the bundle slowly, with his sword drawn.

Reynard shows no such caution. He trots right over to the Princess's bare foot and nudges it with his nose. She comes awake quickly, flipping and flapping like a fish, for the ropes that bind her allow no better movement.

"Have you come to kill me?" she spits. Unlike the people upstairs, she speaks a kind of basic form of Middle Standard. Curious.

"Is there a reason I should?" the Hero asks.

"Monsters need no reason!"

Reynard noses the girl's foot again, and she tries to jerk it away.

"I'm not a monster!" the Hero protests.

"Untie me then, and prove it."

"Tell me why I should first. Then I will be more comfortable untying you."

"My feet are numb. Numb and grimsome. It is a disgrace. You must not look at them."

Politely, he looks over at a shelf full of preserved fruit of some kind. It is impossible to tell, in this light, what kind it is.

She follows his gaze. "And they do not feed me."

A slash of the Hero's sword and a dried sausage falls into his grasp.

The girl glares at him. "Most heroic. I see now. Yes, you are the Hero, with my portrait on your neck. My father sent you, to slay monsters and marry me. Are you done with the slaying? It matters not; I shall not marry you!"

"The feeling may be mutual, madam. But we get nowhere if you are not forthcoming with the reason you are in this situation."

"Give me some meat and I will tell you."

So the Hero cuts off a couple slices and offers them to Reynard, who takes them delicately, and carries them over to the Princess. Still bound, she takes the slices from his muzzle to her lips, and gobbles them down.

"Now," she says imperiously, somewhat spoiling the effect by trying to wipe grease off her chin with her shoulder, "are you going to release me or not?"

One of her pretty feet, which she'd tucked up demurely under the edge of her grubby gown, peeks out a little. Good gods, the Hero thinks; is she flirting with me?

If she is, he knows this game.

"It depends," he says. He slouches elegantly, one hand negligently on his pommel. "If you refuse to wed your rescuer, then what's in it for me?"

"Ah," she snaps back; "but I think you do not yet do the slaying. A braggart is no hero."

"But a hero can still be a braggart. What have you got against heroes, anyway?"

She draws her feet back in. "In the general, nothing. But to be forced to marry the one, just because he knows how to make the Monster go SPLAT with his sword... How is this for me the what's in it?"

The Hero's just a sucker for girls trying out slang. He crouches, loosens the ropes. As soon as she is free, the girl clambers unsteadily to her feet, grabs the nearest jar and pops the lid. She doesn't bother with a spoon.

"Ah!" she sighs happily, licking her lips. "This was the worst! To be looking always, and never tasting." She runs her finger around the bottom of the jar. "This is really quite good. Pumpkin. I like the spice. When I home, these I take."

"Home...? But surely you live here?"

The Princess gapes at him. Her teeth, like her toes, are little pearls. "But surely I do not! You think this—*this?*—is the house of my father?!"

The Hero sits down on a barrel. Between the long journey, the feast, the ale, and the tiny bit of sleep he's gotten, this whole thing is beginning to feel like a dream to him. It has a certain dream logic. If he had to slay something now, he could probably do it on sheer nerve, but untangling riddles he prefers to do by day and well-rested. He pops open another jar of pumpkin jam. It *is* good.

"You may," he says wearily, "remember a certain bargain we made over sausage? I have yet to see your end of it fulfilled. Why. Are. You. Here?"

She sits forward, her posture much improved by food and blood circulation. Oh, he thinks; to be so young as to bounce back that quickly from being tied up!

"You know, I think," she says, "our land it is plagued by the Monsters. And my father, he seeks the Hero to kill them. The men of our land, them we cannot trust—for many of them are with sympathy for the Monsters, yes! Many of them even have the blood in their families, though they will not say. And those that do not, they are villains, lowly men of the soil unworthy. Do you see?"

He doesn't, quite, but he nods to keep her going.

"My father the King, may his name be exalted although I am quite mad at him and wish never to step in his shadow again, he hates the Monsters so much, he wishes them all dead." Another nod; this is par for the course. "My father the King seeks a man to lead us in battle, to slay them in the dawn time. And I would be wed to that man, no matter where his feet have took him!"

She shakes her head. Her ash-colored hair, loose from all her exertions, falls in snaky, dusty ringlets down her modest front. "This cannot be. I will not wed nobody like that. But it is true, my family's throne will never be free if the Monsters are not put down.

"So I think: I will kill them myself! Then I make my own choice." She looks up into his face to see if she is shocking him. He thinks of the Elector and her Heir, and nods sagely, his face a mask of politic sympathy. "Thus I take my little brother's sword, and I climb out my window but I do not have to go through the cactus which is good because I only bring the one dress, and I have a good horse and know to saddle so I make away before anyone know it first. And thus I come here, to their lair! But they—"

"Wait." The Hero holds up one hand. He almost laid it on her shoulder, but you don't do that, not yet. "This house—with the sausage, and the very decent jam—this is the Monsters' lair?"

"Oh, yes."

"The ones who made the jam?"

She nods, unperturbed by the dream-logic of the thing.

Ha! Well, that explains the remoteness and inaccessibility of the 'palace'. It's a hideout, not a royal seat. These people want his protection, probably from the King; no wonder they were evasive about monsters. So did their Envoy deceive the Elector? Or—

She interrupts his thoughts, leaning forward to say earnestly, "Do not be deceive by their looks being like us." Her eyes get very wide. "These Monsters are the terrible. They are—how do you say it?" She utters a word that sounds like *asfdasfddfs*.

At his side, Reynard mutters something softly. He can't quite catch it—and since Reynard has not declared himself yet to the Princess, the Hero knows from experience that it is not his place to ask the fox to speak.

Her next words make it clear that he was right.

"*Animals!*" she whispers. "They are not human, not at all. They wear human face, but their hearts are monster, and too their shape, when they will!"

Reynard bristles, growling.

The Princess goes on heedlessly, "For years they live amongst us, pretending to be like. Because my grandfather's father's father, he conquered this land and made them leave or promise never to do their *asfdasfddfs* tricks again. Ha!" She spits delicately, for emphasis, it seems. "My toe." Curse words never translate well in any language. "But they are true to their nature. Untrue to us. At night, when they wish it, they make the shapes of animals, and then," she breathes, like a child telling ghost stories, "then they run in our villages and eat our young and ravage our maidens and steal our coinage."

Well, isn't that what Monsters always do? He nods gravely, and she continues, encouraged, "They say they own this country before we come here to make them civilized like us. We must defeat them or give up our land. And that may never be. That is what my father says. I wonder sometimes because my nursie she was *asfdasfddfs*. And I love her very much, she no monster. But she had live with us a long time, and civilized. These, they are bad!"

Reynard's growls grow perilously close to speech. The Hero places a cautioning hand on his head, then slices a little of what's left of the sausage. But before he can offer it to the fox, to his surprise the Princess says softly, "Oh! May I feed it to him?"

May she? It's an interesting moment. The Hero hands the Princess the meat, and she holds it out to the fox, very slowly and gently. This, he thinks, is a girl who has not had pets of her own.

Reynard sniffs it for form's sake, as if he did not know what it was, or who was offering. For a second, the Hero thinks he will snap her fingers, but instead, he snaps the sausage, tosses it showily in the air, catches it in his mouth and swallows it whole. The Princess laughs. She has a nice laugh. The Hero lets out a little of the tension of the night. Peace offering accepted, although he's unsure why. He can't wait to hear Reynard's take on everything. Did he really not realize they were in a house of Shifters, himself?

"I like this little one," she says, bending to pet him.

Reynard nips her fingers. She squeaks, then bats him playfully on the ear. He leans in to her. She scratches him behind his neck, which he adores—but seldom lets the Hero do.

"This one," she croons, "he understand. He is very sweet." Reynard leans into her, cuddling. What is he up to? Gaining her trust, the Hero supposes. Playing some foxish game of strategy.

The Princess sighs, looks up at the Hero again. "So we are understanding, now?" She puts the fox aside, clambers to her feet. She leans unsteadily against a pickle barrel. "Your sword you give me, and the Monster I kill."

The girl has sand, the Hero has to give her that. Here she stands in a storeroom, defenseless and covered in jam, and she is sticking to her plan. But he can't give her his sword, of course.

"All of them?" he asks.

"Mmm, no. That is not possible, even to *you*, I think." She taps the barrel, thinking. "I kill just one; then I am Hero. I go home. My father cannot choose for me then."

She's let her foot peep out again from underneath the bedraggled hem of her gown. A ruby ring sparkles on one toe. "Your sword?"

The Hero hesitates. He's a man of action, even of strategy—battle strategy. He is clever about movements, and terrain, and how other people who think that way are likely to jump. It's not his job to figure out who the enemy is. That's Reynard's job. But Reynard is licking the Princess's fingers, seemingly unconcerned with her genocidal plots.

"I make friends with *asfdasfddfs* when I am

Queen, I think," she says. "That will be best for all, and no more killing nonsense. We go, now?"

The Hero has learned one piece of diplomatic strategy from Reynard: the stall. Best to leave the Princess snug in the storeroom whilst he and Reynard discuss their course of action.

"But if I release you, it would be to warn the Monsters of what we plan." (Oh, dear; now he's picking up her diction. He does that, when he travels.)

"Yes," she replies; "that is right. Good thinking, Hero. You tie me up again—but loosely—and I will be so helpless and hungry they will pity me. And then—BAMM! Ha."

The Hero smiles. She's brave, and has a good sense of fun.

So back to the filthy floor she goes, and he ties her up again, but loosely.

He stands up, taking the light with him. Her voice at his feet is suddenly small. "I wonder if... if your fox might like to stay with me? Just a little while? Until light comes again?"

Of course he feels sorry for the girl; but if she wants to be a hero, she needs to learn to wait in the dark, alone. He wants to get Reynard back up to the room, so they can discuss and strategize. He wants Reynard's take on the shifting situation. Ha. He puns when he's tired. But it's Reynard's choice.

"Thank you," says the Princess softly. He lowers the light a tidge, just enough to see the red fox curled at her feet.

DAWN IS BREAKING; there's movement about the house. The Hero heads stealthily back to his room. But when he gets to his door, he finds it open. Inside is a whirl of screeching Illyrians. The bear-skinned 'King' rushes towards him, gesticulating and shouting. He's swept up in the whirl, and borne down the hallway.

Did they discover his discovery of the Princess? Everyone is shouting. Some are waving short swords; others brandish bows. The Hero looks around frantically for the Envoy; he hopes they are not shouting *hang him or chop him* or something equally unpleasant, but without the Envoy he has no idea. No one has disarmed him yet, which is reassuring. They are making enough noise, surely, that Reynard will be warned.

The horde bursts out into the courtyard; the sun is barely over the roof ridge and already its rays feel like hammer-blows on his back. The gate is open; they hustle across the cactus moat, and through the ocotillo stockade to a stand of nervous-looking horses. There's the Envoy, holding the bridle of a beautiful paint horse.

"What is going on?" the Hero demands.

"The Monster! Come, mount, we have no time to lose! He catches the dawn!"

As they ride away, pell-mell, the Hero looks over his shoulder, hoping to catch a glimpse of a small red shape, rushing to catch up with them. But the dust cloud is too thick and obscuring.

EVEN IN EARLY morning, it is hot out on the Illyrian hillside. The smells of sage and juniper mingle with the dust and old, old yellow rock. He wonders where the rubies are. Maybe right underneath him....

They'd ridden to an outcropping of boulders.

There, they dismounted and picketed the horses, and there the monsters—who looked like men and who hadn't acted the least bit monstrous—had given him a club made of some sort of polished hardwood, its tip embedded with shards of black glass as sharp as his sword's blade; and then they insisted that he take a swig from the leather *bota*. A grassy-tasting liquid that burnt the roof of his mouth and made him feel momentarily light-headed. He accepted the club politely, planning to drop it behind a bush when he could.

What is the Monster that the monsters are afraid of? A bigger Shifter? A renegade, a rogue?

From his stance on the hillside, he looks around hopefully for Reynard; but still no sign of the small red fox. This, more than the approaching Monster, makes him nervous. Perhaps he hadn't heard the commotion from the storeroom? No, Reynard can hear a mouse a mile away. It's unlike Reynard to stay so far behind out of choice. He must be working strategy. That's it.

There's sudden silence. The Hero looks up, momentarily blinded by the sunlight. And so he feels it before he hears it, hears it before he sees it. The tremble of rock, the rhythm of hooves. Look up, look right, and across that little hill... and there it is, magnificent and undaunted, against the sun.

A four-legged bird, wings more than the usual two, hard to tell when they're folded back, but jet black, obsidian black, gleaming with a million colors in the sun. Its legs are shiny, but end in spiked hooves. Its eyes are rubies. Its beak is enormous.

The man next to him is trembling. He's breathing a word, over and over again... it's so clearly "HIM!

THAT! HIM!" that the Hero needs no translation. The terror is palpable.

The Monster wheels and cavorts upon the hill, as if announcing itself, as if daring anyone to approach it. It pauses, then, its wheeling more focused, purposeful. The great beak turns from side to side, ruby eyes scanning the terrain. It is looking for them.

This is his moment. Time for thinking, time for planning is over. The Hero charges, sword upraised.

And the Monster draws a weapon of its own.

Oh, six-fingered gods, it's a man! A man robed in feathers and jewels, but a man nonetheless, up on a horse so he has the advantage, but that's easy enough, the Hero has killed plenty of valiant steeds in his time (pity, though, about this one).

Unhorsed, the feathered man leaps to the high ground, defends himself with massive strokes of his strangely serrated blade, formed of a shining black so dark that when the sun catches it, it turns white, or all colors at once. Bastard. The Hero is whistling through his teeth, an old habit from his training days that he's not even aware of doing.

The creature puts up a good fight. He has a hard time thinking of him as a man. The feathers and jewels are beautiful, distracting... they should slow the fellow down, but they seem to give him assurance. Maybe he's using magic. Probably he is. The elaborate mask should be denying him peripheral vision, but instead he seems to see out of the side of his head, like a bird. The cape should be weighing him down, but he's stronger than the Hero; he feels that when their blades collide, and the force of the obsidian blade nearly pushes him off the hillside. Damn.

The others are shouting something at him, but it's

from the direction of his deaf ear. And do they really think they can advise him how to fight?

The Hero begins to work at disrobing his opponent, to separate him from his magic accoutrements. Tricky, but fun. Very tricky. Trying to stay alive while aiming for a shoulder seam... Trying to breathe in the hot sun while figuring out how the headpiece attaches to the neck... The Hero is slowing down. This is not going well.

He seems to have shrunk to the size of a small animal; he is looking up at a huge black blade coming down at him from a cerulean sky. No, he is on his knees, that's what it is. They're going to hurt like seven devils later, but for now he must use them to get up. Up is where he belongs, not rolling and dodging, eating dust like a desert snake. He can't get a purchase. It's like the land is pulling him down, demanding he yield his bones to it before it can even belong to him for the few years remaining to him. He was planning to retire here, not to expire. Not yet.

Dimly he realizes someone new is shouting over the din, and that shouting is not words of encouragement either. He raises his head, sees through the grit a pair of dirty, perfectly formed feet.

"STOP!!!" screams the Princess. The rest of her words, foreign, are lost to him.

The feathered creature stops. The Hero struggles to his feet, wipes sweat from his eyes, finds his fighting stance, watches the other for his next move—and is utterly astonished by the fact that the creature has begun to dance. It's a lively pace, a sprightly jig that seems to be designed to keep his feet from touching the earth—or, no, to get a bright red fox to let go of his legs.

The Hero is touched beyond measure; Reynard has never fought for him before—and he is horrified to realize that means he must need him to.

The creature stamps and shouts, still trying to shake Reynard off his lower legs. The Hero realizes he must try to attack the top half, the feathered cape, flaring into wings, the beaked head. Because of the fox dance, it's hard to say where the feathered man will be from moment to moment.

The creature is ignoring the Hero, now, concentrating on getting rid of Reynard. Which is good, because he's afraid to come in too close, lest he hurt the fox by mistake. And besides, his sword has gotten awfully heavy. Must be the heat. The fox is a flurry of motion. The Hero is mesmerized by the dancing colors: foxfur rust, tailtip black, rainbow obsidian blade, ruby eye, feather black, rainbow blade, foxblood red—

"No!" the Princess is shouting. Is she defending the Monster, or Reynard? He should give her his impossibly heavy sword after all, see how much luck she has with it. She's lifting something dark and bright: the club they'd given him. She holds it high above her head, and flings it over both their heads, right at the feathered creature.

It hits with a huge thud. The creature's arms fly upward. Is it going to take off from the hillside? No; the obsidian blade goes sailing out instead. Empty-handed, the creature seems to shrink. It—he—falls forward, face-plants in the dust, head askew as the beak turns to one side, reaching for but never nailing the fox lying utterly still beside it.

The Hero stands panting, gasping for water, no longer sure of his status. His sword feels right in his hand. The Monster is dead. Why is no one cheering and bringing him a drink?

At his feet, a girl sits in the dust of the hillside, cradling a ragged bundle of red fur in her lap. She is crooning to it, and stroking its bloody pelt.

IN THE END, he decides to return to Asteria.

The King of Illyria is dead, slain on a dusty hillside by a mysterious stranger while out hunting for his missing daughter, to bring her back to her duty. The Princess will become Queen of the land, now—its first female ruler from this line of invaders. She is assured the throne by virtue of the support of the Shifters, whose rights she has vowed to sustain at the price of their sworn loyalty, and a tribute of seventy-seven jars of pumpkin jam each year.

And she will be marrying an Outlander, a clever red-haired man with a beautiful voice, a nice line in verse, and a pronounced limp from a healing wound. Their time together in the storeroom had been short, but intensely romantic. The last of the Princess's antipathy for Shifters had vanished away, and Reynard had realized two feet, when they were so well formed, were just as good as four.

They asked him to stay, of course. He'd make a wonderful ornament to their court, and a godfather to their children. He could help train the new queen in fighting, and later her children, as well.

But he is suddenly homesick for a place he never thought was home. He'd like to swim in the Asteria River again, and to fish in it, too. He'd like to sit in the orchards of Asteria, and pick apples from their trees. He'd like to taste the fine pastries of the Asterian court, and the sweet red wine.

He'd like to see the Elector again.

He takes two of the three hundred dromos from his purse, plus his winnings from last night's game of something enough like euchre for him to have been successful with the younger set, and a gold hairpin from the grateful princess, and goes off to the Bazaar to see if he can find the Elector a really nice ruby ring.

There will be a Bazaar. There always is.

THE HIGH KING DREAMING

DANIEL ABRAHAM

THE HIGH KING is not dead but dreaming, and his dreams are of his death.

The sun is bright in the blue expanse of sky, the meadow more beautiful than it had ever been in life because he sees it from above. The banners of the kingdoms he unified shift in the gentle breeze: Stonewell, Harnell, Redwater, Leftbridge, Holt. The kings who bent their knees before him do so again, and again with tears in their eyes. The Silver Throne is there, but empty. The scepter and whip lie crossed on its seat. His daughter, once the princess and now the queen, sits at its foot, her body wrapped in mourning grey. The pyre on which his body rests has no fuel beneath it. No acrid stench of pitch competes with the wildflowers' perfume. His beard is white, bright in the sun, and as full as frost. His shoulders are thick, as are his arms and his thighs. His eyes are closed, but his lips hold the memory of a smile. The blade Justice rests on his chest, weighing him down in death as it had in life. His cold fingers hold it easily. He is like a statue of himself, and the legend still unwritten below him should be *Grace and Power*.

He does not recall what brought him low, nor does it matter. He rose in an age of war when all nations stood against each other, and he forged peace. The Eighteen Peaks, snowcapped and bright in the spring sun, have not looked down on bloodshed in a decade. The keeps at Narrowford and Cassin store grain now. Any child may walk the Bloody Bridge at Hawthor and return across it at nightfall. Some lands he took at the point of a sword, some with a wise word, some by sharing grief with enemies who had expected their pain to draw forth only laughter, but with Justice in his hand and God in his heart, he remade the world into a better place than he had found it.

All the events of adventures of his life have strung together like individual steps in a long march that they might bring him here. But that march is not done.

In his dream, he sees the court's cunning man, withered by years and buoyed up by an endless and sometimes vicious humor. He is wearing a robe of gold, as one might at a baby's naming ceremony, and so he stands out among the mourners like a candle in darkness.

"Do not weep!" he cries, waving a staff wrapped with sage at the crowd. "Do you wail and beat your breasts when your father naps? Then do not weep! Stand tall and quiet! Be quiet, or take yourselves to the yard and play your games there. There is no call for sorrow here!"

King Abend of Holt rises, his hand on the hilt of his sword. "The High King lies dead, and you say there is no call to weep? What madness has taken you, old man?"

"The madness of knowing too much," the cunning man says. "The High King is not dead, but dreaming. He waits now in places beyond our sight, but he is not gone. All of history remains before us, and we have lost him now only because he must rest. When he is needed, the High King shall rise and Justice shall again protect the land."

His daughter looks up, and the devastation on her face falters. There is something like hope in her eyes. She looks to her father's body, sobs again, and the cunning man's staff raps her smartly on the shoulder. Smartly, but not hard.

"Would you wake him already?" he asks, and his eyes are gentle. The girl who was once the princess and is now the queen smiles as she has not in days. Perhaps that has been the cunning man's aim all along. She holds out her hand, and the cunning man kneels. She stands, her mourning robes made glorious by the sun and the sky, by her beauty and her gravity. She climbs to the Silver Throne, lifts scepter and whip in her hands, and takes the throne for the first time.

One by one, they come before her. They bend their knees. They swear again the oaths they once swore to him. And to each of them, she says *"When he is needed, he shall rise."* For some it is a comfort. For some it is a threat.

The High King dreams, and his dreams move on. Time is a different thing for him now, and he moves through it to places where the threads of fancy and prophecy are indistinguishable. He is aware of the meadow under a blanket of snow, and then he is not.

He is aware of the sepulcher around him, dark and silent. Of his body, as cold and heavy as stone, and as immune to corruption. And then he is aware of nothing, not even of being unaware.

The war boils around him suddenly. Men are dying in the fields where the crops should grow. He sees the obscene, dancing light from the fires that consume Harraw and Gant. The rich land outside the Keep of Stormcoast is barren, its woods chopped down for fires, its grain eaten by the besieging army. From the battlements of the keep, the banner of Leftbridge flies defiant. From the besieging forces, Holt. His bannermen stand one against the other, and the land is churned into a lifeless muck.

His daughter sits the Silver Throne, looking half a child to him in the unkind morning light. Her skin is ashen, her eyes hold a weariness that speaks of her fright and her uncertainty. It is also night, and she is also with the cunning man, sitting on a low stool in his private study among the great webwork of his experiments. The High King wills his eyes to open, the dream to break. Even as he sees her rise from the throne, he tries to grip the pommel of Justice, as if the sword would pull him back to the world. He dreams that his fingers move and take their grip.

"Stop," his daughter says, and he imagines that she means him. Another voice answers her. The captain of his guard. Of hers.

"Majesty?"

"Bring her to me instead."

The captain is older than he was when the High King lived. His dark eyes are webbed by the marks of age and he has fewer teeth. His black hair is white.

He nods, but does not turn away. "She has already been called to the gallows, Majesty."

"Then you should hurry," his daughter says. Her voice carries a joyless mirth that he recognizes as once he recognized her other imitations of him. The captain hurries, his footsteps echoing. The night before, she looks up at the cunning man and says, "He isn't here. I need him."

"If you needed him," the cunning man says, "he would rise. If he is not risen, then this is not the need."

"I don't know anything about war. I don't know what he would do."

"Neither did he," the cunning man says. "Not at the first."

The captain reaches the gallows and leads the prisoner away. The crows look down in disappointment not to have fresh eyes to peck or the taste of a woman's tongue.

"What would he have done?" the cunning man says, sucking at his teeth. He shrugs. "Ridden with blade in hand to the battle and enforced his will over any who stood in his way."

"I can't do that," she says. It is the whine of a child and also the sober assessment of a woman grown.

"Then the question is not what he would do, but what you shall."

The prisoner kneels before the throne. Her hair is the same auburn as Abend of Holt's. The line of her jaw is as his. The daughter of the rebel and the daughter of the unifier face each other, and the air between them holds its breath.

"You are hostage to King Holt's good behavior," the queen says. "Unfortunately your father's behavior leaves a great deal to be desired." The night before, in the cunning man's dark room, she scowls, her mind searching for something. If he is not risen, it is because this is not the need. The High King's hand relaxes from around Justice's hilt.

"Yes, Majesty," the hostage says.

"He has sentenced you to death by his actions. Your life is mine."

"I understand," she breathes.

"Then take your life to Stonewell in my name. You will write a single letter to your father asking his surrender in return for what amnesty I see fit to grant. And inform him that if he refuses, you will become Queen of Stonewell, and all lands of Holt shall devolve to you and your husband upon his death. I will inform King Merrian of Stonewell likewise. Then we shall see if he can't find the men to break this siege."

No, the High King thinks. Stonewell's recalcitrance cannot be rewarded. If he has not come out in force to put down the rebellion, he must be punished. Justice demands loyalty, but the hostage bows her head.

"Thank you, my queen."

"I'm sorry," his daughter says. Her voice is petulant, reluctant, and still she puts her hand on the hostage girl's shoulder. The girl begins to weep again.

It is a mistake, and the echoes of it will haunt her. He is certain of it, but he can dream that he is wrong. And so he imagines that the war fades, and that the deaths of the soldiers and the wounding of the land become something else. Where the bloodshed was worst, the bodies of the fallen feed the brightest grass. The High King feels the growth as if it were rising from within him, a great, warm exhalation that does not stop. For a time, he is the land, and he is rich and fruitful. His own body, sealed in stone, does not fade. A mouse comes and makes its home in the crook of his arm. It lives its full span, giving birth to its young who scatter through the field and dying beside him, its thin bones against his still pale but eternal flesh.

Songs are sung of him, and then songs are sung of the songs, changing every time until the words are like words written in dreams. The High King who brought the land together, who is the land, whose blood still flows in the veins of the queen and the water of the rivers. There is awe in the songs and reverence. And some smut as well. And some anger. He hears them all, seeing the events they recount as if they were true. He sees himself battling with Lord Souther, blade to blade, and remembers finding Souther's body after the battle, crushed under his fallen horse. The truth and the exaggeration and the lies pour together, becoming something larger, richer, and true in ways that know nothing of fact.

He is not dead but dreaming, they sing, and when the need comes, he shall rise.

The captain of his guard dies from an autumn fever. King Erald of Leftbridge dies, and his son Cormin takes his throne. The cunning man does not die but passes into a twilight that leads him out of the world. The High King hears him laughing as he goes, and knows that the old man will never be seen again by mortal eyes. There is cruelty in the sound as much as sorrow. The High King dreams soft, pleasant dreams, until they turn to nightmares.

A ray of warm sunlight heats the rich-smelling earth. Green wheat nods in the soft breeze. The distant buzz of an insect's wing, and the High King feels shrill horror run through him. He tries to scream. The insect is no larger than the head of a pin. Its black carapace is split, its wings beating so quickly they cannot be seen. Its mouth is a sharpness. He hears it land on a stalk of wheat with a boom like great stones hurled against a castle wall. The inhuman mouth touches the soft, green flesh. In the fields, the farmers toil. In the cities, the merchants and traders make their negotiations. Only the dreaming king knows that it is too late, and his cry cannot be heard.

The blight spreads like ink spilled upon a map. The sun sets upon rich fields, and rises to find them blackened and stinking. Throughout the land, the harvest fails. It has happened before. Starving springs have come and passed, but the next year is the same. Mothers make nettle tea for their babies because there is nothing else to drink. Boney cattle are slaughtered in their fields rather than let them suffer as their keepers do. Desperation smells like an empty pot left too long over the fire. He feels it in his breast, profound and sorrowful. Another blighted year, and the kingdoms will be peopled by bones. War is the only hope. A war not of justice, but necessity. A single dusty tear tracks from his closed eye. It is terrible, but it is needed. If it were only him, he might starve and die proud, but it is his daughter and the land she inherited from him. The time of need has come upon them, and he dreams with a bleak certainty that this is his waking hour.

His dreams are of his daughter, her face gaunt,

standing before her lords. Their condition fills him with dread. The great kings are shades of themselves, withered by hunger and by years. Only King Cormin of Leftbridge and Queen Sarya of Stonewall and Holt who have never seen battle are hale enough to lead an army. His peace has lasted too long. There are no war leaders left but him. The irony is bitter.

The banner of the enemy waves in the winter sun. Crimson and gold with a black star in its center. He does not know it. He sees the enemy, tall men—if they are men—with massive black eyes and ink worked into their skins. Their cheeks are too wide, their lips too thin. Their mouths are purple-black. And their teeth as sharp as a hound's. They stand in the throne room, proud and stern. Cruel horns rise from the temples of their leader, and he wears armor of silk layered upon silk layered upon silk, strong enough to stop an arrow or a sword. His voice is human, his inflections strange, musical, and unsettling. With the logic of dreams, the High King knows these are *hraki*, but he does not know what the word means.

Their leader shakes his horned head, as if in bewilderment at the High Queen's words. Her kings stand arrayed about the Silver Throne, starving but stern.

"Two more years, according to the cunning men," his daughter says. Her face is thicker than it was, no longer a girl's but a woman's. Handsome and strong. She holds the scepter and whip with a forgetfulness born of long company. They are as much extensions of her body as a swordsman's blade. "After that, our fields will be as rich as they were before. Our strength will return. But first we must weather those years. It will mean fodder for our horses and cattle. Grain for our people. Seed for our fields when the blight has run its course."

"And in return?" the *hraki* says, though he knows the answer.

The day before, his daughter is in the small council chamber he used himself. She sits at the blackwood table where his wars were planned, and her kings are with her as once they were with him.

"Do not do this," King Tennan of Redwater says, and his voice cracks on the words. "We will find another way. We are strong, my queen. We are hungry, but we are strong."

Her eyes are calm. She is in both places at once, as is her dreaming father.

"What would we *be*?" King Abbot of Harnell asks. The voice that had been strong and rolling once is wet. His eyes are rheumy.

"Changed," the High Queen says. "We would be changed." And the next day, at the same time, "In return, I will take your son as my husband. He cannot be king, for only my father's blood may sit this throne, but he will be the queen's consort. And your grandson will be High King."

Dreaming, the High King calls out. In the sepulcher, his mouth opens for the first time in years. Young Cormin of Leftbridge slams his hand upon the blackwood table. "We need not do this. We are strong. Your father would not have asked this of you. We can take what we need by force." *When he is needed, he shall rise* creaks and whispers, makes the air rich as if it were the scent of blood and smoke.

"We could take it by force. Would that be justice?" his daughter asks, mildly.

"You would take my son?" the *hraki* asks. His voice is torn between amusement and disbelief.

"I would," she says, looking down from the throne.

"Gracious queen," the horned man says, "I thank you, but this cannot be."

"There have been such unions," his daughter says. "They have been fruitful."

"Our honor does not permit that we lay with those not of our kind."

The High Queen smiles, lifts her chin. She looks like her mother. Sounds like her.

"Make an exception," she says, and the day before turns her eyes to the old men at her table. *Would that be justice?* still hangs in the air. That they cannot answer is also an answer. "Mine is not the only way, it's true. We could take to the field. Or we could accept the loans offered by the bankers in Pallan Syrai. One would mean the deaths of the innocent. The other would mean selling ourselves in all but name."

Two silences mix. Grief pulls at the High King's dreaming heart. Grief and shock and something else.

"My father found five kingdoms shattered by war," she says to the kings of the black table, "and forged them into one. You who would have been my rivals are my brother, my sister, my uncles now. My father was strong and he was just, and you changed for him. Will you not also change for me?"

"I will not command my son to do this," the *hraki* says. "But I will speak with him."

The dream shifts, and the High King is aware of a pool of still water. The stink of its stagnation fills his nostrils, and he knows it is not real. It is an image his mind has conjured to see what is too large to see. A drop of blood falls in the pool's center, and where the ripples pass, the water is made pure and sweet. A small black insect floats on its surface, its wings spread like the arms of a drowned man, and he knows the blight is gone. Not defeated, not conquered, but endured until its natural death takes it. Someday, in the way of all plagues, it will return, but for now it is sleeping. It is dreaming. This is not the need, and never was. The unbroken dream goes on. And more than that, it deepens.

Like the ripple, its movement is in all directions at once. *All history remains before us*, the cunning man says. The dream is unmoored in time now. What has been and what will be reach around like arms around the trunk of a great tree, and their fingers interlace. He dreams that he is dreaming, and that he will wake in his rooms. His child is being born, and fear has exhausted him, but the doors will open and the cunning man and the physician and the midwife will wake him with word of the birth. He cannot stay. Redwater's forces are almost at Hawthor, and if his enemy takes the Bloody Bridge all that he has fought for will fail. He knows that he should not be here, and it gives the dream a sense of terrible urgency.

The woman's cries are not of pain, but of purpose. The pain is there as well, but secondary. She is in a place of extremes, a place between being and not being, and her work is vital and profound and punishing. He loves her more than his body can contain. His teeth grind against each other, but he cannot wake. He cannot help her.

There is a desperate choking sound, an unfamiliar cough, a thin wire of a wail as much animal as human, and he weeps. The worst is past. He holds the girl wrapped in soft cloth, looks into eyes that have not yet decided what color they will be. "*I will make this world deserve you,*" he says. He remembers having said, as if it were a thing he had done years ago. And then it is a different baby he is holding, black-eyed with dark lips pulled back in a wide, joyful grin. For a moment, the babe's swimming gaze seems to find him and it shrieks with delight before it looks away again.

"It seems I have a son," his daughter says. Her voice is a tissue of exhaustion and satisfaction.

"We have a son?" a man's odd, musical voice says. He sits at her side. His horns are curved back, and not so large as his father's. His black eyes are wide with wonder.

"Well," the High Queen says, "You likely have a son, but it's certain that I do."

The horned man's expression flickers through confusion, to comprehension, to indignation, and then bursts forth in laughter. "You are a wicked, wicked woman," the queen's consort says, as he cradles her hand to his breast. The love in his black eyes is unmistakable. She chuckles with him, kisses his knuckle, lays back spent from her efforts. Her face is wide from the months of carrying her boy, and her hair is dark with sweat, and she is joyful. The mother of her family and of the land, the center of her people and her kingdom.

The High King looks into his arms, and she is red-faced, stunned, and confused. She is barely formed, helpless, and so vulnerable a chill might take her away. Curled into herself, she fits in his two hands together. The wars must end. Redwater is coming to Hawthor, and he must be stopped. If she is to live in a world that is not rocked by constant battle, Redwater must be defeated. And so, the High King dreams that he will be. For her.

And in the meadow, King Tennan of Redwater bends his knee to the new High Queen. No acrid stench of pitch competes with the wildflowers' perfume. The cunning man in his bright, celebratory robe capers and laughs and spills wisdom in jokes too subtle to fully comprehend. In her young face there is the echo of the babe that has gone before and a promise of the woman still to come. She leans forward, touches the weeping Redwater's shoulder. *When he is needed, he shall rise.*

In the street, men such as he has known mix with the new black-eyed, horned strangers. Unfamiliar dishes share the plate with the foods that once passed his lips. Around the winter bonfires, strange and musical voices rise with the smoke. They who never knew him sing songs he does not know, and also they sing of the High King who once brought peace. They sing of how he shall rise again in some coming age when he is needed. No one sings of the Bloody Bridge or of making peace with Holt, and the man they sing of seems less and less like him.

He dreams of himself in the sepulcher. No rot has touched him, but his skin is drowned in dust. The great blade Justice has rusted away to nothing. His fingers cup the shape of a hilt that has fallen away from between them. The world has moved on. His daughter has moved on. As she should.

The High King is not dead but dreaming. He dreams of his daughter and the dangers that grow from being his child. From being any man's child.

He dreams of an age that knew him. When he was not only loved, but also needed. He dreams that when she needs him again, he will rise, and he dreams that she will need him again.

He dreams, and the dreams go on forever.

ABOUT THE AUTHORS

Daniel Abraham (www.danielabraham.com) was born in Albuquerque, New Mexico, earned a biology degree from the University of New Mexico, and spent ten years working in tech support. He sold his first short story in 1996, and followed it with six novels, including fantasy series *The Long Price Quartet*, SF novel *Hunter's Run* (co-written with George R. R. Martin and Gardner Dozois), the *Black Sun's Daughter* dark fantasy series (as M. L. N. Hanover), the *Dagger and the Coin* fantasy series, the *Expanse* space opera series (as James S.A. Corey, co-written with Ty Franck), which included Hugo Award nominee *Leviathan's Wake*, and more than twenty short stories, including International Horror Guild Award-winner 'Flat Diane', Hugo and World Fantasy award nominee 'The Cambist and Lord Iron: a Fairytale of Economics.' Upcoming are new solo fantasy novel *The Tyrant's Law* and James S.A. Corey space opera *Abaddon's Gate*.

Saladin Ahmed (www.saladinahmed.com) was born in Detroit and raised in a working-class, Arab American enclave in Dearborn, MI. His short stories have been nominated for the Nebula and Campbell awards, and have appeared in *Year's Best Fantasy* and numerous other magazines, anthologies, and podcasts, as well as being translated into five foreign languages. His first novel, *Throne of the Crescent Moon*, was published in 2012 to wide acclaim, earning starred reviews from *Kirkus, Publishers Weekly* and *Library Journal*. Saladin lives near Detroit with his wife and twin children.

Elizabeth Bear (www.elizabethbear.com) was born in Hartford, Connecticut, on the same day as Frodo and Bilbo Baggins, but in a different year. She divides her time between Massachusetts, where she lives with a Giant Ridiculous Dog in a town so small it doesn't even have its own Dunkin Donuts, and western Wisconsin, the home of her partner, Scott Lynch. Her first short fiction appeared in 1996, and was followed after a nearly decade-long gap by fifteen novels, two short story collections, and more than fifty short stories. Her most recent books are Norse fantasy *The Tempering of Men* (with Sarah Monette) and an Asian-inspired fantasy, *Range of Ghosts*, and short story collection, *Shoggoths in Bloom*. Bear's *Jenny Casey* trilogy won the Locus Award for Best First Novel, and she won the John W. Campbell Award for Best New Writer in 2005. Her stories 'Tideline' and 'Shoggoths in Bloom' won the Hugo, while 'Tideline' also won the Sturgeon award.

Trudi Canavan (www.trudicanavan.com) lives in Melbourne, Australia. She has been making up stories about people and places that don't exist for as long as she can remember. While working as a freelance illustrator and designer she wrote the bestselling *Black Magician* trilogy, which was published in 2001-3 and was named an 'Evergreen' by *The Bookseller* in 2010. *The Magician's Apprentice*, a prequel to the trilogy, won the Aurealis Award for Best Fantasy Novel in 2009 and the final of the sequel trilogy, *The Traitor Queen*, reached #1 on the UK *Times* Hardback bestseller list in 2011.

Glen Cook grew up in northern California and served in the U.S. Navy with the 3rd Marine Recon Battalion, an experience that fundamentally affected his later work. Cook then attended the University of Missouri and the Clarion Writers' Workshop. His first novel in the *Dread Empire* series, *Silverheels*, appeared in 1971 and was followed quickly by a broad range of fantasy and science fiction novels, including the humorous fantasy *Garrett PI* series and others. His most important work, though, is the gritty *Black Company* fantasy series that follows an elite mercenary unit over several decades, and which brought a whole new perspective to fantasy. Cook is currently retired, and lives in St. Louis, Missouri where he writes full-time.

Kate Elliott (www.kateelliott.com) has been writing stories since she was nine years old, which has led her to believe either that she is a little crazy or that writing, like breathing, keeps her alive. Her most recent series is the *Spiritwalker* trilogy (*Cold Magic, Cold Fire, Cold Steel*), an Afro-Celtic post-Roman alternate-19th-century Regency icepunk mashup with airships, Phoenician spies, the intelligent descendents of troodons, and revolution. Her previous series are the *Crossroads* trilogy, *The Crown of Stars* septology, and the *Novels of the Jaran*. She likes to play sports more than she likes to watch them; right now, her sport of choice is outrigger canoe paddling. Her spouse has a much more interesting job than she does, with the added benefit that they had to move to Hawaii for his work. Thus, the outrigger canoes. They also have a schnauzer (aka The Schnazghul).

Jeffrey Ford (jeffford2010.livejournal.com) is the author of the novels *The Physiognomy, Memoranda, The Beyond, The Portrait of Mrs. Charbuque, The Girl in the Glass, The Cosmology of the Wider World,* and *The Shadow Year.* His short fiction has been collected in *The Fantasy Writer's Assistant, The Empire of Ice Cream, The Drowned Life,* and *Crackpot Palace.* Ford's fiction has been translated into over 20 languages and is the recipient of the Edgar Allan Poe Award, the Shirley Jackson Award, the Nebula, the World Fantasy Award, and the Grand Prix de l'imaginaire.

Ellen Klages (www.ellenklages.com) is the author of two acclaimed YA novels: *The Green Glass Sea,* which won the Scott O'Dell Award, the New Mexico Book Award, and the Lopez Award; and *White*

Sands, Red Menace, which won the California and New Mexico Book Awards. Her short stories, which have been collected in World Fantasy Award nominated collection *Portable Childhoods*, have been have been translated into Czech, French, German, Hungarian, Japanese, and Swedish and have been nominated for the Nebula, Hugo, World Fantasy, and Campbell awards. Her story, 'Basement Magic,' won a Nebula in 2005. She lives in San Francisco, in a small house full of strange and wondrous things.

Ellen Kushner's (www.ellenkushner.com) first novel, *Swordspoint*, introduced readers to the city to which she has since returned in *The Privilege of the Sword* (a Locus Award winner and Nebula nominee), *The Fall of the Kings* (written with Delia Sherman), and a handful of related short stories, most recently 'The Duke of Riverside' in Ellen Datlow's *Naked Cities*. Kushner's own narration of her *Riverside* novels has just been released by Neil Gaiman Presents for Audible.com. Kushner's novel *Thomas the Rhymer* won the Mythopoeic and World Fantasy Awards. With Holly Black, she co-edited *Welcome to Bordertown*, a revival of the original urban fantasy shared world series created by Terri Windling. A co-founder of the Interstitial Arts Foundation, Ellen Kushner is also the longtime host of the public radio show *Sound & Spirit*, and a popular public speaker. She lives in New York City, and travels a lot.

Scott Lynch (www.scottlynch.us) was born in St. Paul, Minnesota in 1978 and is the author of the

Gentleman Bastard sequence of fantasy novels, beginning with *The Lies of Locke Lamora*. He currently lives in Wisconsin, where he has served as a volunteer firefighter since 2005. He spends several months of the year in Massachusetts with his partner, fellow SF/F writer Elizabeth Bear.

K.J. Parker (www.kjparker.net) was born long ago and far away, worked as a coin dealer, a dogsbody in an auction house and a lawyer, and has so far published thirteen novels (the *Fencer*, *Scavenger* and *Engineer* trilogies, and standalone novels *The Company*, *The Folding Knife*, *The Hammer*, and *Sharps*), three novellas ('Purple And Black' , 'Blue And Gold' and 'A Small Price To Pay For Birdsong', which won the 2012 World Fantasy Award) and a gaggle of short fiction. Married to a lawyer and living in the south west of England, K.J. Parker is a mediocre stockman and forester, a barely competent carpenter, blacksmith and machinist, a two-left-footed fencer, lackluster archer, utility-grade armorer, accomplished textile worker and crack shot. K.J. Parker is not K.J. Parker's real name. However, if K.J. Parker were to tell you K.J. Parker's real name, it wouldn't mean anything to you.

Robert V S Redick (www.robertvsredick.com) studied English and Russian, before earning a Master's in tropical conservation and development. He has traveled extensively in Latin America, and has written a study of park ranger training and management practices. He has also worked as a baker, translator, horse handler, lab technician, and stage critic for the Portland Phoenix and Valley Advocate. His first novel, *Conquistadors,* is set in 1970s Argentina, is unpublished, but was a finalist for the 2002 AWP/Thomas Dunne Novel Award. His first published novel, *The Red Wolf Conspiracy,* launched the *Chathrand Voyage* series of seafaring epic fantasies, which continued with *The Rats and the Ruling Sea, The River of Shadows,* and *The Night of the Swarm.* Redick lives in western Massachusetts with his partner Kiran Asher.

Ysabeau S. Wilce's (www.yswilce.com) first story, 'Metal More Attractive', was published in *The Magazine of Fantasy and Science Fiction* in 2004. Like all of her work to date, it was set in Alta Califa, an alternate California, and is heavily influenced by her military history studies. A second story, 'The Biography of a Bouncing Boy Terror', appeared in 2005 and 'The Lineaments of Gratified Desire' appeared in 2006. Wilce's first novel, a young adult fantasy with a preposterously long title, *Flora Segunda: Being the Magickal Mishaps of a Girl of Spirit, Her Glass-Gazing Sidekick, Two Ominous Butlers (One Blue), a House with Eleven Thousand Rooms, and a Red Dog,* was published to considerable acclaim in 2007, and was followed by sequels *Flora's Dare* and *Flora's Fury.* She currently lives with her family and a large number of well-folded towels in Northern California.

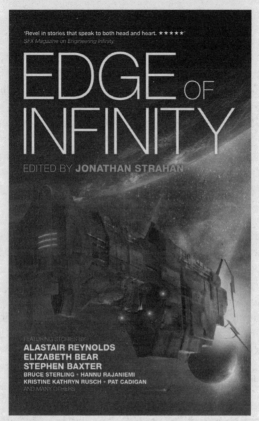

'Revel in stories that speak to both head and heart. ★★★★★'
SFX Magazine on Engineering Infinity

EDGE OF INFINITY

EDITED BY JONATHAN STRAHAN

FEATURING STORIES BY
ALASTAIR REYNOLDS
ELIZABETH BEAR
STEPHEN BAXTER
BRUCE STERLING • HANNU RAJANIEMI
KRISTINE KATHRYN RUSCH • PAT CADIGAN
AND MANY OTHERS

UK ISBN: 978-1-78101-055-9 • US ISBN: 978-1-78108-056-6 • £7.99/$8.99

Edge of Infinity is an exhilarating new SF anthology that looks at the next giant leap for humankind: the leap from our home world out into the Solar System. From the eerie transformations in Pat Cadigan's "The Girl-Thing Who Went Out for Sushi" to the frontier spirit of Sandra McDonald and Stephen D. Covey's "The Road to NPS," and from the grandiose vision of Alastair Reynolds' "Vainglory" to the workaday familiarity of Kristine Kathryn Rusch's "Safety Tests," the thirteen stories in this anthology span the whole of the human condition in their race to colonise Earth's nearest neighbours.

 WWW.SOLARISBOOKS.COM

Follow us on Twitter! www.twitter.com/solarisbooks

ENGINEERING INFINITY

EDITED BY JONATHAN STRAHAN

UK ISBN: 978-1-907519-51-2 • US ISBN: 978-1-907519-52-9 • £8.99/$7.99

The universe shifts and changes: suddenly you understand, you get it, and are filled with wonder. That moment of understanding drives the greatest science-fiction stories and lies at the heart of Engineering Infinity. Whether it's coming up hard against the speed of light – and, with it, the enormity of the universe – realising that terraforming a distant world is harder and more dangerous than you'd ever thought, or simply realizing that a hitchhiker on a starship consumes fuel and oxygen with tragic results, it's hard science-fiction where a sense of discovery is most often found and where science-fiction's true heart lies.

ROWENA CORY DANIELLS

The King's Bastard

BOOK ONE OF THE CHRONICLES
OF KING ROLEN'S KIN

*"Royal intrigue, court politics
and outlawed magic make for
an exciting adventure."*
— Gail Z. Martin, author of
The Chronicles of The Necromancer

UK ISBN: 978 1 97519 00 0 • US ISBN: 978 1 97519 01 7 • £7.99/$7.99

Seven minutes younger than the heir, Byren has never hungered for the throne, and laughs when a seer predicts he will kill his twin. But his brother Lence resents Byren's growing popularity, and King Rolen's enemies plot to take his throne. In a world where the untamed magic of the gods wells up from the earth's heart, sending exotic beasts to stalk the wintry nights and twisting men's minds, King Rolen's kin will need courage and wits to survive...

ROWENA CORY DANIELLS

BESIEGED

BOOK ONE OF THE OUTCAST CHRONICLES

'Page-turning, plot-twisting, breakneck adventure.'

ISBN: 978-1-78108-011-5 • US $7.99 / CAN $9.99

Sorne, the estranged son of a King on the verge of madness, is being raised as a weapon to wield against the mystical Wyrds. Half a continent away, his father is planning to lay siege to the Celestial City, the home of the T'En, whose wyrd blood the mundane population have come to despise. Within the City, Imoshen, the only mystic to be raised by men, is desperately trying to hold her people together. A generations long feud between the men of the Brotherhoods and the women of the sacred Sisterhoods is about to come to a head. With war without and war within, can an entire race survive the hatred of a nation?

Rowena Cory Daniells, the creator of the bestselling Chronicles of King Rolen's Kin, brings you a stunning new fantasy epic, steeped in magic and forged in war.

 WWW.SOLARISBOOKS.COM

Follow us on Twitter! www.twitter.com/solarisbooks

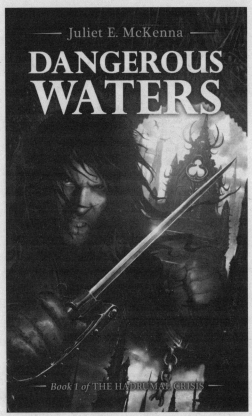

— Juliet E. McKenna —

DANGEROUS
WATERS

Book 1 of THE HADRUMAL CRISIS

UK ISBN: *978 1 907519 97 0* • US ISBN: *978 1 907519 96 3* • *£7.99/$7.99*

The Archmage rules the island of wizards and has banned the use of magecraft in warfare, but there are corsairs raiding the Caladhrian Coast, enslaving villagers and devastating trade. Barons and merchants beg for magical aid, but all help has been refused so far.

Lady Zurenne's husband has been murdered by the corsairs. Now a man she doesn't even know stands as guardian over her and her daughters. Corrain, former captain and now slave, knows that the man is a rogue wizard, illegally selling his skills to the corsairs. If Corrain can escape, he'll see justice done. Unless the Archmage's magewoman, Jilseth, can catch the renegade first, before his disobedience is revealed and the scandal shatters the ruler's hold on power...

 WWW.SOLARISBOOKS.COM

Follow us on Twitter! www.twitter.com/solarisbooks

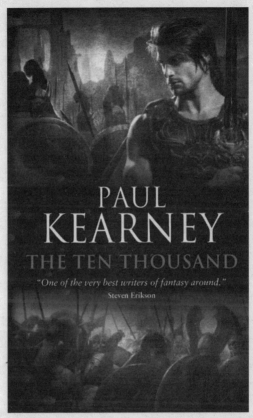

PAUL KEARNEY

THE TEN THOUSAND

"One of the very best writers of fantasy around."
Steven Erikson

UK ISBN: 978 1 84416 647 3 • US ISBN: 978 1 84416 573 5 • £7.99/$7.99

The Macht are a mystery, a people of extraordinary ferocity whose prowess on the battlefield is the stuff of legend. For centuries they have remained within the remote fastnesses of the Harukush Mountains.

Beyond lie the teeming peoples of the Asurian Empire, which rules the world; and is invincible. The Great King of Asuria can call up whole nations to the battlefield. His word is law.

But now the Great King's brother means to take the throne by force, and has called on the legend, marching ten thousand warriors of the Macht into the heart of the Empire.

 WWW.SOLARISBOOKS.COM

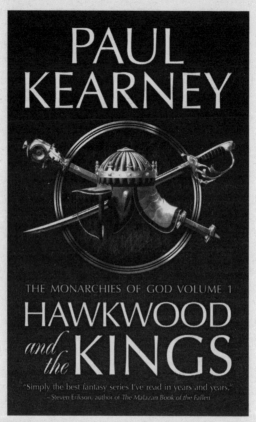

PAUL KEARNEY

THE MONARCHIES OF GOD VOLUME 1

HAWKWOOD *and the* KINGS

"Simply the best fantasy series I've read in years and years."
– Steven Erikson, author of *The Malazan Book of the Fallen*

UK ISBN: 978 1 906735 70 8 • US ISBN: 978 1 906735 71 5 • £8.99/$9.99

For Richard Hawkwood and his crew, a desperate venture to carry refugees to the uncharted land across the Great Western Ocean offers the only chance of escape from the Inceptines' pyres.

In the East, Lofantyr, Abeleyn and Mark – three of the five Ramusian Kings – have defied the cruel pontiff's purge and must fight to hold their thrones through excommunication, intrigue and civil war.

In the quiet monastery city of Charibon, two humble monks make a discovery that will change the whole world...